THE LETHE STONE

THE FAE WAR CHRONICLES
BOOK FOUR

THE LETHE STONE

JOCELYN A. FOX

The Lethe Stone

Book design by Maureen Cutajar
www.gopublished.com

ISBN: 9781519041593

Prologue

Queen Mab, ruler of the Unseelie Court and all its lands, monarch of the Night and the Winter, once the most powerful being in any world, was not accustomed to helplessness. She glanced down at the marble-smooth, pale skin of her hands – hands that had seen centuries, yet bore no sign of age. Hands that had held a blade in the battle against the greatest enemy of her time, yet bore no scars. Hands that had once embraced her sister lovingly, and braided the princess' midnight-dark hair with motherly affection. Hands that now could do nothing to heal the fractured mind and broken body of the rescued Crown Princess.

"My Queen."

Her Vaelanbrigh's voice broke her reverie and she raised her eyes, taking in the sight of the young Knight who had risen to become one of her Three despite his trace of mortal blood. She had become almost fond of Ramel on the long journey through the Deadlands, and he had proven his worth ten times over during the battle in the Dark Keep. At first, she had been wary of this cool affection, cautious that the Knight did not glimpse her increasing favor – for what higher favor could there be other than becoming one of her Three –

and seek to use it to his own advantage. When she had first baptized him, Ramel's steadfast loyalty reminded her with a distant pain of Finnead's fidelity, like an old wound prodded relentlessly. But that similarity had faded with the realization that Finnead had deserted her. No, not deserted…betrayed. He had betrayed her sister, and then he had betrayed Mab by serving the new High Queen. She swallowed against the bitterness rising in her throat like bile.

"My lady," said Ramel again in a slightly gentler voice. The light of the *taebramh* orbs – a habit that, despite Mab's annoyance, her Court had picked up from the Northwoman's – ignited coppery sparks in her Vaelanbrigh's hair. He'd let it grow longer than his custom during the past weeks of travel, yet another vice of the Wild Court that had filtered into the Unseelie ranks, like insidious ink spiraling through still water. She took a deep, composing breath.

"What news?" Mab finally said, her voice as smooth, as cold as ice.

"The Crown Princess is sleeping," said Ramel in that same half-gentle tone, like a rider trying to calm a spooked mount.

"Is she sleeping, or is she unconscious from the potions applied by the healers?" A harsh undercurrent, dangerously close to a growl, lurked in the Unseelie Queen's voice. She clenched her hands reflexively, one hand finding the hilt of her sword since she did not have the cool, carved arms of her throne to grip beneath her grasping fingers.

"My Queen, the healers labor day and night," replied Ramel, "and they are tasked not only with the Crown Princess, but with hundreds of gravely wounded warriors who fought under our banner." He bowed his head slightly in deference even as he reminded Mab that her sister was not the only distressed soul in their camp, though she might be the one farthest beyond any help of their healers.

Mab tightened her hold on her sword hilt until the delicately woven details of the grip dug into her palm and her knuckles felt as though they would burst through her skin. She felt the cold fury rising; at the periphery of her senses, she noted the sudden sharp chill in the air. The plush rug beneath her feet stiffened with frost. Her Vaelanbrigh still stood firm despite the glacial wind pushing at his shoulders, the ruby in the pommel of the Brighbranr glimmering darkly, like a cupped palm full of mortal blood.

"My Queen," he said again in that gentle but firm tone. "The healers are doing all they can, and both Queen Titania and Queen Vell have sent their best..."

"Out," she snarled, ice swirling across the tent as the mention of the other two Queens snapped her control. She'd be damned if a healer sent in pity from one of *their* Courts would help her sister. "*Get out!*"

Ramel bowed and turned, exiting with graceful steps, treading carefully on the now icy ground. Mab clenched her teeth on the sound of pain and fury that frothed up into her throat, instead letting the arctic wind howl through the tent, dagger-sharp icicles puncturing the nebulous forms of the *taebramh* lights with satisfying ferocity. The Unseelie Queen stood in the cold darkness of her tent, gripping her sword, rage and agony coursing through her, feeding the whirling blizzard that screamed through the Unseelie camp.

She had raised her blade against the enemy, and won but she did not bear the scars of the battle. Despair threatened to overwhelm her as she felt, for the first time in centuries, sorrow borne out of the love for another. While her Court drew their cloaks tightly about them and wordlessly endured the biting cold of the furious, unnatural tempest, only a handful of them suspected that the true cause of their Queen's anguish was not her anger, but the pain of a thawing – and broken – heart.

Chapter 1

When the three Queens rode into the City, the commanders of their great army – Gray, Gawain, and Ramel – had already established a place for the wounded in the remnants of what could have been a great cathedral or palace. Even through her exhaustion, Tess gazed up in wonder at the magnificent ruins that rose around them as their small party wound its way through the great army into the city. The widest causeway that passed through the center of the White City had been cleared of the corpses of Dark creatures. When the wind shifted, the scent of smoke drifted over them. Gray informed them that they were still burning the dead creatures in huge pits a small distance outside the City. The Sidhe dead had already been placed on their funeral pyres with honor. It was hard to reconcile the fact that so much had taken place while they were fighting their way through the courtyard in the Dark Keep and facing Malravenar.

The Queens and their warriors rode to the great building used as the healing ward. Its pillars reminded Tess of Greek pantheons, but the skeletons of graceful arched windows, all the glass long since broken, whispered of great cathedrals. It was some sort of cross between Brightvale, Darkhill and the Hall of the Outer Guard, all the most beautiful aspects of Seelie and Unseelie styles blended harmoniously. The white stone bore centuries of grime, and most of the elegantly carved statues had suffered the loss of limbs or heads during the occupation of Malravenar's creatures. Against this backdrop of savaged magnificence, the commanders had erected a great tent in the cavernous main hall.

"The structure is sound, so do not fear it crumbling," Gawain assured the Queens and the Bearer as they crossed the great threshold, "but all the light and heat would be lost into the reaches overhead if we did not have a canopy."

Inside the tent – one of the High Queen's sorcery enhanced creations with nearly unlimited space – the cries of the wounded and the smell of blood and healing herbs enveloped the Queens and the Bearer. Titania immediately swept forward to conference with a fair Seelie healer, and white-haired Maeve paused in her direction of dozens of healers to bow to Vell and make her report to the High Queen. Mab stood silently, the star on her diadem subdued as her eyes swept over the multitude of wounded, long rows of furs and other makeshift bedding stretching down the length of the tent. It was like a miniature city in its own right, hundreds of healers moving purposefully through the ranks of their patients. Tess's mind couldn't comprehend the numbers before her eyes. It felt as though she were surveying the great army from the air with Wisp again, seeing it stretch to the horizons and beyond, but this time, the sight of so much broken beauty and loss stole her breath. She felt cold.

The able-bodied fighters who had traveled into the Dark Keep began to carry the wounded from the Queens' party into the healing ward, with other healers and warriors from the main army streaming outside to help. Tess watched dumbly as two Unseelie carried their Vaelanseld into the tent on a makeshift stretcher. Some of the numbness began to fall away from her body. She thought vaguely that she should make herself useful, but gradually the work of moving the wounded was taken over by the healers and their apprentices. Out of the corner of her eye, she glimpsed Finnead carrying the Unseelie Princess, still cloaked, into the tent. Her shrouded figure seemed much smaller than when she'd stood before the black altar, pouring blood onto it to break the bindings on the Great Seal.

Tess lost sight of Vell and the other two Queens in the industrious activity. Everyone moved so quickly, parting around her like rushing waters of a stream slipping around a rock. The Sword sat silently on her back. She flexed one of her hands, watching the dried blood on her palms crack with the movement. New abrasions crossed the mottled landscape of her scars. Her breath sounded loud to her own ears and a sudden wave of dizziness overtook her. She swallowed and shut her eyes for a moment, willing herself not to pass out or retch. Both would be equally embarrassing.

"Tess?"

She opened her eyes. Robin paused in his supervision of the two healers moving Sage.

"We've got him," the smaller female healer tucked under Sage's good shoulder reassured him.

"I told Sage I'd watch over him," the Bearer said tiredly.

Robin stepped toward her. "Well, come on then."

"Aren't you hurt at all?" she asked as they followed Sage and his healers. It took her a moment to realize that Robin had encircled her waist with one arm, gripping her belt firmly, but she found that she didn't much care. She actually felt grateful for the guidance, since she was fairly certain that she couldn't have walked a straight line under her own power.

"We're all injured in some way or another," replied Robin, "but not all of us dipped into our lifeforce to break and bind the enemy."

"Is that why I'm so tired?" she mused.

"That and we fought for three days and three nights," said Robin with a little bit of a smile.

"Ah, is that the Lady Bearer? Back here, if you please," said Maeve, bustling past the pair and directing Robin to steer Tess toward a curtain marked with a white rune.

"I don't want any special treatment," she protested, noticing in slight surprise that her lips felt oddly numb. She shivered. The cold she'd noticed only a moment ago now seemed glacial. "Sage..."

"You can take that up with the High Queen at a later time, and you're in no shape to watch over anyone right now," said Maeve firmly. "I assume you're comfortable with your red-haired friend here?"

"Comfortable...?" she repeated dazedly as they entered the small compartment. A low table covered with a cloth served as an examination table, and Maeve motioned her toward it.

"It would save us time if he removes your armor while I gather supplies and an assistant," replied Maeve.

Robin maneuvered Tess over to the table and kept his arm about her waist until she was safely seated. "I think we'll manage just fine," he said to Maeve, his deft fingers already finding the strap of the Sword across her breastplate. When Tess didn't contradict him, Maeve nodded and walked away, her small figure radiating purpose.

"Sage," Tess murmured, watching with detached interest as Robin laid the battered sheath of the Sword reverently beside her on the table. The emerald in the pommel didn't flash with that conscious power. It looked like an ordinary emerald in the pommel of a very ordinary, well used weapon. A wave of dizziness swelled over her again. "And Liam. Someone should tell Liam..."

"He's one of Vell's Three now," said Robin as he worked on the straps of her breastplate. She winced as she moved her arm, the movement pulling at the wound across the top of her shoulders that she'd nearly forgotten. "So I suspect that he'll know where you are, because she knows where you are."

"Such a tangled web we weave," she said dreamily. She noticed that her feet didn't touch the floor; she swung her legs a little, experimentally, her head feeling very light.

"Hold still," admonished Robin. He finished unbuckling the other side of her breastplate. As he moved the two pieces of armor that had protected her torso during the battle, the dried blood pasting her shirt and the interior of the armor together pulled with sudden bright pain against her shoulders. She hissed and grabbed at the table, clenching the fabric in her fists. The hot throbbing pulled her roughly back into her body, banishing the floating sensation. She swallowed thickly. Robin held the back piece of the armor in place and carefully removed the breastplate.

"I'm being a baby," Tess said roughly, more to steel her own nerves than anything else.

Robin leaned over her, inspecting the bloody seam between her armor and shirt. "I think Maeve will forgive me if I wait for her guidance. It would be a pity for me to get in trouble so soon after our momentous victory."

"Or it might just be in character," she responded, eliciting a chuckle.

"Your sarcasm survived your duel with Malravenar," he said. "That's a victory in itself."

Tess didn't have another witty reply ready, so she focused on breathing slowly and trying to ignore the growing fissure of pain at the top of her shoulders. Now that the hot adrenaline of the battle had ebbed away, she felt oddly deflated, the numbness slowly transitioning into a dizzying emptiness laced with a keen awareness of her injuries. She rested her hands, palms up, on her thighs, remembering the feel of peeling her hands from the hilt of the Sword. Breaking and binding Malravenar...it had been mere hours since she'd stood before the greatest evil the Fae world had known, and already it felt like a fantastic dream. Had she really defied him and struck him through with the Caedbranr? Had they really bound his shrieking shade into the four gleaming river stones? She pressed the back of one hand against her grimy belt pouch, feeling the shape of the smooth oblong stone through the supple leather.

Maeve swept back into the compartment, trailing an assistant behind her…an assistant with a mane of glinting golden curls that swayed about her head as she moved. Moira raised an eyebrow in question as she placed a steaming bowl on the other table in the room, where Maeve was already busily selecting herbs. Tess managed a lopsided, tired smile in reply.

"Before you chastise me," Robin said, preempting Maeve as she glanced at him with lips pressed into a thin line, "I didn't finish my task because there's a bit of a problem with the backplate of her armor. Or rather, not a problem with the armor, but with what's beneath it."

"It's from the battle in the courtyard," Tess said tiredly. "I didn't even see what kind of creature." She remembered the blur of its grisly, matted fur and shivered at the recollection of its rank breath against her neck as she waited for its teeth to pierce her skin. "Chael killed it."

"So it's been almost three days since you took the wound," Maeve said. "No wonder it's clotted to the shirt and armor." She pressed the back of one hand to Tess's forehead in a poignantly mother-like gesture. "Doesn't feel like you have a fever yet."

"The Sword might have burned any poison out of me," Tess said.

"You don't give yourself enough credit, Lady Bearer," said Maeve, dipping a cup of water out of the steaming basin and tossing powdered herbs into it. "You are strong in your own right." Tess watched the healer's quick, efficient movements with hazy interest. It was like watching a masterful artist mix paints as Maeve selected different colored leaves, crushed them in her fist and filtered them into the water. After a moment, she slid the cup toward Moira, who was waiting with a linen cloth already in her hand.

"This might sting a little," Moira warned softly as she soaked the cloth in the steaming liquid. Tess replied with a sigh, steeling herself. The warm wet cloth felt both soothing and painful at once, loosening the gore-encrusted shirt and armor from her skin but igniting waves of hot pain from the gash as the clots softened, reopening the wound. She clenched her jaw and shuddered. Robin and Moira conferred in quick, quiet words, and the armor slid away from her back. Tess swallowed down bile, shutting her eyes as dizziness enveloped her again. Robin gathered her head onto his shoulder, free from holding the armor in position. She leaned gratefully against him as Moira cut away some of her shirt, still bathing the wound with the wet cloth.

"This is for the pain and the shock." Maeve pressed a rolled leaf into her hand. "Tuck it into your cheek, don't chew it," the master healer said, turning back to her table of alchemy.

Tess obediently tucked the bundle of herbs into her cheek, too tired to fight against the welcome relief from pain. It tasted like mint and lemon. Robin offered his shoulder again, one of his hands gliding feather-light over her hair as she leaned forward, giving the healers access to her back and giving in to the exhaustion sliding over her limbs. With the herbs in her cheek, the pain of her back receded to a dull discomfort and a warm glow chased away the cold emptiness spreading through her body.

"I should be helping everyone else," she murmured into Robin's shoulder.

"You just helped the Queens imprison Malravenar," he replied in a quiet voice, one hand finding her hair again, "and that's quite enough help for a good long while, I think."

"One successful quest...doesn't give me an excuse to be lazy," she said, the words coming slowly. Her mind generated the phrase as sarcasm, but weariness pressed any humor from her voice.

"You're not being *lazy,* Tess," Moira said in gentle rebuke. "It's called taking a moment to gather everything back together. Stitch your wounds, sleep, and let your warriors do the same. There are more than enough hands about to do the work that you think you should be doing anyway."

She hummed noncommittally. The sensible part of her mind that could still think rationally – and it was a small part, at this point – knew Moira was right, but that didn't allay the strange, empty restlessness digging into her stomach. "What will we do now?" Tess frowned slightly as Moira applied a numbing salve to her back. She glanced over to Maeve and saw her threading a silver needle, but the lemon and mint herbs softened even the thought of stitches.

Robin chuckled. "I'm not quite sure. Rebuild what was destroyed, as best we can. Build new and beautiful places for the new and beautiful things that have come out of the war."

"Like the Wild Court," she said, wincing as she felt the pressure of the needle and the pull of the thread. She didn't feel any pain – the salve and whatever magic Maeve had rolled into that little bundle in her cheek made sure of that – but the sensation of the thread sliding through her skin made her feel oddly queasy.

"And the White City," said Moira. "I never thought I'd live to walk the pathways of the White City as our forebears did."

"Not all will see the beauty," said Maeve, speaking for the first time since she'd begun work on Tess's back, her voice sounding…*old*. Tess frowned slightly and raised her head, looking up at Robin. He shook his head slightly, his eyes grim.

"We'll ask later," he murmured quietly into her ear. In such a small space, she was sure that Maeve had heard him with her sharp Sidhe senses, but all fell silent for a few moments. Tess put the pieces together and surmised that one of the twins – or both – must have fallen in the battle, wounded or dead. It was the only thing that came to mind that would shake the unflappable white-haired healer. She felt a cold sort of sadness. Maeve finished stitching her back without another word, gave instructions to Moira in a quiet but firm voice, and left the compartment without a backwards glance.

Tess sat up a little straighter, rolling one shoulder experimentally, her movement rewarded by the tight pull of the fresh stitches against her skin. She much preferred it to the hot aching feeling of an untended wound.

"I'll dress it now and then we'll check it when you awaken," said Moira, her voice subdued.

"Did one of the twins…?" Tess couldn't finish the sentence, her throat tightening despite the fact that she'd thought she was too tired to feel emotions.

"Maire was killed on the first day of the battle," Moira replied, her eyes downcast. "And Niamh lies senseless in the far reaches of this hall. She took a grave wound on the last day. Her *faehal* was also grievously injured. It was astonishing they weren't both killed when they fell out of the sky."

Tess shivered as the memory of the broken and bloody Valkyrie from the dragon hunt rose in her mind's eye. "Quinn needs to be told."

Robin touched her arm. "I'll make sure of it."

She shifted, that strange restlessness surfacing again. "I have to sleep *here*…away from everyone?" Her words sounded plaintive to her own ears. Silence and stillness wrapped cloyingly about her. She crossed her arms over her chest and looked up at Robin and Moira. She didn't miss the look that passed between them, and Moira dipped her head.

"*I'll* make sure that Quinn knows about Niamh, if he doesn't already," Moira told her.

"And I'll stay here with you, if you'll allow me," said Robin, making it sound as though he were asking her permission.

"I'd like to join everyone else," Tess said vaguely. She couldn't corral her thoughts into any kind of sense, but she did know that she wanted to be close to the other fighters who'd experienced the horrors of the Dark Keep. She wanted to stave off the desperate, clawing loneliness that threatened to engulf her each time she remembered that Luca was gone. The thought beat like another heart in the back of her mind, constant and unrelenting: *Luca is gone. Luca is gone. Luca is gone.* She swallowed hard and willed herself not to cry. Tears would feel too much like mourning, and he wasn't dead, she told herself fiercely.

"Most of the company that traveled with the Queens are in their own spaces, or with two or three others," said Moira. "Everyone is eager to hear the story of our enemy's defeat. Those able to talk have been speaking of nothing else but the return of the Queens' warriors, and we thought it best to spirit you all away to give you time to recover."

"I'll stay," Robin said almost gently. The brotherly affection in his voice almost undid Tess, and she was afraid her voice wouldn't work, so she nodded jerkily, pulling at the stitches on her back again.

"I'll let Liam know where you are," Moira continued, "and everyone else of your company, if you wish it."

Tess nodded again, staring down at her still bloody hands, running her thumbs over her raw palms idly. As Moira dressed the wound on her back, Robin took the basin from the herb table and set it next to her. Somehow it was still hot, and the fragrant steam smelled like lavender as it curled about her face.

"Now, Tess, you can wash while I see to Robin," Moira said. She watched expectantly until Tess gingerly picked up the cloth folded over the side of the basin, dipping it into the warm liquid.

"Do you need the table?" Tess asked suddenly, the thought striking her halfway through washing her left hand. She looked up and found that Robin had stripped down to his breeches, letting Moira examine him without any hint of embarrassment. His golden skin was barely visible beneath layers of grime: dried blood that wasn't his, marked by runnels of sweat and mixed with the strange gray dirt of the Dark Keep. Several shallow cuts marked his shoulders, and a mottled bruise spread like an ink stain over his ribs.

"There's quite enough room for both of you to sit," Moira replied a bit absently as she carefully separated a matted section of Robin's hair to reveal a gash as long as her hand. "Almost down to the bone," she said to herself. Robin winced slightly as her long fingers traveled like pale spiders over the rest of his head, returning to gently probe the darkly glistening wound. "I'll need to trim this area to stitch it up."

Robin groaned dramatically. "It's not enough that my skull was nearly split, you must divest me of my dignity as well?"

"Unless you want the wound to become infected because I couldn't properly tend to it, and then *all* your hair might fall out," Moira replied, raising one eyebrow.

"Shear me like a spring lamb," Robin sighed with an air of noble resignation as he sat beside Tess on the table, careful not to jostle her.

Tess began washing her right hand, watching the dried coppery flakes of blood spiral through the water of the basin. "You can ask my brother to borrow one of his knit watch caps. Or maybe Quinn will lend you a baseball cap."

"What is a *base-ball* cap, and does it look dashing?" Robin inquired with narrowed eyes.

"It's from the mortal world. Only Liam, Quinn and Jess would have one." She almost said *and Duke,* but she caught herself in time. Her second heartbeat pulsed at the back of her skull with painful insistence: *Luca is gone. Luca is gone. Luca is gone.* "And I suppose it's dashing."

"Well, I wouldn't want to take anything that might remind them of their home, even if it would cover my unfortunate haircut," said Robin, wincing as Moira deftly cut away locks of his red hair with a sharp little dagger.

"There are far worse things than an unfortunate haircut," Moira reminded him. The undertone in her voice reminded me that she'd fought in the great battle with the Valkyrie. Tess eyed her surreptitiously as she sponged the last of the blood from her hands.

"You needn't stare at me, Tess," she said without looking away from her trimming operation. "I'll have a few scars, but nothing that isn't already on its way to healing." She pressed her lips together. "And my *faehal* survived too, so I'm one of the lucky ones." Her mane of golden curls swayed as she tilted her head, examining her handiwork. A swath of short-shorn hair angled across the back of Robin's head, revealing the ugly lips of the wound.

"Did the blow that gave you that cut knock you out?" Tess asked. Her mind picked up that thread of thought, a glad distraction. It didn't quite silence the drumbeat in the back of her consciousness, but it helped her push it away and compress it into something manageable.

"I think so," Robin replied contemplatively. "Your brother and the *ulfdrengr* with the eye patch saved me, from what I remember. Chael."

"We fought in a courtyard after going through the portal," Tess said in a low voice to Moira. "We were there for at least a day and a night."

"Two days and two nights," Robin said, half-closing his eyes in reflection. "I feel like once we got into the throne room it all went faster. But then again, I was only half-conscious for most of that time because Malravenar was squeezing the air from our lungs."

"It sounds like once you got past the courtyard, there wasn't much for the fighters in the escort to do." Moira threaded a fresh needle. Tess winced, grateful that at least her stitches had been in her muscle-padded shoulder. It wasn't really the needle or the stitching that turned her stomach, it was the thought of the needle scraping against bone, weaving delicate skin together in so sensitive a part of the body.

"Except serve as targets for the wrath of a deity." Robin made a considering sound. "We knew going into it that we were there to make sure the Queens and the Bearer made it to the throne room."

"Steady," Moira said quietly as she leaned close and the needle flashed. Robin's body tightened and he drew in his breath with a hiss. Tess dried her hands carefully, picked up the basin and stood. Her legs were surprisingly steady as she set the basin on the herb table.

"Can I help at all?" she asked Robin. His eyes were closed, his face smooth with concentration and his breathing steady as he used some sort of Seelie meditation to deal with the pain. Or at least that's what she assumed.

"I'll be finished in a few moments," Moira said. True to her word, she finished stitching with remarkable alacrity, tying the final knot and deftly cutting the thread with the same little knife that she'd used to cut Robin's hair. "Done."

Robin opened his eyes and lifted one hand as though he was about to feel the damage – to his hair or the wound itself, Tess wasn't quite sure; but Moira looked at him balefully until he lowered his seeking hand.

"It doesn't look that bad," Tess said in what she hoped was an encouraging tone.

"Somehow I don't entirely believe you," Robin muttered, but he obediently kept his hands settled in his lap.

"We will all have scars," said Moira, grinding herbs with a mortar and pestle.

Tess sighed. "I know. But sometimes it's easier not to constantly think about the terrible price of the battle."

"The terrible price of our freedom," said Robin.

"It might be easier, but it doesn't make it any less real," Moira continued inexorably.

"I know that," Tess said softly, her voice wavering as the reality of Luca's absence once again rose up like a tide in her mind. Moira paused in mixing the salve for Robin's wound, her eyes searching Tess's face as the Bearer swallowed hard and then kept speaking. "There was a moment when the Great Seal was broken. I…there was a lot happening. Luca and Merrick and Duke are…gone. In the mortal world," she added fiercely, willing herself not to give in to the tears pressing behind her eyes. She paused. Moira walked around the table, the little bowl of salve in one hand, and silently began applying the mixture to Robin's head. When Tess was reasonably sure that her voice would work, she pressed on. "So they're not dead. They're in the mortal world. And I'm going to go find them." She looked at the two Sidhe, daring them to challenge her statement. Defiance was easier than sorrow, especially layered over her exhaustion.

But rather than ask how she would find their three lost warriors in the mortal world, Robin reached out and gently gripped her arm, careful to avoid her shoulder. Moira finished dressing Robin's wound and returned the small bowl to the preparation table. Then she turned and met Tess's eyes.

"Well then, let me be the first to volunteer for the search party," she said seriously. "That is, if my lady Queen Vell gives me leave, and you deem me a worthy addition." A hint of a smile colored her last words.

Tess blinked in surprise. "I...thanks." She tried to muster her own small smile but failed. "I haven't...really thought that far ahead.

"No thanks are needed," she replied brusquely. Her mane of curls swayed as she gave Tess a single firm nod. "You're the Bearer. I have no doubt that you'll bring them home, and I'll like to be there with you when you do, whether on this side or the other."

"Vell would approve, I think," Tess said thickly.

"Anyone who assumes they know our Wild Queen's mind is taking his life into his own hands," said Robin.

"Well, you're both patched up as well as I can do for the moment," continued Moira without skipping a beat. "Come on, then." She motioned to a smaller flap in the wall of the compartment that Tess would have sworn had not existed the moment before Moira gestured to it. "You didn't think you're to sleep in *here*, did you?"

Robin gathered his shirt from where he'd tossed it on the edge of the table. Tess went to grab her armor, but her back protested fiercely and she fought back a wave of nausea at the sudden movement. She settled for looping the strap of the Sword over her good shoulder, her motions slow and deliberate.

"Don't worry about the rest of it," Moira said. "I'll find someone to clean it and return it to you."

Tess didn't even have the strength to protest as she and Robin followed Moira through the little doorway into another little room, the walls composed of silvery fabric just as every other room within the maze of the *Vyldretning*'s enchanted tent. Furs blanketed the floor, piled higher in some places, a few pillows scattered in the corners, and the room was dark and just cool enough to make her shiver slightly; Moira pressed steaming mugs into their hands, touched their shoulders briefly and said, "I'll be back to check on you. Sleep."

Robin and Tess settled down onto the furs, sipping cautiously at their mugs. She laid the silent Sword at the edge of the furs. They sat in companionable quiet. The warmth from the tea spread pleasantly through her body.

"A bit of white shroud in the tea, I think," Robin said, swirling the liquid idly as he peered down into the cup.

"Haven't heard of that one," she said. Her eyelids felt heavy. The tendrils of warmth from the tea soothed her aching body.

"Used after battles mostly." Robin took another long swallow. "It helps with dreamless sleep. Some say that it can help heal invisible wounds, make the nightmares less terrible when they do appear. Seelie healers have used it for as long as I can remember. I've heard that Unseelie view using it as weakness." He shrugged. "Personally I'll welcome it."

Tess didn't even have the energy to feel indignant that Moira hadn't told them about the tea. It was probably standard protocol, she thought tiredly, and besides, just because she was the Bearer didn't mean that everyone was required to tell her *everything*. She hoped suddenly that she hadn't been insufferable over the past weeks, demanding to know everything from everyone. Her thoughts flitted disjointedly from one subject to another. She swallowed a last mouthful of the pleasantly warm tea and set her mug down on a little table that had conveniently appeared in a corner of the compartment.

"Thanks for staying with me," she said, dragging a pillow over to her side. Robin dimmed the little *taebramh* lights with a flick of his wrist.

"Of course," he replied, his red hair gleaming even in the darkness. "It was a hard battle. No one should be alone who does not want to be alone."

Tess slid down onto the furs, pulling one over her legs, the pillow impossibly soft beneath her cheek. She curled on her side, wincing as the movement pulled at the stitches in her back. Dimly, she sensed Robin settling down onto the furs as well, a warm, comforting presence within arm's reach. With a little shudder, she gave in to her exhaustion, a tear escaping down her cheek as consciousness faded and she drifted into darkness.

Chapter 2

The air hung heavily over the river, draped like the Spanish moss over the reaching branches of the oaks. Awareness seeped back to him slowly. As he recognized parts of his body – back, chest, one leg, then the other, and finally his arms – the gears in his mind started grinding painfully forward, and he ran through his silent checklist. It wasn't the first time he'd clawed his way out of unconsciousness in dubious circumstances.

He lay face up. Good. Face down was never good, and he felt warm wetness beneath him. His first thought was blood…but no, he lay in a sort of spongy mud. He probed with his mind and felt all his limbs. Also good. But he didn't feel the weight of body armor around his torso, or the pull of a weapons sling around his neck. Confusing, but not necessarily bad. Did he flip his truck or roll an all-terrain vehicle on leave? He brushed aside the questions. Focus. Breathe again, deeply, testing for pain. Dull aches around his ribs, like he'd been in a fight and gotten punched a couple of dozen times, but no sharp announcement of a dire injury…though until he opened his eyes, he couldn't be sure.

Next item on the checklist. Move fingers, and then move toes. Both functional. On to arms and legs. Also functional, though sluggish and leaden. His mind circled back, gnawing at the mystery of how exactly he'd gotten into this mess. Because if there was one thing he was sure of – and there weren't many at this particular moment in time – it was that he was in some sort of mess. What flavor of mess exactly, he'd figure out shortly.

His head ached, the pain intensifying as he rolled his eyes behind closed lids. Had he gotten into a bar fight? It had been years since he'd slept off liquor and bruises in a buddy's back yard, but it wasn't out of the question. He swallowed thickly. And then his mind kindly flashed him a memory along with the next swell of pain inside his skull – the chaos of a battle in a dark cavern, the ground shaking beneath his feet as he ran across slick stones toward a stone altar and a figure holding aloft a shining cup…

Duke inhaled sharply and jerked fully awake, an involuntary sound of pain escaping his lips as he sat up, digging his hands into the soft mud beneath him. A familiar smell surrounded him: heavy wet earth, the humid air thick with the scent of trees and swamp, life and death. God, it smelled like the bayou. It smelled like home.

He opened his eyes, squinting against the morning sun, and when his vision cleared, he inhaled again in shock.

He was home. He was sitting on the bank of the Pearl River – or really a little unnamed offshoot of the Pearl, amid the swamp oak, Spanish moss and heavy air of southern Louisiana. He swallowed thickly, blinking hard. Had it all been a dream? Had he been laid out long enough for his mind to spin that fantastic tale of beautiful warrior women on winged horses, and warriors with the eyes of wolves?

A sudden surge of nausea overwhelmed him. He rolled to one side and retched, emptying his stomach – or what little there had been in his stomach. And then as he wiped his mouth on his sleeve, he froze, staring at the stained and grimy shirtsleeve. He looked down at himself, blinking at the sight of a simple green shirt. And he wasn't wearing his plate carrier and Kevlar, but instead a breastplate made of some sort of fantastically light metal.

"Holy shit," he whispered to himself. "It was…it was real."

The memories rushed back so quickly that he grimaced and closed his eyes again. He'd been reaching for someone when the portal had opened…Liam? He remembered seeing Liam stabbed. A spark of anger at the dark figure that had hurt his teammate whirled in his chest. But no, it hadn't been Liam that he'd been straining to grab before the sinkhole had enveloped them…

He sat up straighter, ignoring his aching ribs. The grass by the riverbank was long and he couldn't see anything beyond the thicket swaying gently around him. He clenched his jaw, rolled to his knees and levered himself upright. Motion to his left, farther into the grassy field, caught his eye. He saw a figure just beginning to stir within a circle of bent and broken grass, as though the man had been thrown onto the ground and rolled with the force of the impact.

Duke swallowed, recognizing the quickening of his heartbeat as the sick feeling of not knowing the location of his teammates. It was one of the worst feelings, second only to the breathless impact of an explosion in the index of his experience. There hadn't been just one of them inside that strange circle; there had been Liam, and then the big wolf warrior – Luca, his mind supplied – and one other. It had all happened so fast. But he knew there were two of them, and he tore his gaze from the stirring figure in the grass. His legs protested slightly as he stumbled closer to the bank of the shallow river. It was only knee-deep in most places, studded with little hillocks of marsh grass. The bank was soft, the mud squelching beneath his boots. He raked the river with his gaze, searching in sectors, and then he saw the prone form laying half in the water. Duke swore under his breath and splashed into the river, hoping that he wasn't too late.

Chapter 3

Warmth enveloped her, wrapping her in a sense of security even as the fog of sleep fell away from her mind. Tess stirred and paused as she felt the arm tucked over her shoulder and the warm body in front of her. Her first thought turned to Luca – but the man with his arm about her didn't smell like wolf and snow and pine. She stiffened as she remembered. *Luca was gone.*

She opened her eyes and waited for her sight to adjust to the dimly lit compartment. Even in the shadows, Robin's hair was unmistakable. They lay facing each other, her head tucked under his chin, his arm protectively wrapped about her shoulder and his other arm pillowing his head. But other than her head against his chest and his arm over her shoulder, their bodies didn't touch. Tess felt the tension leave her limbs as she remembered her insistence at not being left alone, and Robin's brotherly assurance that he'd watch over her as she slept. She felt the comforting rhythm of his heartbeat against her skin, so she closed her eyes and breathed in the warm scent of him – sunlight, and a faint hint of cinnamon – and let herself drift back into dreamless darkness.

The second time Tess woke, Robin and she slept back to back, just close enough that they could feel each other's warmth. She lay still for a few moments, letting the memories of the past days filter back into her awareness. The strained hollow feeling of exhaustion had abated, but she still felt empty. She swallowed hard against the harsh realization of loss as, one by one, the names of those they'd lost in the battle drifted through her mind. Sorrow whirled through her like a cold wind. She curled into herself, drawing her knees to her chest, feeling utterly alone despite Robin's solid form at her back. Her mind started replaying the scene in the throne room of the Dark Keep. Perhaps if she'd resisted Malravenar for longer, or somehow warned the Queens about the Dark Archer taking their blood...

Robin stirred and sat up. Tess curled tighter into herself, a shudder rolling through her.

"Tess?" Robin asked, the edges of his voice still soft with sleep.

"He's gone," she said, her voice barely louder than a whisper, the sound rasping past the tears clogging her throat. With an effort, she pushed herself onto an elbow and then sat up, wrapping her arms around her knees. Robin waited silently. "There should have been something...I should've done something *differently*. Maybe if I'd fought harder, he'd still be here."

"Do you really believe that?" Robin said seriously. He ran a hand through his hair. She felt him watching her, waiting for her reply.

"I don't know," she said into her knees.

"All of us will have those thoughts," Robin continued. "We all saw friends die. You think, maybe if I'd stayed closer, maybe if I had just been fiercer or quicker, they would still be alive." He paused and shook his head slightly. "And maybe it's true. But can you change it now?"

She shook her head. "No."

"No," he agreed. "So why torture yourself with thoughts of what could have been?"

"Because I guess that's how my mind works," she said with a sigh. "The logical part of me knows that I did everything I could have in the moment. I fought hard. *We* fought hard. We knew going into the Dark Keep that some of us wouldn't come out." She stopped and waited for the swell of bone-scraping sorrow in her chest to subside. "It's just…it's not easy. I feel…empty. I can't feel the Sword. I don't know whether it's gone to sleep, or whether it's done with me because I accomplished the mission." She looked over at the plain, battered scabbard of the Sword where it lay silently at the edge of their sleeping furs. The emerald in the pommel didn't blink at her; no primal wolf prowled in the back of her mind and no fiery power turned restlessly in her chest. Just a silence and emptiness that made her ears ring and her head ache dully.

"Nonsense," said Robin firmly. "You're the Bearer. You'll be the Bearer until you pass the Sword on to the next of your bloodline." He caught her gaze with his own bright green eyes. "You're not alone. Whatever you feel, whatever you think, just remember that you're not alone. The days after a battle are hard. And now…with Malravenar defeated, we'll all have to find another purpose." He raised his eyebrows. "I think you already know your purpose, though, Tess."

She blinked. "Yes. I'm going to open a portal and find them." Her voice hardened. "Even if they're dead, they deserve that much. I won't abandon them."

"There you are, Lady Bearer," Robin said with a smile.

She frowned and then had to smile a little too. "Thanks," she muttered, raising one eyebrow. "You did that on purpose."

"Of course I did," he replied, stretching languorously.

Tess tilted her head, testing the limits of motion before she felt the pull of the stitches across the top of her back. Her skin felt tight and dry; she blinked and ran her tongue over her lips, wondering how long they'd slept. The little corner table that suddenly existed again – her eyes slid away from the spot and then it was *there* – now boasting a small brass lantern, not lit with flame but a softly glowing thread of *taebramh*. The lantern emitted the perfect amount of light, not enough to hurt their eyes but enough to let them see everything without straining in near darkness.

"I don't think they're dead," Robin said, running light fingers over the line of neat stitches on the back of his head.

"I don't think they are either," she agreed, "but somehow it makes me feel a little better to just…acknowledge the possibility."

Robin made a sound of agreement, still probing his wound. After another long moment, he dropped his hand and shrugged. "Well, nothing for it…there are worse things than being shorn like an errant lamb."

Tess chuckled, her voice grating dryly in her throat. "It really doesn't look that bad." She winced and swallowed.

"Waking up after a long sleep with white shroud is often a bit unpleasant," said Robin. "Let's go find some breakfast. Or dinner. Whatever time of day it happens to be." He extended a hand to her and she took it, more for the feel of his brotherly clasp than out of necessity. Her body protested as he levered her onto her feet. It felt as though every major muscle in her arms, legs, and back had been put through the most intense workout she'd ever endured – which was true, in a sense – three days of fighting in the courtyard of the Dark Keep, and then struggling against Malravenar. No wonder she felt like she'd been through a double training session with Luca. A little shard of pain lanced into her chest at the unbidden thought, but she took a deep breath and let it settle. She couldn't fall to pieces every time she thought of him. Then Tess revised the thought: she couldn't fall to pieces at all. He needed her to be strong so that she could find him and bring him home.

Tess picked up the Caedbranr from its resting place at the edge of their furs, feeling the familiar grain of the worn leather strap against the tender skin of her healing hands. The smooth spots on the scabbard and bandolier gleamed in the light of the little lamp, a silent testimony to the centuries of Bearers before her who had borne the Sword. How many times had the leather strap of the bandolier been replaced, or the scabbard repaired after a hard battle? She studied it, noticing as if for the first time that one of the buckles of the bandolier was tarnished silver and the other looked to be gold beneath its patina of age.

"You could wear it against your hip," Robin suggested. In the moments that she'd contemplated the Sword, he'd somehow procured a fresh shirt and combed his fingers through his scarlet hair, setting it at a rakish angle to his sharp green eyes.

She pressed a thumb against the cool leather of the bandolier. "No." She pulled the strap over her head, as she'd done so many mornings before this one, as she'd done on the morning of the battle at the Dark Keep. She settled the Sword along her spine, ignoring the sharp ache that reminded her of her healing wound. The blade remained silent, but it was still comforting somehow to feel its weight on her back.

Robin raised one eyebrow. "Don't go strange on me, Tess."

"What do you mean?" She felt her forehead wrinkle.

"Oh, you know, the self-loathing and guilt that you survived a great battle when so many did not. Punishing yourself by choosing pain."

"That's ridiculous." She pressed her lips together. "I just want to wear it the way I usually do. Something normal. Or as normal as things get around here, anyway." She met his eyes beneath his still-raised eyebrows. "If I get the urge to self-flagellate, I'll be sure to let you know."

"Sarcasm *and* a three syllable word," Robin said with a mischievous glint in his gaze. "Now I know you're awake. Come on then, food."

"Finally," Tess muttered. Robin merely chuckled as he pushed aside the curtain to their little compartment. As soon as they stepped into the passageway, the cocoon of silence fell away. Tess heard the murmur of voices, the hum of industry, and every now and again the cry of someone in pain. She jumped a little at the first sound of agony, but steeled herself and followed Robin as he slid down the hall with typical Sidhe grace. She let her thoughts wander aimlessly, marveling again at the ingenious magic woven into the High Queen's great gray tent, although it made her head start to hurt when she contemplated the complexity of the sorcery that would adapt the tent to every person's uses, as it seemed to do. They walked down a short passageway, marked on either side by jewel colored curtains that no doubt led to other sleeping compartments. When they reached the end of the hall, she glanced over her shoulder and saw the rows of curtains stretching as far as her eyes could make out; she blinked and something like a chuckle shuddered through the air.

Tess pushed away a sense of déjà vu as they entered a great room with a long table laden with food. It reminded her of when she'd first been allowed to leave her room after awakening in the Hall of the Outer Guard. She flexed her hands, running a thumb over the lacy scars on her palms.

"Lady Tess!" A red hawk arrowed through the air, the breeze from its wings brushing an errant strand of hair from her cheek.

"May I have the pleasure of accompanying you to your meal?" Forsythe asked as the small, agile bird circled again. "Gyre is restless and I would like to send him for a hunting flight."

"I'd be happy to have you join us," she said, and Forsythe leapt from Gyre's back on the hawk's next pass, landing neatly on her shoulder. His wings extended for balance, he bowed to her, though she could only see him out of the corner of her eye. He sent Gyre off with a sharp little whistle, and the red hawk soared into the upper reaches of the tent, disappearing from view.

"Robin, this is Forsythe," Tess said, motioning to the Wild Court fighter. Robin inclined his head. "Forsythe and his sister Flora were my first teachers in swordsmanship."

"Then I must thank you, Forsythe, for your help in creating such a formidable fighter," said Robin.

A blush heated her cheeks and she cleared her throat. "Formidable isn't necessarily the word I'd use."

"Legendary?" suggested Forsythe gravely. "We have been hearing tales of your prowess in the final battle against the Shadow Throne."

"Legendary," agreed Robin with a devilish gleam in his eye. "That's exactly the word I'd use."

"If your goal was to thoroughly embarrass me before breakfast, you've succeeded," she told them. "Now, can we just get some food?"

"The Lady Bearer gets a bit contentious when she's hungry," Robin said to Forsythe in a mock whisper.

"Insufferable, both of you," she muttered, grabbing a plate and surveying the bounty spread on the table. Most of the food was simple, but there was abundance. Tess single-mindedly filled her plate with bread, roasted meat, cheese and some fruit that looked something like a blueberry but tasted of honey. She added a few more onto her plate after experimentally tasting one and turned to the other long table reserved for eating. A few dozen Sidhe sat at the table. One glance was enough for her to realize that while the Wild Court and Seelie seemed to have no problem mingling, the few Unseelie sat in knots by themselves. She sighed.

"Not enough food for you?" Robin asked, bearing two plates of his own.

"Oh, there's plenty of food," Tess replied, heading toward an empty stretch of table. "I was just thinking that fighting Malravenar together apparently wasn't enough to make the Seelie and Unseelie stop despising each other."

"That is an old, deep wound, and it has festered for a long time," he replied, setting his plates down on the table. He looked at her consideringly, his voice low and uncharacteristically serious. "Have you heard the rumors from the Unseelie Court?"

Tess climbed over the bench, wincing as the movement stretched the tight muscles in her legs. "I don't usually put much stock in rumors, Robin, especially considering that I was the subject of so many during my time in Mab's Court. Some of her subjects seem to amuse themselves by thinking up the nastiest stories they can." She paused. "But considering the fact that I just woke up, no, I haven't had the chance to listen to any gossip."

"I said rumors, not gossip," said Robin mildly, his voice still serious, "and sometimes rumors are just shadows of a truth that is too terrible to view in its entirety."

Tess put down her fork and sighed. "All right. I see I won't be able to eat in peace until you tell me."

A spark of amusement glimmered in Robin's eyes. "I just think it's important for you to know all the latest news."

"I think you just enjoy being the bearer of news," Tess replied with a slightly raised eyebrow.

"That as well," said Robin without skipping a beat. He glanced down the table toward the nearest small group of Unseelie, and lowered his voice to a pitch that would be difficult for them to hear even with their keen Sidhe senses. "There are rumors that Queen Mab is losing her grip on her Court."

Tess blinked. She'd expected something more trivial, some tidbit about a burgeoning relationship between this member of that Court and another. Robin looked at her steadily, waiting for her to speak. "In what sense?"

"In the sense that she grows ever more suspicious of her own subjects, even those closest to her," Robin continued quietly.

A chill ran through her as she thought of her friends in the Unseelie Court. Who was closer to Queen Mab than her own Three? Not for the first time, she wished that Ramel hadn't been raised to that honor. Then she shook her head slightly at her own thoughts. How was it an honor to be bound by blood to a cruel Queen? She took a deep breath, consciously calming her burgeoning anger. She felt Forsythe place one small hand on the curve of her ear in silent support, and she focused on the gratitude she felt for such loyal friends.

"The news is disturbing," said Robin, still looking at her with his clear gaze.

"Yes," she replied honestly. "And though I don't support rumors, thank you for telling me." He nodded, and she sighed. A plaintive note entered her voice. "*Now* can we just eat?"

Robin grinned. "I should know better than to distract you from a meal."

Tess rolled her eyes and picked up her fork again. Forsythe leapt from her shoulder to the table. With a better view of him, she saw that one of his iridescent wings protruded at an awkward angle, like a bone that hadn't been set and healed wrong. He still used his wings to glide gracefully during the arc of his leap, but it was clear he couldn't fly like his Glasidhe brethren.

"Did you injure your wing in the battle?" Robin asked bluntly. Tess almost choked on her mouthful of cheese and fruit – she was used to being the most forthright person in the room.

"No," replied Forsythe. "After the Battle of the Royal Wood, the Vaelanmavar-that-was imprisoned the Vaelanbrigh and the Bearer." The Glasidhe crossed his arms, his aura faint enough for Tess to see the smile of satisfaction on his small, handsome face. "My sister and I and our kinfolk objected to his treatment of Lady Tess."

"He had some terrible things to say about the Glasidhe Queen too," she added, remembering the cold smile on the face of the now dead Vaelanmavar as he told the Glasidhe that Lumina had been tortured because the Small Folk supposedly knew the hiding place of the Iron Sword.

"Which in the end were just to provoke us," Forsythe said, flicking his good wing derisively. "I doubt that Queen Mab, even in her darkest days, would harm Lady Lumina. She would have had to kill all of us to touch our Queen."

Robin offered no opinion other than raising one eyebrow slightly as he completed his focused destruction of the pile of food on his first plate.

"But after all is said and done, a wing is a small price to pay for honor," said Forsythe staunchly.

"I've no doubt you would have given much more than that if called upon," Robin agreed gravely, sliding his first empty plate to the side.

"Many gave much more than me," the Glasidhe warrior said.

Tess swallowed her mouthful of fruit. "How did the Glasidhe fare in the battle?" Her stomach turned a little as she asked the question.

"In truth, better than the ground forces," replied Forsythe. "We were not without our casualties, but we are small and nimble and difficult to catch." His aura dimmed. "Galax fell defending Lady Lumina, and I will have to teach Wisp to ride his own feathered mount." He stepped forward and touched her hand at her stricken look. "It is not so terrible, Lady Tess. He may yet fly again, but only time will tell."

"What about your sister and cousins?" She pushed a lone crumb of bread across her plate to distract herself from the anxiety churning in her now full stomach.

"Farin lost an eye, but she is in good spirits and says she rather likes the look of the eye patch," Forsythe said, his voice warming fondly at the mention of his fierce, indomitable cousin. "Forin will have some scars, but nothing too permanent. And my lovely sister proved her worth in battle ten times over with nary a scratch."

"I'm not surprised," Tess said.

"At which part?"

"All of it," she said, letting herself smile a little. "Farin thinking that her looks are improved with an eye patch. Flora whirling through the battle so fast that nothing could touch her."

Forsythe nodded. "We had many of our kin fall that day, but it seems those closest to the Bearer are touched with uncommon luck."

She pressed her lips together grimly. "I doubt that had anything to do with it, but people will think what they like."

"Aye," said Robin, closing in on finishing his second plate. "Like the fact that you fought for three days and slew hundreds of Dark creatures in the courtyard of the Dark Keep, and single-handedly defeated Malravenar when you thrust the Iron Sword through him."

"It was far from single-handed," she protested. "The Queens were weaving their enchantment, and I wouldn't have made it through the courtyard without the rest of the vanguard."

"Legendary," said Robin to Forsythe, lowering his head slightly.

"If your goal is to annoy me with that nonsense, you're halfway to succeeding," she said mildly, finishing the water in her cup.

"I thought you said she was only contentious when she was hungry," Forsythe said in a low voice to Robin.

"I said no such thing," replied Robin, leaning his chair back and draining his own cup. "I just observed that hunger is simply *one* cause of irritation."

"Dealing with friends who don't know when to leave well enough alone is another," she said with a little grin to take the sting out of her words. In truth, it felt good to banter with Robin and Forsythe. It made the memories of shadows and blood recede just a little, like the ocean drawing back from the sand of the shore with the tides. But just like the sea beyond the safety of the shallows, she knew the memories were waiting, dark and deep, their invisible currents ready to drag her into their cold and lightless depths. Tess collected her plate and cup and stood, listening with half her attention to Forsythe and Robin's continued conversation. For now, she stood safely on the shore, but dark memories would come again as sure as the tide, and she had to be ready to swim.

Chapter 4

"Rosaline Cooper?" The secretary pronounced the name "Rose-ah-leen." Close, but no dice.

"Just Ross, please," said the young woman sitting in one of the chairs against the wall, looking at the fire chief's secretary with composed brown eyes. Ross wondered briefly why the secretary had put so emphatic a question mark after her name – she was the only one waiting for an interview, so was it a matter of pronunciation or disapproval at her application?

"Rose?" the secretary asked, her salt-and-pepper eyebrows rising fractionally.

"Ross," came the unruffled repetition, slightly louder in volume but accompanied with that same steady gaze. "Ross, rhymes with 'boss.'" She let herself smile just a little at the memory of Noah coining the phrase to help him remember how to pronounce her nickname. True, he'd also been fairly concussed and looped up on some nice pain medication after a training accident, but the catch phrase had become a fond hallmark of their relationship. She could even use it without the internal wince of pain now.

The secretary narrowed her eyes slightly, looked down at the open folder on the desk in front of her, and looked back up at Ross. "I just want to ensure that I have this correct before I send you in to the chief's office. You're qualified as a paramedic, but that's not the position you're applying for?"

"That's correct. I would be happy to work Ambulance as a substitute if needed, but I'm applying for a Truck position." Ross kept her voice level, as though she were just discussing the weather.

The secretary – Ms. Evelyn Patterson, according to the nameplate on her desk – pressed her lips together into a thin line, looked down at Ross's application again and back at the composed young lady sitting in one of the cheap plastic chairs that were all the fire department could afford right now with the budget crisis.

"Is the advertised position not open? Or is the chief not available for my scheduled interview?" Ross asked, letting her face settle into the determined expression that she'd honed since childhood. She'd watched herself in the mirror a few times, and it was hard to pin down *exactly* what changed about her face, a hardness in the eyes that most people associated with men, perhaps, and a firmness to her mouth that welcomed challenge. In any case, if she didn't know how to describe the expression, she at least knew how to use it, because people invariably understood that she meant *business* when she was wearing it. It counteracted the initial perception of beauty and therefore femininity that seemed to be the default reception when most people met her for the first time. She couldn't change the "good genetics" (her mother's cheerful term) that had bestowed her heart-shaped face, smooth golden tan skin and almond eyes, but she could damn well change how people viewed her, given five minutes. That, and they invariably noticed the muscles that changed the lines of her petite body from slender to sleek and predatory. She changed what she could with hard work, and if people didn't respect that or looked askance at her strength, well, she didn't have time for them.

"The position is still open," said Ms. Evelyn Patterson slowly, "and the chief should be finishing his conference call with the district chief shortly." The elder lady sighed and took off the glasses that perched on her nose, as though she would be able to see Ross more clearly without the interference of the thick lenses. "All I am saying," she continued in a marginally gentler voice, "is that we *do* have a paramedic position open as well. A different shift, but it might be an easier fit."

Ross smiled thinly. "Ma'am, I've never been one for *easy*." She considered rolling up her sleeve, showing her the furrow that raked across her bicep, the puckered scar a permanent souvenir of her second deployment to Iraq, courtesy of an improvised explosive device that had flipped her Humvee. But she kept her hands folded in her lap and decided not to give the older woman the satisfaction of seeing any emotion. Better to keep it locked up in the black box in her chest. The bare bones of her story were laid out on the black-and-white pages of her resume anyway; she'd tell more if asked, but she didn't owe anyone an explanation.

To Ross's surprise, Ms. Patterson's lips turned upward slightly at the corners in an echo of a smile. The elderly secretary placed her glasses back on her nose and said, "Well, then, perhaps you're exactly what this station needs...Ross." She closed the folder which had *Rosaline Cooper* inked neatly in block letters on the index tab and stood, straightening the hem of her pearl buttoned sweater as she strode over to the fire chief's door.

Ross shook her head slightly and let her smile widen for just a moment as she watched the plump secretary open the door, the steely-haired woman's head disappearing into the office. Then she straightened, feeling her phone vibrate in the cargo pocket against her thigh. Good thing she'd realized she hadn't put it on silent before the actual interview. She deftly slipped it out of her pocket and glanced at it cursorily, her fingers already feeling for the volume button. But as she looked again at the screen, a crease appeared between her eyebrows. She didn't recognize the phone number, but the area code was local. She tapped "Accept" and held the phone up to her ear, a voice on the other side of the line ringing out as soon as they connected.

"Hello?"

It wasn't possible. That voice. It couldn't be him. But all the same her body reacted – she forgot to breathe and her heart stuttered. Wild hope and sharp pain at the impossibility of that hope warred in her chest. She took a deep, shaking breath and ran through the facts of her life in her head. Noah had been killed almost eight months ago in an intense, fiery explosion. They'd told her, off the record, that it had been an IED the likes of which they had never encountered previously, and hadn't since. Noah had been gone for six months before that, deep into another deployment. She hadn't heard his voice in what seemed like an eternity... except for the last voicemail he'd left her the day before he disappeared, twenty-four seconds long, thick with static, and replayed again and again.

Ross slid to her feet in a fluid movement just short of a jump, pacing the small waiting area with long strides. She swallowed hard. Her voice came out more like a growl. "Look, if you're some asshole who thinks he's hilarious for getting this number and pulling a joke, you can go eat a…"

"Ross! Ross, thank God."

Her knees liquefied and she stumbled as she sat down hard in the cheap plastic chair again. The world fell away when she heard his voice, her heart leaping again and banging painfully against her sternum. The growl disappeared, replaced by a whisper. "Noah?"

"It's me, Ross. It's me." She heard him take a shaky breath. His voice sounded hoarse. "I can't talk long. I'm…I need your help."

"What the hell?" she whispered, still not trusting her voice. Tears – of relief or anger or both, she wasn't sure – choked her. Vaguely she registered that Ms. Patterson had finished her conversation with the fire chief and stood looking at her expectantly. "What…what *happened*, Noah? Why are you calling me and not someone from your unit? Did procedure all of a sudden disappear?"

Anger was easier. Anger she could do. "*What* the *hell* happened? You're dead. I helped arrange your funeral. I *went* to your funeral..."

The words choked her as memories rose unbidden in her mind, whirling with savage emotion. She breathed in deeply through her nose and clenched her jaw, compressing the maelstrom into a dense knot in her chest. She would *not* let it overtake her. Not here, not now, not ever again.

"Ross," Noah repeated, "I promise I'll explain everything. I'm on a payphone at the Exxon in Cairn. I need you to come pick me up."

Her entire body went cold and then hot and then cold again.

"Miss Cooper?" the fire chief's secretary said.

She swallowed. "I...dammit, Noah, I'm about to go into an interview."

In some part of her mind, she acknowledged that she was not a 'normal' woman. Her dead fiancé had just called her on her cell phone and she was calmly – *relatively* calmly – considering the impact to her job prospects. The knot in her chest tightened a bit, and she savagely shoved it into a smaller space. Fighting back against the emotion—that, she could do.

"Then come after the interview," said Noah, unshaken, "but I need to know you're coming. Please, Ross." He probably knew what was going through her head, and he accepted her approach: one problem at a time, focus on the immediate issues and press forward. It was one of the reasons they'd gotten along so well from the start. He'd never called her strange for being something different. Some*one* different.

Ross took a deep breath and looked at her watch. "I'll be there before eighteen hundred."

"Thank you." Noah's voice was fervent. Honest. "And Ross? I love you."

"Miss Cooper," said the secretary again.

Ross swallowed hard and ended the phone call. She set her phone to silent and slid it back into her cargo pocket, taking the moment to compose herself. She stared down at the black toes of her Converse shoes and took a deep breath. When she looked up at Ms. Patterson, her face was perfectly composed and courteous. "I apologize, ma'am. I went to check if my phone was on silent and my – my fiancé called to wish me luck."

Ms. Patterson accepted the half-truth without blinking an eye. "Well, Ross, the chief is ready to see you now."

Ross mustered a grateful smile as she stood, her hands unconsciously skimming around her waist, checking to ensure that her shirt was neatly tucked into her waistband and the buckle of her belt was aligned with the seam of her fly. "Thank you, Ms. Patterson."

The elderly secretary raised one eyebrow slightly and said, "Call me Eve, Ross."

Ross nodded, and her smile turned genuine as she walked toward the door of the fire chief's office, confident in the knowledge that she'd made at least one ally in the firehouse. She took one more deep breath as she crossed the threshold of the office, squaring her shoulders and focusing on the task at hand, able at least for the moment to put aside the fact that her fiancé had, for all intents and purposes, just risen from the grave.

Duke hung up the receiver of the pay phone, listening to the quarters tumble through the antiquated machine. He nodded to the gas station clerk, a guy in his late forties with a bristly mustache and grease stains on his faded jeans. "Thanks again for lending me the change. You work this shift every day? I'll pay you back for it." His voice sounded like gravel to his own ears.

"Don't worry about it son, you look you've been drug to hell and back," said the clerk, pausing to spit tobacco juice contemplatively into a white Styrofoam cup. His eyes paused on Duke's face. "Gonna be a nice shiner on your chin there." Duke didn't reply. "Tell you what, you need some water, take a few from the cooler." He motioned with his chin toward the glass door of the refrigerator.

"I...thanks," said Duke. "Really. I appreciate it."

The man nodded. He played the small town hick role well, but his eyes were sharp as he watched Duke take two bottled waters from the case. He spit again into the Styrofoam cup and replaced the makeshift spittoon below the register. His stained fingers drummed on the countertop. "You're him, ain't you?"

Duke paused on his way past the register, looking over at the clerk. "Who?"

"The one that went missin' *over there*." The clerk said the last two words like they were the name of a foreign country… which Duke supposed they were. A country of blinding heat and sand, but also soaring mountains and savage rivers, a land that could be as beautiful as it was treacherous. He tried to move casually, not letting his body tense to give away the sudden surge of adrenaline that flooded him at being recognized so easily. What had he expected? He turned back toward the register and schooled his face to show a mild curiosity in the clerk's words.

"Said you were killed after a while. They had your picture in the paper a few months back. Real nice memorial service." The clerk held Duke's gaze. "Just awarded the first memorial scholarship, too."

Duke took a breath. Well, that was one question answered…as if he hadn't already suspected from the ragged shock in Ross's whisper. The certainty in the clerk's eyes didn't brook any argument; he could deny it but that would only cement the certainty in the man's weathered face. Sometimes the truth was the easiest option. He cleared his throat. "Yeah. I'm him."

The clerk nodded slowly, his hand disappearing, retrieving the cup again. He spat for a third time, sucked on the wad of tobacco in his lip for a moment, and then said sincerely, "Glad you ain't dead."

Duke managed half a grin. "Yeah. Me too." He held up the bottled waters. "Thanks again."

The clerk nodded silently and went back to thumbing through a hunting magazine on the counter, leaning on his elbows and thinking about how his wife would love to be the first with this piece of small town gossip. A small smile turned up one side of his lips beneath his grizzled mustache as he savored the victory warming his insides, kindled by the knowledge that he wouldn't tell the nagging woman a single thing, and she'd never be the wiser.

Duke stepped out into the rising heat of a Louisiana summer day, the humid air wrapping around him with the familiarity of a lover's hands. He swallowed hard, rubbing one hand over his chin. Eight months. They'd been gone eight months and it had seemed like a couple of weeks on the other side of the border between the worlds. Now he'd deal with the fallout. For a moment his mind strayed toward Ross, how it must have hit her when he'd disappeared, whether she'd moved on in eight months… he shook his head. No. Not now. Time enough for thoughts later, when they'd sorted some things out. One problem at a time. He squared his shoulders, glanced up at the sun and started hiking back toward the river, cutting through the long waving grass. When he was out of sight of the road leading to the gas station and its squat white building, he broke into a distance-eating lope, ignoring the protest of his sore body. Time enough for pain later, too, when they were all safe and healing and not out in the open.

He picked out the crooked tree that marked the curve in the river and headed toward it, sliding under the wooden slat of a fence in disrepair. The hum of insects increased as he neared the river, the scent of the swamp intensifying. Lucky they'd been thrown into a relatively remote little bend in the river. He let himself think about the reaction of the gas store clerk if he'd seen them thrown from the portal into the parking lot of the gas station. He winced. Lucky in more ways than one, although it had been a close call with Luca in the river. The big *ulfdrengr* was heavy and hard to move, but Duke had carried guys his size before, in training, with fifty pounds of gear added: vests heavy with loaded magazines and Kevlar plates, weapons outfitted with high-intensity lights and precise scopes, water and food and medical kit all added to a two hundred twenty pound man. Carrying someone that heavy compressed your joints, made you feel every stride in your knees, all the muscles in your shoulders and back straining to keep you upright in the fight against gravity. Back then, in the infancy of their training, he'd cursed the sadistic instructor who'd paired the smallest guy in the class with the biggest guy for buddy carries. But it had become a pattern, one that he'd learned to anticipate and even enjoy a little, in a weird way. Just like carrying the biggest weapon on patrols, carrying the biggest guy for casualty drills became a part of his path to earning the trust and respect of his fellow trainees and then his teammates. They had to know that he'd pull his weight, or carry theirs, in a fight for their lives, and the training had paid dividends several times even before he'd been thrown through a portal back into the swamps of Louisiana.

By the time he'd carried Luca to the bank of the river, the navigator – Merrick, his mind supplied – was there to help heave the motionless *ulfdrengr* through the mud and onto a dry patch of ground. His gray eyes wide, Merrick had watched as Duke slapped Luca's pale face sharply, once, and then a second time. Duke dug his knuckles hard into the larger man's chest, going for the nerve at the sternum that was enough to shock guys awake. In the back of his mind, he had wondered how much time had passed since they'd been thrown through the portal, since Luca had landed face down in the river. But he had a pulse. Duke had checked again to make sure.

"Come on, brother," he'd muttered, Merrick hovering close by. He slapped Luca's face again, lighter this time but still firmly, talking to him now. "Come on back, wake up."

And maybe Luca had heard him, because he choked and Duke rolled him with quick efficiency onto his side as he coughed out the river water from his lungs. But then, as soon as the blond giant had dragged in a full breath, he'd come up swinging, landing a solid punch to Duke's jaw that sent him staggering back for a moment, and fighting off Merrick when the navigator tried to intervene, the smaller Sidhe still no match for a Northman's blind strength.

Duke had seen red and his body had flashed hot after that hit, instincts beaten into him over and over again taking control as he leapt onto Luca. The big man was definitely stronger and plainly well trained – he'd seen enough of his fighting to know that – but he was disoriented and still coming up out of the fog of unconsciousness. Duke had taken full advantage, sliding into position easily and locking his arm around Luca's throat, snugging his elbow tightly beneath his jaw. And he spoke firmly into Luca's ear, holding the choke at just this side of tight, not squeezing enough to cut off air but enough to let him know that it was a good grip that he couldn't escape.

"I need you to calm down, brother," Duke had said into Luca's ear, "you're confused and you wanna fight, but we're not the enemy. Now you gotta calm down or I'll put you out for a few minutes and I can't promise you won't wake up hog-tied like a calf at the rodeo."

The big, muscled body straining against his grip slowly relaxed.

"That's it," Duke said into his ear, noticing, not for the first time, the intimacy of the chokehold. Some didn't understand the bond between teammates, and this was only one of the countless experiences that tied them as close as brothers – their bodies, exhausted and straining against each other, with each other, in training or in combat. They joked that they knew each other better than most women knew them, even though the women got to know them in the biblical sense. Except Ross... Ross had always known him like he knew himself. She had reached into him and found the animal that raged in the cage in his chest, and stared into its eyes, unafraid. He forced himself not to think of her.

When Luca's hands fell away from Duke's arm, he had slowly released him. Both men rolled to their knees, Luca breathing heavily and Duke watching the larger man warily. Luca blinked those unsettling wolf-eyes and swallowed hard. His voice came out in a rasp. "Where are we?"

Duke had sat back on his haunches and chuckled. "Surprised you didn't ask if we were dead. That was *my* first thought when I landed in *your* world."

Luca, though still ghostly pale, had managed a grin. "You are both here, and while I don't doubt you are valiant enough to earn entrance into the halls of the gods, I do not think the halls of the gods would smell like this." He'd wrinkled his nose at the smell of the swamp. Merrick had given a little chuckle at the wry humor in Luca's words.

"Gotta give that one to ya." Duke had smiled grimly too.

Now, water bottles in hand, he glanced at the sun sinking toward the western horizon, lengthening the shadows. The grasses parted against his legs as he tramped through the thickening brush. The bottles of water from the gas station sweated in his hands. As he neared the tree, he caught a glimpse of movement up in the great reaching branches. He stopped, his eyes searching the foliage, but after a long moment he couldn't find anything. Then Merrick dropped out of the tree to land a few paces away, gray eyes glinting in the shadows as he sheathed his sword.

"What are you, a damn panther?" demanded Duke. "What made you think it was necessary to climb into the tree and lurk there?"

"This is not my world," replied the navigator, sliding through the shadows. Luca sat against the trunk of the tree, one knee drawn up to his chest and his eyes closed, though he opened one eye at the sound of their approach.

"Here," said Duke, twisting open one of the water bottles and handing it to Merrick. The Sidhe passed it to the *ulfdrengr* without a second thought. Duke frowned slightly when Luca accepted it without protest, but he opened the second bottle and gave it to Merrick.

"I have a friend coming to pick us up at the gas station in about an hour," he said, glancing again at the sun.

"Who is this friend?" asked Merrick, his voice carefully neutral.

"I trust her with my life," said Duke, "if that's what you're asking."

Merrick gazed at him with unflinching gray eyes. It struck Duke that he'd once thought Merrick looked young. His face was still youthful, but his eyes had aged in the war to save his world. Then a spark of humor glimmered across his expression. "And what's a *gas station*?"

Duke chuckled. "I'll try to explain on the way. It's not far, but I don't want to keep her waiting." He watched Luca out of the corner of his eye as the *ulfdrengr* stood. A light sheen of sweat gleamed on Luca's pale skin, and he put out a hand to steady himself on the trunk of the tree. Duke didn't say anything, but the medic in him made a note. Then again, he thought, he'd felt sick for a solid day after traveling into the Fae world. He hoped it was just that.

Merrick saw Duke eyeing their weapons. Luca's axes hung from their loops at his belt, one of them retrieved from the silt-thick creek, and Merrick still carried his own sword in the sheath at his hip, along with an assortment of daggers.

"It would not feel right for us to be unarmed in a strange world," the Wild Court navigator said, one pale hand touching his sword hilt unconsciously.

Duke took a deep breath and then nodded. "If we run into anyone, just let me do the talking."

"If their accent is as strong as yours, I doubt I'll be able to understand them," Merrick replied lightly.

Duke grinned. "You haven't heard the half of it yet."

They began walking through the long grass in the deepening gold of the evening light, both of them keeping a subtle watch on Luca. The *ulfdrengr*'s movements were somewhat stiff, but his face was stoic as he kept pace with them.

"So now," said Merrick, raising an eyebrow at Duke, "I've read my fair share of texts on the mortal world, but none of them have mentioned *gas stations*..."

Chapter 5

Tess resisted the urge to scratch at the stitches across the top of her shoulders. Though the Sword remained silent, it appeared that the accelerated healing abilities bestowed on its Bearer remained intact. Two days of food and sleep had restored her body, with only a hint of soreness lingering in her muscles. Her hands had healed as well, the new red scars already fading to pink, layered over the silvery ripples from the Crown of Bones.

She'd tried to work a regular shift in the healing wards, queuing with the healers and their acolytes at the long table with all the supply satchels, but one of the younger healers had firmly told her that Maeve had explicitly forbidden the members of the Queens' Company to work for at least three days. She'd sidestepped that edict by visiting her friends in the wards…and if she were to help their caretakers a bit, who would deny her that small task? So now she sat by Sage's side, legs folded neatly beneath her and a leather-bound book in her hand. Every few minutes she glanced up to check the rise and fall of his chest as he slept, and every quarter hour she gently wiped the sweat from his brow. At the foot of Sage's pallet, a pin held a small sheet of parchment in place; each shift's healer wrote notes on this sheet in neat shorthand at the end of every shift. Tess had glanced at the record curiously, but her *taebramh* hadn't helped translate the unfamiliar symbols. Perhaps her *taebramh* would start being useful again when the Sword decided to stop ignoring her, she thought sourly. After her initial surge of annoyance, she thought that she'd ask one of the healers to teach her the shorthand. She couldn't depend on her powers to give her everything, she told herself firmly. Even the Bearer should practice some good old-fashioned studying every now and again.

"Lady Bearer." The young Seelie healer who had charge of this row during the morning shift gave Tess a respectful nod. After a whispered conference with their superiors on the first day of her appearance, they'd accepted her presence. Maybe Maeve had allowed it because she could sense the Bearer's restlessness, but Tess didn't particularly care either way.

"Cora." Tess marked her place in the book with a thumb and returned the nod. "How is everyone today?"

Cora unpinned Sage's record from the foot of the pallet, her quick blue eyes reading the notes left by the healers in the hours since her last shift. "A few better, but just as many worse." She replaced the record and delicately took Sage's good wrist in her grip, counting his pulse just like any nurse would in the mortal world. Tess wondered if Luca had been injured and if he'd been taken to a hospital – would they be able to help him, or would their well-meaning ministration of mortal medicine kill him? The thoughts barely turned her stomach anymore. It was amazing how her thoughts had worn a well-trodden path in just a few days.

"What seems to be making them worse?" Tess asked. She shrugged her shoulders a little to shift the scabbard of the Sword. It pressed against part of the line of stitches and offered at least a moment of relief from the unbearable itching.

Cora pressed her rosebud lips together. She looked entirely too young to have experienced the horrors of war, but Tess could see it in her eyes. "For some, it's the graveness of their wounds; for others, we think maybe poison laced the blades of the enemy."

Tess looked at Sage. He hadn't awoken during any of the time that she'd spent by his sickbed, but that didn't mean she wouldn't continue to watch over him, just as she'd promised. Just as he'd done for her when she hovered between life and death after crowning Vell at Brightvale. "There's no poison in his blood, is there?"

"None that I've been able to see," Cora replied honestly. She paused and then continued. "It's best that he keeps sleeping."

Tess nodded. "I understand. It helps the body heal."

With that, Cora checked the strip of linen at Sage's wrist that protected the ampoule of anesthetic and sedative. It looked like a miniature bottle, shorn in half and filled with the liquid that kept Sage in his peaceful sleep, sealed against his skin with a word of healing magic by Maeve herself. Amber liquid swirled within it.

"Another day, maybe two," said Cora, replacing the bandage and making a quick note on Sage's record. She glanced at Tess. "It will be difficult, when he wakes." She pressed her lips together again. Tess guessed that it was a habit when the junior healer was pushing the limits of her authority. "Would you like us to send for you when it's time? I can pass the word to Verity, she's the next shift…her relief is Faelan, and he would do it too, I'm sure of it."

Tess tried to hide her surprised look at the mention of the other healers' names.

"What, Lady Bearer?"

"Verity. It's a very…*Victorian* name." Tess tilted her head and contemplated the book in her hand. "Very Jane Austen."

"I have very little idea what that means, and I do have others to attend," replied Cora with a considering look. "I think it's a family name, in any case."

"I'm sorry," Tess apologized quickly, "thank you for the offer. I'd very much appreciate it if you could let me know when he's about to wake." She paused. "And if it's not too much trouble, is there a book on the shorthand you use to notate the charts? I'd like to learn it."

A smile touched Cora's mouth. "I'll leave my handbook on the bedside table there during my next shift. It's a standard text that most of the healers learn during their apprenticeship. The section on shorthand should be enough."

"Thank you," said Tess earnestly.

Cora nodded and moved to the next supine figure, an Unseelie fighter with one leg bound from hip to ankle in a splint and most of his face obscured by a swathe of bandages about his head. Like Sage, a bandage covered the ampoule sealed to his wrist, but the liquid in the Unseelie's vial was emerald green. Tess watched for a moment, resisting the urge to offer her help, and then turned back to the book in her hands.

Robin and Calliea had helped her gather a few books that outlined the history of the Great Gate. Tess had been surprised to learn that what seemed like enough books to fill a library had been taken from Darkhill and the Hall of the Outer Guard on the journey to the last great battle. Robin had informed her with a half-smile that most of the Scholars would only leave if they were allowed a stipend of books to bring with them. Some of the tomes had already proven useful, with old maps of the White City tucked among their pages. Tess wondered if the old Chief Scholar – what had been his name? Egbert? – of the Unseelie Court had indeed named Bren as his successor. She smiled slightly at the memory of her early days in Faeortalam, and then the smile faded as she silently recalled the number of her early friends, alive and vibrant in her memories, who had been burned on the funeral pyres of the war dead.

"I thought I'd find you here."

Tess looked up and met her brother's eyes. She managed a tight smile. "You thought you'd find me here, or your Wild Court healers told you that I was here?"

Liam shrugged. "Both, I guess."

She marked her page in the book with the slim ribbon sewn into the little tome's spine and motioned to the space next to her. "Not much room, but I'm happy to share it."

"That's certainly a departure from our childhood," Liam replied as he took the offered seat. He moved with a smooth, sure grace, remarkable for a man of his size. He'd always possessed the surety of movement that spoke of his honed athleticism, but now he held his body with an added elegance that only underscored his strength. It reminded Tess with a painful jab of Luca.

"You move almost like one of them now," Tess said off-handedly, trying to keep her voice casual as she waited for the sting of memory to fade. "I mean, you were always more coordinated than me, I'll give you that, but I guess being one of Vell's Three has its advantages."

Liam made a noncommittal sound. "Or being healed by the fragment of a deity who was one of her Three…"

Tess set the book aside and then didn't know what to do with her empty hands. She rubbed her thumbs along the lacy edges of her scars. "I know I made that decision for you. And if you're…"

"Stop," said Liam gently, his green eyes resting on his sister's face. "We've already been over this, Tess. I'm not angry with you. How could I be? You made the best decision that you could at the time. And so far, I'm pretty happy that I'm not dead." He smiled and leaned back on his hands. He glanced at Tess. "That was a joke. Or at least an attempt at one."

She managed a tight smile at his prompt. "I know. I'm sorry. I just keep replaying everything in my head." She swallowed against the tightening in her throat.

"Doesn't do anybody any good to drown in guilt, Bug," Liam said quietly, putting an arm around her shoulders, careful of the scabbard on her back and her line of stitches.

"I know that," Tess said with a sigh. "The rational part of my brain knows that, at least. But sometimes my mind gets away from me."

"Then don't let it get away from you," Liam suggested.

"Thanks, I'll take it under consideration," she retorted dryly. "I really enjoy reliving the most terrifying day of my life over and over again, not sure I want to cut that short."

"Terrifying? I thought it was more epic and exciting." Quinn stopped at the foot of Sage's pallet.

"That will make me feel better about my difficulty processing it too, thanks," Tess said pointedly. Liam chuckled and Quinn smiled. The tattooed man was less exuberant and sarcastic than before the battle, his ebullient personality dampened by Niamh's injury.

"How is she?" Liam asked. None of them needed to say her name aloud to know that he spoke of the Valkyrie.

Quinn rubbed at the stubble on his strong jaw. "I talk to her. I don't know if she hears me. Maeve stops by at least once a shift."

"No better and no worse?" Tess suggested, thinking of Cora's earlier words.

"No worse," agreed Quinn, "but that doesn't mean that she's not getting better and we just can't see it." The stubborn set of his mouth dared them to argue, but they didn't.

"As much as we respect our...*distinguished*...visitors," said Cora from behind Quinn, "if you would like to socialize, please conduct your gatherings *outside* my ward."

Quinn turned to face the Seelie healer, standing almost a full head taller than slim, white-blond Cora. He bowed his head respectfully to her. "Yes, ma'am. Just saying hello to a teammate." He gave Liam a parting salute, to which Liam replied with a choice single finger. Quinn grinned, gave Tess a nod and strode toward the exit of the healing ward. Cora eyed Liam with a mixture of forbearance and consideration.

"I promise we'll be quiet," said the newest of the *Vyldretning*'s Three in a voice smooth and soft as velvet.

"If you disturb any of my charges, I'll ask you to leave," said Cora, one pale eyebrow raised.

"If I disturb any of your charges, I'll escort myself out without another word," agreed Liam. Tess observed the exchange between Cora and her brother with barely veiled amusement. Cora fixed Liam with an evaluating look, then nodded and swept purposefully away.

"Well, now I know that both your sense of humor and your silver tongue survived the encounter with Arcana," said Tess in a low voice when the Seelie had disappeared from sight.

"Silver tongue? I can't imagine what you mean, dear sister," said Liam with a grin.

"It doesn't hurt that you're a handsome mortal man," she added, making a face. "Though it *does* make my head hurt to even think about that."

"You and I both aren't quite mortal anymore," Liam replied easily. "You know that."

Tess waved a hand through the air. "Right. Remnant of a deity for you, ancient weapon of power for me." She shook her head. "Though I've been pretty much on my own since the battle."

"Maybe it needs to recharge," Liam suggested.

"If it was awake, it would reprimand you for that comment," she replied, "but that's proof of how deeply it's sleeping. Hibernating. Whatever it is." She glanced at Sage and watched him for a moment before turning back to her brother. "Do you feel Arcana at all? Anything left in there?"

"Sometimes." Liam blinked and then shrugged. "Nothing to write home about." He motioned to the leather-bound book by Tess's knee. "Speaking of home, research on the Gate?"

"I have to do something to keep me...well, not even busy, but at least feeling like I'm doing *something*."

"Vell meant what she said, you know. She'll help you."

"I know. I don't doubt her." Tess shifted. "I think Titania will offer her support, but Mab...Mab is the wild card. She doesn't like me much."

"You never really explained that to me."

"Well," Tess said, "there's not really much of an explanation. She doesn't seem to *like* anybody. She uses people. And I didn't let her use me. I escaped Darkhill and became the Bearer when she had other plans."

"I see," said Liam, though his tone made it clear he didn't.

Tess brushed one hand against her belt pouch, a movement now made unconscious by its frequency. The feel of the river-stone pressing against the supple leather reminded her that Malravenar had indeed been broken and bound. "From everything I've read, it will take all three Queens to open the Gate."

"There were only two Queens before," pointed out Liam. "Why can't it just be two Queens now?"

"I don't *know* all the answers, and I may be translating wrong anyway," Tess replied edgily, "but from what the books are saying, the words mean something like 'all those crowned.'" She shook her head. "There's no incentive for Mab to open the Gate. It will require a good amount of her power, and from what I've heard, she's already got her hands full with the reconstruction and her sister."

"What exactly have you heard?" Liam asked quietly. Tess looked at her brother and saw that his eyes had gone chillingly distant, an echo of Arcana's inhuman stare.

"Finnead has been over to the Unseelie camp," Tess replied, vaguely proud of the steadiness of her voice. "Maeve and a few other of our healers have made the journey as well, but they haven't been able to heal the princess." She took a moment to watch Sage again. "And I'm sorry about the fact that it seems like they won't be able to bring her back." She paused, wondering how many of the supposed 'rumors' her brother had heard. "And I've been told that Mab is getting a bit paranoid," she added softly. "She thinks that there are plots against her, apparently. But it still doesn't sit well with me that Mab will most likely refuse to help in opening the Gate."

"First things first," said Liam. "Have you spoken to Vell or Titania?"

"No. They've been...busy." Tess shifted.

"You know that the Queens are never too busy to spare a moment for the Bearer," Liam said.

"Not only do you move like one of them, you sound like one of them too," she muttered.

He smiled. "I'm one of Vell's Three. I have an inside channel, I guess you could say."

Tess waved her hands. "Don't want to know about it. Keep the details to yourself."

Liam's smile widened into a grin. "Oh, because you've heard that Vell and I..."

"Details to yourself!" Tess repeated in a heated whisper, lowering her voice quickly as Sage shifted restlessly on his pallet.

Liam sobered as he glanced at Sage. They sat silently for a moment until he settled. Tess reached out and brushed an errant lock of hair away from Sage's eyes.

"Maybe you need to redirect your research," Liam offered quietly.

"What do you mean? We need to know how to open the Gate."

"Mab and Titania created at least part of the Gate before, didn't they? They created the Seal, at the very least. So I'd leave that part to them." Liam paused. "Maybe you need to find something that would make Mab more...agreeable."

Tess snorted. "I doubt that exists." When Liam didn't smile, she narrowed her eyes. "You're serious. Did you See something?"

Liam shook his head. "No. This isn't part of Seeing or being one of Vell's Three. It's part of knowing people. Part of what I had to know to do my job well."

Tess shifted the scabbard of the Sword again until it rested against the latest patch of skin threatening to drive her crazy with the urge to scratch at it. She grimaced slightly. "So I have to find a bargaining chip powerful enough to lever Mab into cooperating with one of her least favorite people."

"I don't think she dislikes Titania *that* much," said Liam wryly.

Tess chuckled. "I didn't mean Titania and you know it."

"I can't let your head inflate too much with your own importance," he replied. "I've heard the word *legendary* being used in reference to you."

"Are you sure that isn't just hurting *your* ego?" Tess grinned.

"My ego is in no danger of being hurt, let me assure you," said Liam with a Cheshire Cat worthy grin. Tess smacked his arm lightly.

"I told you I don't want to hear about you and Vell. And if one of the two of you wants to talk about it, I'd rather it be Vell."

"As you wish, Lady Bearer," he replied with an affectionately mocking bow. "Just remember that I'll always be your big brother."

Tess pushed down the sudden memory of Liam lying on floor of the throne room in the Dark Keep, a dagger in his side and his lips blue as he gasped for breath. She smiled and stood with her brother, giving him a hug as he said something about a summons from Vell. She sat back down as she watched him glide silently away, her brow creased in thought. Picking up her book, she thumbed it open to the marked page. Finding something to barter for Mab's cooperation seemed like a task more impossible than crossing the gorge over the Darinwel without a bridge, but if it brought her closer to opening the Gate and finding Luca, she'd apply every waking moment to it. "I have a feeling I'm going to need more books," she murmured to herself, settling down for a few hours of reading.

Chapter 6

Ross took another deep breath as she guided her truck down the main road through Cairn in the deepening twilight. The sun didn't set until nearly eight o'clock, the daylight hours lengthening as the humidity and heat increased their summer grip. She'd held it together through the interview, but the moment that she'd shut the door of her truck and thumbed open the GPS application on her phone, her hands had started shaking. She refused to let her mind dig too deep into the phone call. She'd checked the location of the Exxon in Cairn and navigated her way across the traffic clogged bridge over Lake Pontchartrain. Nearly an hour to think about the sound of his voice, the way his words had shot like an arrow into her heart as though she had no defenses at all. She flexed her grip on the steering wheel. That hour had been whittled down to maybe five minutes. Five minutes and she'd either rain down righteous fury on some jerk who thought this was a good practical joke…or she'd be staring into the eyes of the man that she'd thought she was going to marry. That was before he was killed on his last deployment, with only unidentifiable ashes remaining, leaving her with just photographs, memories, and a crisply folded flag.

The smooth, calm voice of the GPS prompted her to turn right onto a side road that could barely be called paved. She tapped the brakes lightly to avoid raising a cyclone of dust around the truck. The gas station rose out of the long grasses about half a mile down the road. She swore softly and pressed her lips together at the rapid hammering of her heart. It felt like the night before boot camp, or maybe the night that Noah had picked her up for their first date. Maybe even the moments before their transport had touched down on the airstrip first deployment.

"Get it together," she admonished herself in a low voice, coasting the last of the distance toward the gas station, tires crunching on the gravelly road as she turned the truck into the little parking lot.

The gas station clerk glanced up as the black pickup truck parked in the far corner of the lot in front of the station. At first look, he would have guessed the age of the woman in the driver's seat to be barely eighteen; she stared at the steering wheel and seemed to be trying to gather her nerve. But then her face changed, hardened, and he was suddenly unsure of his earlier guess. She looked like a person who had seen and done things far beyond her years.

The woman wore a simple black t-shirt, but even so, the clerk could see the outline of the muscles in her shoulders and arms. Again he revised his assessment. This was a woman who could snap most men in two, either with the sharpness of her gaze, the strength of her convictions, or the power of her body. She sat for another long moment in her truck, pulled her shoulders back and killed the engine, opening the door and sliding down onto the hot asphalt with practiced ease. She wore her black hair pulled back in a sleek braid, had clean and pressed gray cargo pants and black Converse shoes. He couldn't tell the color of her eyes from this distance, but he thought that maybe they were gray or green. It would fit with the exotic look of her face.

Ross felt the eyes of the clerk inside the store evaluating her. The distance and the pane of glass between them didn't dull her perception of his curiosity. He watched her like he was waiting for something to happen, like something had already happened and he was waiting for the logical conclusion. Her chest ached as her heart tried to batter its way through her ribs. She scanned the area around the parking lot. There was a stand of a few trees about a hundred yards down the road, and a one-story house that was most likely a converted doublewide trailer barely visible on the horizon beyond the stand of trees. A slight breeze stirred the thick air and brought with it the scent of the swampy river. She resisted the urge to shove her hands into her pockets or cross her arms. Then she saw him, and for a moment she forgot to breathe.

Duke walked out of the shadow beside the farthest gas pump with his heart trying to climb out of his throat. God, either she'd gotten more beautiful or he'd just forgotten the stomach punching ferocity of her: the compact contours of her body and that sweet face aligned into such determined lines, the flash of her eyes, and the tightening of her shoulders as she struggled with the simple task of standing still. Constant movement, that was a part of his memories of her, a whirlwind of soft skin and hard muscle, delightful tenderness and iron will. He knew it the moment that she caught sight of him. Her whole body jerked as if she'd just absorbed a hit, and her eyes widened. He forced himself to keep his strides even, though a good part of his mind wanted to break into a sprint and cover the distance between them as fast as his legs would carry him.

Ross didn't move. She watched him walk toward her with wide eyes, her shoulders rising and falling with huge breaths. He couldn't tell if she was excited, or angry – hell, he couldn't tell what *he* was feeling at the moment, so he closed the last few feet with two strides and stopped an arm's length away from her, giving her enough space to choose her next move and interact with him on her own terms.

Her dark eyes traveled over him once, then twice, her chest heaved, and then she threw herself at him. He barely had the time to brace himself before she was in his arms, head against his shoulder, hugging him so hard he thought that maybe she'd break one of his ribs, and he'd gladly accept it if it was the price he had to pay to feel her body pressed against his again. He felt her heart hammering against her breastbone as though she'd just finished a hard run. The pulse pounding in his own ears was no calmer. He could barely breathe, both from her grip and from the emotions raging inside of him, though he'd never willingly admit it. Except maybe to her. Except maybe to the woman in his arms.

Ross drew back and kissed him hard, her mouth hot on his, her hands sliding up to either side of his face. The feel of the callouses on her palms sliding across his skin drew an incoherent sound of want from deep within him. If she kissed him any longer, he'd throw her over his shoulder and carry her back to her truck. His mind short-circuited, emptying of all rational thought, then suddenly she ended the kiss and his arms were empty. He barely had time to open his eyes before she slapped him.

The grizzled clerk winced as he spit into his Styrofoam cup. Maybe not such a happy reunion after all. He'd thought for a moment that he'd have to fetch the water hose to spray the two of them down. It was the most exciting afternoon he'd had all week. Heck, maybe even all month at this rate.

Duke took a deep breath, the hot sting of the slap still burning across his cheek. "Okay, I deserved that." His voice came out a little hoarse. Ross balled her hands into fists, her glare as hot as the asphalt beneath their feet. He took half a step back. "But I don't think I deserve a punch."

"Start talking," Ross said without relaxing.

Duke glanced over at the gas station and saw the clerk hastily lower his head over his magazine again. "Can we…I mean, this is kind of a very public place…"

"You picked it," she said unrelentingly. "And now you better start telling me the best explanation ever concocted on God's green earth about why in hell you disappeared for eight months and I thought you were dead and now you show up in the middle of nowhere at a goddamn gas station." Her voice, rather than increase in volume, lowered and increased in intensity until she was almost hissing the words, her eyes still hot with anger and unshed tears.

Duke cleared his throat. "Okay. I'll tell you. But just promise me…promise me that you won't call the cops or anything."

Her face hardened fractionally. "I'm not promising shit, Noah."

He rubbed the back of his neck and gave a quick sigh. "Fair enough. I just don't want you to think I've lost my marbles. Anyway, here goes." And he told her the most condensed version of the story that he could manage, sticking to the major points. It sounded crazy to his own ears. He watched her expression change from angry to disbelieving and suspicious, settling into something like sadness when he finished with being thrown through the portal at the Dark Keep.

"You were injured, weren't you?" she asked softly, a crease appearing between her brows. "And you dreamed all this in a coma. Or you're still hallucinating."

He swore under his breath. "I wish it were that simple sometimes."

Ross bit her lip and she pressed her palms against her thighs. It was one of her tells, one of the signs that she was uncertain or anxious. Duke took a tentative step toward her. "Look," he said, hands raised slightly in an unconscious calming gesture, "I'm not trying to freak you out. I'm not trying to pressure you. But it's not just me, Ross. I've got two guys depending on me."

She narrowed her eyes and half-turned away from him. "Two guys?"

"I wasn't the only one pulled through the portal. There are two other guys, and I need to find a safe place where I can really check them over. Transiting between worlds is kinda rough." He smiled slightly at his attempt at humor. Ross didn't smile, eyeing him warily. "They're good guys, guys that I fought alongside." He paused. "I don't really know what else I could say to convince you. But you were the first one – the only one – that I called." He shook his head. "I know I just turned your world upside down, Ross, and I'm sorry, but I didn't know who else to call." He spread his hands in front of him, hoping that she'd believe him.

Ross took a deep breath and gave him a long look, her dark eyes boring into his soul with searing sharpness. Apparently whatever she saw when she flayed him open satisfied her. She shoved her thumbs into her pockets and spread her fingers over her hips. "All right. Let's go pick up these guys. I'm assuming that you've hidden them somewhere while you came to the meet."

Duke smiled. "You know me too well."

She sidestepped his reaching hand. "I…Noah, I'm going to need some time. You're right, you just turned my world upside down. Inside out, I guess." A gut wrenching sorrow filled her face for just an instant. "I thought you were dead. I planned your funeral. It's going to take me a little while to sort things through." And then the sorrow was gone, replaced with a practical air. "But you said you have buddies who need someplace safe, and even if you're crazy, I can't leave you or them out here in the heat." She lifted one eyebrow. "I couldn't even do that to a stray dog."

Duke chuckled. "You're such a humanitarian."

"No," she replied, "I don't like most people." She gave him one last considering look before turning toward the truck. "But I love you, so that tilts most things in your favor."

He thought his heart would stop right then and there when she admitted that she still loved him, and his smile turned into a grin as he followed her toward the truck.

"You can wipe that shit eating grin off your face," she said as he climbed into the passenger's seat, giving him a mock scowl. "I'm still pissed at you for disappearing for eight months and making me think you were dead." The engine rumbled to life and she adjusted the air conditioning. Duke leaned back in the seat and sighed as the cool air flowed over him.

"I never thought I'd feel air conditioning again," he said with a groan of pleasure, closing his eyes.

"Try not to get too excited about it," she replied acerbically. "All right, where are these other two wing nuts that you're bringing along for the ride?"

"Make a right outta the parking lot. One of 'em likes to climb trees to keep overwatch so I put him in that little stand near the river."

As Ross maneuvered the truck out of the parking lot, she almost told him that the doublewide a few miles out from this gas station had been unoccupied for nearly a year, and they could hole up there. But she pressed her lips together. What kind of person would that make her?

"You're thinkin' of telling me to kick rocks and go set up in that trailer out there, huh?" Duke said without opening his eyes. He adjusted one of the air vents slightly.

"Yes," Ross replied honestly. She sighed. "But you know I can't do that."

"Because you love me." He said it almost in a whisper, and she glanced at him to find him looking at her coyly through lowered lashes.

She snorted. "Yes. Because I love you."

"Because I'm your special kinda crazy idiot." He fluttered his eyelashes.

"Yes," she said dryly, "and that story you told brings a new meaning to that." But she couldn't help the smile spreading across her lips. "God, I missed you." She swallowed hard, the amusement nosediving into gut clawing sorrow, an echo of the loss and abandonment that she'd felt when she'd finally accepted that *he wasn't coming back*.

"I missed you too, Ross," Duke said, now serious. "I thought of you every single day. If there was a way I could have let you know what happened, I would have."

Ross cleared her throat. "All right. Enough with the emotional talk." She pulled the truck onto the narrow gravel shoulder. "Let's go get your friends." By the end of her sentence, she'd already killed the engine and had her door open.

"Ross," said Duke, pulling her attention back into the cab of the truck. He smiled, and she saw the tiredness written across his face. "I love you, too."

She managed a small smile. "I know."

They closed the doors of the truck and headed toward the trees, Duke still wearing his smile even though he was exhausted down to his bones. He'd had a lot of crazy days in his life, but being thrown into another world, fighting an ancient deity and then being tossed back into southern Louisiana ranked among the more improbable of his adventures. He frowned and motioned for Ross to pause behind him. He and Merrick had agreed that Merrick would call out with a bird whistle when he saw Duke approaching, and with a vantage point in the tree, Merrick should have seen them by now, but no bird whistle had split the thick, humid air. Long grasses swayed in the slight breeze. The tree's low limbs and the Spanish moss created a dappled thicket, perfect for concealment but also not ideal to jump into without any idea what had happened.

"What's wrong?" Ross murmured, already instinctually crouched into her ready stance. One of her hands drifted toward her cargo pocket, where Duke had no doubt she carried a knife. She always carried a knife. One of the many reasons why he loved her.

"No call and response," he replied in a low voice. His mind raced. Had they been followed through the portal? Had a local stumbled upon this remote place in the short time he'd been gone? He wet his lips and trilled a short whistle, breathing a sigh of relief when the response call sounded from somewhere in the grasses. Duke ran forward, picking his way over the gnarled roots of the trees, Ross following closely behind him. He almost tripped over Merrick, the Sidhe was that silent and well hidden, but one look told him why Merrick wasn't up in the tree.

"He had a shaking fit," the navigator said, kneeling beside an unconscious Luca, "and I thought it better to keep watch over him."

"You did the right thing," said Duke, evaluating the big *ulfdrengr* visually.

"How long did the seizures – the shaking fit – how long did it last?" Ross asked, sliding past Duke to kneel beside Luca. She quickly checked his vitals. "Rapid, shallow pulse. Clammy skin." She looked up at Duke. "He's in shock, I'd bet on that, but I don't know about the seizures. Let's get him in the car."

Merrick had leaned protectively over Luca when Ross had dropped to her knees, watching her with wary gray eyes, but he settled back as he watched her work.

"We just can't catch a break," said Duke in frustration, running his hand through his hair. In the back of his mind, he noticed how his heart swelled with pride in his girl: someone in trouble and she was right there, no matter what. "All right. Merrick, this is Ross. Ross, this is Merrick and the big guy is Luca."

Ross gave Merrick a curt nod but remained focused on counting Luca's pulse, two fingers pressed against the artery in his neck.

"Merrick, help me carry him," said Duke, positioning himself at Luca's head. The *ulfdrengr* was bone-pale, his skin alarmingly cool to the touch.

"I'll get the truck ready," said Ross, bounding off through the long grass.

It was one thing to drag Luca out of the creek with the aid of adrenaline. It was another thing entirely to carry the *ulfdrengr* the hundred yards to the truck. But between Duke's stubbornness and Merrick's Sidhe strength, they managed it, and Ross had the back seat of the cab ready with a blanket and pillow.

"I'll ride in the back with him," Duke told her, and she nodded in agreement. Luca was so big that Duke ended up putting the *ulfdrengr*'s head and most of his shoulders across his lap, using the pillow to make sure Luca's head wouldn't hit the door if they hit a bump in the road.

"We should be going to a hospital," Ross said as she jumped into the front seat. Without skipping a beat, she fastened Merrick's seatbelt for him. The Sidhe navigator ran his long fingers over the straps of the restraint, a considering look in his eyes. He grimaced slightly and took a deep breath; Ross hoped he wouldn't be sick in her truck.

"No hospitals," said Duke. In less than an hour, Luca had gone from walking and talking with them, though not without some discomfort, to comatose. Every instinct directed him to find the nearest Emergency Room and let a doctor handle it. But he shook his head. "He's not human, Ross. I don't know what would work for him and what would kill him."

"Northerners are much like Sidhe," said Merrick from the front seat. "You can test anything you need to use on him on me first."

As soon as Duke had said "not human," Ross looked more closely at the lithe young man in the front seat of her truck. His clothes were outlandish – they looked like they had gotten a flat tire on the way to the nearest Renaissance festival – and he wore a sword at his hip. There were several other sheaths holding daggers. She saw one at the top of his boot, another on his forearm, and she was sure there were more weapons she couldn't see. They were all encrusted with the remnants of grime and gore; she wrinkled her nose as she suddenly acknowledged the smell of unwashed men and blood filling the enclosed space. But more than that, there *was* something inhuman about Merrick in the alabaster perfection of his skin, the strange masculine beauty of his face, the gleam of his dark hair. He caught her eyes and tucked his hair behind one ear, offering more evidence of his otherworldly appearance: the tips of his ears were delicately pointed.

It crossed her mind to laugh and commend him for a great costume, but that thought died as she really *looked* at him. Her skin prickled in goose bumps as her instincts recognized the *otherness* of him, the alien power flickering in the air around him. She swallowed hard and tore her eyes away from Merrick, twisting to look into the back seat. Duke looked up from examining Luca and caught her eyes. "You weren't…you didn't make this up," she whispered.

"No," he replied steadily. "I didn't. We need to get somewhere safe, Ross. Somewhere we can help him."

She nodded jerkily and turned around, swallowing hard.

"For what it's worth," Merrick said quietly, "I may not be human, but I am not your enemy. I will defend you along with my sword brothers, in this world and my own."

Ross blinked at the sincerity in his voice. "Thanks." Her voice came out hoarse, and she focused on starting the truck. As she pulled away from the little copse of trees with her newly resurrected fiancé, an unconscious man who could have come from the world of Conan the Barbarian, and an alien-elf in her front seat, Ross almost laughed at the thought that when she'd gotten up this morning, her biggest worry had been what to wear to her interview at the firehouse.

Luca shuddered and Duke adjusted his grip on the *ulfdrengr*. "Drive as fast as you feel comfortable, Ross." A low urgency undercut his calm words.

"Got it," she said, and she didn't miss the little yelp of surprise that came from Merrick as she jammed her foot down on the gas and the truck leapt forward, roaring down the road through the deepening dusk of the southern night.

As the pale dust settled onto the still warm asphalt, a shadow detached itself from near the dumpster at the side of the gas station. It was as though an oil slick had been draped over a man. Thick darkness oozed around the figure, absorbing the fading rays of the sunset. The man shaped slice of darkness slid toward the wall of the convenience store and melted into it.

At the register, the grizzled clerk looked up from his magazine. The grainy black and white footage that showed the security camera's view of the pumps and the back two corners of the store flickered. He reached up and tapped the side of the old pendulous monitor, but rather than fixing the problem, the picture disappeared entirely with a faint *pop* and a little burst of acrid smoke. He sighed and cursed under his breath. One more thing for him to fix.

One of the lights in the back of the store flickered. The clerk looked up, squinted, saw the figure gliding toward him when a moment before his shop had been empty. He reached for the pistol in the concealed holster beneath the counter, but then the light over the register exploded, shards of glass showering him like deadly raindrops. He ducked, covering his face with his hands, and when he looked up again, a faceless black figure stood before the register. The thing reached out something that was almost an arm, and the clerk's blood ran cold. He fumbled for the pistol, but then the thing touched him, and the world went black.

Chapter 7

Tess stood next to the kitchen table in her childhood home and rubbed her fingers lightly over the grain of the wood. Her father read the newspaper at the table, the ancient coffee maker that he refused to replace rattling as it heated up water in preparation to brew. Lila sprawled in a patch of sun in the adjacent dining room, eyes closed in canine bliss.

The sound of a scream, a voice stretched thin with agony, rippled through the house. Tess turned toward the sound.

"Just ignore it," her father said in an unconcerned voice, turning the page of the newspaper.

Why would he tell her just to ignore it? The scream came again and the voice plucked a chord of memory. She couldn't recall the name but deep down she *knew* the person to whom the voice belonged. Tess walked quickly through the dining room, past Lila, who raised her golden head and gave half a wag of her tail, and opened the front door, stepping out onto the porch that her parents had built themselves, sanding and staining the planks with painstaking care. The scream echoed again. A jogger continued down the street, undisturbed, giving Tess a friendly wave. She listened, straining to place the scream, racing down the front steps when it came again from someplace to her left.

Her vision went black and the world whirled sickeningly around her. When the darkness receded, she stood once more next to the kitchen table. The scream came again, and then another. One man, one woman, both sounding as though they were being tortured.

"I told you to ignore it," said her father.

"I have to find them," Tess said. "I have to...I have to stop whatever it is that's hurting them." Another voice joined the chorus of agony, and then another. Tess felt sick as the cacophony rose in volume, surrounding her with a sensation bordering on tangible.

"Their pain will end soon enough." Her father folded the paper neatly and laid it on the kitchen table, making a motion of dismissal with one hand.

She began to pick out words in the screaming. And she remembered their names. She could hear Calliea and Merrick, Sage and Finnead, Robin and Moira, all of them crying out to her to rescue them, to save them from their torment at the hands of Dark creatures. She ran out the front door again, only to have the world dissolve and reform around her, placing her neatly back at the kitchen table.

"You thought you'd saved them, but I will still claim them," said her father, standing up from the kitchen table. His face changed, shifting with a horrible liquidity into the coldly beautiful face she recognized as Malravenar. Darkness pooled beneath him, tentacles reaching out from the blackness to slide over the objects of the room, transforming everything it touched into that dark, glimmering substance from which the Dark Throne had been made.

The chorus of torture intensified, the screams whirling around Tess like bats. Panic rose up within her. She couldn't escape. She couldn't defeat him, not this time, and everyone she knew and loved would pay the price.

"Tess!" Robin's voice sounded distant, but it was different than the screams and cries of pain.

The room around her was completely black, glittering with Malravenar's power. He looked at her, drinking in her distress as though sipping fine wine, and then he laughed.

Tess jerked awake, Malravenar's laugh echoing in her ears, a cold sweat soaking the blanket that had tangled around her legs in her fitful sleep. Robin sat back as she took a few measured breaths and pressed the heels of her hands to her eyes.

"Nightmare?" he asked quietly.

She swallowed thickly and nodded, not trusting her voice.

"Part of the battle or something else? Though of course you don't have to talk about it if you aren't inclined. I've found, though," Robin continued as he delicately adjusted the *taebramh* lantern to give a little more light, "that talking about my nightmares helps."

"You've had nightmares?" asked Tess, disentangling her legs from the blanket.

"Yes. Mostly of the battle in the courtyard. I thought it would never end, and in my dreams it doesn't. Or at least, not until I've seen everyone I know killed by the monsters." His green eyes flickered. "Sometimes they are resurrected, only to be killed again because I'm too slow to save them."

"When I stood before the Dark Throne, Malravenar took me to my childhood home. He showed me my mother and father…actually, he tried to *be* my father. He told me he could give them back to me." Tess drew her legs up and rested her chin on her knees. "I said no. In my dream, I'm there again. I can't escape. But I can hear the screams. I can hear everyone being tortured." She shivered. "And then Malravenar speaks through my father as though he's not broken and bound into the river stones. He says that he will still claim all those I know and love." She took a deep breath, trying to calm her racing heart. "It wasn't real," she said, more to hear the words aloud than anything.

Robin folded his legs beside her. "It wasn't real, but dreams have a way of illuminating very real fears."

"Malravenar is bound and broken in the river stones," Tess said. She ran her thumbs over the scars lacing her palms. "I shoved the Sword through him myself."

"You experienced his power first hand," said Robin.

"He must have thought I was the weakest, because he focused on me."

"Quite the opposite, I'd think," replied Robin. "He didn't give any of the rest of us a second glance. He focused on you because he knew you were the key to his downfall. And you broke free. You and the Queens defeated him."

"Then why is he still in my head?" whispered Tess, feeling almost as forlorn as when she'd first woken up in Darkhill in a new and strange world. "It doesn't *feel* like I defeated him."

"I don't have the answers to that, Tess," Robin said, "but what I *do* have is a sword arm itching for some sparring."

Tess folded the blanket and half-heartedly ran a hand over her braided hair. It would do, especially if she'd be sweating during a sparring session soon. "I should check on Nehalim too."

"Oh, he's getting fat in the paddocks," said Robin. "I think he has his eye on a few pretty mares."

Tess smiled. "Let me grab a quick bite before we head out." She slipped the strap of the Sword over her head. Moira had pulled out the stitches across the top of Tess's back before she'd gone to sleep, and the scar was tender but not unbearably so.

"Already covered." Robin tossed her a neatly wrapped little packet that she found to contain an apple and a cold meat pastry from the prior night's dinner. After buckling the scabbard of her plain blade to her belt, she followed Robin through the wending halls of the tent, eating her breakfast contentedly as they walked.

When they passed through the great columns of the entrance to the hall, Tess realized that it was the first time since they'd returned from the Dark Keep that she'd ventured outside. The sun shone brightly overhead, thick golden light pouring down over the ruins of the White City, gilding the pale stone and banishing all but the most harmless of shadows. Tess marveled at the marked difference just a very few days had made in the appearance of the city. New glass glimmered in the arched windows of the cathedral, and the stones of the path beneath their feet and the buildings rising around them gleamed alabaster in the sunlight, cleaned of the grime of decay and the Dark creatures' occupation.

"There's been talk of the *Vyldretning* setting up her Court here in the White City," said Robin as they walked side by side down the causeway. "For now, Queen Mab has taken the western portion of the citadel and Titania the eastern. The Wild Court has made their place much where they please, but most of us are helping in the Queen's Cathedral."

"So it is a cathedral," said Tess, tilting her head back slightly to better feel the welcome touch of the sun on her face.

Robin shrugged slightly. "That is the best word that I can find to describe what it once was. Something of a palace but also something of a place of worship. A sanctuary and a place of learning."

"Like the Saemhradall?"

"All respect to the Seelie, but the Saemhradall was a pale copy of what this place once was."

They passed a handful of Sidhe on the paved path, most of whom touched their foreheads in obeisance to Tess, who gave them a nod in return.

"I don't think I'll ever get used to that," she muttered.

"Well, you'll only have to deal with it for the rest of your life," replied Robin cheerily.

Tess rolled her eyes as she followed Robin off the main path and through a carved arch. They walked down the smaller path – alleyway? Tess wondered – and then passed through another, larger arch into a huge square.

"Now tell me that doesn't put a smile on your face," breathed Robin as they paused to take in the sight of the practice yard, large enough to hold hundreds of fighters and hosting at least three score warriors engaged in various activities. White chalk marked out sparring circles on the hard-packed earth, and at the far end of the square were targets painted with bullseyes for archery. The smell of wood smoke drifted briefly over the yard, and Tess traced the source to a building along the periphery of the practice grounds. A handful of fighters formed a queue just outside the open door, and she glimpsed the glow of a forge, the ring of a hammer on metal distant across the expanse of the practice yard.

"Chael has set up shop?" Tess asked as they made their way toward a practice ring.

"Some days," replied Robin. "His apprentice Thea has taken on most of the simpler repairs to weapons, and Conall is there to help with the more complex work."

Tess wondered if that meant that Chael was spending most of his time with the wolves – she hadn't seen the one-eyed *ulfdrengr* or any of the three wolves in the great tent in the cathedral – but her thoughts were cut short as they reached an empty practice ring. She pulled the strap of the Sword over her head again, her hands lingering on the battered sheath for a moment longer than necessary as she stared into the emerald in the pommel. How many times had she growled in annoyance at the Sword's presence in her head and the turn of its power behind her breastbone? Now she willed the Sword to give her any sign that it wasn't just a dead instrument, a weapon that served no other purpose than to draw blood. If the Caedbranr was only a sword now, what did that make her? At least she still had her own *taebramh*, her reserves depleted but replenishing as she regained her strength.

"Tess?" prompted Robin.

She set down the Caedbranr just outside the practice ring and turned to face Robin. "Sorry. Got lost in my thoughts there for a moment. Would you like to start with a warm up sequence?" She drew the blade that bore the names of the dead, light rippling down its length, and they stepped into the ring, swords meeting in a choreographed dance.

After an hour of sparring, Robin grinned at Tess and motioned with his head toward the fountain in the corner of the yard. She sheathed her sword and nodded, catching her breath as she retrieved the Caedbranr and they walked the perimeter of the yard toward the water. Copper cups hung on hooks above the burbling fountain, once again giving Tess cause to appreciate the elegant simplicity of Sidhe design. Robin handed her a cup and she gratefully filled it with water, her eyebrows shooting up in surprise as she found that the water was ice-cold.

"That tastes almost as good as the water from the river in the Northern wilds," she said with a smile.

"No water will *ever* taste *that* good," retorted Robin with a grin.

Tess pulled her shirt away from her sweaty skin. The morning had grown warm, but not uncomfortably so, and a slight breeze brushed against her skin every now and again. Her eyes roamed over the Sidhe practicing in the yard. As they'd learned the hard way while traveling to the Dark Keep, appearance alone was not a sure way to decipher Courts anymore with the mixture of Seelie and Unseelie in the Wild Court. The *Vyldgard* did tend to set themselves apart voluntarily, though, wearing bright colors and complex braids with feathers and strips of dyed leather interwoven with their hair. Tess spotted a few of the *Vyldgard* sparring with some of the Seelie warriors. "Is everyone playing nicely together?"

Robin shrugged. "There is always a bit of tension, but the Unseelie have been rather withdrawn. We haven't seen many in the common areas."

Tess took another draught of the icy water. "Why?"

"Far be it from me to guess at Queen Mab's motivation, but I have heard that she has...*discouraged* her subjects from mingling with the other Courts."

"Whatever her motivation, that does sound like her." Tess finished her water and wiped her cup clean, replacing it on the hook to be used by the next parched swordsman or archer. She frowned as they began the walk around the perimeter of the practice yard back to their circle. "Have you heard anything else about the Unseelie Court? I'd think that the rescue of the crown princess would improve Mab's mood, but…" She let the sentence fade and shrugged.

"Rescue is a strong word," said Robin. "Her body is here, yes, but her mind is gone. Or so I've heard."

Tess pressed her lips together as she set down the Caedbranr. "I wouldn't wish madness on anyone. But madness is her best defense right now. She killed *Vyldgard*."

"And took part in the harrowing of the North, apparently," said Robin grimly. "So both the *Vyldgard* and the *ulfdrengr* lose no sleep over her fate."

"We sound ruthless, don't we," mused Tess.

"We are," replied Robin without any sarcasm. "We've seen war. We stared into the face of evil and came out alive. That changes a person."

"When did you become so serious?" she asked, shaking her head.

"When we stepped through the portal into the Dark Keep." Robin paused and then grinned. "But I'll tuck away the serious side for now. Another bout?"

"Sounds preferable to listening to your somber statements," replied Tess with an answering grin. They stepped into the circle and leapt into another sparring match, this time almost at full speed. Tess found in surprise that she was almost as fast as she'd been before the journey into the Dark Keep, even without the Sword's power rumbling in her chest. Apparently, she had been changed thoroughly and indelibly, and even if the Sword never awoke again she would remain not quite mortal. For the first time since she'd raced Vell down the mountain toward the White City, she let go of conscious thought, letting her body flow into the practiced motions of swordplay, the burn in her muscles and the slide of sweat down her back a welcome counterpoint to that feeling of impotence that had lingered in the back of her mind. Robin launched into a quick attack, driving her back across the circle, but she locked blades with him and slid away, dancing to the side. He turned and she slid her sword beneath his guard, resting the point neatly just below his rib cage. They remained in their frozen tableau for a quick moment, the only movement the rise and fall of their chests and the slow smile spreading across Tess's face. She lowered her sword and Robin relaxed.

"You have lost none of your quickness, Lady Bearer," he said with a grin and a playful bow. "Though your counters are still a bit sloppy when you're tired."

"And *you* have lost none of your cheek, Robin," said a new voice from just outside our practice ring. Tess turned and her smile widened as she saw Moira.

"And you have lost none of...your..." Robin narrowed his eyes, grasping for an appropriate ending to the sentence. "Hair," he finished triumphantly, grinning as Moira rolled her eyes.

"How observant," the spritely *Vyldgard* fighter chuckled. Several strips of red leather bound back her mane of tightly coiled curls, keeping them out of her face but letting them spring free in a golden halo around her head, like a painting of a Byzantine saint.

"Well, keeping hair isn't a given these days," said Robin, raising his eyebrows. He raised his free hand to the back of his head, where stubble of scarlet hair had begun to grow around his still healing gash.

"I know, since I cut your hair myself," replied Moira, grinning. "Unless the knock to your head made you forget that." She slid her bow down from her shoulder. "Mind if I join your session?"

Robin promptly stepped out of the ring and threw himself emphatically down on the ground, leaning back on his elbows. "By all means, try to counter the supernatural quickness of the Bearer."

"Thanks for asking me whether I wanted a break," Tess said dryly.

"I need to warm up, in any case, so there's ample time for you to recover," said Moira, her curls swaying about her head as she completed a few slow patterns with her sword.

"I'll be fine. I just wanted to see whether I could make Robin blush." Tess raised an eyebrow at the red-haired *Vyldgard* warrior.

"Takes a lot more than that to make me blush, dear Tess," Robin replied with a lazy smile, watching the sun gleam on Moira's sword as she increased the speed of her strokes.

"Well, you know the saying. Or maybe you don't," amended Tess. "If at first you don't succeed, try, try again!"

The sunlight and good companionship did wonders for her spirits as noon approached, their shadows shortening beneath them to daubs of darkness on the hard-packed earth. Tess sparred with Moira, losing two out of three matches.

"There goes any chance of my ego growing too big," she said, only half-joking, as she watched the tip of Moira's blade lower from her throat.

"If you were fresh, it would have been a different story. As it was, we are very evenly matched. Perhaps you should consider being more willing to switch sword hands," Moira said.

"I don't want to rely on my left hand too much," Tess said, wiping sweat from her forehead with her sleeve.

"You're not relying on it. You're using it to your advantage. In any case, I think I shall challenge Robin to a few matches." Moira raised one eyebrow and pointed her sword beckoningly at Robin.

"And I shall gladly accept such a ravishing sparring partner," Robin replied, springing to his feet.

"And *I* shall gladly accept a break," said Tess, mostly to herself. She wiped her face again and smoothed back the tendrils of hair that had escaped her braid. There was no shade to be found, but she didn't mind much as she took Robin's place at the perimeter of the circle. She hadn't yet tired of the warm sunlight. Perhaps she would never tire of warmth, she thought idly, since she'd felt the cold touch of Malravenar trying to wrench the life from her body. As she watched Robin and Moira spar, her mind circled back to the problem that occupied every spare moment – the opening of a Gate between the worlds. Could they open the Gate as Malravenar had tried to do, by breaking the Seal? Or was the Great Gate so poisoned that it needed to remain sealed by Titania and Mab's enchantment? If that was so, Tess thought, they could most likely open a lesser Gate like the ones that had existed in the Seelie and Unseelie lands even after the closing of the Great Gate centuries ago.

She rested her unsheathed blade across her knees and watched the sun shine on the silver between the engraved names of the war dead. The names rippled slightly, moving beneath the smooth surface of the sword like the reflection of clouds moving across a still lake. Tess watched the names intently. Murtagh's name eventually appeared, and a few moments later Kavoryk. They were still compiling the records of the dead. She had checked with the Scholars of the Seelie Court once already, adding the names of their dead to the sword. Each Court kept a great scroll as census, births and deaths, and a separate column for the coming of age ceremony in which their Queen publicly acknowledged the Sidhe as adults. In the Unseelie Court, the tradition involved drinking water containing Mab's blood, binding them to her and allowing her to sense any disloyalty. Tess wondered if any of that had changed with the resolution of the war. During the bleakest days of the struggle with Malravenar, Mab had resorted to draining the life force from members of her Court chosen by lottery, Murtagh among them.

Tess swallowed back the tightness in her throat and touched the smooth surface of her sword lightly with two fingers. She'd freed Murtagh from Mab's hold, but in the end, *she* had killed him by draining his power to free Queen Titania from Malravenar's ethereal prison. In a way, she was no better than Queen Mab. The thought rankled her. She clenched her jaw and took a deep breath. To distract herself, she plucked a small spark of her *taebramh* from the recovering well by the pulse of her heart, sending the bit of power rolling down her war markings like a marble on a spiral chute. She rested her chin on her shoulder and watched the intricate whorls of her markings flash emerald beneath the white cloth of her shirt. The little spark split into four different pulses of light, sliding over the paths of her war markings like a bit of captive lightning. The sparks reached her hand and jumped from her skin to the smooth surface of her sword, disappearing with a little ripple into the shifting engravings of the names of the dead.

Tess shifted her focus and watched Robin and Moira lock blades, both of them moving with liquid grace, springing toward each other and then dancing away. She thought of the training session on the great flat plain of the Deadlands where they'd pitted the vanguards against one another in good-natured contest, and all the warriors had watched the twins Niamh and Maire battle fiercely for the victory. It still didn't seem real to her sometimes that Maire and Elwyn and so many of those she had known were dead. Somehow she expected the twins to come prowling into the practice grounds, golden and beautiful and alive. Her chest ached dully at the thought.

"All right, Tess?" Robin asked, the two fighters taking a quick break between matches.

Tess smiled half-heartedly. Robin narrowed his eyes at her. "Thinking serious thoughts," she admitted under his skeptical gaze. "I was just thinking that I have this feeling of expectation. This feeling that Luca will walk around the corner or the twins will burst into the practice yard and raise havoc. That I'll see Elwyn conferencing with Vell." She shrugged. "I remember the feeling from when my father died. It goes away eventually."

"That doesn't mean it's particularly pleasant," said Moira, taking a swig from a flask.

"Never said it was," replied Tess. "Only that it will fade."

"The pain fades, but the loss will be there forever," said Robin in his somber voice, staring down at the sharp edge of his blade.

"The loss will be there forever," agreed Moira, and to Tess's ears it sounded like the solemn conclusion to a recited prayer.

"Shall we see if they can find anything useful for us to do back at the palace?" said Robin after a long moment of silence.

Tess clambered to her feet and brushed the dust from her legs. "Maybe we can convince Maeve to lift the restrictions on the Queens' company working in the wards." They began walking back toward the palace, their shadows lengthening as the sun progressed toward the western horizon.

"Well, I don't know if I want to be *that* useful," deadpanned Robin, and the two women chuckled as they threaded their way through the once great city, ruined statues gazing down on them with sightless eyes, the wind brushing through cavernous empty buildings, moaning quietly behind the stone walls.

Chapter 8

"I don't exactly live by myself," cautioned Ross as she pulled onto the interstate, glancing in the rearview mirror to catch Duke's eyes.

"If you'd be more comfortable setting us up in a motel, I'll figure out how to pay you back," he replied without hesitation. "I just need to get these guys somewhere safe and figure a few things out."

"No," Ross said quickly, changing lanes to pass a slower driver. Merrick grabbed the handle above his door, his face pale as Ross pushed the needle of the speedometer over eighty. "It's fine, we have a three bedroom and Vivian is gone right now, but I'll have to talk to her before she gets back."

"Right," said Duke, taking another set of Luca's vital signs.

"How is he?" she asked.

"Respiration shallow and pulse is fast, and he's still clammy. Shock, like you said before."

"There's another blanket under the seat."

Duke carefully shifted Luca's weight and reached under the seat, his questing hand finding one of her ubiquitous brightly patterned Mexican blankets that appeared at festivals and lazy days on the beach. He shook it out from its neat folds and draped it over Luca. It only covered down to the *ulfdrengr*'s knees, but it was what they had. Luca wasn't shivering, like most in shock did, but Duke wondered if the Northerners ever felt cold. Did their bodies even react to it like he expected of humans?

"Better?" Ross asked, her eyes flicking up to the rearview mirror again. He'd forgotten her habit of making eye contact even if a person was in the back seat.

"Better than nothing," Duke said honestly, a thread of frustration thickening his drawl.

Ross frowned. "What's wrong?"

"Realizing that I know jack shit about these guys' physiological markers and systems," muttered Duke, his mind running at full speed through the knowledge that he'd learned as a medic. How much of it was applicable and how much of it was garbage when it came to the Fae?

"Hey," she said in a firm voice, "we'll figure this out together, okay?"

He nodded.

"I will help as much as I'm able, though I'm not a healer and I haven't encountered the *ulfdrengr* when they are wounded," said Merrick, his knuckles still white as he gripped the overhead handle.

"This is your first ride in a car, huh?" said Ross as she passed a truck towing a speedboat on a trailer. Merrick gazed with interest at the other vehicles and the passing signs.

"Yes," the *Vyldgard* navigator replied. A slight sheen of sweat glistened on his pale skin. "It is very...enclosed."

"You could have ridden in the truck bed if you'd preferred. Sometimes May likes to ride back there on short trips."

Merrick frowned and glanced through the rear window to the truck bed. "I don't think that would have been an advisable solution, given our speed."

Ross narrowed her eyes at him. "Are you sure you're not Vulcan?"

"Vulcan?" Merrick looked over his shoulder at Duke for help with the unfamiliar word.

"He's not Vulcan," Duke answered for him. "He's Fae."

"Fae," repeated Ross blankly. "Like faeries and legends kind of Fae?"

"Something along those lines."

"You're still going to have a lot of explaining to do after we put out the fires," Ross said under her breath. A convertible cut in front of the truck, forcing her to slam on the brakes. Duke's shoulder crashed into the back of her seat but he managed to keep Luca from hitting his head or sliding entirely off the back seat, and Merrick closed his eyes, bracing himself with his elbow against the window. Ross punctuated her tirade of full-volume curses with a middle finger directed at the balding driver of the convertible as she passed him in the other lane. Her oaths decreased in volume until she muttered a few more to herself and then sighed. Merrick opened his eyes and seemed relieved that everything was much the same as when he'd closed them. Silence settled over the truck cabin for a moment. Then Merrick tilted his head, his silvery eyes contemplative. He glanced at Ross, observed her for a moment and then slowly unwrapped his fingers from around the grab handle, settling his hands in his lap.

"Who is May, and *why* would she enjoy riding in the bed of the truck?" he asked, pronouncing the foreign words with delicate care.

Ross smiled briefly. "You'll meet May soon. She's the third roommate. And she likes riding in the bed of the truck because she's a dog."

"That makes much more sense," said Merrick thoughtfully. "I didn't know that mortals still kept hunting hounds."

Ross laughed, which seemed to startle him. "You really did drop out of medieval times, didn't you?"

"I…no," replied the navigator in surprise. "From what I understand, time is fluid between our worlds, but it's much the same. I don't believe that there is a significant…"

"It was a joke," said Duke, smiling a little despite his worry for Luca. "Kinda like I thought I'd been dropped into Valhalla when I popped out in your world."

"Valhalla?" Ross arched an eyebrow.

"There were warrior women on flying horses, okay? It was all very Final Fantasy."

"Was Quinn with you? That would be his wet dream," she said with a chuckle as she took an exit off the highway. "We're about five out."

"Yeah, Quinn was having a nerdgasm the entire time," drawled Duke. "Totally his thing…armor, swords, dragons, the whole nine. We didn't actually see the dragon," he clarified. "They just told us about the hunt."

"Oh, you didn't actually *participate* in the dragon hunt. I see," said Ross with mock sincerity. "That makes *much* more sense." The truck hit a pothole and Merrick's hand jumped reflexively toward the grab handle, but he set his jaw and put his hand back in his lap. Ross turned the truck again from the main road onto a smaller two lane road much like the one on which the gas station had sat. Gnarled oak trees reached their limbs over the road, branches trimmed away from the power cables. The lush green of riverside land overflowed in places, long grass spilling onto the shoulder of the road, a riot of greenery climbing up around the tree trunks and the mailboxes that stood along the road every hundred feet or so.

"Still technically Cairn," said Ross, "but it's a little closer to the city."

The city, of course, meant New Orleans. They'd spent a few nights of drunken debauchery in the Crescent City on his predeployment leave. It was a city of memories for them. He'd proposed in the gardens of Jackson Square over a year ago, the scent of camellias and honeysuckle heavy and sweet in the humid air. The ring hadn't been large, Ross had never liked flashy. She preferred classic and understated when she chose to wear jewelry. He glanced at her hands on the wheel but couldn't see if she still wore the ring.

The crunch of gravel beneath the tires cut into his thoughts as Ross pulled the truck into the driveway. The small house sat a few hundred yards back from the road, shielded by a few large oaks dripping with Spanish moss. Like most houses on the edge of the bayou, it sat on cinderblock stilts, nothing like the elegant, stork-like legs of the summerhouses that looked out over the lake by the city, or stood by the shores of the Gulf. Just enough that if the bayou heaved a couple of feet of muddy water toward the road, the little house wouldn't be flooded, except maybe in a hurricane. In a hurricane, pretty much everyone was screwed anyway, so Duke didn't quite understand the expensive houses built on soaring twenty foot poles. But people with money to burn would do what they pleased. Ross threw the truck into park, jammed down the parking brake with her foot and reached over to release Merrick's seatbelt. He gingerly extricated himself from the belt, watching it automatically retract like one would watch a snake slithering across the ground.

"Let me put May into the guest room quick before you come in," Ross said, jumping out of the truck. She crossed around the front of the truck and opened Merrick's door as well, a small part of her empathizing with him. She couldn't imagine being thrown into a world where everything was strange and new, though she could grasp at the sensation from her experience overseas. That was as close to another world as any, she supposed. "You got him?"

"Yep, we'll handle it," said Duke. Merrick leapt out of the truck and then stumbled, his usual poise deserting him as he caught himself, swaying. Duke watched him warily. Apparently it wasn't only Luca having trouble with the mortal world. Merrick took a few breaths with his hands braced on his knees and then clenched his jaw in determination. He caught Duke's look of concern and raised his chin challengingly, daring Duke to comment. The wiry medic shook his head slightly and filed the observation away for later.

Luca stirred as Duke carefully shifted him. Merrick managed to open the back door of the truck's cab. The *ulfdrengr* jerked and tried to lever himself upright, only Duke's quick shielding of his head preventing him from knocking himself out on the ceiling.

"Easy, big guy," Duke said. "I *really* don't want to fight you in the back seat of a pickup truck. Brings back some bad memories."

Luca coughed and swayed, his surge of motion receding as he sat on the seat. "Where am I?" His blue eyes were bloodshot as he took in his surroundings.

"Someplace safe. The house of a friend," said Duke. "How are you feeling?"

"Like I fought a cave troll and lost," said the *ulfdrengr*, tugging experimentally on one of the loose seatbelts and tapping on the glass of the open door's window. "What is this?"

"It's a truck. I'll explain more later, but I really want to get you inside so I can make sure you're good to go." Duke watched Luca cautiously. From the other side of the *ulfdrengr*, he heard the sounds of Merrick retching, but he couldn't see the Sidhe navigator. "If you can walk, that'd help us out."

"Stop staring at me as though I'll keel over at any moment," said Luca hoarsely, smiling a little.

"Well, that's what already happened, so…" Duke shrugged. "It's tough to carry you, man."

Luca chuckled. "I'll try not to inconvenience you further."

Duke opened his door and hopped to the ground, circling around the back of the truck. He got there just as Luca climbed down without flourish or fanfare, his face set in concentration. Merrick straightened and unceremoniously wiped his mouth.

"You're looking green around the gills," Duke commented. "Just try not to barf on the carpet inside. Ross hates the smell."

Merrick swallowed and nodded gamely. "I take your expression to mean that I look terrible, which is an accurate reflection of how I feel."

"You aren't alone in that," said Luca. Duke shadowed the big warrior as he began walking toward the front door of the little house.

"It took me a few days to adjust when we got thrown through," said Duke, "but the worst of it was over after the first few hours."

"There are things in your world that are poison to us," said Merrick, following behind them. "I'm not sure that it's quite the same."

"Valid point," conceded Duke. "Do you know exactly what you should avoid?"

"Iron, for the Sidhe," grunted Luca, reaching the small wraparound porch. He eyed the four steps for a brief moment, then heaved himself up the incline.

"It's better now that I'm not in the...*truck*," said Merrick.

"Well, shit, we just put you in a metal box for that ride, didn't we," said Duke.

"It had to be done." Merrick paused at the top of the small flight of steps, taking several deep breaths. He'd lost the sickly green tint to his pallor, but sweat still stood out on his forehead.

"All set, Ross?" called Duke through the screen door.

"Yeah, bring them in," came the reply.

Merrick reached for the handle of the screen door and then drew his hand back quickly as if burned. "I can't...touch it."

"I got it," said Duke, looping two fingers through the wrought-iron handle of the wood-frame screen door. Many houses in this part of Cairn were over a century old, and vestiges of the past appeared in small details...like a nostalgic handle on the screen door.

"Iron won't kill *ulfdrengr*," said Luca, "but something...something is not right with me." He looked pained as he said it, as if admitting his weakness bothered him more than the physical cost of being thrown into the mortal world.

"We'll figure it out," Duke replied in his calmest, most encouraging medic voice. Luca placed a huge hand on his shoulder.

"I have no doubt," the *ulfdrengr* said. "I'm certainly glad we have a friend and guide in this strange world."

"You did the same for me," Duke said, the gratitude in Luca's voice making him uneasy – if he couldn't help, that gratitude would make him feel guilty as hell. "Now get your big ass inside before you pass out on me again." Luca chuckled and moved past him into Ross's house. Duke followed, closing the screen door carefully behind him.

Ross had already set her emergency bag by the couch. Duke motioned the other two men to take a seat. They both took a few more steps into the house, but remained on their feet, their eyes exploring the details of the first human dwelling they'd ever seen. Duke closed the front door behind him, turning the deadbolt and hearing the satisfying click as it slid into place. Ross frowned at him as she emerged back into the open main room of the house.

"You expecting unwelcome visitors?" she asked, a crease marring her forehead. She looked at the three of them and when Duke didn't answer, she continued, "Shoes off. I'd prefer you don't track swamp mud all over the floor."

"Just like you, to be worryin' about mud on the floor when I'm tellin' you about other worlds," Duke drawled in an undertone as he complied. Luca and Merrick both pulled off their boots with varying expressions of bemusement and forbearance. Duke set all their boots in a row by the doormat. "There. Happy?"

"It's a start," Ross said blithely, arching an eyebrow. She wrinkled her nose. "After the initial assessment, all three of you need a shower. You smell like a pack of wet dogs."

Merrick smelled himself surreptitiously and Luca merely grinned his wolfish grin.

"The couch is secondhand anyway," she said. She pointed to it. "Sit."

Luca glanced at Duke and chuckled as he obeyed the much smaller woman's command. Ross didn't even reach Luca's shoulder, Duke himself had to look up to meet the *ulfdrengr*'s eyes, and he was taller than Ross by a few inches. But he'd seen a lot of people make the mistake of assuming that her stature and beauty limited her capabilities. They'd been set straight in a hurry.

Merrick remained standing, silently surveying the room. The house was decorated with an artistic flair – colorful tribal rugs from far-flung lands covering the hardwood floors played counterpoint to a sleek dark ladder that had been converted to a bookshelf, and edgy framed prints hung at intervals on the walls. Some of the artwork was from local tattoo shops, mostly pin-up girls with a military theme, but a few reprinted advertisements from the Roaring Twenties hung on the walls as well, interspersed with antique travel posters enticing travelers to exotic destinations. The front of the house had been remodeled into an open floor plan, no walls separating the main living room from the dining room and kitchen. A narrow hallway led back to what Duke assumed were the bed-rooms.

Ross had busied herself taking Luca's blood pressure. The *ulfdrengr* watched her with thinly veiled curiosity, and Duke heard her explaining the basics of the device to him in a low voice. For all her prickliness, she was a damn good medic. A damn good *person.* He felt his heart give a strange lurch as he watched her.

"Would you mind taking off your axes before my couch gets ripped?" she asked as she pulled the blood pressure cuff off of Luca's arm. Luca obligingly took his two axes from their loops on his belt, handing them to Duke. Merrick grudgingly unbuckled his sword, sheath and all, and Duke stowed the weapons in the little closet by the door, out of sight, but still easy enough to reach if they needed them. Trust Ross to put the men at ease and get them to take off their weapons without a word of argument. He kept the knife he wore on his belt. Ross was more than used to his state of perpetual readiness for a violent confrontation.

"Mind if I take a look around back?" he asked, reaching for his boots again. He should've thought about a perimeter check before taking them off, but everything was upside down in his head. Better make that right, he told himself firmly. Other people were depending on his ability to make clear-headed decisions. He couldn't let the reunion with Ross distract him to the point of clouding his judgment.

"There's not a back door," Ross answered, pulling a stethoscope from its pouch in her kit. "But the bedroom windows are close enough to the ground that they'll serve in a pinch. Take a lap if you want, I'll be fine for a few minutes."

He nodded and caught Merrick's eye. "You good for now?"

"If by that you mean that I'm reasonably certain I won't embarrass myself by retching or fainting, then yes, I'm *good for now*," replied the navigator dryly, crossing his arms and leaning slightly against the wall by the couch. Duke smiled and slid out the front door, shutting it firmly behind him. He stood on the front porch for a long moment, gazing out into the riotous wet green of the foliage around the house. Then he took a deep breath and straightened his shoulders, setting off on a perimeter of the house's exterior. No fence marked the extent of the property, but Duke did spot the little flags that denoted an invisible fence for the dog. What had Ross said the dog's name was? May. He stood at the back of the house and estimated the distance to the river. Ironically, it was the same river in which Luca had nearly drowned, a little offshoot of the Pearl that threaded its way through Cairn before rejoining the larger river and emptying into Lake Pontchartrain. He examined the windows. Like the screen door, they were old but well maintained. In some old windows, you could turn the manual lock from the outside by sliding a knife between the seams of the frame; Duke's hand strayed to his belt as he thought of testing the method, but then he saw the simple bit of wood, painted to match the window frame, fitted vertically against the sill from the inside. Even if anyone managed to turn the lock from the outside, the small beam would prevent the window from actually opening. He smiled a little and thought that he should've expected no less from Ross.

After completing the circuit of the house and noting all the pertinent details, distance to the trees, distance to the road, visibility and coverage at all angles, Duke walked back up the stairs of the front porch and went inside, throwing the bolts again. He pulled off his boots and lined them up again with the other two pairs. The main room was quiet. Luca sat on the couch, head leaned back against the wall. He didn't open his eyes at the sound of Duke's return. Ross wasn't in the living room, and neither was Merrick. He felt his heartbeat increase with a little jolt of adrenaline, even though the rational part of his mind knew that Ross was perfectly capable of taking care of herself, and this was *her* house, after all. It wasn't that he suspected Merrick of any ill intentions, either. It was just his protective instinct rearing its head again after the time apart. He took a deep breath and evened out his heart rate with calm focus.

"She said that she couldn't bear the smell any longer," Luca said. "Though I think she was partly joking." The *ulfdrengr* fixed Duke with his pale blue gaze. "She's your wife?"

"Fiancée," said Duke. "Engaged to be married. I left for deployment, and then I got thrown into your world. They told her I was dead. So I guess you could say things are…uncertain."

"Why would things be uncertain? Does time change the love in your heart?"

Duke felt half a grin on his lips. "I swear, sometimes you sound like a bad Hallmark movie."

"I have no idea what that means," Luca said bluntly.

"I know. Sorry. I get what you're saying. I just…it's a lot for her. Missing for eight months and we were gone for a few months before that." Duke ran a hand through his hair and took the other half of the couch. "So she hasn't seen me in over a year, they had a funeral and everything for me. And then I drop out of the blue with you two in tow." He smiled humorlessly. "I think she's handled it really well, considering."

"Yes." Luca nodded, his eyes thoughtful. "There was a time when I thought that all I loved was destroyed, when I was held in thrall by the darkness." He raised his scarred hand and looked at it contemplatively. "Death seemed preferable to a world without all I'd ever known. And it was preferable to allowing evil to control me and use me for wicked deeds." Settling his hand back on his thigh, he gazed at Duke again. "And then Tess freed me. All my people were not dead, and I fell in love with the mortal woman who had saved my soul." There was something pained about his smile. "Even now, with the veil of the worlds between us, I love her. I would die for her. And if you love Ross, she will know that you never stopped loving her, not even a world away."

"She was my first thought in the morning and the last thought before I closed my eyes," said Duke in a low voice, his drawl imbuing his solemn words with a prayer-like cadence.

After a moment, Luca commented, "You are actually more serious in your own world, I think, than you were in mine."

Duke gave half a laugh. "Well, that was because at first I thought it was all a dream. Or that I was already dead." He shrugged. "I've been told that humor is my defense against feeling too much emotion."

"It makes sense," agreed Luca companionably.

Ross emerged from the hallway, drying her hands on a small towel. "It's more difficult than you'd expect, explaining a shower to someone who's never seen one before." She raised her eyebrow at the two men. "Luca, you can use my shower. I'll leave the instructions to Duke this time. Unless you need me to explain the niceties of civilization again to you, too?"

"I think I can handle a shower, darlin'," drawled Duke with a lazy smile. Ross blinked and didn't smile at the term of endearment. Duke swallowed down the hot disappointment burning in his throat. "Come on, big guy. Let me introduce you to the wonders of indoor plumbing." He stood with a sigh. Soreness was settling into his muscles with every passing moment, and he was beginning to agree with Luca's cave-troll assessment.

"Your clothes are still here," said Ross in a strangely quiet voice. "In the closet of the study, the guest room. But May's in there…let me move her to Viv's room."

"I'm not afraid of dogs," Duke said lightly, watching as Luca levered himself to his feet.

"May is a sweetheart most of the time but she doesn't know you," said Ross. "She's got a protective streak. And it's not you I'm worried about, it's those two. Pretty sure that they smell different than anybody she's ever encountered."

"True," conceded Duke. "Well, let me get Luca set up in the shower and then you can introduce me to her."

"I… okay," said Ross, pressing her lips together. She rubbed her palms down the front of her cargo pants and motioned with her head. "My room is the last one at the end of the hall. It's the master so the bathroom is attached."

"Fancy," he replied with a waggle of his eyebrows. He eyed Luca. "I might have a shirt and shorts that will fit you mixed in somewhere. But I'll get you started. Come on."

Ross's bedroom was cool and dark, gray satin curtains covering the window. He recognized the furniture and most of the artwork from her last apartment. She favored dark polished wood and gold accents, splashes of jewel tones tastefully interspersed with muted dove gray and slate. The silver-framed photo on her nightstand caught his eye and pierced him as surely as a dagger to the chest. It was one of his favorite pictures of them, both of them covered in mud and dirt and sweat at the finish line of an obstacle course race. He'd grumbled that anyone who *paid money* to run ten miles and climb through mud pits was crazy, but he'd relented after she'd raised an eyebrow at him and kissed him thoroughly. In the photo, he had his arm around Ross's shoulder and she hugged him around the waist, both laughing into the camera, the medals in their hands forgotten amid their punch drunk enjoyment of each other. They'd both decided that they'd liked that picture better than their engagement photos. He'd had a print of that photo tacked up next to his bunk on base.

"All this space for one person?" asked Luca guilelessly.

Duke grinned and shook his head. "Yeah. Just wait 'til you see the shower."

The bathroom was decorated in a tastefully nautical theme. Duke wondered if Ross had taken design pointers from her roommate Vivian. He remembered Vivian as a friend Ross made after she'd moved down South to finish school and take a job when she'd gotten out of the military. If he had the right girl, the most vivid detail about her was her hair, long and the color of a fox's tail, wavy when she tamed it and a riot of frizz when she didn't. His thoughts kept speeding along at a breakneck pace as he demonstrated the shower to Luca and explained the other essential functions of the bathroom. To his credit, the *ulfdrengr* listened with intent focus, showing little surprise at the stream of heated water flowing from the shower-head... or at least he was very good at concealing his curiosity. Duke popped open the top of Ross's shampoo and body wash; both of them smelled fresh but neutral.

"We're lucky she doesn't like girly scented stuff in the shower," he told a slightly bemused Luca. He pointed to the bottles. "That's for your body, and that's to wash your hair. You only need a bit of it, so don't go crazy. Towels are there. I'm gonna leave the door unlocked just in case, I'll be back to check on you."

"You hover like a mother wolf over her newborn cubs," said Luca, shedding his shirt and tossing it unconcernedly to the tile floor.

"Yeah, well, I just don't want you to drown in the shower," muttered Duke. "And I'm gonna take a look at those bruises on your ribs later."

Luca slid the shower curtain back with comical delicacy, his eyes narrowing as he watched the brass rings move along the shower curtain rod. Then he shrugged slightly. "As you wish."

"All right then...I'm just gonna go," Duke said as the *ulfdrengr* began unlacing his breeches. He shook his head slightly and left the door to the bathroom open a crack. Before he walked away, he heard Luca step into the shower, an unabashed sigh of enjoyment accompanied by wordless humming of a Northern song that Duke thought he remembered from around the fires of the *Vyldgard* camp. He smiled as he walked back through Ross's room, thinking for the first time since they'd been thrown through the portal that maybe, just maybe, everything would turn out all right after all.

Chapter 9

Finnead padded down the dark streets of the city, making no more noise than a shadow passing over the paved path. Vell knew where he was going – he could keep nothing from his Queen. But unlike the Unseelie Queen, the *Vyldretning* let even her Three have their privacy most of the time. He could still feel her through their shared bond, but it was not the constant watchfulness and cold, efficient collection of his thoughts that he had experienced with Mab.

The sentry knew him by sight and let him pass with a grave nod, though Finnead thought he saw a flicker of disdain in the Unseelie Guard's eyes. The man's gaze settled for a moment on the sapphire in the pommel of the sword at Finnead's hip, the sword that had once been the Brighbranr of the Unseelie Court and was now the Brighbranr of the Wild Court. None of the Guards or Knights showed outright malice, but none of them welcomed him on his visits to the Unseelie stronghold. None of them except for loyal Ramel, he amended silently to himself. He brushed a hand against the hilt of the Brighbranr as his feet led him surely down the dim passageways.

The Unseelie Court had found what had once been an armory carved into the hill on the western side of the White City. It had reminded them of Darkhill, he knew, because it reminded him of Darkhill as well, though he didn't quite feel sadness at the memory of his former home. The golden age of the city must have been splendid indeed for the Sidhe to put such care and skill into such an expansive project. He admired the smooth curves of the passageways and the subtle details of the carved vines about the arched doorways as he walked. He encountered no one as his strides led him down a passageway that sloped downward at a noticeable angle, burrowing deeper into the hillside.

Finally, he turned the last corner. Two Guards stood at either side of a great wooden door. He felt the same familiar disgust welling up within him. What did Mab think, that her sister was capable of breaking her chains and slaughtering grown men with her bare hands? The memory of another prison cell in Darkhill nudged at him. He took a deep breath as he contemplated the barred door and let the memory wash over him. He'd learned long ago that it was easiest to let the darkest parts of his past break over him like a wave, swirling about him and then dissipating as he accepted its pain and absorbed it back into himself. Once, Mab had chained *him* in a cell in the depths of Darkhill. He had survived and escaped the Enemy, but she had not trusted him. The rebellion had eaten away at her faith in her subjects, and the death of her beloved sister had dealt the final blow to her magnanimity. She had locked him away still broken and bleeding. For the safety of all her Court, she had said, or so he had been told later, when he regained his senses. That had been the first time that Ramel had proven his unswerving loyalty and friendship.

He took another deep breath and addressed one of the Guards. "Are they here?"

The Guard gave a silent nod.

"Good. I will enter." Finnead watched the Guards lift the bar from the door, opening one side enough for him to pass through.

One of them lit a torch from the sconce in the wall and handed it to Finnead. When he stepped through the door, it slid shut immediately behind him, and he heard them settle the bar back into place. His breath plumed in the air before him. The passageway on the other side of the door was glacially cold. A rime of frost glimmered on the walls, and even with his natural grace he slipped a few times on the increasing layer of ice on the floor. Finally, he reached the small door at the end of the passageway. The door had no knob or handle, nor any visible hinges. It was a door merely because it fit in the space at the end of the passageway. He switched the torch to his other hand and sketched a rune on the icy surface with the tip of a finger. Numbness crept up his hand as he worked, though he tried to ignore it. The painful prickling extended nearly to his elbow before he finished drawing the symbol, and he grimly pressed his palm to the center of the rune, clenching his jaw as the cold bit deeper into his arm.

In the back of his mind, he felt Vell stir at his pain, stretching herself down their link for a moment. He knew that she sat before the fire in her chambers, reading another ancient text. Her insomnia rivaled his own, some days. She opened their bond enough that for a brief instant he felt the warmth of the hearth. He smiled a little at the jest. Liam cast a bit of attention toward him as well but drew away when he recognized the cold sensation of the rune casting. Gray must have been asleep or ignoring him.

Rather than glowing as most runes did when completed, this particular rune sizzled softly and sank into the door like a charred scar. He thought it appropriate that the rune sealing the door to this prison revealed itself in such an ugly way, an ugly rune to keep an ugly scene contained. He straightened his shoulders as the door silently swung inward.

The prison deep in the heart of the armory looked more like it was carved from ice than stone. Frost glimmered on every surface, even the small table and chairs placed near the roaring fire. Two figures sat by the fire. Neither of them turned as the door opened – there were only three of them now that entered this chamber. Mab had stopped coming after the first few days, her face hard and cold with the finality of her despair. The healers had still hopefully persisted, but even the most optimistic could not say that their ministrations had any effect, and they, too, stopped traveling to the icy chamber deep underground.

"Once more into the breach," said Ramel in greeting, the firelight glinting off his coppery curls. The light of the fire did not penetrate the deepest shadows of the room. The silver bars of the cell, coated in ice, glinted in the darkness, looking like icicles grown from the ceiling at neat intervals.

"I wish it weren't so cold," the dark-haired woman sitting with Ramel said without rancor. She stood and slid closer to the fire, offering Finnead the seat closest to his former squire. He tossed his torch into the fire. They had stocked new, unlit torches beside the firewood, and a branch of candles flickered on the table.

"If she could understand us, she could make it so," Ramel said, glancing at the darkened corner beyond the silver bars.

"I don't think understanding is her problem," Molly said, still without any trace of spite. They had fallen into the habit of speaking bluntly.

"I agree," said Finnead as he walked closer. He didn't sit down, instead regarding Molly intently. "Something is different about you," he said slowly.

The *fendhionne* swallowed and glanced at Ramel. He couldn't recall ever seeing her show nerves. Finnead looked at Ramel, too, and discovered that the other man wore an expression of mingled pride, satisfaction and embarrassment. The emotions passed over Ramel's face with the speed of a hawk's shadow sweeping over the ground, but Finnead caught them. He had long training in recognizing the emotions of even the most smooth faced of his brethren.

To his credit, Ramel composed himself and said in a measured voice, "We did it."

Finnead gazed at him expectantly, waiting for him to continue.

Ramel looked at Molly, his expression once again inscrutable. Two spots of color appeared on the *fendhionne*'s pale cheeks.

"I restored her memories." Ramel said the words slowly, savoring them, his eyes still resting on the dark-haired, pale woman whose body swayed toward him at the sound of his voice.

Finnead felt as though the ground shifted beneath him. He gripped the edge of the table for support, his hand sliding on the damp wood. He cursed himself for the hope that surged in his chest and filled his eyes. Damn it all, he was a fool thrice over. He shut his eyes briefly to regain his balance. When he opened them, Molly had taken a step closer to him, her cat-like eyes intent on his face.

"Are you all right?" she asked with genuine concern.

"Are you?" he returned, straightening.

"If you mean to ask me whether I'm crazy from what Ramel did, I don't think I am," she replied with a little smile. "Or if I am, I don't realize it. Is that the same thing?"

Incredibly, Finnead heard himself chuckle. Ramel crossed his arms over his chest and leaned back in his chair. Molly's smile widened as she looked fondly at Ramel, the heat from her earlier gaze only an echo in the depths of her eyes. She pulled her cloak tighter about her shoulders. She felt the cold more acutely than either of the Knights. Finnead supposed that was her mortal half.

"How?" He directed the single word at Ramel. His hands suddenly felt empty and useless. He gripped the hilt of the Brighbranr and it pulsed comfortingly under his touch.

"I combined three of the restorations that we had tried in the past," said Ramel, his eyes alight. He leaned forward in enthusiasm, but before he began his explanation, rattling chains sounded from the dark cell. Finnead swept up the branch of candles from the table, not flinching as the hot wax spilled onto his wrist. With three long strides, he crossed the chamber, the halo of light around the candles flickering. It seemed as though the light struggled to beat back the shadows beyond the silver bars. They had learned that the light of one candle was not enough to strain through the darkness.

The chains rattled again, an almost bell-like sound. Finnead tasted the bitter tang of old anger at the back of his throat. The chains were silver, and delicate as far as chains went, but worked with the Queen's own power. It still angered him that Mab chained her own sister like a convict...but then again, she had chained him as well. And, he reminded himself staunchly that in the most literal sense of the word, the princess was a killer. Though she'd been under Malravenar's power, she had still killed dozens of Sidhe fighters.

The flickering candlelight spread over the floor and finally reached the figure in the center of the cell. It looked like the princess had leapt from her narrow bed to the center of the small space, landing in a predatory crouch. She growled as the light wavered over her, turning her face away from the candles and hissing.

"Andraste." Finnead said her name in a low voice. He wasn't sure why he tried to speak to her anymore. She showed no recognition, no spark of rational thought. It was as though they had chained a wildcat in the silvery cell. The only sign that she recognized her imprisonment at all was the bitter cold that rolled through the room and the passageway beyond. At first, Finnead had thought it had been Mab, and the Queen may have indeed reawakened part of Andraste's power with the touch of her own. But it had not been cold at first, not until Queen Mab had left and failed to return. Finnead tried to tell himself that the ice encasing every object in the room proved that Andraste still thought and felt. He tried to tell himself that it was her rage and bitterness at her abandonment that led her to freeze her prison.

But the cloaked figure squatting in the center of the cell bore little resemblance to the lithe, graceful princess who had once been the future of the Unseelie Court. She growled again, louder, one clawed hand darting out to paw at a shadow created by the dancing candle flame. The silver chains pooled about her as she pressed her hands flat on the floor and shifted her weight in one direction, then another. She made nonsense sounds in a low voice, stopping to growl at another shadow that slipped across the floor.

"I do not know if it will work on her," said Ramel quietly from beside Finnead, his voice grave.

Andraste whined softly to herself.

"I know," Finnead replied in a tight voice.

"We thought it might be best not to discuss this with anyone else," Molly said, the candlelight bringing out the gold flecks in her eyes. "It might raise hopes that we can't afford to disappoint." She looked away. "Not even Tess. I want to tell her, I know she'll be happy, but I'm…afraid." Ramel touched her shoulder comfortingly.

Finnead nodded woodenly. "I understand."

Something like relief passed briefly over Molly's face. "Thank you."

He shook his head and turned away from the glittering cage. "No need to thank me. You two are the only ones who still come."

"We'll keep trying," promised Ramel.

The frost glittered on the walls of the cell as the Unseelie princess began to laugh, her voice echoing around them in a cacophony of madness.

Chapter 10

"Lady Bearer."

Tess marked her place in the leather tome. She'd returned from the practice yard to find a stack of books on the small table in her sleeping quarters, an accompanying note tucked under the base of the little *taebramh* lamp.

Tess –

These volumes are about to be in high demand. As far as I know, they were lost in one of the fires set during the battle, so no one will be expecting them to be returned.

P.S.: You still owe me some updates to our records, and not only of the mortal world at this point.

The message hadn't been signed, but Tess had recognized the handwriting as belonging to Bren. She'd left a stack of books in Tess's room once before, what seemed like years ago at Darkhill. Now Tess used this carefully folded note as a bookmark; she'd meant to burn it after reading it, but somehow the words written by one of her oldest friends in Faeortalam held a strange comfort. After insomnia had sunk its claws into her again tonight, she'd slipped out of the little compartment, leaving Robin sleeping peacefully. The dining hall had been nearly deserted in the early morning hours; a *taebramh* light provided just enough light for her to read. She blinked muzzily, her eyes refocusing after so long reading the small, precise calligraphy of the Unseelie Scholars. The Glasidhe messenger waited courteously, his light dimmed in the darkened dining hall . He hovered an arm's length away from Tess, hands clasped neatly at the small of his back like a soldier waiting for his orders.

"I don't believe we've met," said Tess, her voice hoarse from disuse.

"No, my lady, and it is my distinct honor to serve Queen Vell and thus the Lady Bearer," replied the Glasidhe. "My common name is Haze, my lady."

Tess squinted at him, blinking again. "You bear a very strong resemblance to a very dear friend of mine, Haze."

From within the nebulous light of his dimmed aura, Haze grinned, cementing the connection that Tess had already made between his elfin, pointed face and Wisp's boyishly pretty looks. "Wisp is my cousin, my lady. He has always been the more fortunate of the two of us."

Tess already felt the smile stretching her lips, but she raised an eyebrow and asked, "And why is that, Haze?"

"Because he has met more mortals than any of our kin, and he was the messenger who brought the summons to the Bearer," Haze replied guilelessly. He paused and then bowed. His downy hair shone silver. "Forgive me if I have been impertinent in lamenting my cousin's good luck."

Tess leaned back in her chair, stretching. "Nothing to forgive, Haze, unless you're interrupting my late-night reading simply for the thrill of it." She smiled to soften the sarcasm.

"Oh! Forgive me once again, my lady. I am usually much more prompt in delivering my messages, but meeting the Lady Bearer for the first time is exciting, even to one as experienced as I," said Haze, a hint of an impish gleam whirling in his aura. "Queen Vell sent me to ask if you'd be so kind as to meet her in her quarters."

"Imagine that, both of us insomniacs," replied Tess, linking her hands together above her head to stretch more thoroughly before standing.

"My instructions are to lead the way for you, if you wish to accept the Queen's invitation."

"I can catch up on my reading anytime." She stood, tucking the book under one arm and grimacing slightly at the lingering stiffness in her knees. With her free hand, she picked up the Caedbranr's strap from where it had hung over the back of her chair and slipped it over her head in a practiced motion. "Lead on."

Haze led her through the maze of the great tent's hallways. Tess thought, not for the first time, that the pathways shifted according to the identities of those traveling through them. It was also strange that she rarely encountered others in the halls, though she knew hundreds, probably thousands, of Sidhe dwelled in the great tent beneath the ruined dome of the palace. If she concentrated, she glimpsed motion at the edges of her vision, a barely visible rippling as though some great hand shifted the fabric of reality, or maybe just the fabric of the tent, amended Tess, remembering Vell's words when they'd first used the great tent on the journey through the Deadlands. *A bit of sorcery in the weft and weave,* she'd said with that gleam in her golden gaze. Tess stopped trying to watch the ripples, a headache gathering behind her eyes.

Haze led Tess to a magnificent scarlet tapestry. A black wolf prowled on the field of red, so life-like that Tess blinked again, wondering for an instant whether it was actually Beryk standing in front of this great tapestry. She put a hand out and felt the smooth, silky surface of the magnificent work, reassuring herself that the golden-eyed wolf was simply a life-like depiction of the fierce Northern *Herravaldyr.* But then the tapestry warmed under her touch and the wolf moved beneath her hand, his fur sliding beneath her palm and the sting of seeking sorcery bubbling over her skin. She withdrew her hand as if burned and hastily stepped back from the tapestry, a growl of surprise rumbling in her throat.

"Ah, I did not know you had not encountered one of the *Vyldretning*'s sentinels before," Haze said from over her shoulder. "I apologize once again, Lady Bearer."

Tess stiffened. Her growl of surprise died in her throat and her eyes widened as emerald light blazed down her war markings, throwing the tapestry into sharp relief and illuminating the corridor with sudden brightness. The Caedbranr reached out and investigated the wolf on the tapestry, its *taebramh* circling once in an emerald swirl and then *entering* the scarlet field, taking the form of the primal wolf that Tess had seen a handful of times when they'd first encountered the *ulfdrengr*. The black wolf in the tapestry suddenly looked very two dimensional, then the Caedbranr tilted its wolf head and the black wolf was suddenly no longer solid, but a writhing mass of runes flowing over one another in silvery bands. Haze made a sound that could have been interest or shock. Tess watched warily. The Sword-as-wolf nosed at the rune wolf, eliciting an indignant exclamation from somewhere behind the tapestry.

Vell stormed into the hallway, brushing aside the tapestry and nearly barreling into Tess. The *Vyldretning* spun on her heel and looked at the Sword-as-wolf, which peered back at her out of the tapestry, the rune-wolf now seemingly frozen.

"You've proven your point," said Vell. "I'd appreciate it if you didn't ruin my rune crafting."

The Sword-as-wolf swung its primal head toward the two-dimensional impression of a wolf, the runes flowing more sluggishly now. Tess shook herself and reached for the Sword. It was like flexing a muscle that she'd forgotten she possessed. In the end, she wasn't sure whether the Caedbranr was heeding her or just being polite, but the Sword-as-wolf gave a very lupine grin, stepped out of the tapestry and padded back to Tess. It stood beside her for a moment before dissolving into a rush of emerald fire that whirled back up her war markings. Vell touched the image of the wolf on the tapestry with two fingers, and the black wolf shook itself, a few silvery runes dripping from its fur as though it had just emerged from wading in a river.

"Good evening to you too," said Vell pointedly, raising an eyebrow.

Tess shrugged. "Sorry. It was being...cantankerous."

"That's a really big word to say that it was being a pain in the ass," the *Vyldretning* replied dryly.

The Sword's chuckle vibrated through Tess's ribs. She smiled. "Never thought I'd be happy to feel it laughing in my bones again."

The black wolf in the tapestry yawned, its pink tongue lolling over sharp silver teeth, and settled down onto its belly, ears still pricked watchfully.

"Well, no harm done," said Vell, brushing away a fading rune from near the wolf's tail. She chuckled. "Though I don't think I've felt anyone poke at one of my craftings quite like that before."

"Like you said, pain in the ass." Tess grinned.

"Come on then. I have *khal,* if you want some. Calliea is actually getting quite good at making it." Vell slid past the tapestry and Tess followed, Haze still hovering just over her shoulder.

The room on the other side of the wolf tapestry reminded Tess of both the *Vyldretning*'s old tent, in which she'd held her war councils and planned the dragon hunt, and the rooms at the Hall of the Outer Guard. Embers glowed in a stone hearth, and great beams supported the hexagonal ceiling. Rather than the chandelier that had graced the Queen's tent, Vell had somehow fashioned the ceiling of this tent to look like the night sky, stars providing dim light from overhead. A full moon hung suspended in the center of the room.

"Is this still in the tent?" Tess mused aloud.

Vell made a noncommittal sound. She motioned to the assortment of seating arranged in a haphazard semicircle around the hearth. "Take your pick. Oh, and thank you, Haze. Would you like to join us for *khal?*"

"It would be my honor, my lady," said the Glasidhe.

"It'll be here in just a moment." Vell took one of the seats by the fire. The sitting area was really little more than a circular platform piled with furs and a few cushions. Tess chose the oversized cushion between Vell and the hearth. The slow, pulsating warmth of the smoldering fire felt like a cloak draped over her shoulders.

"So this is where my brother spends his days," Tess said conversationally, adjusting the Sword's sheath so that the strap didn't dig into the tender scar at the top of her back.

"Your brother spends his days leading one of my reconstruction teams and tending to other tasks," Vell replied smoothly.

"Reconstruction teams?"

"A very...*new*...term, yes, one that he taught me," the Wild Queen said. Vell somehow looked like she'd settled into her new role, despite the fact that she wore her hair in a simple braid and dressed plainly in a white shirt and dark breeches. Her only jewelry was the thin golden circlet gleaming across her brow. No additional ornaments spoke of her power, but a quiet self-assurance and acceptance radiated from her. She caught Tess gazing at her with circumspection and raised an eyebrow. "Something you'd like to tell me?"

"You look like you've grown into being Queen," Tess replied with a little smile.

"I don't know whether to be offended or take that as a compliment," Vell said. Haze flew to the other side of the room under the pretext of inspecting one of the rafters, but Tess heard his bright chuckle.

"I guess it's a compliment." Tess shrugged and smiled. "Means you look...*queenly*."

"Fantastic." Vell rolled her eyes.

"Okay, that just squashed it." Tess grinned.

"What, you mean rolling my eyes isn't *queenly*?" Vell placed her hand over her heart melodramatically. "I am *wounded*."

Tess chuckled. "It takes a lot more than that to wound you."

Vell sobered. "True, and I'm glad for that." She glanced at the leather-bound volume sitting by Tess's knee. "Some light nighttime reading?"

Hefting the tome in one hand, Tess passed it to Vell for her inspection. "One of the more senior Unseelie Scholars is an old friend from my time in Darkhill."

"Didn't know you still had friends in Mab's court," Vell murmured, reading the title of the book and opening it to the first page.

"Not all Unseelie are quite as misanthropic as Mab," Tess pointed out.

"Cantankerous...misanthropic...you're talking like quite the Scholar yourself tonight."

Tess waved a hand. "Sorry. It's something my brain does when I'm tired, mostly after I've been reading a lot." She grinned. "I can't think of normal words, only the ones with more than three syllables."

"And that is exactly the reason why I am not going to have any Scholars in the *Vyldgard*," said Vell, her golden eyes intent as she continued reading. "I'll leave the stuffiness to the other two Courts. It seems they've got it covered." She turned the page and read for another moment, then snapped the book shut.

"Easy," said Tess. "That's an old book."

"If it's withstood the centuries, it'll withstand me," said Vell with half a gleaming grin, handing the book back to Tess. "But I'm glad to see you're researching the Gates."

Tess nodded. "It was slow going until Bren left these for me. Her note implied that the material referencing opening the Gates would either be destroyed or restricted soon."

"Mab being difficult," Vell said, staring into the embers of the fire.

"No surprise there," agreed Tess with a sigh.

"Ah, I hope I've brewed enough," Calliea said, crossing the room with a tray bearing a copper kettle and mugs.

"Where did you come from?" Tess demanded, searching the walls of the room for other doorways and finding none. She realized that the entrance concealed by the scarlet tapestry had also melted away.

"I thought you'd gotten lost, Laedrek," Vell commented with a glimmer of humor in her eyes.

"No, just scorched the first batch," Calliea replied with a grin. Her bright hair was braided and pinned about her head, and at her belt Tess glimpsed the coil of her golden whip. "Oh, and I, ah, *convinced* the watch rotation at the kitchens that we routinely sample the first batch of scones."

"Of course. How else would we ensure that our fighters are being fed a quality breakfast?" Vell said.

"Breakfast *is* the most important meal of the day," agreed Tess. Her stomach rumbled as the scent of the freshly baked scones reached her nose. Calliea set the tray down on the low table in the midst of the chairs and moved to pour the *khal*, but Vell waved her away, grumbling something about letting others *brew* the stuff but certainly being able to *pour* her own damned *khal*. Calliea watched as Vell took a sip; apparently it was acceptable, because Calliea grinned, grabbed a scone and sat in one of the higher chairs with a satisfied flourish.

"All right, now that we have some *khal*, it's time to talk seriously," said Vell. Tess poured her own cup of *khal* after Calliea. She moved to help Haze with the kettle – it was as tall as he was – but the Glasidhe courteously waved away her attempt to pour for him. He hooked his cup onto a little line as gossamer as a spider's thread, pushed aside the lid of the kettle and adroitly dipped his thimble-sized mug into the *khal*. The line and hook disappeared into his miniscule belt pouch. Tess smiled at the ingenuity of the Small Folk – she still had much to learn about the everyday details of life at peace in the Fae world.

Vell looked at the Glasidhe. "Haze, if you would speak to what you know, whenever you're ready."

Haze stepped delicately over the lip of the tray, his mug of *khal* in hand, and bowed to Vell before turning to Tess. "As you wish, my lady. Lady Bearer, while I was running messages for Queen Vell to the Unseelie Court, I happened to overhear some conversations that may be of use to you."

"Happened to overhear, eh?" Tess raised an eyebrow at Vell. Vell shrugged innocently.

"Yes," answered Haze seriously. "My cousin is very conspicuous now with his hawk, but most of us can still move about unnoticed." He took a sip of his *khal*. "The attempts to heal the Unseelie crown princess are not progressing well."

"So I've gathered." Tess frowned and took a sip of her *khal* as well, the fragrant steam caressing her face as she raised the mug to her lips.

"Queen Mab has come to believe that there is a solution to her sister's madness," Haze continued in a somber voice. "It is an object that she believes was in Malravenar's possession, an instrument which he used to twist the minds of his captives and bend them to his will."

Tess shifted uneasily on her cushion. She might have imagined it, but she thought she felt a strange little tug in her belt pouch, as though the river stone holding a piece of Malravenar's fractured spirit had jumped at the mention of his name. "Another magical object. Sounds familiar."

"Our world isn't like yours, Tess," Vell said. "My people had many relics and objects of power, and so did both the Courts. They are heirlooms to us, just like beautiful paintings or jewelry are passed down through families in your world."

"I've never heard of a painting that could help control a captive's mind," Tess said, raising an eyebrow. "But I see your point."

"There are still a few items in the mortal world that bear traces of sorcery," said Haze seriously. He looked at Vell, who nodded for him to continue. "In any case, Lady Bearer, Queen Mab believes that this object could be turned to her will and used to...cure...her sister. In a sense."

Tess frowned and glanced at Vell. "What does this object do?"

Calliea handed Vell a small but well-worn book. Vell opened the little volume and quickly found the right page, handing it in turn to Tess. Her hands dwarfed the tiny tome, and she held it gingerly, estimating that it looked like the oldest book she'd ever seen in the Fae world. The page was yellowed with age despite the preservation runes inked at the borders, and it took Tess a moment to translate the Sidhe tongue. "This is like reading Old English," she muttered, squinting at one word in particular. She peered at the illustration that took up the entire right page. She read aloud the caption, "The Lethe Stone."

"*A* Lethe Stone," corrected Vell, "but most likely the only surviving one. For a few centuries, they were banned. Most were destroyed."

"I can understand why," said Tess as she finished translating the text in her head. "An instrument to erase memory…that sounds like it could very easily be used for dark purposes. As it was, I suppose."

"Luca actually mentioned this as a possibility," said Vell, her voice almost gentle as she said the *ulfdrengr*'s name.

Tess swallowed, feeling the familiar jolt in her chest that she felt at each harsh reminder that Luca was gone, that he and Merrick and Duke had been thrown defenseless into the mortal world, the portal slamming shut behind them. Victory, but at what cost?

"He didn't say anything to me about it," she said finally, her voice steady. "But we didn't talk much about the time he'd spent as a prisoner."

"One of Malravenar's sorcerers became particularly adept at using the Lethe Stone on prisoners," said Vell. "He would take their happiest memories so they could not escape their despair in their minds."

Tess shook her head, a sickening pit opening in her stomach at the thought of losing all her joyful recollections. "And Mab wants to possess this object? How do we know that she won't use it for her own purposes?" She stopped short of saying *like Malravenar*, but the silent comparison pressed down on them all.

"Because at the end of all things, I must believe that she is not evil," replied Vell quietly. Calliea sighed, one hand on her coiled whip as she stared into the glowing embers of the fire. Haze looked somberly into his mug of *khal*.

"That's the bargaining chip we need to convince her to help open a Gate," Tess said softly. Her voice hardened. "If that's the price, I'll pay it."

"It's not a price that will come easily," said Vell.

"Binding and breaking Malravenar did not come easily, and we do our men a disservice if we do not fight just as hard to bring them home," said Calliea in a low, fierce voice.

"And I need something to keep me busy anyway, now that we've corralled the Big Bad." Tess hoped that her face didn't betray the sudden surge of hope in her chest at the possibility of finding Luca, now suddenly tangible for the first time since the battle. She thought for a moment. "So what, we have to find where this sorcerer was standing when Malravenar bit the dust? Find where he dropped the Lethe Stone?"

"Not all of Malravenar's creatures imploded when he was bound and broken," said Vell darkly. "Especially these sorcerers. Some of them existed before he came to power, and they were drawn to him like moths to a darkly burning flame. But they didn't draw their power only from him. They became stronger through their alliance, yes, but they didn't depend on him for their existence."

"As long as there is light, there will be darkness," Calliea said quietly, her fingers caressing the coil of her whip.

"The Unseelie Court is not our enemy." Vell's voice matched Calliea's volume. As Tess watched her old friend, it looked as though the sparks of a fire leapt in Vell's golden eyes, kindled by the glow of the embers in the hearth. "We must remember that. There is too much hatred, too much division. The Seelie groom us to be their allies, but perhaps only to build their strength against the Unseelie."

Tess blinked. She felt as though she was standing on the cliff at the Darinwel again, staring down into the raging river with the wind plucking at her hair. "The enmity between the Seelie and Unseelie is truly that deep? We just fought a war, all as one."

"It was an uneasy truce between them. You know that as well as me, Tess," replied Vell, crossing her arms over her chest.

"I thought the whole *source* of the enmity between them was the kidnapping of the crown princess and the rise of Malravenar." Tess looked sharply at Calliea as the Valkyrie commander gave a mirthless chuckle.

"We have been enemies for so long that the *source* of it all has been lost in the depths of time," Calliea said musingly. "Under the extraordinary circumstances of the past few centuries, some of us have looked past our mutual dislike to work together against the Shadow." She shook her head. "But most of us who held no malice toward the other Court belong to a different Court entirely now."

Tess sat back in her chair, the small ancient book still held carefully in her hands. She glanced down at the sketch of the Lethe Stone.

"It was not my choice to be crowned," said Vell in a soft, serious voice. "But a Queen must choose her Court. A wolf must have her pack." She touched the silver marks on her neck where the teeth of the White Wolf had baptized her as the key to her people's survival, even before she had been crowned the High Queen in a wash of fire and power in the trembling throne room of Brightvale.

"You're the High Queen," Tess said slowly, still staring down thoughtfully at the illustration. "Can't you…mediate?"

Vell snorted. "I will not play nursemaid to the Sidhe Queens, or their Courts." She pressed her lips into a hard line. "If it comes to blood, perhaps. But I have my own people to tend, my own Court to build." Her hard expression softened slightly. "I must find a home for us."

Calliea smiled slightly. "For a Northern mercenary, you suddenly sound very soft-hearted, my lady."

One dark eyebrow rose infinitesimally, but the barest hint of a smile touched Vell's lips. "Watch your tongue, Laedrek, else you'll be answering for your words with your blades."

"If you wish to match skills with me, my Queen, you have only to ask," replied Calliea, the Fae-spark flashing through her eyes and an answering smile on her lips.

"Soft-hearted," muttered Vell, shaking her head. She narrowed her eyes at Calliea. "Is that truly what is being said of me?"

"Since when have you cared what others thought of you?" asked Tess as Calliea bit her lip, hedging, though amusement still glimmered in her eyes.

"Since there is no more war to fight and I must learn the intrigues of politics," growled Vell.

"All think you are most fierce, my lady," said Haze gallantly, punctuating his statement with a regal bow. Vell glanced at Calliea suspiciously once more, and then nodded to Haze.

"Thank you for your forthrightness, Haze," she said, her voice now more of a purr than a growl. "It is good to know I may rely upon you to tell me true."

"Always, my Queen," said the Glasidhe graciously. "Now I must beg my leave of you, to deliver the midnight message to the watch without and within."

"You have my leave, and my thanks," replied Vell. She settled back against her seat as Haze bowed to Tess, who gave him a nod. He inclined his head courteously to Calliea, and then leapt from the table and was gone in a silver blur.

"The midnight message?" Tess finally closed the small, old book and offered it back to Vell.

"A polite name for my orders to all my Glasidhe spies," replied Vell with a little grin. "I have a handful now, you know. Lumina professed that she could not deny me the Glasidhe who wished to serve me, since both Mab and Titania have Small Folk in their service as well."

"But neither Mab nor Titania command the same loyalty that you do among your Glasidhe messengers," said Calliea, a hint of pride coloring her voice.

"We shall see if Lumina allows them to truly join the *Vyldgard*." Vell drew up one leg, resting her elbow on her knee and her chin in her hand.

"With your leave, my lady, I'll ensure the watches are set as well and then take my rest." Calliea stood and moved to gather the empty *khal* cups and the still-warm kettle, but Vell waved her away.

"I'll get it," the *Vyldretning* said, the slim golden circlet almost hidden amidst her dark hair suddenly catching the low light of the flickering embers. "And yes, by all means. Ensure our watchstanders aren't becoming comfortable." She paused and then added, "Vigilance is the eternal price of safety."

Calliea bowed slightly from the waist and silently padded from the room, leaving Tess and Vell alone by the hearth.

"Liam taught you that saying." It was more of a question than a statement. Tess smiled slightly as she said it.

Vell chuckled. "You still don't want details, do you?"

Tess made a face. "Well, if I have to hear it from one of you, I'd rather it be you, I suppose. I love my brother, but we've never been the type of siblings who share the sordid details of our romantic conquests."

"Well, if it was a conquest, *he* was not the one who conquered *me*," replied Vell with a wicked gleam in her eyes.

"Good for you," Tess said mildly. "He's never found a woman who was tougher than him...until now, I guess."

"I wouldn't say I'm tougher than him," Vell said musingly. She tilted her head and looked at Tess, her queenly mask falling away. They were two old friends talking about the latest happenings of their lives, oddly comforting to Tess, just as seeing Bren's handwriting had felt comforting. "I think it's very much like what you and Luca have," continued Vell in a quieter voice. "We're equals."

"You're the High Queen and he's one of your Three. I don't think that makes you quite equals," commented Tess.

Vell waved a hand as though brushing the sound of Tess's words away like smoke in the air. "Do you and Luca love each other any differently because you're the Bearer?"

"No. I love him more because he doesn't look at me with that…that awe and bit of fear." Tess smiled even as she felt her throat tighten. "So I suppose I just refuted my own statement there."

"I suppose you did." Vell grinned.

"Thank you," Tess said quietly.

"For what?"

"For talking about Luca. For not avoiding him. For not talking about him like he's dead." Tess swallowed hard, feeling pressure building within her chest, like a dam about to burst. "Even Robin slipped this morning. He said, when Luca *was* here to teach us." Her voice wavered, balancing on the hard knot of sadness and anger and longing in her throat. "And I know he probably just meant that…Luca isn't here *now*. He *was* here when we were traveling across the Deadlands. I get that. But every time someone talks about him in the past tense, I feel like they're saying he's dead."

Vell shook her head. "I don't believe he's dead." She looked keenly at Tess. "I'm not saying it isn't a possibility, but they were alive when they were thrown through the portal, as best we know. A Gate, even a Gate made by a broken Seal, usually doesn't kill those who pass through it."

"I'll face that if it's a reality, not if it's a possibility," Tess said firmly, ignoring the aching emptiness within her chest. The knot in her throat loosened slightly. "I *have* to think that he's alive." She drew a sharp breath. "I'm not ready to face what my world would be without him." And just when she thought she'd reined in all her traitorous emotions, they burst through the dam and tears sprang into her eyes. She pressed her lips together and looked away from Vell, cursing under her breath.

"It's all right, Tess." Vell's voice sounded a little uneven. "You're the Bearer, and I'm the High Queen, but before that we were just an outcast Northern mercenary and a slightly awkward mortal girl." Her voice softened even further. "These past weeks have not been easy, and I have not been there for you as a friend. Let me be here for you now."

The gentleness in Vell's words, the emotion from the tough Northwoman, undid Tess. She felt her face crumple, hot tears streaming down her cheeks, a great shuddering sob shaking her shoulders. No sound of movement betrayed Vell, but somehow the Northwoman was there beside Tess, smelling of snow and pine and the sharp scent of sorcery as Tess let Vell gather her head onto her shoulder. It was not a tight embrace, but to Tess it said more than words ever could. For the first time since the battle at the Dark Keep, she let her tears flow unchecked in front of another person. She tossed aside the mask of tough endurance and, for a few moments, let the swift current of grief sweep her away.

Finally, she sniffed and scrubbed at her face with her shirtsleeve pulled over one palm, her eyes swollen and scratchy. "I'm not crying because I think he's dead," she clarified, her watery voice still defiant.

"I know." Vell nodded.

"It just…it *feels* so unfair. It feels *wrong* that he's not here." Tess gave a hiccupping sigh. "I miss him. All the time. Every minute of every day, it's a constant ache. And I hate that it reminds me of how I've missed people I've loved after they died." She swallowed and wiped at her nose again. "And I'm frustrated that I'll have to strike a deal with Mab to open a Gate."

"I love Luca too," Vell reminded her, the gentleness gone but her voice far from brusque. "He's one of my brothers in the pack. He is an *ulfdrengr*, a loyal warrior, and for that alone I owe him my best effort to bring him home."

Tess nodded, blinking.

"Calliea will ask to go with you," continued Vell. "She has already spoken of it to me. As long as you wish it, she has my blessing."

"Of course," Tess said. "How is she? I didn't want to...bring it up." She smiled in self-deprecation and spread her hands. "Which I know makes no sense since I just thanked you for talking about Luca."

"Everyone handles it differently. The Laedrek is a bit withdrawn. I think she is still grieving the loss of her Valkyrie who fell in the battle, and she sits at the bedsides of those who are still fighting to remain on this side of the veil."

Tess pressed her lips together, thinking of Maire and her twin, still clinging to life. "How is Niamh?"

"No better and no worse. Liam brings food to Quinn sometimes; otherwise I don't think he would remember to eat. The healers have given up on trying to get him to leave her side for the night."

"I hope she pulls through."

"As do I." Vell looked into the glowing embers in the hearth and twirled a finger idly, sending a molten stream of sparks flaring from the remnants of the fire.

"Moira volunteered to go," Tess said.

Vell said nothing for a moment, staring into the hearth. Finally she sighed. "I cannot give leave to everyone who merely wants an adventure in the mortal world." She smiled a little wryly. "I don't think I'd have a Court left if I did that."

"Moira was a good friend to me during our ride through the Deadlands, and she helped rescue the men in the Northern wilds," Tess pointed out.

"I understand." Vell's eyes, when she turned her gaze to Tess, looked more wolf than woman; a slight shiver ran through Tess. "But what I also know is that I cannot give you the entirety of the *Vyldgard*'s young and strong fighters. I know Moira is just one, but it will open the floodgates." She shook her head. "I will allow Calliea to go, because she has a stake in the outcome. Just as I could not let all go with you to the Northern mountains, it is the same now." With a deep breath, she visibly set aside the topic, her face smoothing again into the visage of the Northern woman rather than the Wild Queen.

"And other than what we've already discussed, how are *you*, Tess? I wasn't surprised when Haze reported that you aren't sleeping much."

"Haze has been spying on me?" Tess couldn't muster the energy to feel indignant. She felt like a wrung-out sponge, dry of any more emotion.

"Just observing," replied Vell. She grinned a little. "And reporting his observations to me."

"It's hard for me to sleep. It's just…different." Tess shrugged. "I don't like feeling alone. Even with Robin there, falling asleep feels very lonely."

"Nightmares?" Vell asked bluntly.

"Yes." Tess shrugged. "But I'm no different than anyone else who fought in the war. We all saw things. We watched friends die, we faced terrible creatures and stared into the face of evil. Or at least that's what someone told me."

Vell made a noncommittal sound. "Everyone is different," she repeated. She stared into the fire. "I don't have nightmares about the battles that I've fought. We are raised from birth to fortify ourselves for war." Her gaze was distant. "But I do have nightmares about my sister. About Arcana." She pressed her lips together and fell silent.

"What do you do?" Tess asked.

A humorless smile tugged at one corner of Vell's mouth. "You're not curious about the exact nature of my nightmares?"

"I have enough nightmares of my own without digging into ones that belong to other people," Tess said lightly. In a more serious vein, she added, "And I don't think it much matters what the nightmares really *are*. I'd just like to know if you've found a way to manage them that works for you." She took a deep breath. "Because even though I have a lot of research to do on Gates and Lethe Stones, I'd prefer to get some good sleep every now and then."

"Ever practical, Lady Bearer," Vell said dryly. She pulled another string of sparks from the hearth as she thought. "I've tried a few things so far. White shroud works, but I don't like the thought of not being able to wake up if I'm needed."

"It leaves me groggy in the morning," agreed Tess.

"Sometimes a hard practice session a few hours before I want to go to sleep works, but not always." Vell shrugged. "Mostly Liam wakes me up and soothes me back to sleep." She smiled at Tess's look of surprise at the tender admission. "You know we're lovers, Tess. Did you think we just rut like wild animals and go our separate ways? Although we certainly do that as well." She winked.

Tess's look of surprise transitioned into a look of mingled shock and comical disgust. "I…I did *not* need that visual. Metaphor. Whatever." She shook her head.

Vell chuckled. "Well, it certainly shocked you out of your self-pity."

"Um, you can just *tell* me when you're tired of my moping. You don't have to scar me with a description of your love life with my brother." But Tess was grinning despite herself.

Vell settled back into her seat. "Now that we've got the emotions out of the way for a while, I think we should discuss our approach to the next council meeting."

"Agreed." Tess straightened and looked at Vell. "So how are we going to make Mab do what we want?"

As the embers in the hearth spit sparks every now and again, the two women talked, pouring lukewarm *khal* into their mugs and examining every possible course of action that came to their minds. Tess felt a profound gratitude for Vell's friendship and unshakable determination, and she let the thread of hope in her chest spread its roots as they meticulously built their plan.

Chapter 11

By the time all three of the men had showered, thick darkness pressed against the windows of Ross's little house. Duke stitched up a few cuts on Merrick and Luca that had been revealed beneath the lingering grime and gore. The most serious wound was a series of puncture marks on Merrick's ribs where a creature had grabbed him.

"We'll have to keep an eye on these, make sure they don't get infected." Duke looked dubiously at the tube of antibiotic ointment in Ross's kit. "I don't want to use something on you that might make it worse."

Merrick shrugged slightly. "If you have anything that's made from a plant, that might be the least dangerous. As far as I know, there aren't many plants in your world that are deadly to us. If it's good for you, I'm willing to try it."

Duke glanced at Ross, who raised her eyebrows as if to say that Merrick had a point.

"I might have some hippie stuff that could be useful," she said. Then she smiled slightly. "And by that I mean Vivian might have some hippie stuff that could be useful." She disappeared down the hallway. Duke heard her speaking firmly to the dog as she slid through the door to Vivian's room.

Merrick sat back slightly on the couch, holding a blue t-shirt in one hand. Both he and Luca had fit into pairs of Duke's gym shorts, thanks to the modern miracle of elastic waistbands. After some digging, Ross had found an old shirt that fit Luca – Duke thought that it might have been Liam's at one point, mixed into his pack during one training evolution or another. Luca sat on the other side of the couch, the cloth of the t-shirt straining over his broad shoulders. Although he still looked like he could wrestle a grown bull with his bare hands, he had fallen asleep almost as soon as he sat down. Shadows darkened the skin beneath his eyes in stark half-circles, and rather than making him look better, the shower had only revealed the motley assortment of bruises, scrapes and cuts from the battle, which stood out vividly against his pale skin. At least when they'd all been coated with a light layer of grime, he could pretend that Luca didn't look like he was sick, Duke thought darkly.

"Found some things that might be useful," announced Ross as she breezed back into the room. "Vivian's a big fan of the whole natural movement, which I don't think is a bad thing, but…anyway. Here's an antiseptic ointment – eucalyptus, tea tree oil and calendula." She held up a small jar as she read off the label and set it on the arm of the couch. Merrick picked it up, unscrewed the cap and smelled it gingerly. "Pure tea tree oil, some lavender oil and I know she has some tea and things in the kitchen."

"I'll do a test with the ointment," said Duke. He took a cotton swab and scooped out a small amount of the opaque salve. "I just want to make sure that I'm not poisoning you, especially letting something into your blood that could be harmful."

"Our healers would approve," said Merrick, offering his arm when Duke gestured. The Wild Court warrior watched speculatively as Duke smeared the ointment on the skin at the inside of his wrist.

"Tell me if you feel sick or the skin starts to itch," Duke said, screwing the cap back onto the jar. "I'll look in the morning and if you haven't reacted to it, I think it'll be safe to use." He sat back on his heels and looked at Luca, grateful that the *ulfdrengr* didn't have any serious wounds from the battle but wishing all the same that he could do something concrete to help Luca regain his strength. A cut he could stitch back together. He didn't know how to treat this invisible drain on the *ulfdrengr*'s strength.

"It might be the separation from his wolf," said Merrick, pulling his t-shirt back on after Duke finished taping a gauze pad to the puncture wounds on his side.

"Kianryk is not my wolf," said Luca, eyes still closed.

"I thought you were asleep," replied Merrick mildly.

"Resting," countered Luca. Then he opened his eyes and sat up a little straighter as Ross walked back into the room with several thick sandwiches stacked on a plate.

"It's been a long day," she said, "and I'm sure you're hungry by now."

Duke was long past the point of hunger, long past the point of exhaustion, but the sight of the sandwiches prodded his stomach back to life. Luca and Merrick both took half of a sandwich and Duke grabbed one as well. "Thanks," he said to Ross. She didn't reply, looking at him with the expression that meant they'd be talking later, having a *serious discussion*, as she often termed it. But even the prospect of that conversation couldn't dampen the simple pleasure of that first bite of the ham sandwich. He noted that despite Luca's wan appearance, the big man ate two of the sandwiches, which was heartening.

They finished the plate of food in industrious silence. Merrick sighed and leaned back against the couch, chewing his last mouthful. Luca stared into the distance with pale eyes. Ross watched him as she polished off the remnants of the last sandwich.

"I'll go make up the study into the guest bedroom," she said to no one in particular.

Merrick looked at Duke. "Does she believe you?"

"About what? That you're Fae, or that I was in your world for almost a year by the time measured here?"

"I think starting with our existence," replied the navigator. He took out his scrying-glass from its case on his belt, holding it in one palm and running a finger lightly over the delicate knobs.

"I don't know." Duke shook his head. "It's a lot to ask of anyone. Your world is just legends and fairy tales here. Bedtime stories told to kids."

Merrick smiled a little. "When I was young, my mother would tell me tales of the mortal world before I went to sleep at night."

"So you pointy-eared bastards *do* have parents," said Duke, raising an eyebrow.

"I think by definition that means we are not bastards, doesn't it?" Merrick's gray eyes gleamed.

Duke chuckled. "And you're fast on the uptake. You'll do fine here, as long as we can keep you away from iron."

"That might prove to be difficult. It is a constant feeling, the nearness of it." Merrick shifted. "It feels a bit like the morning after drinking too much *laetniss*."

"A constant hangover?" Duke shook his head. "That blows."

"It makes it difficult to concentrate at times, but I'll manage," replied Merrick. "I believe Luca is faring worse."

"I can still hear you," rumbled the *ulfdrengr*, sliding out of his trance to look at the *Vyldgard* warrior.

"I didn't say anything offensive." Merrick shrugged slightly.

"Has this ever happened before to you?" Duke asked Luca. "The seizures, the sickness...do you have any idea what it could be?"

"My best guess is that it is the withdrawal from Kianryk. The stretching of our bond." Luca paused. "When I was a prisoner, they held Chael and Kianryk while forcing Rialla and me to track the Bearer. I felt something akin to this then, but much less severe. And I had a dagger imbued with a Dark spirit bound to my hand, so..." He spread his hands. The scars on his right hand looked fresher, redder, than Duke remembered. Perhaps it was just because Luca was paler.

"So what happens if this bond continues to be stretched?" Duke asked.

Luca took a breath. "Most likely I will become weaker and weaker, until I die. The bond between a warrior and their wolf is normally like…like a loop." He searched for words. "My energy goes into the bond, and into Kianryk, but I receive his energy back. It is a balance. It does not *take* from either of us." He paused. "If man or wolf is killed, the bond is broken. It ceases to exist. But since we are both still alive, in different worlds…I believe it's draining my life force. And that of Kianryk." He smiled tiredly. "Though it has been said before that wolves are much more resilient than men, and I hope it is so."

Duke felt cold dread settle into the pit of his stomach like a stone. "How long do you have?"

Luca met his eyes. "I don't know."

The wiry Southerner looked at Merrick. "Can you open a portal back from this side?"

Merrick sighed. "If I could, I would. But I feel as though I can barely light a candle right now."

Duke muttered under his breath and ran his fingers through his hair.

"Well, one of you can sleep on the futon and I inflated the air mattress next to that," said Ross, walking back into the room. "There's a few extra blankets on the chair by the desk."

Merrick stood and nodded gracefully to Ross. "Thank you for your hospitality. We are grateful." He placed a long-fingered hand over his heart.

"You're welcome," said Ross, two spots of color appearing on her cheeks.

"I do have another favor to ask," continued Merrick. "I'd like to put up some wards on your house, and it would be easiest if you had chalk or charcoal. I will clean it in the morning."

"Some wards," said Ross faintly. "Um, sure." She walked over to a chest of drawers standing by the entryway and fished out a cardboard packet of chalk. "Here. I hope the color doesn't matter, it's just plain white chalk."

"It will serve its purpose." Merrick took the chalk and walked over to the door, studying it for a few moments before beginning to sketch runes on the doorframe. The chalk was almost invisible on the cream-colored paint. Ross watched him, seeming more amused and perplexed than anything else, and then her eyes found Duke. She raised her eyebrows in silent question. He tilted his head and motioned for her to watch.

Merrick worked on the front door industriously, the chalk scratching against the paint as he marked runes with quick, sure strokes. He stepped back, surveyed his handiwork, and then marked a complex rune in the center of the door itself. He held out a hand to Duke. "Your dagger, please."

Duke had an idea about what was going to happen with his blade, but he handed it to Merrick hilt-first anyway, hoping that Ross wouldn't completely freak out with the faerie voodoo going on in her entryway. Merrick finished chalking the circular rune, pricked his finger decisively with the tip of Duke's dagger, and pressed a bloody print into the center of the door. The hairs on the back of Duke's neck stood on end as the air tightened in the room, and he saw Ross stiffen as she felt it too. Two small sparks of silver flashed out from the center of the door, tracing the frame and then zipping away in opposite directions around the walls, outlining the window frames in the living room and dining room like frenetic fireflies before zooming away toward the bedrooms. Duke heard May's sudden barking in Vivian's room.

"There," said Merrick, a sheen of sweat glistening on his forehead. He swallowed and swayed, reaching out to steady himself on the chest of drawers and missing. Ross grabbed him, grimacing as she kept him from falling. Duke quickly rescued his dagger, wiping it clean before sliding it back into its sheath.

"I think that's enough of whatever that was for one night," said Ross, guiding Merrick toward the study-turned-guest-room.

"Didn't want…anything…coming in during the night," gasped Merrick, letting her steer him down the hallway. Duke watched them for a moment, thinking, and then retrieved Merrick's sword and one of Luca's axes from the hall closet. He'd slept with his rifle beside him in the mountains of the Northern wilds, and though a little house in southern Louisiana was a bit different from that untamed wilderness, Luca and Merrick were still in a world not their own.

"Come on, big guy," Duke said to Luca, offering him his free hand. "Might as well get you settled for the night too." To his surprise, Luca took his hand. Duke grunted as he hauled the *ulfdrengr* upright. "Feels like you weigh more than half a mountain."

Luca chuckled as he stood for a moment and made sure his legs were steady. "If you think I'm big, you should have seen my brothers."

Duke opened his mouth to ask – it was rare that the *ulfdrengr* talked about their families – but then he pressed his lips shut. If he'd lost everything and everyone, he sure wouldn't want some curious asshole digging into the wound. He shadowed Luca to the guest room. May still whined low in her throat behind the door of Vivian's room, uneasy after the sweep of Merrick's spell over the walls of the house.

Merrick stood by the single window of the study, Ross watching him with a hint of wariness. The room was small and simply furnished with a desk, a tall silver lamp, a bookshelf and an old leather wing-backed chair in the corner. Ross had pulled the futon away from the wall and made it up like a proper bed; the air mattress, too, had sheets and pillows and a blanket, situated a few steps away from the futon against the other wall.

"I'll take the…air mattress," said Merrick, tasting the words on his tongue. The navigator gazed out the window for a moment more, staring into the heavy darkness of the Louisiana night, and then let the curtain fall back into place.

Luca didn't argue, padding over to the fold-down bed. He paused and turned to Ross. "As Merrick has already said, thank you for opening your home to us. We are strangers here." He smiled faintly. "I am sure you have many questions. I think Duke can answer most of them, but I am also sure he will not tell you of his courage and steadfast loyalty in the battle for our world."

Duke felt his neck heat with a flush as he laid Merrick's sword by the air mattress and positioned Luca's axe within easy reach of the futon. He hated the part of war that came after the actual fight, the talking and the evaluation and the assignment of awards. It was one thing to talk about it with his brothers. *That* he didn't mind. It was when someone tried to talk him up or an outsider offered their analysis that he bristled. Well-intentioned on Luca's part, and he did feel a prickle of gratitude – maybe it would help Ross believe him – but it made him uneasy all the same. War was ugly. People died, in ugly ways. He didn't like it when people tried to romanticize it and package it in pretty words. But he bit his tongue. If anyone had earned the right to talk about the battle, it was Luca.

A slight frown creased Ross's brow. "What do you mean, the battle for your world?"

"If I tried to tell the whole story tonight, I think I'd keel over in the middle of it," said Luca with another faint smile. The shadows under his eyes looked even more pronounced in the light of the study's lamp. "But Duke and his companions helped to save our world. I saw the destruction of my people and my homeland, and I was held captive by this evil. I thought I had seen the last of light and hope in my life. But then the Bearer freed me from the darkness, and her brother and his companions helped free us all." He paused as if to gather his strength. "It was a great battle, and not one easily won."

"We don't rightly know if it was won," Merrick pointed out in a carefully smooth voice.

"The portal closed behind us," said Luca wearily. "I think that means the Queens bound and broke Malravenar." He sat experimentally on the edge of the futon, testing to ensure that it could handle his weight.

"It's held two people before," said Ross reassuringly, pretending she didn't see Duke's sudden pained look at her statement. "I think you should both get some rest. Noah can explain the rest to me." She walked across the room and showed Merrick how to switch off the tall lamp. He nodded, gray eyes glimmering in his pale face as he stared out again into the darkness. Luca laid down on the futon, the bed creaking slightly but holding steady beneath his weight.

"I'll be on the couch in the living room if anything happens," said Duke to Merrick. The Sidhe nodded, his gray eyes flickering to Luca, who looked like he had already fallen asleep. Duke walked back out into the hallway and Ross followed, shutting the door behind them.

"You're sleeping on the couch?" Ross asked in the painstakingly neutral voice that she used when she had a very strong opinion on something but didn't want to show it.

Duke took a deep breath. Traditionally, he treaded lightly when Ross used that voice, but he was so damn tired. He ran a hand through his hair again. "I thought it would be easiest for tonight."

They drifted to a halt in the middle of the living room. Ross shoved her thumbs into her pockets and swallowed. "Yeah, you're right."

"If I take another step toward you, will you just promise not to slap me again?" Duke said gently, a smile in his voice and on his lips. God, he wanted to hold her. He ached to touch her. He had thought that he hadn't forgotten her beauty, but the details blurred after months apart. Now he marveled again at the subtle golden flecks in the irises of her dark brown eyes, the smooth sharp plane of her cheekbones, the tawny gold of her skin, the sprinkling of freckles across her nose.

She didn't reply, so he slowly closed the distance between them, giving her plenty of time to say something or step back. She didn't move away, but she crossed her arms over her chest, hugging herself.

When she looked up at him, her almond-shaped eyes were wide with pain.

"They declared you dead, Noah. Your whole team." Her voice trembled slightly. "The investigation took months. They wouldn't tell us much, other than you'd been attacked and, they thought, hit by an IED. They found your vehicle and some of your kit. Or the shell of it, anyway." She swallowed hard and looked away but continued doggedly. "They told us that your bodies were burned with some kind of accelerant or explosive they couldn't identify. The fire burned so hot that they couldn't get anything reliable for DNA testing." She hugged herself harder. "They folded a flag for me at your funeral, Noah. It was my worst nightmare."

He couldn't stop himself. He couldn't watch her try to fend off the tears and comfort herself, as she'd had to do while he was gone. He reached out and folded her into his arms; she stiffened for a breath and then melted into him as though her bones had disappeared, pressing her face into his chest so hard that he felt the sharpness of her cheekbone against his sternum. The warm wetness of her tears soaked through the thin fabric of his t-shirt. She was shaking. He guided them to the couch and carefully sat down, cradling her against his chest. She freed one arm and slid it under his arm, her hand gripping his shoulder with an almost painful urgency, like she was afraid that he wasn't real, or that if she let him go he'd evaporate, a figment of her imagination. He stroked her dark hair and said softly, "I'm so sorry, Ross. I'm sorry you had to go through that. I..." He didn't have words. There was nothing to say. He'd followed Liam into the Fae world out of loyalty; he'd had a choice to make and in the heat of battle he couldn't let the leader of his team be dragged away by those faceless monstrosities.

After a few minutes, Ross raised her face from his chest, her eyes red. "Tell me what happened. Tell me what really happened."

"Half of it's gonna sound crazy. Some of it I still don't know if I believe myself, and I saw it with my own two eyes."

"I don't care," Ross said with sudden vehemence. "I need to know what happened. I spent almost a year thinking that you...you were killed and then burned. *Burned*, Noah." Her voice was shaking with anger now. "I didn't know whether those bastards had done anything else to you and the boys. Nobody could give me any answers." She sucked in a sharp breath. "Anything you tell me will be better than what I thought happened to you." Her hand tightened on his shoulder again. "And even if you're fruit-loops crazy, you're *here*. You're...here."

"I'm here," he agreed softly, "and I'm alive, and I'm only as fruit-loops crazy as when I left." He gave her a lopsided grin. "At least I think."

She smacked him lightly on the chest with her free hand. "Start talking, mister."

"Yes, ma'am," he said, and despite the exhaustion aching in his bones, he reached back in his mind to the day that they'd been on patrol. The ground had shaken and the sky darkened like some unnatural storm, an earthquake and a hell-raising tempest swirling around them, sweeping them into what felt like another realm, complete with its own monsters. It had happened once before, but not as harshly, the ground shaking, at least, and that's when they'd first met Finnead and Luca. They'd known Liam's sister. Luck had been strangely calm about Tess's disappearance. It was like he'd flipped a switch. He got up one morning, sent a few emails out on his laptop, and then that evening he relaxed for the first time since he'd gotten the word that his baby sister had vanished. Run away, their mother postulated scornfully. Duke had heard part of that Skype call, even through his noise canceling headphones.

He told the story to Ross as best he could. His mouth went dry and his voice became hoarse from talking for so long, but he pressed on. If he'd had to go to Ross's funeral...he didn't know what he'd have done. If he'd had to watch the flag draped over her casket folded with solemn precision, and then handed to him, a heavy triangle of lost possibilities, torn dreams and the strange hard pride of sacrifice. She had survived it, and he'd survived his foray into Faeortalam. He told her about the Northern mountains, the skirmishes with the strange, deformed creatures and the sense that Liam wasn't telling them everything. But they trusted each other with their lives, so they let Luck have his secret. And then knowing they were being tracked, knowing that they couldn't overcome these ravenous monsters in the wilderness for long, finding the ledge and deciding that's where they would make their last stand. He told her about the Valkyrie and about the sword wielding woman who had leapt her horse over the rocks bordering the ledge, killing one of the deformed wolves that had been tracking them. Ross's eyes widened slightly when he told her that the sword-wielding woman was Liam's sister, Tess.

"Wait," she interrupted. "So Tess…she disappeared too, with her friend Molly. And you're telling me they both traveled to this other world, too?"

"Yes," said Duke. "Like I said, half-crazy. But I saw her. I fought alongside her." He smiled a little at the memory. "She got damn good with that sword. And she had another sword, a…a *magic* sword. She said that she was the descendant of a priestess who had been the last one to bear the Sword, a couple of centuries ago."

"A couple of *centuries* ago," repeated Ross. She sat up straighter and slid back a little in his lap so that she could see him without straining her neck.

Duke shrugged. "I didn't see that part. I don't know."

"Okay," said Ross slowly. She'd met Tess when the unit had returned from their last deployment, and she'd liked the younger woman, but she hadn't pegged her as a warrior, tough as nails. Then again, that had been almost three years ago now, and Tess had just finished her freshman year of college, bright eyed with possibility. Ross had gotten back from her final deployment a few months before the homecoming, and she admitted now that she'd probably been a bit prickly. Maybe she'd judged Tess too harshly. "I wouldn't have…never mind. Go on."

Duke grinned. "Looking back to when I met Tess, I wouldn't have expected it either."

Ross smiled and they looked at each other quietly for a moment.

"What's this battle that Luca was talking about?" she asked softly.

Duke took a deep breath and dove into the rest of the story. He told Ross about the journey across the Deadlands, traveling with the Wild Court and seeing Queen Titania and Queen Mab from a distance. Her dark eyes kindled with interest as he described Vell and the *ulfdrengr*, trying to capture the bond between the warriors and their magnificent wolves. He attempted to explain the darkness and evil that they'd felt after crossing through the portal into the courtyard of the Dark Keep, time undulating around them as they fought what felt like an unending tide of his dark creations. His words ran dry when he got to the part in the throne room.

"I'm sorry," he said, "I just can't…words don't do it justice. I'm not good with words anyway."

"You've done fine," said Ross quietly. "Thank you."

Duke heaved a frustrated sigh. "We saw her opening the portal. I heard Tess shout to stop her. She had a cup of blood…Liam got there first and she… she stabbed him. I didn't see her move, but she stabbed him. I tried to stop her but she…" He mimed picking something up and throwing it with his free hand. "She just *grabbed* me and slammed me into something. The altar, I think. I blacked out. When I woke up, I was laying in the grass by the river a couple miles down the road from the gas station in Cairn."

"How did Luca and Merrick get drawn through too?" Ross asked.

"I'm guessing that the portal opened and sucked me through. One of them must have grabbed me to try and pull me away from it. Chain reaction. And we all ended up here." Duke shrugged. "I don't know how it works. But it closed behind us."

"You're sure? You're sure it's closed and there's not any of those creatures that can come through?"

"I thought you wouldn't believe me," Duke said wonderingly,

"and here you are askin' all the questions that I should've thought of." He smiled slightly. "Kinda like old times."

Ross made a noncommittal sound and chewed on her lip distractedly. She slid off his lap and stood, stretching her arms over her head. "Whatever Merrick did…that was real. That was…magic, I guess. I don't know what to call it." She shook her head. "God, what a day."

"Not every day your fiancé returns from the dead," agreed Duke, arching an eyebrow.

"Don't joke about it," she snapped. Then she softened. "At least…not yet. I'm just…still processing."

"Sorry." Duke leaned his elbows on his knees. He felt like he was screwing everything up and he hadn't even been back a full day, like he was trying to find solid ground in the swamp, testing the hillocks of marsh grass and half expecting to be plunged into the warm, brackish waters.

"No…no, it's okay." Ross sat down on the couch beside him and sighed. "I just…I don't know how to navigate this." A sliver of a smile appeared on her lips. "There's no standard operating procedure for your dead fiancé suddenly appearing with a Viking and an elf in tow."

Duke chuckled. "First of all, you *just* said no joking."

"So? I can disregard my own rules," Ross said primly.

"And second, I'd like to see you tell Luca and Merrick that to their faces."

"Maybe I will," she said in that same mockingly proper voice.

Duke swore softly under his breath and scrubbed at his face with one hand. He itched to scoop her into his arms and kiss her silly…his mind slid down that rabbit hole and he wanted to do so much more than kiss her but he reeled himself back. Easy. Just like coming back from deployment. They had to get to know each other again. It wasn't all sunshine and roses and rainbows. And this time he was coming back from the grave, not from an overseas combat zone.

Ross interrupted his thoughts by placing her hands squarely on his thighs. He froze and slowly opened his eyes. She slid her body between his knees. He swallowed hard, keeping carefully still as she leaned toward him and kissed him. His hands gripped the cushion of the couch as he forced himself to let her set the pace. After a long, gentle kiss – tasting, reacquainting – Ross drew back. Duke stared up at her, breathing raggedly, not caring that she could plainly see his intense desire.

"Are you sure you want to sleep on the couch?" she asked, her voice barely more than a whisper. Her eyes were drowning-dark and kiss-drunken, but the thread of uncertainty in her words only confirmed what he knew he had to say.

He closed his eyes and groaned. "God, Ross, I don't wanna sleep on the couch. I wanna...well, you know what I wanna do." He gestured to himself. "Goddamn Exhibit A." He forced himself to take a deep breath. "But what I want more than that...and *God,* do I *want* that...what I want more than that is to do this right. To not screw it up." Another deep breath and the riptide of desire receded just slightly. Enough for him to firm his resolve. "You've been through a lot. I don't wanna push you too hard too soon."

She reached out and touched his cheek, a rare soft gesture from the hard as steel woman that he knew and loved. "You know me better than I know myself. You're right."

He smiled a little ruefully. "Wish I wasn't."

She smiled in reply. "It'll make it better in the end, I think."

"Cold comfort now," he said, and then hastily backpedaled. He didn't want to make her feel as though he was only doing this because it was what *she* wanted. He knew it was the right thing to do. "I mean...I'm tired as all get out. Wouldn't be my best performance anyway." He gave her the best smile he could manage.

"Let me grab you some blankets and a pillow," she said, padding across the room and disappearing momentarily into the hallway. She winced as she tried unsuccessfully to fluff the lopsided pillow and

Duke unfolded one of the rather threadbare blankets. "Sorry. Scraping the bottom of the barrel. It's not often we have three guests at once."

"No worries. I've slept in worse places." He smiled.

"You and I both know that," she retorted. She tossed down the pillow and contemplated the front door, Merrick's white chalk runes barely visible against the light frame. But his bloody fingerprint, now preserved in silver, still glowed faintly in the center of the intricate spiral rune in the center of the door. She looked at Duke. "If you're sure nothing came through, why did Merrick want to put up these protections?"

"I'm not one hundred percent sure," Duke said heavily. "I just...I think that if something had followed us, we'd have run into it by now."

"From what you said, the enemy might be smarter than you give them credit for," Ross murmured. Then she looked at him with a businesslike air. "May will sleep in my room tonight. I'll introduce you to her tomorrow morning." Without an explanation, she walked quickly down the hallway. Duke heard her open a drawer in her bedroom. She returned with a pistol and two magazines. "Remember how to use one of these?"

"This is a new Glock," he said approvingly, watching as Ross showed him clear and safe – that the weapon was unloaded – and handed it to him, grip first. He checked the rounds in the magazines.

"I have the Beretta in my room still," she said. "Oh, and May is a retired working dog. So if something gets in and you hear me let her out, just get out of her way."

"Shepherd?" Duke asked about the dog, contemplating the best place to stash the pistol and magazines. He wasn't sure if bullets would work against any sort of monster that had followed them through the portal, but they sure as hell couldn't hurt.

"Malinois," replied Ross. She smiled faintly. "Brett got in touch with me after your funeral. Thought I could use some company, and I have to admit I like having her around."

"May is a weird name for a combat dog," said Duke, half to himself.

"Oh, that's just her nickname," said Ross with a grin. "Her full name is Mayhem."

Duke chuckled. "That's more like it." He settled on a place to stash the Glock and magazines, and then sat down on the couch. "So you've got a magic spell on the house, a working dog named Mayhem, and me with a Glock on the couch by the front door. I think you're pretty well covered."

Instead of smiling, Ross looked serious. "I hope so." She stepped close again. Duke stopped breathing. She kissed his forehead. "I love you." She said the words softly, like she was afraid if she said them louder she'd break the spell that had somehow brought him back to her.

"I love you, too," Duke said as she straightened. They smiled at each other for a long moment.

"See you in the morning." Ross turned off the light as she walked back toward her bedroom.

Duke settled onto the couch, pulled the threadbare blanket over him and closed his eyes, knowing that sleep would be difficult despite the tiredness seeping into his very bones. He hoped that he didn't mess things up with Ross. He hoped that he could navigate a world that thought he was dead. And he hoped most of all that he hadn't brought danger to this small, sleepy Louisiana town. His thoughts whirled, but shortly his body succumbed and he drifted into sleep.

In the hot heavy darkness outside the small house, a lone figure stood on the road. The lanky man stared at the house through the shadows, an inky blackness sliding unnaturally in the whites of his eyes. He spat a stream of tobacco juice into a white Styrofoam cup and thought to himself that his master would be very pleased.

Chapter 12

Darkness pressed close around the cloaked figure sliding with quick grace through the shadows. Breath plumed in a frosty cloud from within the hood of the cloak, and spidery veins of ice transformed the stones of the courtyard into a treacherous wintry path. The figure navigated the ice surefootedly, looking almost like a dancer whirling across the flagstones.

Ramel watched from within the concealing blackness of a deep arched doorway on the other side of the courtyard. He kept his thoughts tightly controlled; he could not think her name or let his love wash through him at the sight of her slim form slipping swiftly through the night. Their meeting was clandestine, held in the outer reaches of the claimed Unseelie territory, but even the farthest corners of Mab's claimed part of the city felt her cold wrath. Winter had descended on the Unseelie portion of the White City, proclaiming their Queen's rage and despair almost as loudly as Mab's declarations of treason against one or another of her subjects.

Finally, Molly reached him. He kept the hilt of the newly made Brighbranr covered beneath his palm; the ruby set into the pommel, awake and rolling like a bloody scarlet eye, seemed to give Mab more purchase on his thoughts. Ramel despised the fact that he was suspicious of even his own blood-bound weapon, but he kept his hand on the ruby all the same, feeling a little shiver of displeasure from the blade.

"I was not followed," she said in a low voice as she reached the doorway. She stood an arm's length away from him, her body coiled like a spring as she glanced about for another long moment. Then she reached up and pulled back the hood of her cloak.

"Even that is not certain," said Ramel in a voice thick with the concentration of keeping his thoughts free of her. Meeting clandestinely was so great a danger that he had almost balked, but in the end he couldn't deny that ignorance of what was happening to Mab was more dangerous to many more than just her. In a way, he was proud of her courage.

It had been terrible, when Mab had plucked the knowledge that Molly had regained her memories from Ramel's mind. He'd let his guard down, and he still cursed himself for it. The Queen had not been herself for some time, but after the battle at the Dark Keep and the first desparate days of attempting to bring back the Unseelie Princess, Mab had plunged into a deep and unrelenting spiral of seething sorrow and bitterness. Eventually, that sorrow and bitterness had hardened into rage and suspicion. Rage at her inability to cure her sister, and suspicion that even her closest advisors were plotting against her. Queen Mab had planted the seed of what seemed to be a self-fulfilling prophecy as her moods became even more unpredictable and her fury even more terrible. Ramel feared what would happen at the next Winter Solstice, when it came time for all to renew their blood oath to the Queen.

When she had drawn the knowledge from his mind that he had restored Molly's memories, Mab had summoned him before her throne. He hadn't had time to send a missive to Molly warning her of the Queen's knowledge, and he had feared for her more than himself as he strode toward the throne room. The young Vaelanmavar had not been there, but the Vaelanseld had stood by the door.

Mab sat on the throne that her artisans had carved from black stone, her fingers gripping the elaborately engraved finials at the end of the throne's arms. Ramel had seen in alarm the scores in the stone, each set of four shallow gouges the perfect distance apart to match Mab's clawed fingers. He could not say for certain, but he had thought that her fingernails shone a little blacker, a little more like the talons of a predator rather than a graceful Sidhe Queen. Mab's face, too, changed a little more every day, the planes sharper and more angled, her eyes burning with a dark and furious intensity.

Ramel remembered the blazing eyes of the *syivhalla* in the barracks at the Royal Wood, what seemed like a lifetime ago; and he quickly pushed the comparison from his mind.

"Vaelanbrigh." Mab's voice had rung out coldly in the cavernous room.

He had dropped to one knee before her throne and bowed his head slightly.

"I can taste your fear, my Knight," the Queen had said, the words sliding through the bitterly icy air like snakes, flicking their tongues into his ear.

A shudder ran through him. "Yes, my Queen."

"Why are you afraid, Vaelanbrigh?" Her voice had remained stony.

He had taken a slow breath, watching a spiral of frost form on the stone before him. His knee ached from the cold. "Because I fear I have displeased you, my Queen, and my greatest desire is only to serve you."

She had laughed then, a frightening sound that started low and rumbling like the beginnings of an earthquake, rising until her voice summoned the fury of a raging winter storm shrieking around the throne room. Ramel had stoically bent his head against the physical onslaught of her mad laughter. The edge of insanity in his Queen's voice shook him deeply.

"Serve me?" she had said finally into the echoes of her laughter. "It seems you wish to serve yourself, restoring memories to your half-mortal whore."

He had dared to glance up at her supplicatingly, his eyes taking in the sight of her beautiful face twisted into an ugly mask of fury, her dark nails biting into the stone of her throne. "My Queen," he said, "I wish to serve you. I restored the *fendhionne*'s memories only to test a method that I believe will restore the Crown Princess."

Nausea turned his stomach as he said the words, even as he suppressed his own disgust at his own cowardice before the fury of the Queen. But if supplication could save Molly's life, he would abase himself before Mab in any way the Queen desired. He had focused his thoughts on his loyalty, his desire to serve, hoping that Queen Mab would rake her claws through his mind and draw those bits of his consciousness out like a hawk disemboweling a rabbit.

"The *fendhionne* was not willing," he continued, "but I forced her." He had tasted bile at the back of his throat but kept his face carefully earnest. "I wish to serve you, my Queen, and restore your sister to you. I did not wish to harm the Crown Princess, and so I bade the *fendhionne* be my subject for my experiments." He had bowed his head again. "I beg your mercy if I displeased you by using the mortal girl."

Mab had fallen still, her dark eyes fixed on Ramel with cold consideration. "You have succeeded with the *fendhionne*, and you shall succeed with the Crown Princess."

Coldness had spread to every part of Ramel's body at the unspoken threat in Mab's words. "Yes, my Queen. I hear, and I obey."

"If I commanded you to kill the *fendhionne*, as I have no more use for her, would you obey?" Mab had asked the question almost lazily.

He had raised his head and saw the glittering amusement in her gaze. "My Queen," he had answered steadily. "I am yours to command." He paused. "The *fendhionne*, though, might be suffered to live a bit longer, that I may perfect certain other methods on her. The restoration of her memories did scar her mind, but I believe it to be a result of her mortal weakness." He had spoken carefully.

"So she is mad?" asked Mab, digging one talon into the dark stone.

"At times," Ramel had allowed. "I wish to study her further so that I may better help the Crown Princess."

"Study her further," Mab had repeated mockingly. "I suspect that you do indeed want to *study her further*, Vaelanbrigh." She suddenly stood, sweeping down from her throne. She had seized Ramel by the face, her fingers digging painfully into the tender underside of his jaw, one of her sharp nails piercing the skin of his throat. He had held his body carefully still as she wrenched his head up, his gaze downcast in respect.

"Look at me," she had hissed, the faint scent of carrion washing over him with her breath.

He obeyed, gazing up at her darkly blazing eyes and sharp face, keeping his mind carefully blank.

"Fail, and I will make you wish you were dead, Vaelanbrigh," she said in a low voice. "Betray me, and you *will* be dead, along with your mortal whore."

He had not been able to speak with her hand gripping his face, but in his mind he thought clearly, *I live only to serve you, Majesty, Queen of Winter and Night, my one true Monarch. My life is yours as is my loyalty.*

She had given a low hiss that could have been satisfaction as she released him, sweeping back toward the throne. He had dragged in a few breaths, feeling the cold burn of her phantom touch and the blood sliding down the side of his neck. Then she had settled back onto her throne and dismissed him with a flick of her wrist. He had bowed and walked away; the Vaelanseld did not meet his eyes as he passed him at the door.

Now Molly gave a hiss of her own as she glimpsed the raw burns on his face, the imprint of Mab's fingers clear in the pattern. One of her hands moved as if to touch him, but she let it fall to her side. His terse missive had cautioned her against any display of affection; he was afraid that feeling her touch would break his control over his thoughts.

"We have little time," Ramel said in a low voice, "so please don't waste any on pity."

"Not pity," said Molly, "anger."

Ramel took a breath and nodded. "Anger is good. Anger will help us survive." He took another breath. Holding his thoughts in alignment while he spoke of a different subject had always been difficult, but he was glad he had practiced the discipline. Perhaps it would save at least her life now. "Mab knows. I told her I had forced you." He couldn't help the bitterness that entered his words; he controlled his thoughts at the expense of showing emotion in his voice. "I also told her you are a bit mad and I wished to continue to experiment on you, to better help the Crown Princess."

"You already tried the restoration on the Crown Princess," said Molly in a low voice of agony. "It didn't work."

"The Queen doesn't know that yet," Ramel replied wearily. "She might still kill me, and she might still kill you. But I'm trying. I'm doing my best."

"I know you are," said Molly, her words thickening with unshed tears. Then she straightened, drawing back her shoulders, and he had to suppress his sudden pride in her. "Tell me what must be done."

"You must act a bit mad, and I will have to keep you as a sort of prisoner." Ramel let the words fall heavily into the bitter cold. He wished briefly that he could apologize, but all his will was focused on the serenity of his thoughts to feed the connection to Mab. Perhaps that was why his next words surprised even him. "If you begin to hate me," he said, "it might be easier for you when she kills me."

"I won't let her," Molly said immediately, her voice fierce. Her fists clenched by her side. "And I will *never* hate you."

He nodded. "I won't be able to show that…I won't be able to show any of it." He couldn't even speak the words for fear that his thoughts would follow.

"I will always know," she said in that same fierce voice. "Even if you cannot show it, I will always know that you love me."

He took a deep breath. Exhaustion pressed down on him, and his face burned from Mab's touch. "We cannot meet again like this."

"I know." Molly gazed at him for a moment and then her face hardened in resolve. "You aren't alone, Ramel. I won't leave you, not even if she threatens me. We'll fight together." She drew her hood up again. "Come and collect me as your prisoner in the morning. I'll be sure to act properly mad."

And with that, Ramel watched her ghost away again across the frost-laden courtyard. The ruby in the hilt of the Brighbranr pulsed sharply, and he drew his hand away, staring at the cut that the sword had bitten deeply into his palm. For a long moment, he watched the pulse of blood from the cut, and then he walked away without even bothering to bind it, heedless of the dark trail of blood dripping onto the icy stone.

Chapter 13

"I still think this is overkill," muttered Tess, tugging at the hem of the long tunic and wishing for her plain, well-worn shirt and breeches.

"If I can wear this frippery without complaining, then so can you," said Vell pointedly. One of the Wild Court fighters who had some skill as a tailor had suggested to the *Vyldretning*, in sly jest, that she wear a gown to the council; and the answering growl had ignited sparks of amusement in the eyes of all in the room.

"Frippery," repeated Calliea with a chuckle. They all stood in one of the rooms behind the wolf tapestry, not the great room with the hearth, but something more like a dressing room. There was even another scarlet tapestry enchanted to reflect their images as surely as any silver mirror. Tess glanced at it; the scarlet rippled and parted like a curtain, revealing her reflection. She wore an emerald green tunic – thankfully, no one had suggested a gown to *her* – and a tailored vest of mahogany leather. The vest contained echoes of a corset in its snug design: the top of the vest reached to just below her breasts, and it flared slightly at her hips so that she retained freedom of movement. She had to admit that it was beautiful in its simplicity and it complemented the green of the tunic. As a bonus, she'd discovered that the tailor had added a small hidden sheath under her left arm, so she could wear a slim dagger to draw with her right hand. Her only jewelry was Gwyneth's pendant, the rubies that had once been her blood catching the light, and Vell had braided her hair as they'd done while traveling. Tess slid the Sword and its scabbard from its bandolier to wear it at her hip. Vell had said that this was not a council of war, and so they would not be wearing armor. But Tess would be damned if she'd leave the Caedbranr in anyone's hands but her own, especially after it had awakened again. She felt its power sleeping behind her breastbone. Sleeping was better than absent.

Tess caught Vell's reflection behind her own. For all the muttered protests and growls, the *Vyldretning* looked magnificent, dressed in velvety black breeches and boots, a high collared scarlet tunic, and a sleeveless surcoat worked with rippling golden runes, fastened at the waist with a wide, braided black belt. Aside from the glistening runes on her surcoat, the only ornaments Vell wore were her plain golden circlet and a woven gold net pinned about the coils of her dark hair at the nape of her neck.

"Are you done ogling us both?" the High Queen asked, pausing in her restless pacing to arch an eyebrow at Tess.

Tess smiled. "You look fantastic." She raised her own eyebrow. "Has Liam seen you?"

Vell waved a hand. "He will soon enough." Her golden eyes sharpened. "You know Finnead will be there."

"I'm not a schoolgirl with a crush," Tess replied serenely. Though she *did* feel a faint tug somewhere in her chest, it was nothing like the maelstrom of conflicted feelings that she'd once harbored for the former Unseelie Knight. "Anymore," she amended with a self deprecating smile. Then she sobered. "How is he?"

"He's...withdrawn," replied Vell, showing no surprise at the question. "He acts much more like he did when he was at the Unseelie Court as one of Mab's Three. Not that I question his loyalty, I would know if he was disloyal without any words." The High Queen's golden eyes flashed as she spoke of the invisible bond that allowed her to feel her Three's innermost thoughts. "He's just…different."

Tess tilted her head, considering. "When he drowned in the Darinwel, he was freed from Mab's control. Making him one of your Three, part of the Wild Court, made him part of something new and young."

"New and young," repeated Vell with a chuckle.

"The Crown Princess draws him back toward Mab," said Tess softly. "Or back toward what he used to be when he was in service to Mab, at least."

"I think perhaps I've been allowing him to spend too much time in the Unseelie camp," Vell said, a hint of agreement in her voice as she resumed her pacing. "But there's a fine line between the discipline of a fair ruler and the cruelty of a jealous one." The sound of a knock echoed through the room, despite the lack of a proper door. "Enter," Vell called.

"My lady." Gray bowed. She wore a red tunic, so dark it was almost black, a simple black belt, and black breeches paired with her well-used black boots. She'd set a scarlet feather like a jewel in her fair hair, the length of the feather curving against her braids. Her golden beauty remained undiminished by the scars she bore from the battle over the White City. A thin red line traced her jaw from her left ear to her chin, and then trailed down her neck. Only Gray's Sidhe reflexes had saved her from choking on her own blood, thought Tess. If that cut had been just a bit deeper, Vell would have lost one of her Three. The Sword thrummed a little at her hip, as if to draw her from her morbid thoughts.

"Finnead and Liam?" Vell asked.

"Waiting just outside the door," replied Gray. A knowing smile touched one side of her perfect cupid's bow lips. "Awaiting your pleasure, my Queen."

"My *pleasure* is not to deal with your sarcasm at this particular moment," said Vell firmly. "Come on, then. Let's get this over with." She strode past Gray.

Gray bowed slightly to Tess. "Lady Bearer."

"It's good to see you, Gray," said Tess, and to her surprise she actually meant it. There hadn't been any particular love lost between them in the past, but Tess thought that Gray's casual indifference toward her had warmed into a wary…something. *Friendship* was too strong a word. Perhaps it was because Liam was now one of Vell's Three. But in any case, Gray accepted Tess's words without qualm.

"And you as well, Lady Bearer," she replied, falling into step just behind Tess as they made their way toward the invisible door of the room. Tess forced herself not to wince or hesitate, walking through the spot in the wall where Vell had just disappeared ahead of her. A prickling sensation not unlike what she'd felt when passing the Sentinel Stones coursed over her, and then she stood in the hallway.

"Can we ever just have doors?" Tess asked Vell, rubbing her shoulder where the prickling lingered. "Or would that be too ordinary for you to bear?"

Vell merely grinned her wolf-like grin. Liam walked forward to meet them. His tunic was a deep green, not jewel-bright like the color of Tess's tunic but shadow dark, like the duskiest parts of a forest, and he wore a short axe in his belt. The sight of the axe reminded Tess painfully of Luca. She was fairly certain that the *ulfdrengr* had given her brother that very weapon.

"My Queen," said Liam to Vell with a small bow from the waist. Vell nodded to him, and Tess resisted the urge to roll her eyes. Vell and Liam still played their roles flawlessly in public, never a glance or word straying beyond the expected boundaries between a Queen and one of her Three. Tess didn't know who exactly was within the trusted circle that understood the true relationship between the *Vyldretning* and the newest member of her Court, but she guessed that Gray knew from the laughter dancing in the Sidhe woman's vibrant eyes. She wondered briefly how much was shared through the bond with the Three, and then she shook her head, clearing it of the thought.

Her hand found the hilt of the Sword and she rubbed two fingers along the crossguard absently. Her brother had adapted well to this new world, blending in almost seamlessly now. Then again that was part of his training, adapting to survive, learning quickly and correcting mistakes. His experience in the mortal world had served him well. And there was the fact that he had an echo of Arcana in his head. Tess hadn't mustered the courage to ask him about that yet. She didn't want to waste what little time she was able to spend with her brother delving into sensitive subjects. There was more than enough of that to go around already.

Finnead emerged from the shadows a bit farther down the hallway, falling into step beside Gray without a word. Tess glanced at him and felt a little twinge of empathy. He looked paler than usual, his eyes distant and his raven-dark hair slightly unkempt. She'd heard that he spent more than half his waking hours over in the Unseelie portion of the City. Other than their healers taking shifts in the healing ward, the Unseelie had withdrawn into their own encampment –even the healers kept to themselves, tending only the most gravely wounded Unseelie fighters that still could not be moved to the convalescent ward in the Unseelie camp. Tess resisted the urge to reach out and touch his shoulder. He looked so…alone. The Sword stirred.

He is no more alone than before the battle, the Caedbranr said in her head.

Oh, so we're back to providing commentary on my thoughts? Tess asked silently, raising one eyebrow. Liam and Gray were discussing something as they walked, but she couldn't focus on both conversations.

You have seen and done much more than many Bearers past, replied the Sword in its androgynous layered voice, *but you are still young.*

And so you're my sage guardian, making sure that I don't relapse into an infatuation with Finnead? she retorted.

The Sword's silent chuckle vibrated through her ribs and down her spine. She shivered a little, half in annoyance, but realizing once again that she'd *missed* the feeling of the Caedbranr's amusement rolling through her bones.

Empathy in the face of tragedy can sometimes relight the embers of a past romance, the Sword told her.

Tess couldn't help the snort that escaped her. Liam looked over at her questioningly but Vell murmured to him and he just smiled and shook his head.

So you're an expert on romance now, are you? Seen much of that, being a Sword and all? Tess pressed her lips together to keep from laughing at her own sarcasm.

You are being impertinent, said the Sword, managing somehow to sound haughtily offended, like a very proper schoolmarm who'd just heard a dirty joke.

Indeed I am, she replied with a grin. The Sword grumbled something she couldn't quite make out – how exactly did that work, not being able to hear something that was in her own mind? But in any case, it circled and settled again in her chest, its voice falling silent.

"Enjoying the conversation that none of the rest of us can hear?" Liam asked, falling into step beside her.

"Oh, yes, I love it when inanimate objects give me unsolicited advice," said Tess with a smile. Finnead, she noticed, hadn't so much as looked at her during the traverse down the long passageways of the tent palace. He kept his eyes fixed straight ahead, his face smooth, his eyes distant.

"I hear that's the best kind of advice," her brother said. "The unsolicited kind, not the kind from inanimate objects. And besides, does the Sword count as inanimate? I think that's a gray area."

Tess shrugged. "It can't get up and walk away. It was stuck in a tree for a couple of centuries and I had to go fetch it. I think that meets the definition of inanimate." The Sword thrummed in protest at her flippant description of the quest that had nearly killed her after she'd first tumbled into the Fae world and landed in the web of intrigue and danger that was Queen Mab's Court. She looked at Liam. "How are you? I haven't seen you in a couple of days."

"I've been busy with the reconstruction teams," he replied.

"And busy with…other things," Tess guessed, raising her eyebrows lasciviously.

"Vell warned me that you were still a little weirded out by the whole thing, and here you are making jokes about it." Liam narrowed his eyes at her.

"I'm your little sister. I get to tease you about your love life. But I *do not* want to know details."

Liam chuckled. "That I can deal with." He slowed their pace slightly so that they fell behind Vell, Finnead and Gray. "Are you ready for this council?"

Tess shrugged, although a little thrill of anticipation coursed through her at the thought of going head to head with Mab again. "As ready as I'll ever be. It isn't my first rodeo."

"Well, it's mine," he said in a low voice. "I only know Titania and Mab from seeing them at a distance and then in the Dark Keep."

"Titania has always been gracious to me," she said. "That might be because I rescued her, but..." She shrugged. "Mab, on the other hand, doesn't like anyone who doesn't serve her purposes."

"You're trying to strike a deal with her," said Liam.

"Yes. A trade of sorts."

Liam drew in a breath. "And that trade is going to send you diving into danger again, isn't it?"

Tess smiled slightly. "Is this the obligatory 'protective older brother' talk?"

"I'd prefer you didn't mock my concern for your safety," said Liam.

"Pot, meet kettle," countered Tess.

He sighed and nodded to a pair of passing Wild Court fighters that Tess vaguely recognized. "If we open a Gate to our world again, what will that mean?"

"In what sense?" Tess asked carefully, glancing at her brother.

"None of us can go back to our old lives. My team was probably declared dead, killed in action in that firefight when Malravenar's creatures tried to kidnap me." Liam said the words calmly, as though he were discussing the weather. "You disappeared almost two years ago. Once I knew you were safe, I…I convinced everyone that you'd just wanted to try things your way. Live your own life."

"I guess that's mostly true, if you count being dragged into Queen Mab's Court and being bound to an ancient weapon of power 'living my own life.'" Tess raised her eyebrows. Part of her wanted to ask whether their mother had so easily accepted that her daughter had just…disappeared. Did she really matter so little that she could vanish without a trace and people would just shrug after a while?

"I think there's some sort of…reaction, when someone is pulled through a Gate," said Liam. "I know you're wondering why everyone would just accept it. It seemed strange to me too, almost too easy. So I think that something happens when a mortal goes through into Faeortalam."

"Most of the Sidhe in Vell's Court are too young to have experienced travel between the worlds," Tess murmured, almost to herself.

"If there *is* some sort of…*forgetting*, on a cosmic scale, that happens when a mortal travels through the Gate, what happens when you go back? Is there any blowback?"

"We're talking metaphysical blowback here?" Tess took a deep breath. "I have absolutely no idea. I feel like I'm still figuring out how I fit into everything here."

"That's what worries me. Not the fact that *you* don't know, Tess, but that *someone* might, and they might not be forthcoming," Liam said.

"If Mab knows," Tess said slowly, "Titania must as well. They must have had some sort of procedure to deal with it back when the Great Gate was open and they…invited…mortals into their Courts. But we're assuming that there *is* some kind of metaphysical exchange. Maybe a Gate is just a Gate, like a door that gets you from one room to another." She shrugged slightly. "We might be manufacturing worry, if we just let ourselves imagine everything that could go wrong."

"I just don't want you to rush into this." Liam touched her shoulder lightly. "I can't go with you."

"I know." Tess nodded as they emerged from the great doors of the palace.

A flat sheet of gray clouds pressed down on the city, muting the morning sunlight. Vell looked up balefully at the dark sky but said nothing, striding onward without a word with Finnead and Gray on either side of her.

"I've already been doing research," continued Tess. "Mostly into the precautions that Sidhe take when they go through a portal. But we can't delay much longer. Luca and Merrick might not have much time. We don't know if they were wounded before they were pulled through, and having Kianryk on this side and Luca on the other…" She swallowed hard. "Vell said that it will kill them eventually."

This time when Liam touched her shoulder, it was a brotherly squeeze of support. "She told me as much. She's worried too, you know."

"I do. Without her, this all falls apart. I don't think I would be able to convince the Sidhe Queens to open a Gate on my own." The Sword stirred a little at that statement. Tess kept walking but frowned slightly, cataloguing that small movement. Was the Sword trying to keep itself from telling her that *she* could open a Gate? She brushed the idea aside. She'd already discussed that with Vell. There was no record of any Bearer opening a Gate, and it was arrogant to assume that just because she was the Bearer, she could solve everything. Maybe the Sword just disagreed with her thought that she wasn't powerful enough to convince the Queens on her own.

After a few moments more of walking, they reached the site of the council. The Glasidhe messengers had flown missives for two days straight during the negotiations for the location of the meeting. In the end, the Queens had settled upon a pavilion nearly equidistant from the Seelie, Unseelie, and Wild Court camps. Despite the destruction wreaked on the city by Malravenar's creatures and the damage inflicted during the battle, the pavilion stood in a small courtyard, four paths – one at each point of the compass – winding away from it into the streets of the city. The stone shone whitely even in the pale light struggling through the thick layer of clouds. Banners emblazoned with the wolf of the *Vyldgard*, the sun of the Seelie Court and the moon of the Unseelie Court hung from the roof of the pavilion between the pillars, rippling gently in the light breeze. Between the banners, long diaphanous curtains draped from the ceiling to floor, creating an airy semblance of privacy for the council.

Vell strode without hesitation up the small flight of marble steps that led to the pavilion. The air undulated as she crossed the threshold of the pillars. Tess set her teeth and endured the feel of small hands sweeping over her yet again, though this was a lighter touch than the door of Vell's chambers.

The floor of the pavilion looked almost like a mirror, but its silvery surface didn't reflect anything. Rather, it looked like the surface of a pond or the ocean, traces of blue waves rolling through the silver, bracelets of foam encircling the legs of the chairs placed around the circular table in the center of the room. Tess resisted the urge to touch the illusion. And rather than *taebramh* lights, as Tess had expected, the domed ceiling of the pavilion emitted a soft light that she would have sworn was natural sunlight.

Titania sat at the circular table, magnificent in a cerulean gown. The simplicity of the gown and the richness of its color complemented her ethereal beauty. Miniature white roses adorned her intricate braid, and a white-gold circlet gleamed against the ripe wheat of her hair. The Seelie Queen stood when Vell entered, gliding around the table and extending her hands to the High Queen. Vell took Titania's hands and smiled, though it was the smile of the High Queen playing her part. Finnead, Gray and Liam greeted Queen Titania's Three, each clasping the hands of their counterparts in the Seelie Court. Tess stood a pace behind Vell, feeling slightly awkward and wishing that she had Farin or Wisp on her shoulder, whispering into her ear. Should she go greet Titania's Three, or wait until the two Queens were finished with their conversation? She'd met Niall, Ailin and Gawain at the Hall of the Outer Guard, so they weren't strangers…but she wasn't one of Vell's Three. She was the Bearer of the Iron Sword.

Fortunately, her dilemma only lasted for another minute, as Vell nodded to Titania and moved to greet the Seelie Three. The beautiful Sidhe Queen turned to Tess, her golden radiance more pronounced than Tess remembered.

"Lady Bearer," said Titania with that familiar sisterly smile. Tess remembered the shining warrior Queen who had sliced through the enemy in the Dark Keep, a beacon of vengeance in the battle. Had Mab once been able to slide between faces as easily as Titania? Her own thoughts startled her and she pushed the musings away, placing her hands in Titania's, feeling a familiar, warm glow as her skin touched that of the Seelie Queen.

"Queen Titania," Tess said, trying to match the Queen's smile.

"I have been told that you took no lasting scars from the great battle," Titania said, motherly concern lacing her voice.

"No visible ones, at least," Tess replied with a tight smile. "I wish I could say the same for all of our warriors."

Titania nodded. "As do I. But loss is the price of victory over the darkness."

Tess noticed that Titania wore a small golden pouch at her belt, and she felt the river stone within her own belt pouch tremble suddenly. She took a breath and bit back the reply that rose readily to her lips. Luca was not a *price* to be paid for victory. He was the man she loved. And she had loved as friends many others who died. Perhaps Titania's heart was just as cold as Mab's after all. Tess steadied herself before she spoke. "Vell has told me that you will support us in opening the Gate."

"I can see why you and she are such friends," said Titania, her blue eyes glimmering. "You have the same affinity for bluntness."

"I suppose you could say that." Tess drew back slightly, touching the river stone through the well-worn leather of her belt pouch.

"The river stones react to their nearness to each other," Titania said. "But a fractured spirit is not conscious, so you need not worry about that."

Tess wondered how Titania could be so sure. "It's still a bit strange to me."

Titania didn't reply, studying Tess's face. "I will support you in opening the Gate, Lady Bearer...because we are friends, are we not?" She smiled brilliantly.

The question caught Tess off guard. She blinked. The Sword stirred at her hip, the emerald in its pommel pulsing with a soft light as it awakened. *Careful*, whispered the Caedbranr in her mind, its voice so quiet that Tess couldn't be sure it had spoken at all. Tess forced herself to smooth her face of any surprise and ensured that an answering smile curved her lips. "I hope that the Bearer of the Iron Sword is counted as a friend to all three Queens and their Courts," she said in what she hoped was a gracious voice.

Something flashed in Titania's eyes, just for an instant. "Well said, Lady Bearer."

Tess inclined her head to the Seelie Queen, and Titania turned away from her, leaving her with the distinct feeling that she'd just missed something important. But then she turned to the Seelie Three, who greeted her with grace and courtesy. Ailin wore a sling on his right arm, a lingering wound from the battle in the courtyard of the Dark Keep; Niall and Gawain seemed whole, though Gawain walked stiffly and Niall seemed more withdrawn than Tess remembered from their first meeting. Titania's Three had nearly died in Brightvale, giving their life force to sustain their Queen while Malravenar had kept her Walker form captive. When Tess freed Titania, her Three were freed as well, though the strain had washed them of their golden Seelie coloring and given them ghost-pale eyes.

As Tess watched Vell and Titania move toward the table in the center of the pavilion, Gwyneth's pendant warmed at her throat. She took a deep breath and braced herself slightly as the edges of her sight faded and the Sword showed her the vision, the tall woman dressed in a flowing scarlet gown, standing before what looked like the intricately carved frame of a mirror. A wind seemed to emanate from the mirror, frothing the woman's skirt into waves. The woman didn't carry any weapons that Tess could see. Tess wished the Sword would show her the woman's face – her golden hair could have marked her as Seelie, but Tess felt a pang of familiarity at the wavy texture of the woman's hair, the way it fell over the woman's shoulders in half-curls, tendrils with a mind of their own.

Was the woman a Bearer? She couldn't see the Sword, if she was. And from Tess's vantage point, looking over the woman's shoulder into the strange mirror, she saw a strikingly modern mortal scene: a cobbled street in some historic city, the buildings speaking of early colonial times but the cars parked along the side of the street firmly placing the city in the last half-century. Wrought iron lampposts held glass lanterns at intervals along the street. Tess fought a wave of dizziness. Who was the woman, and how was she traveling into the mortal world? The Gates had been closed.

Not all the Gates, not until just recently, the Sword reminded her, the words drifting around her in the vision.

Who is she? Tess tried to move in the vision but only succeeded in unbalancing herself, and the Sword hastily withdrew her from the scene to save her from falling onto the enchanted floor of the pavilion. She swallowed and glanced around surreptitiously; no one had seemed to notice her brief sojourn from reality. Then Liam caught her eye and raised an eyebrow inquiringly – of course her brother had picked up on it. She shook her head slightly to signal him that she was all right.

Just like you to give me a vision that explains absolutely nothing, she said to the Sword a bit grumpily.

Perhaps it will teach you patience, the Sword replied serenely.

Tess snorted slightly. *Fat chance.*

The Sword chuckled in its sheath. *Now, we must focus on this council, my Bearer.*

A cold wind suddenly shoved its fingers into the pavilion, snapping the banners and twisting the gauzy curtains. The sunlight emanating from the dome overhead wavered, storm cloud darkness curdling at the edges of the sky illusion. Titania turned to face the eastern entrance to the pavilion, standing regally with her Three ranged in a crescent behind her. The Seelie Queen motioned with one hand – a small motion, barely more than the curl of one finger – and the sunlight from the dome strengthened, the blinding blue of a cloudless noon sky pushing away the lurking thunderheads at the edges of the pavilion.

Tess felt the Sword coil watchfully. She stepped closer to Vell, who stood off to one side, hand casually resting on the hilt of the ceremonial dagger at her belt. Gray looked bored. Finnead watched without any sign of interest, his handsome face perfectly unreadable. Out of the High Queen's Three, Liam seemed the most engaged, but he'd never witnessed a meeting between the Seelie and Unseelie Queens.

"I thought that perhaps this was happening," murmured Vell without turning her head.

"Thought *what* was happening?" Tess asked, sliding her words back toward the *Vyldretning* like smuggled coins.

"The makings of another war," the High Queen said in a low voice.

A chill ran through Tess as Vell's words echoed in her head. She drew back her shoulders and forced herself not to show her horror at the thought of a war between the two Courts. There was no love lost between she and Mab, but she still had friends in the Unseelie Court. And just because they were Mab's subjects didn't mean that they deserved to be thrust into a needless war, not to mention the cost to the Seelie. Where would the *Vyldgard* fit into a war between the Sidhe? Goosebumps raised the skin on her arms as the cold in the pavilion deepened from a chill to a biting wintry cold. The curtains tangled about the pillars, and the wind whipped froth into the sea illusion on the silver floor beneath their feet. Tess looked away before it could make her dizzy. Her breath plumed in a frosty cloud. The Seelie Three and their Queen seemed unaffected, and the High Queen and her Three still held their looks of casual observation.

Mab strode into the pavilion in a swell of icy wind, the stars in her diadem shining coldly. At the edge of her senses, Tess heard the crashing waves and baying hounds that had once overwhelmed her in Darkhill. Mab had raked through her mind on that first meeting, rifling through Tess's thoughts and memories with her cruel touch. The Sword's power expanded in her chest, warming her ribs and sending a comforting tendril of power down her war markings. Tess raised her chin. Vell stood perfectly still, her golden eyes shifting between Mab and Titania.

The Unseelie Queen wore a gown as dark as night, the skirts embroidered with gems that pulsed like miniature stars. Her Three wore all black, and Tess noted with another chill that they all wore breastplates that did not shine with a gloss or lacquer like those of the Seelie and *Vyldgard*, but rather seemed to suck the light into them with a dark hunger. She thought that it had been agreed not to wear armor to this council. Ramel walked at Mab's right hand, half a pace behind the Unseelie Queen. His green eyes, usually flashing with humor, were cold and hard when he glanced at Tess. The change in Ramel shook Tess more deeply than the iciness of the air. Donovan, anointed as the Vaelanmavar during the battle in the courtyard, walked at Mab's left hand, and her Vaelanseld stood behind her, as if guarding against an attack from the rear. All of Mab's Three wore their swords. Finnead stiffened slightly.

When Mab stepped onto the silver floor, its surface darkened to the steely gray of a stormy sea. The hint of a smile touched Titania's lips. Tess forced herself not to grip the hilt of the Sword for comfort as the air in the pavilion hummed with tension. The roiling thunderheads gained purchase again on the eastern edge of the pavilion, pushing into the bright noon sky, a midnight darkness cloaking the ceiling behind them.

"Crown Sister," said Titania, her mellifluous voice somehow still beautiful but hard as steel.

Mab said nothing in reply, striding across the floor until she stood opposite Titania, her Three standing closer to her than the Seelie Three. At closer range, Tess noticed the change in Mab's face: sharper angles and a darker fire in the eyes of the Unseelie Queen. Mab didn't acknowledge Titania, but rather turned slightly to Vell and said without inclining her head, "High Queen."

"Queen Mab," replied Vell, still perfectly neutral. Somehow, Tess realized, Vell had positioned herself exactly between Mab and Titania, standing at the seam between the two Sidhe Queens yet still maintaining the distance of a few paces. Tess stood closer to Mab, though she was clearly within the High Queen's radius. She wished she'd positioned herself on the side closer to Titania as glacial cold seeped into her boots from the floor. Then Vell made a small motion, similar to what Titania had done, and the cold receded. The frost creeping across the tempest tossed gray floor met an invisible wall arcing around Tess and the High Queen's Three. Tess thought she saw a small smile lift one corner of Vell's mouth, but she wasn't entirely sure. The Sword prodded her, and she turned her attention back to the Sidhe Queens.

"This is not a council of war," Titania said, locking gazes with Mab. The enmity between them crackled through the air like a fork of lightning.

"I cannot be sure of my enemies in these days," replied the Unseelie Queen, her beautiful cold voice echoing in the pavilion.

Titania arched an eyebrow even as her Three took a step closer to her. "You believe me to be your enemy?"

"We have long been enemies, you and I," said Mab.

"Yet not a sennight ago we fought in the Dark Keep together." Titania remained serene. The storm clouds reached the center of the pavilion's ceiling, and there they stopped their advance, roiling higher but leaving the sky over Titania and her Three untouched.

"The enemy of my enemy is my friend," said Mab. She turned slightly toward Vell again. "Is that not the *mortal* saying, Lady Bearer?" The word *mortal* sounded like the worst kind of insult from Mab's lips.

Tess clenched her jaw, meeting Mab's eyes. She let a moment of silence hang suspended in the pavilion, and then she said calmly, "Yes."

Mab waited, as though she expected Tess to say more, but then she turned back to Titania. "Now the enemy is vanquished, and there is no need for the pretense of any love between us."

Titania laughed, the sound as lovely as a brightly chattering waterfall and the chimes of delicate bells. "There was never any pretense of love between us, Crown Sister."

Tess couldn't be sure, but she thought she saw Mab whiten further at every mention of the word *sister*. Was Titania deliberately baiting Mab? She felt like she'd stepped into a whirlpool and couldn't stop herself from careening toward its center. The vision of the woman in the scarlet dress had knocked her off balance, and now she felt that she couldn't recover.

Then Vell spoke before the Sidhe Queens pressed further with their veiled threats. "If you wish to hold a council of your two Courts, by all means you may, after we have concluded this council of three." She gestured to the table, around which were ranged four chairs. "Let us sit and hold council, as is our purpose here."

"By all means," murmured Titania, her eyes never leaving Mab.

"As the High Queen requests," said Mab, her voice a low and deadly purr.

Mab and Titania swept over to the table, taking seats opposite each other, leaving Vell and Tess to sit between them. Tess took a breath and sat down, Titania on her right and Mab on her left. The tension in the pavilion hadn't lessened.

"I shall open this council with discussion of its most pressing matter," said Vell without preamble. "We wish to open a Gate into the mortal world."

"You and the Lady Bearer wish to open this Gate," said Titania, making it more of a statement than a question.

"Yes," replied Vell. "Three of our warriors were lost through the portal opened by the breaking of the Seal during the battle in the Dark Keep. We wish to open a Gate in order to search for them."

"They are most likely dead. Why should we waste our effort?" said Mab, looking at Tess and *smiling*. Tess clenched her jaw so hard she thought that her teeth would break, and she knew in the back of her mind that she was glaring murderously at the Unseelie Queen, but she didn't care.

"Because it is what is owed to our warriors," said Vell, her voice slightly louder. The scent of snow and pine slowly drifted around the table.

"They are not *my* warriors," Mab said silkily.

"Merrick was, once," said Tess, the clipped words escaping before she could contain them.

"And so was your Vaelanbrigh, once," replied the Unseelie Queen, shifting her gaze to Finnead. "Or do you go by a different title at the High Queen's side?"

Tess frowned slightly at Mab's venom toward Finnead. He'd rescued the Crown Princess in the battle, and he'd already spent countless hours in the Unseelie camp trying to find a way to mend the Princess's broken mind. Then she realized that Mab blamed

Finnead...perhaps even considered him a traitor.

Vell raised her chin slightly. "If you have any quarrel with one of my Three, Queen Mab, you shall address it to me."

Mab's gaze slid to the *Vyldretning*. "You have been crowned over us," she said in a low voice, "and you steal our warriors away from us to create your own Court."

"You are approaching treasonous words," said Vell calmly. "I would tread carefully, Mab."

"So we must bow and scrape to you now, even as you pick away at our courts to feather your own nest?" said Mab derisively. She smiled coldly. "I will not bend the knee to a Northern wilding brat barely off the teat."

Tess tensed as Liam, Finnead and Gray took a step forward. Rage flickered behind Liam's eyes, and Gray looked as though she wanted to leap across the table. But Vell tilted her head, considering Mab as she took a long breath and let it out slowly. Then the High Queen smiled a dangerous, unsettling smile and her power burst through the room in a silent explosion, shattering the illusion of the sky overhead and the sea beneath their feet, sweeping away the evidence of the struggle between the two Sidhe Queens in undeniably spectacular fashion. The diaphanous white curtains suddenly dripped scarlet, as though blood poured from the ceiling. The frost disappeared, wiped away neatly. Tess felt Vell's power rush around her without touching her. It felt like standing on a rock in the middle of a frothing river. She saw Titania pressed back into her chair, and Mab whitened even further, but both Queens maintained their calm expressions despite the power crashing over the pavilion.

Then Vell took another deep breath, and her power receded, gone as quickly as it had appeared. She looked hard at Titania and then at Mab, keeping her gaze on the Unseelie Queen. "I shall assume your...*rudeness* is sparked by the unfortunate circumstances of your younger sister, for which you have my empathy. I have lost a sister and found her again, only to have her taken from me." Vell paused. Tess couldn't help the small smile that stole its way onto her lips at her friend's magnificent handling of the Sidhe Queens. "Now, I have had enough of the posturing and insults. We shall discuss the Gate now." The *Vyldretning* looked again at Mab and Titania. Titania managed to nod gracefully, but Mab merely stared at the High Queen with hooded eyes. Tess thought that perhaps this was the first time in a long time that Mab had been effectively reduced to a bully.

As the scarlet drapes rippled slightly in the breeze, Vell continued. "I believe it is in our best interest to open a Gate to the mortal world. The balance between our worlds was long kept by careful maintenance of the Great Gate. Both your Courts and my people have benefited from our interactions with the mortal world, though the good that came of it might be easily forgotten over the centuries."

"Centuries are not so long a time," said Titania in a quiet velvety voice.

Vell acknowledged Titania's words with a slight nod. "I propose that we construct a warded, mobile Gate. Travel into the mortal world and returning to this world will be restricted, the list approved and amended in subsequent councils or by another method upon which we agree."

"And you will force us to help you in building this Gate?" Mab's words contained a hint of sulkiness.

"I would not *force* you," replied Vell. "I am not a tyrant. But I ask you to consider it, and I am willing to hear requests for aid in kind."

Tess kept her face carefully smooth even as her heart rate increased: Vell had just laid the bait. Now they had to see if Mab would take it.

"I need no aid in kind to assist the High Queen if she asks it," said Titania, smiling beatifically at Vell. "I shall assist in the creation of this Gate. I give my word." The smile faded from her face as she stared across the table at Mab, her eyes challenging the Unseelie Queen. Mab ignored her and looked at Vell.

"If you truly offer an...exchange," the Unseelie Queen said, "then I take it."

Tess held her breath.

"I would not say it if I did not truly offer it," replied Vell, arching one eyebrow. "What exchange do you propose?"

"There is an object of power," said Mab. Tess felt her heart hammer against her ribs. "Perhaps the last of its kind, and perhaps the only solution to my sister's...pain."

"And what is this object?" asked Vell, though she knew perfectly well. She had been the one to send Haze into the Unseelie Court, planting the seed of this idea. Wisp's cousin was not so well known as a Wild Court messenger, and he had clearly succeeded in his task.

"A Lethe Stone," said Mab, and Tess pressed her lips together, swallowing down the hot triumph bubbling up in her chest.

"Lethe Stones are outlawed by every code in both our Courts," said Titania.

"So are mortals, and yet one is standing behind the High Queen as one of her Three, and one sits between us as the Bearer of the Iron Sword," replied Mab smoothly.

"I believe neither of us is quite mortal anymore," Tess said lightly, "but I would like to hear more about your request for this Lethe Stone." She leaned forward, clasping her hands together on the table and looking at Mab. "What exactly is a Lethe Stone, and why was it outlawed?" She forced herself to hold Mab's narrowed gaze. She was the Bearer, and Mab could no longer dig her claws into Tess's mind to ascertain the truth of her words. But all the same, a tiny thrill coursed through her when Mab leaned back slightly and began speaking.

"A Lethe Stone holds the power to erase memories."

"And why was it outlawed?" asked Tess when Mab fell silent.

The Unseelie Queen gave her a humorless smile. "Because it was dangerous for anyone to have the ability to wipe clean someone's mind. Memories make us who we are, do they not? If we do not remember our past experiences...have we lived?"

Tess pressed her lips together. "So if it is outlawed, why is there even a Lethe Stone that still exists? Weren't they all destroyed?" All hollow questions, adornment of their carefully laid trap. But she wanted to hear Mab's answers.

"I believe there is a sorcerer who bore one of these Lethe Stones in the service of Malravenar," said Mab. "Not all of Malravenar's servants were laid waste at the Dark Keep."

"What do we know of this sorcerer?" Vell asked.

"I would think you would be most familiar with his work," said Mab. "He was the architect of the recent harrowing of the North."

If Tess didn't know that Vell had already known, that they'd done their own painstaking research and reconnaissance, she would have thought that Vell's indrawn breath and the slight flicker in her golden eyes were real signs of surprise or distress, or both.

"I believe he is a bone sorcerer," continued Mab blithely, "making him especially suited to wield the Lethe Stone."

Vell had explained to Tess that bone sorcerers were a particularly nasty breed of Dark mage, versed in using blood and bone to weave their spells.

"A bone sorcerer roaming our lands is cause for action in itself," murmured Titania.

"Oh, he is not in *our* lands," replied Mab. She looked at Tess, a predatory glee spreading over her beautiful face. "He is in the mortal world."

Tess didn't have to feign shock. Mab's words hit her like a punch to her stomach; she hadn't known this. All their preparation hadn't revealed that vital piece of information.

Or Vell hadn't told her. She raised her eyes to her brother, who stood behind Vell dutifully. She couldn't read Liam's expression. Had he known too? Tess swallowed and the Sword's power expanded, filling her bones, fortifying her. She looked squarely at Mab. "Then as the Bearer, it is my duty to travel into the mortal world and kill this bone sorcerer."

"Another dangerous quest for our intrepid Bearer," purred Mab.

"One that requires a Gate to the mortal world," replied Tess steadily. She'd been prepared for a lightning fast mission into the Northern wilds or the far reaches of the Deadlands; she'd even talked to Calliea about using the Valkyrie. They'd been prepared to hunt and destroy this sorcerer with all the might of the *Vyldretning* and perhaps the Seelie Queen behind them. Now…now Tess thought of returning to her old world to battle an enemy she knew nothing of, in a world where she didn't know how her powers would react, and her stomach curdled. She forced herself to think of Luca. This was the only way to save him.

"You shall have your Gate," said Mab, "but you must bring me the Lethe Stone that this bone sorcerer bears."

"I cannot agree with this exchange," said Titania. "The Lethe Stone must be destroyed with the bone sorcerer."

"The Lethe Stone offers a chance to save the Crown Princess," replied Mab.

"Not save her," said Finnead from behind Vell, a slight tremor in his voice. "It will not restore her. It will destroy her." He fell silent as Vell held up a commanding hand.

Mab glared at Finnead, white with fury. "I need not justify myself to you."

"Peace," commanded Vell as Finnead stiffened. Mab looked away. "Queen Titania, is there a compromise to which you would be amenable?"

Titania stared across the table at Mab. "I cannot condone the use of a Lethe Stone. It breaks fundamental laws laid down between our Courts centuries ago."

"Centuries are not so long a time," Mab echoed with cold venom.

Tess took a deep breath, feeling as though she were about to step off a cliff. "As the Bearer, I am not bound by the laws of your Courts." She looked at Mab. "As an exchange for the construction of a warded Gate to the mortal world, I will retrieve this Lethe Stone from the Bone Sorcerer." She shifted her gaze to Vell. "And for the safety of both our worlds, I will destroy this dark mage."

"And so it is made as a pact before the High Queen," said Mab, triumph in her words.

Vell nodded slowly. "So it is made as a pact."

Tess swallowed against the mingled excitement and confusion rushing through her. In the end, it had worked. In the end, they'd gotten Mab to agree to the Gate…but somehow she felt as though *she* had been the one trapped. She sat back in her chair and listened as the Queens began to discuss the details of the Gate-building, Titania with anger behind her golden beauty, Mab with a hint of satisfaction lurking in her words. Vell glanced at Tess and gave her a slight nod. The important thing was that they would be rescuing Luca and Merrick – she'd face whatever dangers she needed to bring them back into their world alive and whole. The Caedbranr trembled in its sheath as if in anticipation of this new adventure. Tess rested her hand on its hilt and smoothed her face, thinking that at least in the mortal world she wouldn't have to endure any more councils.

Chapter 14

Ross woke to the rumble of May's low growl and a strange scratching noise, like branches from one of the rose bushes brushing against the window. She struggled out of sleep, fumbling for her phone on the bedside table, groaning when she saw that it was just past two in the morning. Her entire body ached in the way it did when she didn't get enough sleep between shifts. Darkness pressed around her in the bedroom, and her eyes tried to slide shut again.

"May," she said drowsily, thinking that the dog had to be growling at the three strange men in the house, "knock it off. They're friends."

At Ross's voice, the dog's growl subsided for a moment, but then resumed, the sound more insistent. The strange scratching sound came again at the window. Ross blinked and realized that May wasn't standing at the door to the bedroom, to the right of the bed. The dog was standing to the *left* of the bed, growling at the window.

A surge of adrenaline swept away the haziness of sleep as Ross kicked away the quilt, reaching for the holster bolted into her headboard. Her hand curled around the familiar grip of the Beretta, forefinger pressing the button on the holster that released the weapon with a practiced motion. She slid out of bed, the gun held in in her right hand and pointed it at the floor as she made her way in a low crouch toward the footboard of the bed. The window was between the foot of her bed and the door of the closet. Her eyes adjusted to the darkness, Ross peered around the edge of her bed and saw Mayhem, all four paws planted in a wide stance, facing the window squarely. The black-and-tan Malinois who had once worked to sniff out bombs and flush out enemies from abandoned buildings looked every inch a working dog, her hackles raised, lips drawn back from her white teeth, frozen in a crouch and ready to spring.

Ross looked up at the window. Her breath caught in her throat and she brought up the Beretta, gripping it with both hands, her thumb sweeping off the safety even as a scream bubbled in her throat. She clamped down on the scream and reduced it to a guttural exhalation of shock, sounding as though she'd been punched in the stomach. Mayhem's growls escalated.

Dark liquid smeared the exterior of the window. Blood. Ross couldn't catch her breath. She kept her finger straight and off the trigger. The scratching sound came again. It was a hand. A human hand scratching at the glass of her window, nails broken and bleeding.

"Noah!" Ross shouted, keeping her voice just calm enough that it wasn't a scream. She heard a thump from the living room, a pause, and quick footsteps down the hallway. The doorknob rattled once and she thought numbly that it was locked and that she should unlock it, but she didn't move, staring up at the window, her Beretta pointed steadily at the creature scratching at the glass. The darkness and the blood smeared across the glass made the figure ghostly and strange. She made out the pale oval of a face, the thing's motions jerky, like a life sized puppet violently controlled by its master. Bile rose in her throat as the thumping and scratching continued, scenes from zombie movies flashing in her mind's eye.

"Coming in," came Duke's muffled warning. *That* spurred her into action; she slid forward and took a knee by Mayhem, telling the dog with a quiet command to keep her position facing the window. May didn't waver, not even when the door burst inward with the force of Duke's kick. He slid into the room with practiced quickness, hugging the wall and striding toward the closet even as he cleared the other sectors of the room.

"Window," said Ross, resting one elbow on her knee so she could keep steady aim.

"Roger," responded Duke automatically.

Whatever was outside the window had backed away momentarily, leaving only the rusty streaks across the pane of glass. But Mayhem didn't relax, so neither did Ross.

"Something trying to get in at the window," said Ross, squeezing out the words. Her chest ached and her head began to pound.

"What was it?" asked Duke tightly.

"Not sure," she replied. "I was asleep and May woke me up…it was *scratching* the window. All I saw was its hand."

"Did it look human?" Duke didn't take his gaze from the window, but he lowered his pistol slightly, pointing the gun at the ground in the ready alert position. She followed suit.

"I…I don't *know*." She pressed back the panic welling up within her. Work through it. Sort it out. Take a deep breath. "All I saw was its hand."

"It's important, Ross. What exactly did you see?"

"You think I don't *know* it's important, Noah?" she snapped, and then she gulped down a huge breath, let it out slowly. "I'm sorry. It…it scared me." She gathered her thoughts. "From what I could see," she said slowly, "it looked human. But not normal."

"How not normal?" asked Duke.

"What normal person claws at a window until their fingers are bloody?" she asked. Mayhem's stance relaxed marginally, but her amber eyes still watched the window.

"I'm going on a perimeter check," said Duke. "Stay here with the dog and stay sharp."

Ross opened her mouth to protest but then swallowed instead.

"You shouldn't go alone," Merrick said from the doorway, gray eyes luminous in the shadows. He held an unsheathed sword. A huge shadow that had to be Luca leaned against the wall behind him.

Duke nodded curtly. "Stay tight on my six."

Merrick didn't ask what it meant. He followed Duke down the hallway. Ross gave Mayhem a low command and the dog peeled away from the window, standing alertly by Ross's knee. Ross kept the Beretta in her right hand and rested her left hand lightly at Mayhem's neck, purely for her own comfort. She'd learned a few of the commands that May had utilized during her time as a working dog. It had seemed a good way to bond with the dog and keep her from missing her old job too much. Now Ross was grateful she'd stuck to the discipline as she walked toward the bedroom door. May tensed when Luca stepped in front of Ross. And then, to Ross's bewilderment, Luca crouched in front of the well-muscled dog. He said a word that sounded vaguely Scandinavian to Ross's ears and held out a hand.

Ross watched in amazement as Mayhem stepped forward and smelled Luca's palm. May didn't like strangers. She wasn't aggressive – she was too well trained for that – but she didn't voluntarily approach people. She always waited for Ross to give the okay. Luca let the dog sniff his hand thoroughly, and then he reached out and clasped May's face with his huge hands. Ross sucked in a breath, expecting the Malinois to wrench herself from his grasp, growl or even snap at the big man. Instead, Mayhem sank into a crouch and whined low in her throat as Luca pressed his forehead to hers. The dog licked Luca's face as he drew back, and he chuckled. Then he said another strange word to Mayhem – definitely not one of the words that she knew from training – and nodded at Ross. Mayhem *wagged her tail* a few times and backed up until she sat at Ross's knee again.

"What did you just do?" Ross asked in a low voice, distracted for the moment from the shock of that hand scratching at her window.

"I said hello," replied Luca with a wolfish grin, his teeth very white in the darkness.

"Okay," Ross said slowly.

"She loves you," Luca said. "Do not worry, I am not trying to steal her away."

"Good," said Ross in that same slow, suspicious voice.

Luca put out a hand to steady himself on the wall. May whined deep in her throat and Ross stepped forward to help. "Come on, you shouldn't be up. How are you feeling?" She swallowed down her fear for Duke and guided Luca to the living room couch, glancing uneasily at the window, but no disembodied hand reached out of the darkness. No sooner had she settled Luca onto the couch than the crack of a gunshot split the night. Luca surged to his feet, an axe in his hand, and May moved between Ross and the front door. Her heart leapt into her throat and then sank back down into her chest, leaving her a bit light-headed, but she planted her feet and held the Beretta with both hands, watching the door. After what seemed like an eternity, someone walked up the front steps.

"It's Duke," came the familiar voice. "Coming in!"

"Come in," responded Ross automatically, relaxing her grip on her gun.

The doorknob turned and the runes on Merrick's protective spell flared silver. Duke made a face as he slid through the doorway. The smell of cordite lingered around him.

"You fired your weapon," said Luca, his axe still held in one hand.

"Yeah," said Duke. He looked at Ross. "It was the guy from the gas station. The clerk."

"Oh my God," Ross said, remembering the grizzled clerk who had peered out with such interest from behind the register, his curious gaze drawing her notice even through the glass.

"He's not dead," continued Duke. "I need you to call an ambulance."

Ross drew in a shaky breath, and then her mind clicked back into gear. Her thoughts roared ahead at breakneck speed. "Okay. Get him up onto the porch." Duke turned, and she caught his sleeve. "You can't be here. And Merrick and Luca..." She shook her head. "Take them out back. There's a shed down by the river."

"I don't want to leave you," said Duke tightly, his eyes fixed on her face. "And like hell I'm gonna go out back without a weapon." He raised his eyebrows slightly at his last words, almost daring her to contradict him.

"Well, you don't have a choice about leaving me because that's what needs to be done," she said in a businesslike voice. "Look, Noah, I know you want to protect me but what if the police recognize you? Your photo was in all the papers, all over the local news. Most of the town came to your funeral, and that included the local cops." She thought quickly. "Take the Beretta. I need the Glock."

They exchanged pistols in efficient silence. Duke pressed his lips together and nodded, disappearing again out the front door.

Mayhem padded alongside Ross as she quickly walked a circuit through the house, checking the details of her story in her mind. After quickly adding a sports bra under her loose t-shirt, she grabbed her phone from the bedside table and dialed 9-1-1, her hands beginning to shake as she held the phone up to her ear. "Operator?" She made her voice breathless and summoned the thickness of held back tears. "I need the police. I need someone right away...there was a man who tried to break into my house, he tried to break my bedroom window and then he somehow got in the front door and...please send someone. I... I shot him."

Hot tears gathered in the corners of her eyes as the operator asked the standard questions. Ross quickly gave her name and address, walking back toward the living room with Mayhem on her hip. When she neared Luca, static suddenly laced the call. She stopped and took a step back, the operator's voice wavering in her ear. "I... I'm sorry, you're breaking up, the guy's still alive... I need to help him, I don't want him to die." It was almost too easy to sound semi-hysterical. She stepped closer to Luca again and static swamped the call like a tidal wave. Experimentally, she held her phone out toward him and watched the screen flicker and fade into blackness.

"Well, I hope I didn't just fry my phone," she muttered, and then she felt terrible. Duke just shot a stranger who had bloodied his fingers in some bout of insanity clawing at her window, Luca looked like he was about to pass out; the cops would be arriving in short order, and she was making flippant remarks about her phone. She slid the phone into the pocket of her gym shorts and considered the door. Should she leave the runes or try to clean them off before the police arrived? She decided against it, grabbing her medical kit instead. "Be ready to move," she told Luca, who braced his elbows on his knees and nodded. Frustration and exhaustion etched lines onto his face.

Ross opened the door just as Merrick and Duke carried a limp figure onto the porch.

"His shoulder, didn't hit anything major," grunted Duke. "Not bleeding much, but I think he's passed out just from the shock. Something…something was *in* him."

They set down the lanky clerk by the front door. Duke held something out to Ross. "The brass."

Ross stared down at the spent bullet casing gleaming in her hand. Then she shook herself and wiped it with the edge of her shirt, holding it between two fingers to put her prints back on it – she was the one who loaded her own magazines, after all – and dropped it onto the porch with a metallic clink. Then she looked at Duke. The heavy night air pressed around them. "What do you mean, something was *in him*?"

Duke crouched by the unconscious man and pulled the man's unbuttoned shirt aside enough for Ross to see the ugly blackened skin on the man's chest. "The worst burn is over his heart. There are others at his wrists and one on his ankle." He shook his head. "I have no idea what it means."

"A bone sorcerer," said Luca from the doorway of the house.

Ross blinked. "A…*what?*" Mayhem sniffed at the prone man and growled low in her throat. Ross gave her a quiet command and the dog subsided. The distant wail of sirens echoed through the humid darkness, spurring them all into action. Merrick reached for Luca, offering his shoulder to the *ulfdrengr* as they made their way down the steps of the porch. Duke stopped, looked down at the blood on his hand from holding pressure on the man's wound, and smeared it onto the wrought-iron handle of the screen door and the doorknob of the front door. Then he strode into the shadows without saying a word. The sirens grew louder, and she gripped the Glock, suddenly realizing that if the police took prints from the gun, they'd find Duke's prints, too. She had only purchased the weapon last month. Her mouth went dry but she held the gun in her left hand and grabbed a gauze pad from her medical kit with her right, tearing the package open with her teeth. The man didn't even stir when she pressed the gauze to his shoulder.

Two police cars careened down the small road, their flashing lights painting the oaks with garish hues of white, blue and red. An ambulance followed close behind, its siren splitting the night. Ross swallowed hard and winced when the first officer's flashlight nearly blinded her. Her heart pounded in her chest as she calmly told them that she held her Glock in her left hand and set it on the floorboards of the porch. Two other officers fanned out and searched the darkness with their bright lights, their weapons unholstered.

"Are you hurt, ma'am?" said one officer.

She blinked. "No." She couldn't find the energy to say anything else. May pressed against her side, watching the men moving about the house, a soundless growl vibrating in her chest.

After the policemen ascertained that the scene was safe, the paramedics wheeled a stretcher out from the ambulance. One of them, an older man with a moustache, did a double take when he saw Ross. "Cooper? This guy tried to break into *your* house?"

The other paramedic knelt by Ross and took over the pressure on the gauze, giving her a small nod.

"Um," said Ross, feeling sick. She must've run into the older paramedic during training or one of the temporary fills she'd taken at one of the smaller firehouses. "Yeah. I think…I think he's on drugs or something, he broke his nails trying to claw through the glass on my bedroom window."

Two of the policemen glanced at each other when she mentioned drugs.

"Are you hurt?" asked one of the policemen again, a younger guy that she vaguely recognized.

"No." She drew in a shaky breath. "No, I'm fine." Sudden inspiration struck her. "Um, if it's okay, I'd like to put my dog in the house. It's already been a rough night for her."

"Sure," said the younger policeman, shadowing her as she opened the door with shaking hands and motioned May into the living room. She gave the command to stay, and Mayhem whined low in her throat but settled down onto her belly to watch the door. When she shut the door, she looked down at the crimson smear on her hand. The officer saw her staring at her hand, frowned and then directed the beam of his flashlight at the door, picking up the smears of blood.

"Would you mind telling us what happened, Miss Cooper?" he said slowly, glancing between the unconscious man's bloody fingers and the gore smeared on the front door of Ross's house. Ross took a deep breath and silently promised that she'd go to confession and light candles in the cathedral at Jackson Square in penance as she started to tell one of the biggest lies of her life.

The paramedics wheeled away the unconscious clerk as Ross described how she'd awakened to Mayhem growling at the window, and she saw the hand clawing at the glass. Then she heard him at the front door and she shouted at him that she had a gun…She let a few tears slide down her face as she told the officer how the man had somehow opened her front door, maybe she'd left it unlocked accidentally, she didn't know, but she yelled at him to stop and get back, and then she fired. She mentioned that she'd stopped at the gas station earlier that day on her way through Cairn, and she'd seen the guy behind the register watching her.

"Do we need the techs out here to process the scene?" the youngest-looking policeman asked the one interviewing Ross, who shook his head.

"Pretty cut and dried. Home invasion, self-defense. The guy's gonna live, no reason to waste department resources." The officer looked at Ross. His businesslike tone gentled. Ross estimated him to be in his late thirties, early forties. "Do you want to come get checked out at the hospital?"

Ross swallowed and shook her head. "No. No, I'm good. He didn't touch me, he..." Then she glanced at her hands. "Um, but I didn't wear gloves when I pressed the gauze to his shoulder." She cursed in her head and then sighed. "No open wounds or anything though so I should be okay."

"They can start you on a preventative course of meds if you come in now," said the older policeman almost kindly. "Especially since it sounds like the guy might have been a drug user."

The other officer muttered something about worthless junkies. He crossed his arms and watched the second pair of policemen pull away in their marked car, lights no longer flashing.

"I'd really like to just take a shower and get some sleep," said Ross honestly. "Unless you need me to come in to the station or take any evidence from me." She held up her bloodstained hands, hoping that they didn't want any evidence. A quick swab with a special kit would show that she didn't have gunpowder residue on her skin from firing the Glock...but if she showered, it was a moot point. She tried to reel in her racing mind; the officers already seemed sympathetic, and she didn't even know if they used the residue kits in the field.

The older officer considered. His nametag read *Anderson.* Ross let him have a moment to think, and then hugged herself, despite the blood on her hands, as though she were cold. "Officer Anderson, thank you so much for responding to the call. All of you. I thought...it was scary. I didn't know what was going to happen, when I realized he was probably on drugs."

Officer Anderson nodded. "Just doing our job, Miss Cooper. Is there anyone you can call to come and stay with you?"

"I have Mayhem. My dog." She smiled. "If the guy had taken one more step toward me, she'd probably have gone after him."

"Well, let me just call into the station and get the go-ahead to close this up." Officer Anderson nodded brusquely and walked a small distance away, lowering his head to speak into the radio transmitter clipped to the collar of his uniform.

"You sure you're all right?" the younger officer said. He was good-looking in a generic way, blonde hair combed to one side, only a few inches taller than Ross. She wondered if he got teased for his lack of height as she read his nametag: Burch. Then she swallowed and nudged her mind back on track.

"I'm a little shaken up," she admitted, "but I'll be okay." She leaned back against the house. "It was just…creepy." She shook her head. The disgust in her voice was real. "I wake up and some crazy guy is clawing at my bedroom window. That's *creepy*."

"I probably would've shot him through the window," Officer Burch said in a conspiratorial tone, leaning slightly toward her.

She took a deep breath. "I couldn't see him clearly. I didn't…I didn't want to shoot him if I didn't have to."

"You have more trigger discipline than some cops I know," he replied, and she couldn't tell whether he was joking. He walked casually down the porch and glanced through the living room window. "You said you're here by yourself?" A different light entered his eyes as he turned back to Ross.

The couch. He'd seen the couch made up with a pillow and blankets. "Yeah." She smiled a little sheepishly. "I like to have a pillow and blankets when I watch TV. I fell asleep last night watching some reruns." She shrugged and fervently hoped that he couldn't see the men's boots by the door. "Didn't clean it up when I went to bed."

Officer Burch smiled. "Just have to cover our bases. You sure you don't want us to check the house for you?"

"I'm good, thanks," she said, smiling in reply. "Mayhem does a pretty good job of letting me know if there's strangers around."

As if on cue, the Malinois' black and tan face appeared in the living room window, her ears perked and her tongue lolling out of her mouth. The dog looked like she was grinning at the mention of her name. Ross shook her head and chuckled, thanking the dog silently for the diversion. "Just look at that face. I can't even yell at her for being on the couch."

Officer Burch grinned. His partner had gone back to the car to check something in the computer; he hooked his thumbs in his belt. "We always had Labs growing up, but I've heard great things about Shepherds and Malinois."

"Doesn't the Cairn Police Department have a K9 unit?" Ross asked, seizing the opportunity to change the subject.

"Yeah, but you can imagine it's a struggle with funding…." Officer Burch elaborated for a few minutes, prodded along by Ross's strategic questions. Finally, his partner returned from the police car.

"Just got approval to close up shop. No crime scene tape or anything," said Officer Anderson with a fatherly smile to Ross.

"That would have *really* given the neighbors something to talk about," she replied. Then she sobered. "Did you get an update from the paramedics? Is the guy gonna be okay?"

"You're a better person than I am," Officer Burch said, shrugging his shoulders at his partner's warning look.

"Paramedics said that he was stable when they dropped him off at the hospital. He'll have to have surgery to get the round out, but it didn't hit anything major from the looks of it," Officer Anderson said.

"Good." Ross sighed in relief.

"Those burns though…that's some weird sh – stuff. Weird stuff," the older policeman said.

"I wish I could be more helpful." Ross looked up at them earnestly.

"You've given us all the information we need," said Officer Anderson. "And if you're all right, we'll be on our way." He walked down the steps of the front porch, heading toward the car.

Officer Burch leaned in a little closer to Ross, so close that she caught a faint whiff of his pine-spice aftershave mixed with body odor. Her stomach turned uneasily. "Next time just aim center of mass," he told her in that same friendly voice. "Do us all a favor and put another meth-head out of his misery."

Ross went very still. "I'll keep that in mind," she replied sweetly, forcing a smile. The policeman held her eyes for just a second too long, and then he followed his partner down the steps, leaving the scent of pine and sweat in his wake. Ross put a hand out to steady herself on the wooden siding of the house, drawing in a shaky breath, a tidal wave of exhaustion crashing over her as she stared at the blood staining her front door and wondered what new, tangled world she had just entered.

Chapter 15

"Did you know?" Tess stared at Vell. The *Vyldretning* stood before a crackling fire in her quarters, still dressed for the council. "Did you know that the bone sorcerer was already in the mortal world?" A coil of dread tightened in her stomach.

"I suspected," said Vell quietly. She faced Tess. "But I didn't know for certain. I needed Mab to confirm it."

Tess unbuckled her sword belt and threw herself into one of the chairs, staring at the fire with the sheathed Caedbranr laid across her knees. "So you were playing me just like you were playing her."

Vell sighed and pinched the bridge of her nose between two fingers. "Please don't be difficult, Tess."

Tess snorted. "Right. *I'm* the one being difficult."

"What would you have me do?" demanded Vell, spreading her hands and taking a step closer to Tess. "I can't confide *everything* to you, Tess. There's already talk in both Courts about the Bearer being an instrument of the High Queen."

"Better they think that I'm an instrument of the *Vyldgard* than of the Seelie or Unseelie Courts," countered Tess. She took a deep breath and looked into the fire for a long moment. "You're right. It was just a shock." She shook her head. "I don't like it when Mab shocks me. It reminds me of when I was first at Darkhill."

"And she invaded your head," finished Vell. "I know."

"How?"

"Finnead."

Tess rubbed the smooth leather of the Caedbranr's scabbard. "I don't know how anything works in the mortal world."

Vell chuckled. "Don't be melodramatic. Of course you know how things work in Doendhtalam. It was your world for over twenty years, wasn't it?"

"Yes," answered Tess grudgingly, "but what I *mean* is that I don't know how my powers work there. I don't even know *if* I'll have powers."

"I think it would be a bit silly to have a Bearer as emissary to the mortal world when her powers are useless there, don't you think?" Vell arched an eyebrow as she unpinned the golden net from about her hair, shaking out her dark tresses.

"I thought the Queens' Named Knights were their emissaries," muttered Tess.

"Are you hungry?" Vell asked, hands on her hips.

"What? I…*no*, I'm not hungry." Tess stared at her best friend in confusion.

"Sometimes you get irrational when you haven't eaten, and I was wondering if that's what this was," said the High Queen, unbuckling her wide woven belt with nimble fingers and shedding the surcoat worked with golden runes.

Tess groaned. "You sound like Robin."

Vell grinned and moved to the table, pouring *khal* from the copper kettle. "In any case, you'll probably need this. We have a lot of preparations to make over the next day."

"A day still feels like too long," said Tess, standing and accepting the cup of *khal*. She left the Caedbranr leaning against the chair by the fire, feeling oddly light without its weight on her back or at her hip.

"It will seem *very* short," said Vell. A stack of books anchored one side of the table. She ran her finger down their spines until she found the one she sought. "All right. Ailin and Gawain have been helping us in our research. I've asked them to come by in an hour, so I want to make sure you understand how we're going to be building the Gate." She flipped open the leather-bound book, thumbing through the thick pages. "It's going to be a Summoned Gate. It's a compromise between the Great Gate and the portals that were used by the Seelie and Unseelie in their own lands."

"Also called a warded Gate?" Tess made it a question.

"Yes. One and the same. It's a Gate that remains open, but it isn't accessible to anyone wishing to travel from the mortal world into Faeortalam unless they have the proper Summons."

"It's a locked Gate and the Summons is the key," said Tess in understanding.

"Exactly. The Summons will also have three different components, and you need to employ them at precisely the right time in order to make it work." Vell slid the book toward Tess.

"All this information is just readily available in these books?"

"Not *readily* available. They were under lock and ward for centuries. And I'm sure the Sidhe Queens would have killed anyone trying to open a Gate."

Tess sipped at her *khal,* reading the pages marked by Vell. A frown creased her brow. "So…I have a question. We just talked about this bone sorcerer, about how he uses flesh and bone to amplify his power. How is that any different than most of the spells that you've done, or I've done, for that matter? We've used our blood countless times. And the Summons requires blood, too."

"We've always used our own blood," replied Vell without hesitation. "It's different. You can use your own blood to augment your workings. There's never been a law against that. It's when you start taking blood from unwilling victims that it crosses over into bone sorcery."

"So blood magic is not necessarily bone sorcery," said Tess slowly, mulling the explanation over in her head. It made a strange sort of sense. She looked at Vell. "Is what Arcana did bone sorcery?"

Vell pressed her lips into a thin line. "Do you mean wearing my sister's body or healing your brother?"

"Both, I guess."

The *Vyldretning* shrugged. "I don't know. Perhaps. But even if it was, she's gone, and Liam is alive because of it."

"It could be a slippery slope," murmured Tess, feeling a prickle of morbid fascination. It was a feeling similar to the interest she'd felt after her discovery that she could Walk to the Gray Cliffs and bring a soul back from the brink of death. But retrieving a spirit meant Walking, and she hadn't Walked since the battle at the Dark Keep. She had no intention of Walking anytime soon, either.

"Why do you think bone sorcery is outlawed?" Vell raised an eyebrow.

"Point taken. All right, so this Summons has three parts…" Tess bent over the centuries old text before her and committed its details to memory, talking through the spell with Vell to make sure she understood every part.

Ailin joined them after what seemed like a very short hour. The Seelie Queen's Vaelanbrigh spoke easily with the High Queen and the Bearer, his pale eyes bright with the Fae-spark as he explained the preparations that the Named Knights undertook before venturing through a Gate into the mortal world. He showed them the runes that they inked upon their skin to protect them against the sickness caused by the amount of iron in the mortal world; Tess amused him by asking why they didn't just get them tattooed on their bodies.

"Not all of us are so well suited to have such permanent decoration on our bodies," he said with a smile, motioning to Tess's arm, where her emerald war markings surged out of her sleeve and onto her hand in a complex pattern. "But if we start making longer trips into Doendhtalam, it's an idea worth considering."

"Would it have to be a special kind of ink?" Tess asked musingly.

Vell tapped the table with two fingers. "We have precious little time, Tess."

"Focus. Got it. I'm focusing." Tess sat up straighter and looked at Ailin, waiting for him to continue. They worked for another hour before the Seelie Vaelanbrigh was satisfied that he'd imparted the necessary basics. He gracefully took his leave and Tess sat back in her chair, rubbing her temples.

"That was a lot of knowledge." She sighed. "My head hurts. Why isn't Finnead teaching us all this, by the way?"

"I'll verify everything with him while you're asleep," said Vell, "but he's struggling. He truly believes that the Lethe Stone will destroy the princess, and it's nearly driving him mad."

"So he doesn't want me to go into the mortal world," Tess said softly, toying with the handle of her now cold mug of *khal*.

Vell shook her head. "It's not that. He knows that you need to destroy the bone sorcerer. He just believes the Lethe Stone should be destroyed, too."

Tess thought for a moment. "What will happen, once Mab has the Lethe Stone? What's to prevent her from turning it into a weapon?"

Vell looked at her levelly. "Because *I* will use it on the Crown Princess, and then I will destroy it."

"That's not what Mab thinks is going to happen."

"If she truly only wants it to heal her sister, she'll have no objections. It will help pacify Titania as well." Vell shifted in her chair and then let out a low growl. "I hate the palace sometimes. I miss the forest."

"Not the forest we passed through on the way to Brightvale," said Tess with an exaggerated shudder, thinking of the skin wraiths that had tracked them. She remembered Merrick's valiant actions when he'd been the newest addition to their small band of travelers: throwing himself between Tess and an attacking skin wraith, impaling it on his sword at the cost of a dislocated shoulder.

"No," said Vell, "the Northern forests." She took a deep breath. "I wish I'd been able to go with you into the Northern mountains. Luca said it almost felt like being home again."

Tess smiled slightly. Then she straightened again in her chair. "I'll be taking Kianryk with me, won't I?"

"Yes."

"How is he?" she asked softly. "I haven't seen…"

"The City feels too much like a cage to them," said Vell. "Beryk tolerates it for my sake sometimes, but Rialla and Kianryk have been roaming the lands to the north of the city. There's a bit of forest and some grassland there. It seems my presence here is helping to speed the recovery of the lands."

Tess thought about telling Vell that she was avoiding the question, but she decided against it. Worry would only distract her from the preparations for the Gate. She swallowed the last of her cold *khal*, grimaced and reached for another book.

She awoke with a start in one of the chairs by the hearth in Vell's chambers without remembering when she'd fallen asleep. As she blinked dry eyes, her fingers found the hilt of the Caedbranr leaning against the chair and she drew in a breath, letting her eyes close again.

"Lady Tess," came an insistent whisper.

Tess cracked open one eye to find Haze hovering at eye level a respectful distance away from her. So *that* was why she'd awakened – she certainly didn't feel like she'd gotten enough sleep. She sat up straighter and cleared her throat, scrubbing at her face with one hand. "Yes, Haze?"

"I was sent by Faelan in the healing ward, my lady."

Tess swallowed and grimaced. She felt like cotton stuffed her head; it made thinking very difficult. The name Haze mentioned plucked a distant chord, but she couldn't grasp the memory. "And what message did Faelan send?"

"He is the healer tending to your companion," said Haze with a slight bow. "Sage is awake, my lady, and his healer sent me to notify you."

"You're a very busy messenger," Tess commented as she stood and picked up the Sword, slinging it over her shoulder by its bandolier.

"It is not so hard to be in the right place at the right time," Haze said enigmatically. "Would you like me to accompany you to the wards, my lady?"

"I'd appreciate the company," Tess said with a small smile. She left the pile of books by her chair, thinking that Vell's quarters were more secure than the healing ward, but she did take her small leather-bound notebook and poured herself a cup of cold *khal* for the walk. She waited until they were wending their way through the darkened passageways and then said, "I have a question for you, Haze. Well, more than one question, actually."

"Of course, my lady," said the Glasidhe messenger, who hadn't yet shown his cousin's fondness for riding on Tess's shoulder. Perhaps he was too courteous, thought Tess with affectionate amusement. Then she brought her mind back to the question at hand.

"Did the High Queen know that the bone sorcerer was in the mortal world before the council?" she asked.

Haze remained silent for so long that Tess thought he hadn't heard her, although the passageways were completely silent at this time of night. They passed a pair of *Vyldgard* fighters, probably rotating out of a guard post, and Haze waited until they'd rounded another bend to speak.

"I do not think I can rightly answer this question, Lady Tess," he said.

"Because the High Queen instructed you against answering questions about it?" Tess swallowed down the guilt burning in her throat. She didn't like the feeling of calling into question Vell's loyalty or friendship – she wasn't even sure *what* exactly she was calling into question. If Vell had known about the bone sorcerer in the mortal world, what would that change? The *Vyldretning* had already given her own explanation.

"My lady," said Haze carefully, "I would prefer not to have to answer this question. I do not wish to be caught between you and the High Queen."

Tess pressed her lips together. "I see."

"From what I have heard," said the Glasidhe, flying just ahead of Tess on her left side, "Queen Vell only desires what is best for her Court."

"I'm not a part of her Court," Tess pointed out, her voice tightening. She wasn't sure if her feeling of betrayal was a product of her lack of sleep, the stresses of navigating the Fae world after Malravenar's defeat…or if it was a perfectly normal result of a friend withholding such a crucial piece of information.

"No, you are not part of the *Vyldgard*. You are the Bearer," continued Haze bravely. "But you are also her friend. She wishes you to be happy and whole, just as she wishes for her *Vyldgard* to be happy and whole."

Tess took a deep breath as they neared the entrance to the healing wards. There would be time enough later to unpack her feelings about the negotiations to open the Gate…or perhaps there wouldn't be. She shook her head to clear it of her oscillating thoughts. "Thank you for accompanying me, Haze. And there is another question I'd like to ask you."

"My lady." Haze bowed as Tess came to a stop, still hovering precisely at eye level.

"Would you join the party venturing into the mortal world?" Tess asked.

Haze's aura flared and sparked in surprise. He quickly regained control over his aura but his wings beat double time and his precise positioning wavered. "I… my lady, I … I will have to…"

"Ensure that you have permission from Lumina, I assume," said Tess with a small smile as Wisp's cousin trailed off. "I think she'll see the benefit in sending another one of her finest messengers to gain experience in the mortal world."

"I shall ask her this morning," said Haze faintly.

"You don't think Wisp will be upset with me, do you?" Tess asked, raising one eyebrow. "Forin and Farin might be coming along as well, and they're capable messengers, don't get me wrong, but I think they would be quite happy if their duties were reduced to scouting and fighting."

"Wisp acknowledges his new limitations, such as they are, with...well, I would not say with *grace*, but at least with honesty," Haze replied. "But I vow that if I travel with you to the mortal world, Lady Tess, I shall serve you with the utmost honor and dedication."

"I have no doubt of that," she replied. Then she sobered. "Please let me know what you decide, Haze. I'm going to go see Sage, and then later today it is planned that we'll open the Gate."

"I will seek you out as soon as I have Lady Lumina's blessing," said Haze.

Tess walked toward the entryway to the healing ward, and then paused, looking over her shoulder. "Oh, and Haze?"

"Yes, my lady?"

"I don't like formality with my traveling companions, so it's just Tess from now on."

Haze bowed quickly, but not before Tess saw the delighted grin on his puckish face. "Yes...Tess."

Tess gave him a nod and a smile, and then turned back to the healing ward. She walked quickly past the supply stations at the entryway. Most of the healers didn't give her a second glance. The night-dimmed *taebramh* lights glowed softly at the foot of each wounded fighter's pallet. She noted with quiet satisfaction that more of the pallets were empty since her last visit to the ward.

A healer that Tess recognized as one of the *Vyldgard* met her before she reached Sage's pallet. She forced herself to stop, waiting silently for him to speak.

"Lady Bearer," said the healer quietly. "Cora told us that you wanted to be notified when Sage awoke."

Tess nodded. "I appreciate it." She took a step forward, but the healer – Faelan, Tess reminded herself – raised a cautionary hand.

"Lady Bearer," he began again, "just another moment of your time. Sage is having difficulty."

"Difficulty? What kind of difficulty?" She wanted to push past Faelan and see Sage for herself.

"Sometimes," Faelan said, "awakening from a white shroud infusion is difficult. Sage is suffering from some…confusion."

"Confusion," Tess repeated slowly. "Do you mean loss of memory? That kind of confusion?"

Faelan paused. "It isn't a problem of memory. Sage knows who is and he remembers parts of the battle. I think it is more a problem of separating reality from his hallucinations."

"He's having hallucinations?" Tess frowned. She didn't like the idea of the wry, compassionate Seelie healer suffering from hallucinations. It sounded like the worst kind of punishment, not a physical wound but a mental one.

Faelan nodded. "I believe so. Please just keep that in mind. Some of the things that he says don't make sense, and some of them are outlandish. Some of them even border on treason."

She stiffened. "Surely Titania wouldn't truly think it's treason. Not in this circumstance."

"I don't believe so," said Faelan. "But I'm no longer part of the Seelie Court."

"I understand." Tess took a deep breath. "I don't have much time, so I'd like to spend what time I can with him now. Hallucinations or no."

The *Vyldgard* healer bowed his head in acceptance. "I understand, Lady Bearer. If he becomes too agitated, I may have to give him a light infusion to calm him, but I hope that doesn't happen."

"I hope that doesn't happen as well," Tess replied softly, looping one finger through her pendant as Faelan stepped aside and she approached Sage's pallet. There was already a figure sitting by the bed, but she saw that the other visitor was dozing, his elbows on his knees and his chin propped on his hands. The dim light of the taebramh globe reflected off his hair with a fiery red sheen. She touched his shoulder gently. "Robin."

He startled awake and then relaxed as soon as he saw her. "Tess. Thought you'd come soon."

"How long have you been here?"

"Most of the night. I knew you were preparing for the Gate and I'd been told that they were bringing him off the white shroud soon." He combed his fingers through his tousled hair, delicately avoiding the tender scar at the back of his head.

Tess offered him her half-full cup of *khal*. "It's cold, but it's better than nothing."

"That's certainly true." He took the cup without hesitation and downed it one draught.

While Robin drank, Tess looked down at Sage. She couldn't convince herself that his pallor and the shadows under his eyes were entirely due to the dim lighting. His eyes were closed, but his eyelids trembled with fitful movement and his good hand plucked at the blankets. Sweat dampened his skin. A sling and thick swathes of bandages bound his right arm across his chest, and a line of stitches marked an almost-healed gash just above his left eye. Tess resisted the urge to reach down and brush his fair hair from his forehead. "So you were here when he woke up?"

Robin nodded. He put aside the empty cup and motioned for Tess to sit. "Yes."

She folded her legs and sat on a few piled furs. "Tell me what happened."

"Faelan told you?"

"Faelan told me that Sage seems confused, but I don't really know what that means. So please, tell me what happened."

Robin took a slow, deep breath and looked steadily at Tess. "I don't think he's confused."

"Why?" She felt a crease appear between her eyebrows.

"Because I'm not confused." Sage stared up at her with fever-bright eyes, and his attempt at a smile only emphasized his hollow cheeks and sallow skin.

"Sage," said Tess, leaning forward quickly. "I'm so glad you're awake."

He grimaced. His voice was so low and hoarse that it was almost a whisper. "I guess I should say I'm glad, but..." He stopped and swallowed painfully. Without a word, Robin lifted a cup of water to Sage's lips and helped him drink.

"How's the pain?" she asked, unpinning the sheet of parchment at the foot of his pallet. She scanned it quickly and pressed her lips together.

"It's...not good." Sage again attempted to smile. "But you know...they can't give me anything...coming off of white shroud. Have to...cleanse it all out."

Tess replaced the record, stabbing the pin into the parchment a little more violently than strictly necessary. "I don't understand why they use it, then."

"It helps...in the long run," said Sage in his dry and crackling voice. He stiffened, clenching the blankets in his good hand as he bit down on a sound of pain. Robin leaned forward and covered Sage's hand with his own.

Taking her seat again, Tess frowned and mulled over Faelan's warning. Sage didn't *seem* confused, and she hadn't seen any evidence of hallucinations yet. She sat silently until Sage took a long, shuddering breath and turned his head to her again.

"You're going into the mortal world," he said.

She blinked in surprise. "Yes. How did you...?"

He chuckled mirthlessly, a rasping sound that ended in a cough and another sip of water. "I wasn't so deep under the white shroud that I couldn't hear the healers sometimes."

"Okay," Tess said quietly, thinking that the heavy sedation sounded less and less appealing. "Yes, I'm going into the mortal world."

"Have they told you?" Sage's eyes widened with fervor.

"Told me what?" Tess glanced at Robin, but the *Vyldgard* fighter didn't meet her eyes.

"They haven't told anyone," Sage continued, his voice cracking. "Mab hates you and Titania is protecting herself and they haven't told anyone."

Tess leaned in closer to Sage, hoping that it would encourage him to keep his voice down; a prickle of unease raised the hairs on the back of her neck. "What haven't they told anyone? I don't understand."

"My father was a part of it," Sage said. "He was young, he wanted to rise in favor with Titania..." He trailed off and groaned, his hand tightening around Robin's.

Gwyneth's pendant warmed at Tess's neck. Her eyes widened – the pendant rarely made itself known anymore. "What was your father a part of, Sage?"

The Seelie healer seemed not to hear her, his eyes clenched shut. She waited a long moment and then reached out, touching his good shoulder. Robin pressed his lips together but said nothing.

"Sage, please. I need you to tell me."

Sage seemed not to hear her, breathing heavily in the throes of his pain. She reached for his shoulder again but Robin gently caught her wrist with his free hand.

"He already told me," he said. "Or I heard him. He's talked about it twice since he awakened. The healer heard some of it, but he's *Vyldgard*."

"He's talked about *what*?"

Robin glanced up, his eyes finding Faelan at the far end of the row. He spoke in a low voice completely different from the loud and exuberant fighter she normally knew. "Sage said that before the closing of the Great Gate, there was a handful of Sidhe that rebelled against Mab and Titania. The last Bearer was thought to be sympathetic to them."

"I don't believe that Gwyneth would have supported an uprising," said Tess through numb lips. But then again, how much did she truly know about her ancestor?

Robin shook his head. "I don't think that it was an attempt to *overthrow* the Queens. These Sidhe just wanted their freedom. A few of them had traveled north and spoken to the *ulfdrengr*. Some of them had even lived among them for a few seasons. They'd seen how the Northmen lived and they chafed under the rule of the Queens."

"It doesn't sound like this is the first time you've heard about it," she said quietly.

"There were rumors. Half-truths passed down through the centuries. But it was forbidden to speak of it. Except now, with the Wild Court breaking the bonds between Sidhe…things are different."

"Sage is still Seelie." Tess felt a sudden surge of concern for her friend.

"Yes." Robin looked down at Sage. "Which is why it is dangerous for him to be speaking of it, but he won't be quieted."

Sage's eyes rolled open again. "Not until you know, Tess."

"So there was a rebellion against the Sidhe Queens long ago," she said softly, her voice almost a whisper. "Mab and Titania blamed the *ulfdrengr*?"

"In part," said Robin quietly. "That was the start of the enmity between them."

Tess shook her head. "I don't understand what all this has to do with me if it happened centuries ago."

Sage caught her eyes, his gaze glossy. "Because, Tess, the rebels were exiled."

"Exiled…to where?" Tess asked slowly, though her mind had already supplied the answer.

Sage's voice was barely loud enough to hear, but his words seared into her as though he'd shouted. "To the mortal world. They were exiled to the mortal world and the Great Gate was sealed soon after." He licked his dry lips. "The Queens expected them to perish in Doendhtalam."

"Let me guess," said Tess. "They didn't."

"Some survived," said Sage.

"They survived their exile for centuries in the mortal world," said Robin, his voice grim. "But it's doubtful their sanity is intact."

Tess shivered. "How would they have survived?"

"Blood," whispered Sage. He let out a long breath. "My father told me on his deathbed that he regretted it." He gazed into the hazy darkness overhead. "They rounded them up and put chains of iron on them and thrust them through the Gate."

"They used iron on their own people?" Tess couldn't help the incredulity in her voice.

"They were traitors," said Robin. He lifted an eyebrow fractionally. "Or so they were called."

"Why is it so important to warn me?" she asked. The Sword thrummed on her back. Sage shifted his eyes to the sheath of the Caedbranr, staring at it until Tess patiently asked her question again. He blinked and looked at her.

"Because," he said, "the Exiled will want revenge."

Chapter 16

Ross picked her way through the overgrown brush in her back yard carefully, cursing under her breath as she stepped into the mouth of some animal's burrow. Pausing, she switched the Glock into her left hand and pulled her phone out of her pocket. She pressed down on the power button again, watching the screen hopefully and giving a little sigh when the glowing silver emblem appeared and the device powered on. She flicked through to the flashlight function and used the little light to illuminate the ground before her feet, switching the phone into her left hand and the gun into her right.

The old shed sat far back on the property, almost on the bank of the river. When Ross moved in, Vivian had explained that there had been a little dock on the river once upon a time, but the upkeep had been too much. So the boat shed had been converted into a sort of garden shed, not that Vivian or Ross used it much. When she'd first moved into the house, Ross had harbored a brief fantasy of outfitting the shed with a pull-up bar and some kettlebell weights for training, but the thick humidity and plethora of insects that resided near the river quickly quashed any desire to use the shed as her gym. She'd admitted a bit ruefully after the first month of summer that air conditioning was her new favorite creature comfort.

The thin beam of her phone's flashlight cut out sharp shadows behind the blades of grass and the climbing vines reaching out from the trees along the river. Ross felt the darkness of the night pressing in around her; a bubble of incoherent fear rose into her chest, but she pushed it away and focused on the physical task of walking. One foot in front of the other, don't step in any more holes, don't think about what else could be lurking in the inky blackness. Don't let the primal survival instinct take control of your mind and send you running. Steady breathing, steady footsteps, and then she was at the shed, the worn planks gray in the shadows. She reached out and knocked three times on the wall of the shed. Two knocks sounded from inside; she smiled a little. She hadn't used a deconfliction knock in almost three years, but the old training was always there in the back of her head.

The door of the shed swung open. "All good?" Duke asked, her Beretta held in his right hand – finger straight and off the trigger, safety on, pointed down at the ground.

"For now," Ross replied. "The cops are gone. Everyone okay here?"

"We should get back to the house," said Duke. No smile, no joke about how she'd probably been waiting to use that deconfliction technique for the past three years. They hadn't turned on the one bare light bulb in the shed, leaving the only illumination the weak moonlight filtering in through the small square window. Ross spotted Merrick and Luca by the paleness of their skin when they moved.

"What's wrong?" she said. Duke shook his head slightly and moved through the door, holding it open for Merrick and Luca. Merrick slipped through first, conspicuously avoiding the old wrought iron hinges on the door, turning back to watch Luca. The *ulfdrengr* walked stiffly, as though every step cost him, and he held a piece of cloth, ripped from the bottom of Merrick's shirt, Ross saw, to his nose. Even in the shadows, Ross saw that the cloth was dark with blood.

"It's getting worse," Duke said quietly to Ross.

"You guys just can't catch a break," she murmured, reaching out instinctively as Luca wavered; but Merrick was there, silently pulling the big man's arm over his shoulder. The flashlight from Ross's phone flickered and then died with a pop and a small curl of white smoke. She shoved the phone into her pocket again, thinking that she probably wouldn't be able to revive it from its second close encounter with whatever strange energy field surrounded her otherworldly visitors.

When they reached the house, she made them wait while she slid around to the front porch and ensured that none of the patrol cars had returned and no neighbors had made their way over out of curiosity. She walked quietly back toward where the men waited, pausing as she passed her bedroom window. An acrid smell lingered in the air, setting her teeth on edge, reminding her of charred flesh and burnt hair. Dark streaks marked the pane of the window. She knew in the morning light they'd be rust-colored: dried blood, a gory echo of stained glass. With one last glance, she drew her shoulders back and strode toward the back of the house.

May waited for them in the living room, sitting patiently by the couch watching the door. She whined low in her throat as they crossed the threshold. Luca stumbled, and the big dog inserted herself under his hand as he reached for something to steady himself. Ross shivered at the strange rippling feeling that washed over her as she stepped past Merrick's runes on the doorframe. As she watched May with Luca, the sight only added to her certainty that Duke was telling the truth about his fantastic adventure.

Duke shut the door behind them and threw the deadbolt. He surveyed the runes. "Do these need reinforcement or anything?"

Merrick shook his head as Luca sat down heavily on the couch. The *ulfdrengr* experimentally removed the wadded cloth from his nose and sighed when blood slid down over his lip, pressing the cloth to his face again and muttering what Ross thought were curses in some language that sounded a bit like Norse. She noticed with detached interest that the blood on the cloth wasn't red, but a dark blue, almost black. So they were indeed very physiologically different, if their blood didn't oxidize to red in the open air, she thought clinically.

Mayhem whined, looked at Luca on the couch and then up at Ross, shifting her weight between her front paws. Ross smiled a little at the dog's steadfast obedience, even though there was clearly a connection between the *ulfdrengr* and the former war dog.

"Go ahead," she said to May, giving her a nod and a discreet hand signal. The dog leapt up onto the couch and settled herself across Luca's legs, laying her head on her paws. Luca opened his eyes and gazed down at Mayhem, his face unreadable. Then he leaned his head back against the couch and his free hand made its way to Mayhem's head. He idly stroked Mayhem's ears, and the dog made a low, approving sound. Ross smiled a little at the image the two of them made, but then she felt a twinge of loss. It looked as though Mayhem wouldn't be sleeping at the foot of Ross's bed tonight, despite Luca's earlier words.

Merrick stood in front of the door, surveying his runes. He said a foreign word in a low voice and the silver thumbprint in the middle of the door flared. Ross started slightly when the silver sparks raced out again around the house, but no one else, including Mayhem, so much as batted an eye.

"The runes will hold," said Merrick. "If it had tried to cross the threshold, it would have been killed."

Ross swallowed. "Don't get me wrong, I'm all for protection...but sometimes killing things causes more trouble than just scaring them off."

"The bone sorcerer has not been *scared off*, as you say," said Luca, taking the cloth away from his nose again and nodding in satisfaction when no blood slid down to his upper lip. He looked up at Ross, one hand still stroking Mayhem's ears. "He sent a scout. The destruction of that scout will matter little to him. He'll just make another."

"Why? Why will he make another?" Ross shook her head. "I don't understand. Why does he care about you at all?"

"We are the first of our kind to enter your world in hundreds of years," said Luca.

"That's not entirely true," demurred Merrick, his luminous gray eyes contemplative. "The Queens still sent their Named Knights into the mortal world after the closing of the Great Gate, and the Glasidhe have still passed through the veil as messengers."

"Why do you think the Queens only send their Named Knights?" asked Luca, arching one eyebrow. His hand slowed and then stopped gliding over Mayhem's pointed black ears. The dog opened one eye, waited a moment, opened her other eye and nosed his palm in clear suggestion.

"Diva," muttered Ross at the dog. Duke smiled tiredly. Luca chuckled and obligingly resumed indulging the dog.

Merrick frowned slightly. He glanced down at the naked sword he still held in his right hand, studying his reflection on the gleaming silver blade. "The Named Knights must be protected," he said slowly. "There must be rituals…runes, perhaps." He shook his head. "It wasn't necessary for us to learn any of that when we were younger. When I was apprenticing as a navigator, I asked about the mortal world…but all it got me was boxed ears." He gave half a rueful grin and then sobered. "It would make sense. There would *have* to be precautions taken against iron poisoning, and discovery…and the other dangers of the mortal world." He shook his head slightly. "I never thought to ask again."

Ross tried to stifle a yawn and failed. Her jaw popped and she winced as the exhaustion pressed down again. "Are we safe until dawn, at least?"

"Dawn is only a few hours away," said Duke.

"A few hours that I think everyone should spend getting some rest," she returned. He raised his hands slightly in a signal of deference.

"The runes should hold." Merrick looked at Luca and then at Ross. "We will stay out here."

Ross wasn't sure whether it was because Luca looked like he was already falling asleep with Mayhem laid across his legs or that Merrick wanted to guard the door, or both. She didn't particularly care. Duke and Merrick made quick work of moving the air mattress to the living room floor. Merrick laid his sword within reach and set about rearranging the blankets to his liking. She checked the deadbolt on the door out of habit, a strange warm buzz vibrating through her skin when she touched the lock. It wasn't unpleasant, but it was strange.

"See you in the morning," she said to the two men. Luca didn't reply, but Merrick smiled at her in response before turning back to his preparations for sleep. He pulled his shirt over his head and Ross had to turn away to prevent herself from staring at his bare torso. Whatever else she thought about these alien guests, she acknowledged two things: they were definitely not from her world, and they were beautiful in a way that only confirmed their alien nature. She wondered if phones would short out around Merrick, too. Then she sighed, walking down the hallway toward her bedroom.

"You all right?" Duke touched her shoulder gently.

"Mind's racing like it does when I need to go to sleep," she said honestly. They stood just outside the open doorway of the guest room.

Duke glanced at the rumpled futon. "Guess that's mine for the rest of the night." He smiled crookedly.

Ross turned her head and looked down the hallway toward her room. She imagined how the blood on the window would look from the inside as she laid in her bed, and she shivered.

"Hey," said Duke softly. His hand lingered on her arm, warm and reassuring. "It's over. He's gone."

"For now," Ross whispered. She turned back to Duke and sighed in frustration. "All I want to do is sleep, but I don't want to go in there. Stupid, huh?"

"It's not stupid," said Duke. "You saw some weird stuff tonight. It's okay to be creeped out. Heck, *I'm* creeped out and I wasn't the one who woke up..." He trailed off and rubbed the back of his neck, realizing too late that it probably wouldn't help Ross's frame of mind to rehash her first glimpse of the bone sorcerer's minion.

"You weren't the one who woke up to a guy clawing his fingers bloody on your bedroom window," finished Ross with a hard smile. Her head ached and her eyes felt like half a sandbox had been dumped under her eyelids. God, all she wanted was sleep but each step toward her bedroom wound the knot of anxiety in her stomach even tighter.

"Hey," said Duke, rubbing her arm slightly to get her attention. He nodded to the guest room. "You said this futon has held more than one person before, right?" Something surfaced in his eyes again when he said it, but he made the joke gamely.

She suddenly realized what he'd thought when she'd made the statement earlier. "Noah, I didn't mean that I'd...or that anyone..." She kept trying to figure out a way to say it and stopped, taking a breath. "I haven't slept with anyone since you...went away, if that's what you thought I meant earlier."

Duke rubbed the back of his neck the way he always did when she pinpointed one of his thoughts. "Well, I mean...I wouldn't say...it would've been perfectly..."

"We can talk about it tomorrow," she said with what she hoped was a smile. Her face felt numb. "But do you really mean it?"

"Mean...? Oh, of course," stumbled Duke. "Wouldn't have offered if I didn't."

"Okay. I'm going to wash my face and then I'll be in." She walked like a sleepwalker to the hallway bathroom, feeling like her legs weren't her own. As she stood in front of the mirror, she realized dully that she still held the Glock in her right hand. She placed the gun on the counter by the sink. Flattening her palms against the cool countertop, she braced herself on her arms and stared into the mirror at her reflection. She looked like she'd expected herself to look, exhaustion written on her face in the shadows beneath her eyes, the lack of color in her cheeks and the pinched corners of her mouth. But there was something else, something in her eyes. The closest she could come to describing it in her own head was that it looked like she'd seen a ghost, and now she expected a poltergeist to appear at any moment.

She reached to turn the faucet on and stopped, staring down at the dried blood on her hand. Then she turned on the water, waited until steam rose from the sink basin, and scrubbed her hands until they were stinging and red.

Ross padded down the hallway toward the guest room, face freshly washed, one of her raw hands clasped around the Glock. Duke sat on the edge of the futon, staring down at his own hands. She wondered when he'd washed them; they looked clean. He looked up at her, she shut the door behind her, and crossed the space between them.

"I don't know what else is going to happen," she said. "I'm still processing what's *already* happened." She set the Glock down on the end table by the futon and then turned back to Duke. "But no matter what happens, it's worth it to have you back."

His hands found her hips, and he drew her down onto the futon. She twined her arms around his neck as they lay down, her legs tangling with his.

"The light's still on," she whispered, her head finding the spot between his neck and shoulder where she fit perfectly. She pressed her forehead against his neck and breathed in the warm scent of him.

"Do you want me to get up and turn it off?" His arms tightened slightly around her and his voice rumbled through his chest into her cheek.

"No," she murmured drowsily, eyes drifting shut. She vaguely felt him pull a blanket over them, then his chest rose and fell in a quiet sigh. His warmth melted the knot in her own chest, and she finally relaxed, letting herself slide into sleep.

Ross awoke to the smell of bacon drifting through the door of the study. She stirred and yawned, expecting to find Duke out of bed already and making breakfast, as he tended to do. He woke up earlier than her most days, even on the weekends. He usually cooked breakfast and then woke her up with a kiss. But when she moved, stretching her stiff neck and shoulders, she found that there were still warm, muscled arms wrapped loosely about her. She sat bolt upright and Duke awoke with a start as she scrambled off the futon, almost falling in the process.

"What's wrong?" he demanded as she untangled the blanket from around her legs.

"They're going to burn down the house!" she exclaimed, running for the door.

"What…who?" Duke rubbed his eyes as he followed her hasty steps toward the kitchen. "Oh." His eyebrows rose of their own accord as he took in the scene: Merrick, still shirtless, tending bacon in a stainless steel skillet, and Luca experimentally sniffing at an opened carton of milk. Mayhem sat at Merrick's feet, gaze glued to the skillet. Duke winced and glanced at Ross as Luca started to drink milk straight from the carton. After a few swallows, Luca made a face of approval. Merrick jumped a little and muttered something under his breath as a crackle of bacon grease leapt from the pan and singed him.

"Cooking bacon shirtless is never a good idea," said Ross in an only slightly strangled voice. Duke couldn't tell if she was trying not to laugh or just arrested by the sight of the Sidhe man and *ulfdrengr* in her kitchen.

"I did not want to dirty your shirt anymore," said Merrick to Duke.

"That's what a washing machine is for," Ross said in that same strangled voice.

Merrick raised his eyebrows. "I'd like to see this…ma-chine. It sounds like it is a convenient invention."

"Like your ice-box," contributed Luca. Ross spied a loaf of bread already on the table, half of it gone, with an open jar of peanut butter beside it and a knife stuck in the spread like a claimant's flag.

"I'm going to have to go get more groceries," she said faintly.

Duke stepped past her. "It's called a refrigerator," he told Luca. He opened a cabinet, found a glass and set it down in front of Luca, who looked at it questioningly. Duke sighed, took the carton of milk from Luca's hand and poured him a glass of milk.

Ross gulped down a giggle. "Um, I…how did you know how to...?"

Merrick glanced at her, holding a baby-blue spatula in one hand. Vivian was a fan of kitchen accessories in pastel colors. Ross pressed her lips together firmly to suppress the smile that threatened to curve her mouth.

"We may be new to your world," Merrick said seriously, arching an eyebrow, "but we're not idiots."

This time she couldn't contain the spasm of laughter. Duke looked at her as though he couldn't decide whether he should ask what was wrong or join her in laughing at the absurd tableau. Merrick's eyebrow rose fractionally higher and he turned back to the skillet, unsmiling. Ross thought suddenly that maybe she'd offended him. "No," she gasped, finally able to catch her breath. "I'm not laughing because I think you're idiots. Really, Merrick, that's not why I laughed."

He looked at her with consideration.

"I just…my roommate, Vivian, she…." Ross bit her lip to keep herself from laughing again. The thought of Vivian's reaction to these beautiful men casually tearing apart the kitchen was enough to whip up another frothing geyser of giggles.

"You're giggling," said Duke flatly. "You usually don't giggle. Are you sure nothing is wrong?"

Ross couldn't catch her breath. She'd never heard of a panic attack inspired by helpless laughter, but there was a first time for everything. Then a sound cut through everything, making her stand up straight and stop laughing. It was the sound of a key turning in the door.

"Merrick," she said quickly, "will your runes kill *anything* that comes through the door other than us?"

"Of course not," he said, sounding slightly affronted. "Only things of Dark origins."

"Okay, I have no idea what that means but another human won't be hurt?"

"No, not unless they are inhabited by a Dark spirit."

The doorknob turned. May wrenched her attention from the bacon in the skillet and trotted toward the door, tail wagging slightly. Luca and Merrick both turned toward the door, Luca with an axe in his hand and Merrick with the baby-blue spatula held like a dagger.

"My life has turned into a sitcom," Ross said breathlessly, trying not to dissolve into giggles again as the door opened. Her roommate, Vivian, walked into the living room, talking as soon as she crossed the threshold. She focused on taking off her shoes and depositing her car keys in the little dish on the table by the door.

"Ross, did you drop your phone in the toilet or something? And there's a stain on the door. Gross. I texted you and called this morning but there was no..." She finally looked up and her voice died as she saw Luca with his axe; Merrick with his spatula; Ross with her hand clasped over her mouth and her shoulders shaking in silent laughter, and Duke leaning against the wall, arms crossed. "...answer," she finished. Her eyes performed another circuit of the room and lingered on Merrick, her mouth forming a little circle of astonishment. She dropped her backpack by the door with a thud.

"Hey, Vivian," said Ross, her voice choked with restrained laughter. "I didn't know you'd be home this soon."

"That's why I tried to text," said Vivian, her eyes never leaving Merrick. She blinked and glanced at Ross. "You didn't tell me you had…guests." Her eyes flicked back to the two beautiful men.

"Nice to see you again, too, V," said Duke dryly. "Not like everyone thought I was dead or anythin'."

Vivian straightened and her gaze snapped to Duke, eyes widening. "Oh…*oh my God!*" Her voice rose high enough in octave that Luca winced. One hand flew to her mouth. "Jesus, Ross, no wonder you weren't answering!" She grinned puckishly and waggled her eyebrows.

Ross smiled. "Thanks, V. I knew I could count on you to bring the innuendo."

"That's why we're such good friends," Vivian replied brightly. "I bring the innuendo, you bring the…*man candy*." She lowered her voice, waggled her eyebrows again and grinned at Merrick, who looked at Duke questioningly for help with the slang. Duke found himself biting his lip along with Ross to keep from laughing.

Luca stepped forward, axe still in hand but lowered. He directed his question at Ross but kept his gaze on Vivian. "Do you trust this woman?"

"With her deepest, darkest secrets," Vivian answered him with a cheeky wink, but Luca waited for Ross to nod. He slid his axe back into his belt yet continued to watch Vivian warily. Ross's roommate was almost the exact opposite of Ross physically: where Ross was barely five and a half feet tall, Vivian stood as tall as Merrick; Ross's dark, sleek hair contrasted with Vivian's shock of bright red curls; and Vivian was so pale she might have been able to pass for Unseelie, rather than the golden-tan of Ross's varied heritage that placed her closer to Seelie coloring. A smattering of freckles brushed the bridge of her nose, and her long face was interestingly handsome rather than conventionally pretty. Her eyes, too, were interesting: a strange sort of hazel, they were green around the edges of her iris and a golden-brown near her pupil.

"Are you done inspecting me yet?" Vivian tilted her head to one side and struck a pose, extending one leg with a delicately pointed toe.

"I do not mean to cause offense," Luca said. "We're just…new here."

"Yeah, Ross will have to explain that to me. Why haven't I ever seen these gorgeous boys before?" Vivian cocked her head in the opposite direction, looking questioningly at Ross.

"This is the first time they've been in town," Ross replied. Vivian didn't miss the look exchanged between Ross and Duke. For all her bubbly exuberance, she was a sharp observer. But she let them have their secret…for the moment, at least.

"Well, they're being good guests and cooking breakfast, I see," she said, striding forward and flipping her hair over one shoulder, "but, honey, you're burning the bacon." She smiled at Merrick, who regarded her like some unknown creature that could attack him at any moment. She cleared her throat and stepped closer to him. Merrick held his ground but raised the spatula as though to ward her off. Ross snorted with swallowed laughter. Vivian glanced at her roommate over Merrick's shoulder, then delicately slid the spatula from the *Vyldgard* navigator's grip and went to work attempting to rescue the bacon, that puckish grin lingering on her lips.

Chapter 17

Tess hooked a finger into the pendant at her throat, brushing her thumb over the three small rubies that had once been drops of her blood. She paced again in front of the fire in Vell's chambers. The Sword thrummed a little on her back. It seemed to be awake more often now that her journey into the mortal world was imminent.

A little shiver slipped down Tess's back at the thought, equal parts excitement and foreboding. She had sat with Sage and Robin for a long while, discussing the Exiled in a low voice with them both and trying to offer Sage what comfort she could as he sweated through the gray hours of the early morning. Finally, Sage had drifted into a fitful sleep, and Robin had told her that she'd better go catch a few hours of rest herself. The healers had changed shift by the time she made her way out of the healing wards to catch a few hours of uneasy sleep in her little compartment.

She woke gasping out of a nightmare – not a nightmare of Malravenar or the battle. It was a new nightmare that disappeared like fog under the morning sun, leaving her only the impression of grasping, clawed hands and a bloodstained mouth. But she pushed it into the back of her mind as she twisted the *taebramh* lantern into brightness and packed her bag for the journey. Somehow, it felt very different from when they'd been on their journey to Brightvale, across the Deadlands. It felt like she was about to set sail in a ship across an ocean, leaving all she knew behind. Silly, she chided herself, since she'd spent the first twenty years of her life in the mortal world. But somehow those oft-repeated words rang false in her mind. Her life before she'd been carried through the Lesser Gate into Mab's kingdom had faded like a dream. This was her world now, she was the Bearer.

Slinging her traveling pack over one shoulder, she looked about her little room and thought that perhaps she'd never see the little table and its lamp again. It was a strangely poignant thought. Her pack was relatively light, bearing only her small book of notes, two changes of clothes, a cloak and two of the more arcane books that contained useful bits about the role of the Bearers in the mortal world, *taebramh* in the mortal world, and Fae reactions to mortal objects. Tess ran her hands over her assorted weapons: long dagger at her belt, one in each boot top, plain sword at her waist and the Caedbranr in its sheath on her back. She had decided against bringing a bow, thinking that the quiver might prove to be unwieldy. As she pulled aside the curtain and stepped out into the hallway, Haze drew up short, aura sparking at the sudden change in direction.

"Impeccable timing, Lady Bearer," he piped brightly, sweeping an elegant bow.

Despite the anxiety twisting her stomach, she smiled. "The same could be said for you, Haze. I assume that Vell sent you?"

"The High Queen wishes to meet you in her chambers this morning before the Summoning," confirmed Haze, taking station above Tess's right shoulder as she began walking briskly in the direction of the *Vyldretning*'s quarters. She felt vaguely proud that she'd finally mastered the intricate workings of the ensorcelled pathways but then she wasn't sure that the pathways didn't shift themselves for her, sliding her toward her destination by their own magnanimous volition rather than her sense of direction.

As her feet carried her toward Vell's quarters, Tess thought about whether she would ask the High Queen about her knowledge of the Exiled. Vell was *ulfdrengr* and *volta*, but Finnead had been one of Mab's Three. Wouldn't that mean that Vell would have known through her bond with Finnead? Tess still wasn't sure how deep the bond between Vell and her Three extended. Clearly it was just as deep as the Sidhe Queens and their Named Knights, but did Vell choose to know their hearts and minds in the same way as Mab and Titania, who reached into the very core of their Three?

After ruminating on how exactly to broach the topic of the Exiled for the time it took to traverse a few corridors, Tess turned her mind to the party traveling with her through the Gate: Calliea, and she hoped Haze; Forin and Farin, as she'd told Haze, though she hadn't seen hair nor hide of the twins lately. One *Vyldgard* warrior and three Glasidhe seemed a spare rescue party. Then she almost slapped herself. Of course she had to ask Liam whether Jess or Quinn wanted to come with her. She thought that Quinn would most likely stay here – Niamh had shown slow signs of improvement in the past few days. But she could at least fulfill the promise she'd made to Jess to return him to his family in the mortal world.

Haze, for his part, remained silent throughout the walk to Vell's quarters. Deep in her own thoughts, Tess didn't remark on it until they reached the scarlet tapestry emblazoned with the rune wolf. "I apologize for being so unsociable, Haze," she said, pausing before the entrance.

"Make no further mention of it, my lady," Haze answered gallantly. "I have been lost in my own musings as well, faced with the prospect of leaving my world for the first time."

Tess raised an eyebrow, stifling the smile that tried to creep onto her lips. "Does that mean you've accepted my offer to accompany me?"

"I have received permission from Lady Lumina," said Haze, "but I also would ask leave of Forin and Farin. They have traveled with you before, and I would not wish to cause them displeasure."

Tess let herself smile. "Well, as I said before, I'm sure that they'll be delighted to be asked to simply scout and fight…though I doubt there will anything 'simple' about this journey," she added.

"And that is why I could not pass it up," Haze said in a conspiratorial voice, laughing brightly at Tess's grin.

"You'll probably be able to wrest the title of having met the most mortals from your cousin," she said. The wolf on the tapestry stood and circled, sitting down again and yawning as if impatient for her to pass through the entrance.

"Wisp will always hold the title of First Messenger for the Bearer," replied Haze.

"That he will," agreed Tess, touched again by the Glasidhe's chivalrous hearts. Their fierce loyalty and even fiercer sense of honor and duty expanded the Glasidhe beyond their small statures.

"I will leave you to your meeting with Queen Vell," said Haze, "and I will go prepare myself for the journey." His grin shone even through his aura. "And I am looking forward to this adventure, Lady Tess!"

"As am I," she replied with a smile, though she swallowed down a tangle of unease even as she said the words. Haze gave her a little salute and zoomed off down the passageway. Tess turned back to the tapestry and shook her head at the rune-wolf, which flicked its tail at her and settled down on its belly. The Caedbranr only stirred within her chest as she passed through the entryway into Vell's quarters.

The circular chamber was empty, but the copper kettle beckoned with fragrant steam on the table. Tess poured herself a cup of hot *khal* and made a rough sandwich out of a few pieces of bread and cheese from the tray beside the kettle. She forced herself to eat the food despite the nerves souring her stomach. Each mouthful felt like it took an eternity to chew. She didn't particularly enjoy the food, even though she knew in the back of her mind it was as delicious as any of the *Vyldgard*'s simple fare. But she did notice that the bread and cheese filled some of the vague hollowness in her body, and the *khal* at least warmed her pleasurably.

She set her pack on one of the empty chairs but couldn't bring herself to sit. The fire danced on the logs in the hearth. Her mind turned again to the Exiled. Robin and Sage hadn't agreed on whether the Exiled would be hostile to *her*, the Bearer; they made it sound as though they were most concerned for Merrick, since he was of Unseelie blood. Were the Exiled completely immune to iron at this point, after so long a time unprotected in the mortal world? And if they were…how exactly did one kill a Sidhe who was immune to iron? Tess felt a little sick at the thought. For all her experience in war, she'd never had to kill a Sidhe. She'd driven the Sword through Allene, but she was already possessed by the *syivhalla*. What would it be like, to watch the life fade from eyes so similar to her own? Perhaps Liam could offer her some advice on the subject. She shook her head and brushed the thought away. Liam's advice to her during the journey to the Dark Keep had been the closest they'd ever come to discussing his experiences in battle in the mortal world.

Tess paced in front of the fire, rubbing the cool curve of Gwyneth's pendant between two fingers. The pendant didn't respond, but the Sword thrummed softly in its sheath. She drew back her shoulders and addressed the Caedbranr silently. *Will you help me, once we're in the mortal world?*

The Sword vibrated a little. *You will not need help.*

Tess blew out a frustrated breath. *I feel like I will. I don't know how anything works in the mortal world as the Bearer.*

Why do you think it will be so different than here? The Caedbranr's androgynous voice remained carefully neutral.

Well, for one thing, apparently there are bloodthirsty banished rebels from both Courts who may or may not be insane from their centuries in the mortal world, she replied acidly.

The Sword's amusement rippled through her ribs. *That is a good line. You should use that in your conversation with the High Queen.*

"Fat lot of good you are," Tess muttered, turning again to pace down the opposite length of the chamber. She paused as she heard voices in the hallway, and several people emerged through the wall in quick succession. Suddenly the empty chamber was humming with activity: Vell swept in first, followed closely by her Three, and then Calliea and Haze.

"Good, Tess, you're here," Vell said, unclasping her scarlet cloak and tossing it onto the back of an empty chair. "The preliminary workings are done, and we've made the objects that you'll use to Summon the Gate back in the mortal world." She pulled a black silken pouch from her belt. "I convinced them to make three sets. It's always good to have extra."

"Very practical," Tess said. Liam grinned as he poured himself a cup of *khal*.

Calliea wore her battered breastplate, the robin's egg blue still marred by scratches and dents. She'd polished the breastplate until it gleamed, but she wore the scars almost proudly. Gray joined Liam at the table, talking to him in a low voice as they both selected their breakfast. Tess envied Liam's easy camaraderie with the *Vyldgard*. He fit in so naturally. She stood awkwardly in front of the fire, trying to corral her scattered thoughts.

"Oh, I had your armor brought for you, I hope you don't mind," Vell continued. "It's just over there." She motioned with one hand, and then seamlessly accepted the cup of *khal* offered by Liam. "Thank you." She took a sip and made a considering face. Liam and Gray watched their Queen closely. "Decent. Whoever made it didn't burn it, at least."

Gray smiled, her eyes flashing brilliantly as she arched an eyebrow and looked at Liam with an expression of triumph. Liam only chuckled and shook his head.

In contrast to Liam and Gray, Finnead stood silently behind Vell, hands clasped behind his back. His handsome face conveyed dutiful obedience to his Queen, but there was no light in his dark eyes. He looked even more haggard than at the council.

"We'll be Summoning the Gate at noon in the pavilion." Vell glanced at Tess. "Are you alright? You're awfully quiet."

"Just…thinking," Tess managed. Vell searched her face with her golden gaze for a long moment and then turned back to the table. She emptied the black pouch onto the table with nimble fingers.

"Three objects, each with one of the Queens' blood imbued in it," said the *Vyldretning*. Tess stepped closer, gazing at the objects that would open the portal again, grouped into neat threes. Each was contained in a small glass orb only a little bigger than a marble. One of the orbs shone brilliantly blue, a tiny white rose curled within; another sparkled like the night sky, dark and mysterious; and in the third orb, snow swirled about a miniature tree. Tess carefully picked up one of the orbs between her thumb and forefinger, marveling at the intricacy.

"Now, you remember the Summoning that Ailin went over? You have to use them in the right order: Mab, Titania, me. And then once you break the three orbs and say the incantation, seal it with your own blood. Just a drop will do, nothing extravagant."

"I remember." Tess nodded, placing the little orb back on the table. Vell swept them back into the pouch and handed it to her. She opened her belt pouch and nestled the little silk bag next to the river stone containing a piece of Malravenar's spirit. She might have imagined it but she thought that the stone shuddered a little as the Queens' orbs settled next to it.

Vell took another long drink of *khal*. "We also discussed your traveling companions."

At that, Tess raised her eyebrows. "I thought that I'd be choosing my own company."

Vell smiled humorlessly. "We already had to drive a bargain with Mab to secure her cooperation. They each want to send an emissary to ensure the proper handling of the Lethe Stone."

"Because I can't be trusted to handle it properly?" Tess asked, resisting the urge to fold her arms over her chest. The scars on her palms itched.

"That's not what I said," replied Vell, raising her own eyebrow. "It makes a certain kind of sense, Tess, however much we both may dislike it."

"So I'll have to play peacemaker between a Seelie and Unseelie in addition to...everything else?" demanded Tess, almost mentioning the Exiled right then and there. Vell's eyes narrowed at her hasty correction.

"That's part of what I'll do," said Calliea. "I don't mind treating them like children if they act like children." She grinned. The Valkyrie commander was in much higher spirits now that the day for action had arrived.

"The Laedrek will be my emissary," continued Vell.

Tess sighed. "And whose company do I have to look forward to from Mab's Court?"

"I believe you're on good terms with him," said Vell. "Ramel."

Tess swallowed her sound of surprise. She hadn't expected Mab to send one of her Knights that had interacted with the Bearer and even been rumored to continue a friendship with her.

"She also wishes to send the half-blood girl," Vell said.

"Molly?" This time, Tess couldn't hide her shock.

"She wishes to get rid of her, more like," muttered Gray. Calliea snorted.

"Who from the Seelie?" Tess pressed on, trying to regain her footing.

"Niall. He has the most experience in the mortal world."

Tess remembered the Seelie Vaelanseld favorably; she'd met him in the Hall of the Outer Guard, and seen him only peripherally after that during the journey across the Deadlands to the Dark Keep. "I suppose I don't have much to say about it."

"On the contrary," said Gray, "I think you should say whatever you please about it."

Liam nudged Gray – like he nudged Tess when she was being especially difficult. "Don't be rude."

"I'm not being rude," retorted Gray. "I'm just letting the Lady Bearer know that she's not without a voice on the subject."

Tess thought for a moment. Ramel was too young to have known about the Exiled, but Niall was the Seelie Vaelanseld. "How long has Niall been with Titania as one of her Three?"

Vell looked at Finnead, her silent command plain.

"He was chosen as her Vaelanseld only shortly after Mab's Vaelanseld was baptized," Finnead said.

Tess took a deep breath. "Was that before or after the uprising and the exile of the rebels?"

Vell grinned wolfishly. "And here I thought I was going to have to tell you myself."

"So you knew?" The Sword hummed quietly to Tess, perhaps advising caution.

"Only within the morning," replied Vell. "My people had our own stories about the Sidhe who abandoned their Courts to live among the wolf-chosen."

"I guess it doesn't really matter who knew what and when," Tess said, mostly to herself. "But the thought of the Exiled really doesn't bother you, it seems."

"Well, I'm not the one journeying into the mortal world," replied Vell with a raised eyebrow, "but I don't think you should be particularly afraid. The Sword will be an effective weapon against them."

The reality of Vell's statement hit Tess like a slap across the face. She felt stupid that she hadn't thought of it herself – of course the Sword would be her weapon against the Exiled. But then her thoughts circled back to her musings while she'd paced before the fire. "Unless they're immune to iron at this point."

"That's highly doubtful," said Finnead, speaking of his own volition for the first time. He shook his head. "There are extensive protections that are laid on each Knight by their Queen before they travel into the mortal world. As the years have passed, the protections have gotten more and more complex. Without any sort of shield against the poison in the mortal world, the rebels will most likely be very weak if not dead."

"Rebels. Sounds like you approve of their treatment." Tess let herself cross her arms this time.

Finnead met her eyes, his gaze cold. "They were traitors to their Queens and their people. By all rights, they deserved to die."

"They deserved to die for wanting their freedom?" she retorted. The room went still.

Finnead didn't reply, merely raising his eyebrows slightly in a look of dismissive disdain that somehow cut Tess deeper than any stinging words. She pressed her lips together on a nasty comment that rose to her lips – she didn't let herself think it fully, or else she might have said it, but it had something to do with the princess and the Lethe Stone and what Mab intended to do with it. Instead, she swallowed and turned back to Vell.

"Haze, Forin and Farin are coming with me," she said in a measured voice. "They've all been granted leave by Lumina. And Jess, too, if he'd like." She directed her last comment to her brother.

Vell nodded. "That's good." She looked at Tess for a long moment and then said, "Leave us for a few moments."

Without a word, all the *Vyldgard* melted through the wall, even Liam. Vell pressed one hand to her temple as if to ward off a headache.

"I don't want us to part on bad terms, Tess," she said, sounding almost weary.

Tess felt a pang of sudden guilt. She hadn't thought of what it must have cost Vell to play the diplomat and mediate between Mab and Titania. "I'm sorry," she said, her own voice tired. "It just seems like there are curve balls being thrown at me every waking minute."

Vell sat down in the chair that Liam had vacated. "You and me both." She sighed.

"One thing we haven't discussed this morning," said Tess, taking the chair opposite Vell. "I'm taking Kianryk with me, aren't I?"

She nodded. "Yes. It's the surest way to help Luca."

"Would it be strange if I said that I'm most nervous about that, and not the Exiled or the Lethe Stone or anything else?" Tess felt a lopsided smile lift her mouth.

Vell chuckled. "Not at all. But the care and feeding of an *ulfdrengr* wolf is much simpler than you might think."

"I don't know how I'll keep him hidden," Tess said honestly. "Carrying swords and dressing like this is bound to arouse enough suspicion already. Adding a wolf to the mix will probably set off alarms."

"I'll take care of it. He won't like it, and neither will Luca, but it's what has to be done." A hint of sadness touched Vell's words.

"Nothing permanent, I hope." Tess frowned at the unhappiness in her friend's voice.

Vell shook her head. "No. Nothing permanent, thank the White Wolf, though I may never forgive myself."

Tess pressed her lips together. "That sounds pretty permanent to me."

The *Vyldretning* chuckled wearily. "Look at you, trying to make *me* feel better when it should be the other way around." She sobered. "We'll miss you here, Tess. I'm hoping that I can keep the Seelie and Unseelie from starting anything that isn't easily undone while you're gone."

"You really think they'd go to war against each other?"

"I don't know. I hope not. But even my power could not keep them from each other if they want to fight."

Tess hummed. "Probably for a little while, at least."

Vell laughed. "You're right. But in any case, it'd be best if you're quick about this mission in the mortal world. I think you'll have more in the future, but this first one is more important than the rest. Things aren't settled yet."

Tess took a deep breath. "Will things ever be settled?"

"With these difficult Queens, probably not," muttered Vell.

"That was rhetorical." Tess laughed. It felt good to laugh. Her mind was heavy with the knowledge of what lay ahead, but for the moment she let herself enjoy the company of her good friend, trying not to acknowledge that if she didn't succeed, it could very well be the last time they sat and laughed before a merrily crackling fire. Her own words came back to haunt her as she remembered her caution to Liam and his teammates – *You die here in this world, that's it. You're dead.* It worked the same for her in the mortal world.

"Why aren't you sending one of your Three with me?" she asked Vell after a moment of easy silence. "Not that I'm asking you to…but it's just that…"

"The other two want to outmaneuver each other. It's not that they don't trust you – well, maybe for Mab that's the reason," Vell amended. "But she distrusts Titania as well. Titania might have started off sending Niall as a goodwill gesture to the Bearer, but Mab takes it that she wants to interfere somehow with the procurement of the Lethe Stone."

Tess shook her head. "Intrigue upon intrigue."

"And you thought you'd be leaving all the politics behind when you stepped through the Gate," said Vell with a grin. "Besides, Calliea is going with you. I'm not *sending* her – she would stay if I commanded her, but what type of Queen would that make me?" She shrugged, her golden eyes contemplative. "As far as anyone can tell, Merrick helped save Liam's life. If Merrick hadn't pulled him away, he'd be in the mortal world, and probably dead at this point from the dagger in his side. So I owe him a debt for that."

"Merrick was the only one who dove past those iron wards set around the altar," Tess said. "Apparently no one guessed the strength in our young navigator."

"I did," replied Vell simply. "That is why I baptized him the Arrisyn."

Tess smiled. "I was so proud that day. Of him and Calliea both."

They let the conversation glide into recollections of their past adventures, taking comfort in the memories. After too short a time, Vell's Three reappeared. Liam stepped forward, addressing both of them. "It's almost noon." He nodded to Tess. "I let Jess know. He's ready."

Tess nodded. "Good." At least she'd be able to fulfill her promise to one of the men. She slid the strap of her pack over her shoulder, wishing suddenly that she'd had the time to say goodbye to Nehalim. She was lost so deeply in her own thoughts that she almost didn't notice the strange sensation of sliding through the wall into the passageway beyond.

"Hunting a bone sorcerer isn't difficult," said Gray, unexpectedly falling into step beside her. "I've spoken to my cousin about the particulars."

"Thank you," said Tess cautiously, unsure what to make of Gray's sudden forthrightness.

"Don't thank me yet," said the beautiful *Vyldgard* warrior blithely. "Tracking him isn't the hard part. It's killing him." She tilted her head. "But then again, you're the Bearer, so *that* part should be easy for you, too."

"Reassuring," Tess said drily. She wasn't sure how to continue the conversation. To her relief, Liam appeared on her other side and gave Gray a meaningful look; the golden-haired knight serenely moved to take position just behind Vell.

"You forgot your armor," said Liam with a smile, holding up her breastplate in one hand.

Tess chuckled. "Look at you, still making sure I'm dressed for school even in the Fae world."

"It's what big brothers do," said Liam with mock seriousness. They paused, standing to the side of the passageway, and he quickly helped her don the light breastplate. Tess ran her fingertips over the surface of the armor, feeling the various scratches and dents where the armor had protected her from the fangs and claws of Dark beasts. It felt like greeting an old friend, and she smiled at Liam in thanks as she rearranged the strap of the Caedbranr across her chest. They lengthened their strides to catch up to the rest of the company. Jess seamlessly joined them as they reached the great double doors of the palace. He nodded to Tess, dressed in his camouflage pants, boots and a black shirt.

They didn't encounter any others in their walk through the streets of the White City to the pavilion.

"It's like in the old Western movies when everyone disappears before the big showdown," murmured Tess to her brother, rewarded by his chuckle.

"Let's *hope* this doesn't turn into a showdown," Liam said quietly in reply. Vell glanced over her shoulder at him, one eyebrow raised slightly. Tess nudged Liam's shoulder, lips pressed together to quash the grin trying to wriggle its way into existence. To her surprise, Liam colored a little.

"Are you *blushing*?" Tess demanded in a low voice, letting the grin blossom. "You never blushed before when you were…ahem, *involved* with other women."

Liam smiled a little sheepishly. "This is different."

"Different because you have a mind meld with her, or different because….?" Tess raised her eyebrows. A slight breeze whispered down the deserted path.

"Different because it's the first time I've been with a woman that can kick my ass," he replied with a little chuckle.

"That in itself isn't enough to make you blush." Tess narrowed her eyes. "Are you *in love*?"

"Yes," said Liam quietly. "Though I haven't said so much in words to her."

"Well, she's already implied it, and apparently you two get along well in all the ways that count, from what she's said," Tess replied with a little smile.

Liam groaned. "Now you're just twisting the knife. This is why I don't talk to you about my love life."

"You had no problem giving me advice about Luca and Finnead," Tess pointed out.

"Well, that's different. I'm your older brother," Liam said with exaggerated sternness.

Tess snorted. She saw Jess glance at her, amusement in his usually serious eyes.

"Doesn't matter. I think we're past the age where that's the trump card," she retorted.

"We're never past the age where that's the trump card, Bug." Liam smiled as she rolled her eyes.

Then Tess sobered. "No matter what happens, take care of her, Liam. She's always been there for me, even before I was made the Bearer."

"I will. But don't talk like you're not coming back. I won't allow it." Liam put a hand on her shoulder. She leaned into him slightly as they kept walking, and he gave her half a hug.

"So how've the visions been?" she asked as they separated.

"Smooth change of subject. And they haven't been bad since I died."

She hit him lightly in the arm. "Don't say it like that."

"Okay, they haven't been bad since I died and an ancient deity resurrected me. And by not bad, I mean…non-existent."

Tess sighed in forbearance. "I'd have appreciated a head's up on whatever I'm stepping into in the mortal world. It sucks that your mojo is out of whack."

"I would've loved to have given it to you. And it's not common knowledge that my visions haven't returned since the deal with Arcana. Finnead and Gray know, of course, but that's about it."

"The Sword felt that way for a while too. They'll probably trickle back." Tess let her eyes find Finnead, walking with his usual cat-like grace opposite Gray on Vell's left side. "And…I know that he and I aren't necessarily on great terms, but keep an eye on Finnead, too? This whole thing with the princess seems like it's hitting him pretty hard."

"It is. And I will." Liam nodded but didn't elaborate.

"Thanks." Tess smiled, and then they fell into comfortable silence as they traversed the last few paths to the pavilion. The scarlet curtains still hung between the pillars, the three sigils of the Queens vivid on their banners. Inside the pavilion, the ceiling overhead still held the image of night and day, divided neatly down the center. The large round table was gone. The pavilion was empty save for a small silver bowl in the center of the gleaming floor.

Titania stood with her Three at the eastern entrance of the pavilion. Mab faced her at the western entrance, flanked by her own Knights, though the two Queens did not look directly at each other. Tess glanced up at the ceiling again and picked out three bright glows that she'd mistaken at first glance for stars in the night sky. She had enough time to recognize them as Glasidhe before Farin dove for her, trilling in her bright voice. Forin and Haze followed at a more dignified pace.

Farin had braided her hair, weaving two small red feathers into the white-gold plaits at her temples, and she wore her Glasidhe armor and war paint, cobalt symbols covering all her visible skin. Even her eye-patch had not escaped adornment: she'd painted it a bright blue to match the runes on her skin. Forin wore his war paint as well but Haze had abstained, looking no less war-like in miniature gauntlets with his bow slung over his shoulder.

"You look very fierce," Tess told Farin as the High Queen's party came to a halt.

"I am most excited for this foray into the mortal world," Farin replied, baring her pointed little teeth. "I am eager to hunt this bone sorcerer!"

"I'm grateful you're coming along," Tess said honestly.

"We would not miss it for all the gold in the Seelie Court!" the indomitable Glasidhe replied gleefully.

Tess chuckled and then turned her attention back to the Queens. Mab and Titania had not moved. Vell, however, looked to the northern entrance of the pavilion and whistled piercingly. After a few moments, Beryk loped up the steps to the pavilion, looking as large as a small horse. The black wolf flowed sinuously across the floor to Vell. Kianryk followed behind him.

Tess caught her breath at the sight of the tawny wolf. While Beryk seemed to fill the extra space in the pavilion with his presence, Kianryk seemed smaller than usual, his golden fur lank and lusterless, his blue eyes lacking their usual fire. He walked gingerly, as if every step caused him pain, yet he held his head high as he traversed the pavilion and stopped before Vell. The High Queen knelt and murmured words in the Northern tongue softly. Kianryk whined low in his throat, breaking something in Vell's demeanor and she threw her arms around the tawny wolf's neck. Beryk stood grandly at her side, staring at the other two Queens with a challenge in his eyes, as though daring anyone to comment on Vell's display of emotion.

The Caedbranr stirred with interest. Tess padded cautiously forward, and no one stopped her. Vell released Kianryk; the wolf whined again low in his throat and lowered himself to his belly, laying his great head in her lap. Vell still spoke softly in the Northern tongue as she drew an object from the folds of her cloak: a scarlet collar, runes flowing over its surface. Tess's chest ached as she saw the pain on Vell's face. Kianryk heaved a great sigh and closed his eyes in submission. Vell's hands shook as she fastened the collar about Kianryk's neck, and wetness gleamed on one of her cheeks as she took the tawny wolf's face in both her hands and kissed him between his ears, pressing her forehead to his for a long moment. Beryk maintained his steadfast watch on the other Queens, an obsidian guardian at her side.

Finally, Vell pressed another kiss to Kianryk's head and raised her face, her golden eyes glimmering with hard light. With an effort,

Kianryk stood, the scarlet collar stark contrast against the white gold fur at his neck. He didn't look any different to Tess's eyes, but perhaps it would only take effect in the mortal world. The wolf stood stoically on Vell's other side.

The High Queen looked at Titania and then Mab. Her voice rang out through the pavilion. "Let us open the Gate."

Chapter 18

"So let me get this straight." Vivian lounged on one of the armchairs in the living room, arranging her lanky body with insouciant grace. She pointed at Duke. "You didn't die, you were abducted into another world."

"Followed Liam into another world. But yes," replied Duke.

"And you two are natives of this other world." Her long finger switched to Luca and Merrick.

"Yes." Luca nodded. He, Merrick, Duke and Ross had held a quick conference in the kitchen when Vivian went to put her backpack in her room and change out of her traveling clothes after breakfast. Ross had vouched for Vivian's trustworthiness, and they couldn't see any way other than telling the truth, which, as Ross had pointed out, sounded more fantastic than any story they could come up with anyway.

"You got thrown through this portal during an epic battle, and now you're being hunted by this bone wizard." Vivian ran her fingers through the end of her long, curly ponytail, her habit when she was deep in thought.

"Bone sorcerer," corrected Merrick. He'd quickly reclaimed the shirt Duke had lent him after Vivian's appraising glances during the preparation of breakfast.

"This sounds like it would be a *fantastic* novel, doesn't it?" Vivian asked Ross with a cheeky smile. "Just the right amount of smoldering heroes and dark magic."

"Something like that," Ross agreed. "Vivian is a writer, among other things," she explained to Luca and Merrick.

Vivian watched Luca and Merrick thoughtfully for a long moment. "You know, my grandmother used to tell me stories. *Her* grandmother was from Ireland. Immigrated during the Potato Famine." She smiled and shrugged. "Or so the family lore goes. In any case…I've heard about the Fae and your tendency to view mortals as playthings." Her eyes rested on Merrick. "You look like you'd be Unseelie."

Surprise flickered for a bare instant across Merrick's face. Then he drew his shoulders back. "I was born Unseelie, but I'm *Vyldgard* now."

"*Vyldgard*. Never heard of that one." Vivian thought. "Sounds Norse. Viking or something." She shifted her focus to Luca. "And what about you? You don't look Sidhe." The words rolled from her tongue with aplomb.

Merrick shot Ross a look that plainly said, *How does she know all this?* Ross shrugged. Duke watched the whole exchange with a bit of amusement – he hadn't expected Vivian to accept the story so completely, much less start throwing around her knowledge of Fae folklore.

"I am *ulfdrengr*," replied Luca. "Also *Vyldgard*, at this point."

Vivian hummed in thought. "*Ulfdrengr*." She wrinkled her nose and then grinned. "Got it. Thought it sounded familiar. Wolf warrior, or something like it." The redhead widened her eyes innocently at the nonplussed expressions of Ross and Duke. "What? I took an ancient mythology course at Tulane. More than one, actually. And an Early Western Literature course. You'd be surprised at the depth we went into with *Beowulf* and some of the other Viking sagas." She crossed her legs and then folded her hands atop her knee. "This is fascinating. So the stain on the door is blood?"

"From the gas station clerk," confirmed Duke.

Vivian raised an eyebrow. "From what?"

"The gas station clerk," he repeated.

"No, I got that part. I mean, did you stab him? Shoot him?"

"Jeez, V, Ross never told me you were this bloodthirsty," the wiry man replied.

"I just want to know the details in case I'm asked about it." She looked at Ross. "I mean, I'm your roommate. It makes sense you'd tell me the whole story, especially since you called me after it happened and I rushed home to be at your side." Her impish grin reappeared.

Ross couldn't help but smile. "As far as anyone knows, I shot him in the shoulder with the Glock." Her smile faded. "He clawed his fingers bloody on my bedroom window."

"That's not creepy at all," deadpanned Vivian. Then she took a deep breath and looked between the four of them. "All right. How can I help?"

Duke blinked in surprise, but Ross just smiled again. Leave it to Vivian to swallow their story whole and then demand a part of the action. It was part of why they had become such good friends after Ross had answered the ad for renting a room. "You could start by letting them stay here."

Vivian waved a hand. "That's already a done deal. Of course they can stay here."

"Aren't you both renting?" Duke looked at Ross. "I mean, I just don't want your landlord to get his knickers in a knot."

"*I'm* renting. Vivian *owns* the place," she explained with a smile.

"And I won't be getting my knickers in a knot." Vivian grinned. "Grandparents willed it to me along with the coffee shop," she elaborated. "Besides that, anything else I can do, you just let me know." She nodded seriously.

"Will do, V. Thanks," Ross said honestly. She wasn't one for frequent displays of affection, but she felt the strange urge to hug her tall roommate at her unquestioning acceptance of Duke, Luca and Merrick.

"No problem." Vivian squinted at Luca. "You don't look too good, big guy. Maybe you should lie down."

He smiled faintly despite the bruise-dark shadows beneath his eyes. "I've survived worse." But he took a seat on the couch, ensuring that his axe didn't dig into the cushions.

Ross crossed her arms and looked at the members of their makeshift council. "So. What will this bone sorcerer do next?"

Merrick shook his head. "I haven't encountered a bone sorcerer before, but if he was in the service of Malravenar…I think he will either try to build his power in the mortal world, or seek a way back to the Fae world."

"This bone sorcerer," said Luca heavily. "I believe I know of him."

Everyone went still, waiting for him to continue. He kneaded his scarred hand, eyes distant.

"He was once a Northman. Not wolf-chosen, as he desired. He passed the age of Choosing, and he could no longer stand at the ceremonies where the pups choose their life partners." Luca grimly traced the puncture scars on his palm. "So he decided to learn the ways of the *volta*."

"I thought the *volta* were all women," said Merrick.

Luca shook his head. "Most of them. The power seems to favor the girl children. And it is possible to be both wolf-chosen and *volta,* as with our *Vyldretning*, though it isn't common and most don't pursue both paths."

"And *volta* are…?" Ross raised her eyebrows and looked at Duke, who shrugged and directed her attention back to the *ulfdrengr*.

"The keepers of the power of our people," said Luca, searching for the right words. He thought for a moment. "Sorceresses, perhaps you would call them."

"*Now* we're talking," breathed Vivian softly, transfixed. Luca seemed not to hear her.

"But just as not all are wolf-chosen, not all are *volta* either. In the case of this boy...the *volta* did not want to teach him. He had power, but he also had cruelty in his bones."

"Let me guess, they started finding small animals that had been tortured around the camp," said Vivian, raising a pale eyebrow.

Luca chuckled mirthlessly and shook his head. "For a boy that had been brought up to be a warrior – wolf-chosen or not – animals presented no challenge. He had been hunting with his father since he could walk."

The sarcastic smile faded from Vivian's face as she began to sense the direction of the story.

"The *volta* of his village began to teach him despite her misgivings. He was quick to learn, but his blood did not have much power." He shrugged. "Sometimes that is the way of things. It was a constant source of anger to him. He did not understand why after he had been insulted by not having been wolf-chosen, he could not rise to the highest ranks of the *volta*. The old *volta*'s formal apprentice, Kiri, was nearly ready to take the rites that would make her an elder in the *volta* and begin to train her own apprentices." Luca paused. "Kiri never took her rites. She disappeared like snow into the mountain air. The old *volta* had her suspicions, but nothing could be proven."

"What did he do to Kiri?" Vivian almost whispered the question.

"They never found her. But to take her power...which is what the boy did...he would have had to carve out her heart and drink her lifeblood."

Vivian paled and swallowed hard.

"He found that rather than work hard to make the most of the gifts he'd been given, he would rather take the gifts of others for his own. Two children from neighboring villages disappeared, but again nothing could be proven, even before a council of the elders." Luca took a breath. "If a Northman is accused of a crime, he has the right to face his accuser, and the right to *sjofnod*." He thought for a moment as he translated the Northern custom. "Trial by a group of Northmen in good standing in the village. Or from neighboring villages, if the accused does not think his peers will be able to judge him fairly."

"Other than this blood-drinking and heart-carving, it sounds like you're pretty civilized," commented Vivian in an attempt at lightening the mood.

"Or if the accused and the accuser both agree, they may determine their fates through *aenvig*." Luca grinned wolfishly. "A…duel, I think is the word." He looked to Duke for verification. He waved a hand, becoming serious again. "But the boy grew sloppy with arrogance. He killed the old *volta,* but before she died she marked him with the symbol for kinslayer on his forehead, a mark that will never fade. He fled into the wilderness, knowing that he would be named outlaw. Eventually, he was taken into the service of Malravenar."

"Does this bone sorcerer have a name?" Ross asked.

"They named him Stone Soul. Gryttrond."

"Gryttrond," Ross repeated. "So what will Gryttrond do next?"

Luca smiled faintly. "He is probably sick with hunger, and we represent a great feast to him. A Sidhe, an *ulfdrengr*, and a mortal who has walked in the Fae world."

"Do you think he would kill us, or use us as bait?" Merrick asked in a measured voice, his gray eyes clear and focused.

Ross frowned. "Why would he use you as bait? Or I guess, *who* would he be using you as bait *for*?" She stopped as Luca looked at Merrick and both men glanced at Duke; she let her mind digest the question, and then she tilted her head. "Tess. He would be setting a trap for Tess."

Luca nodded wearily and Merrick cursed under his breath.

"Okay, now I'm lost. Who's Tess?" Vivian asked bluntly.

"The Bearer of the Iron Sword," said Merrick. "She is a descendant of Gwyneth, the last Bearer, and she recovered the Sword after it was lost for centuries."

"It is a weapon of great power," said Luca.

"So it sounds like this bone sorcerer shouldn't be much of a problem for her," Vivian said with a toss of her vibrant mane.

"It isn't that simple," Merrick said. "This will be the Bearer's first journey into the mortal world. Everything feels different here."

"Her power will be less?" Ross asked. "Will it not work at all?"

"I wish I knew," replied the dark-haired Sidhe fervently. "But what I do know is that I cannot let this bone sorcerer set a trap for her. I will not cower in hiding while he prepares his snare."

"How do we know that the bone sorcerer really has power in this world, if he's from *your* world?" Vivian asked, brow wrinkled as she worked through the logic.

"Because blood magic is one of the few things that remains the same between the worlds," Luca replied grimly. "Blood and death are the constants of our universe."

"Cheery," Vivian muttered, but she swooped down into the wing-back chair again, propping her chin on her hand and her elbow on her knee. "So on the one hand, we don't know if Tess's sparklers will work in the mortal world, hence the concern. On the other hand…what can *we* do against the bone sorcerer?"

"We sit here and let him hunt us, or we turn the tables," said Merrick. He locked eyes with Luca.

"*We* hunt *him*," the *ulfdrengr* said in a low voice that was almost a growl. Mayhem appeared in the living room; there was a break in the conversation as the Belgian Malinois greeted everyone and then leapt up onto the couch, settling across Luca's lap with a happy sigh.

"Okay, hunting him. That sounds…very bold. But again…how are *your* powers holding up?" Vivian raised an eyebrow.

"V is certainly throwing herself into this headlong," Duke murmured to Ross.

Vivian pointed at Duke. "I heard that. And yes I am. Unlike you two, I've been stuck in the swamps most of my life and haven't had a chance for adventure." She smiled. "I can totally use this as source material for a book when it's all over."

"You would reveal our existence to all your fellow mortals?" Merrick's eyes sparked with a Fae light and he took a step toward Vivian.

She held up a hand. "First of all, I'd let you guys read it beforehand. Second of all, not 'all my fellow mortals' would read it. Let's be real, I'm not Rowling. And third of all…it would be a *fantasy* book. Everyone would think it's *not real*." She grinned, pleased with herself. "Isn't that *brilliant*? I totally get to have a real adventure and write about it but everyone will think it's fiction!" She put her arms up in a 'goal' gesture.

"I…did not fully understand that," Merrick said in defeat, looking at Ross in supplication.

"I'll explain later," Ross said, silently chuckling at her roommate's enthusiasm. "But basically she's saying that she won't reveal your existence, so don't worry too much about it."

Merrick nodded, looking suspiciously at Ross. "Good. Because it would be an unpleasant task to convince her that she cannot do this."

Vivian seemed not to hear him, lost in thought as she stared at the chalk runes on the doorway. She tapped a finger against her lips. "So. Geek brain thinking now. Can you build your own trap for the bone sorcerer with runes like those?"

Merrick blinked. "I'm not a rune-master…"

"Modesty doesn't do anyone any favors," Vivian said, cutting him off. "Seriously, Ross, back me up on this."

"On the rune plan or the modesty comment?" Ross smiled.

"Both, obviously, because I'm right."

Merrick frowned slightly. "I'll take your rudeness as a particularly mortal trait. The Lady Bearer is considerably more courteous than you."

"Yes, yes, and she was the solution to all of your problems. I'm just a gangly red-headed girl who happens to own the house which is your only sanctuary right now." Vivian smiled sweetly at the *Vyldgard* navigator.

Ross smiled. "She's got you there, Merrick. But just remember…she's mostly all bark. Isn't she, May?"

The black dog raised her head from Luca's lap and grinned at Ross, her pink tongue lolling out of her mouth. Luca smiled and smoothed back the dog's ears with his huge hands, eliciting a comical expression of canine bliss.

Vivian smiled. "Well, if May says so…" She chuckled and shrugged. Merrick slowly relaxed, and then he, too, stared thoughtfully at the runes on the door.

"Luca," he said, "If we are to attempt this, I might need your help to create this runetrap…"

The group splintered as Luca and Merrick began to discuss the particulars of the trap for the bone sorcerer. Duke went to go check the perimeter of the property; Ross didn't protest, but she watched him go silently. Vivian touched her friend's shoulder. "Hey. Don't look so gloomy. He's back, right?"

Ross smiled. "Yeah. He's back. All of this, though…it's a bit overwhelming."

Vivian rolled her eyes. "You can say that again. Want a beer?"

"V, it's not even noon yet."

Vivian shrugged as she opened the refrigerator and surveyed the selection. "So? We're setting a trap for a bone sorcerer and stuff. Requires libations."

"Libations." Ross shook her head and chuckled, accepting the craft beer that Vivian opened for her. "You already sound nerdy. Hanging around these guys isn't going to help your case."

"It's a risk I'm willing to take," Vivian replied with a grin. She popped the cap off her own beer and held it up. "Here's to trapping the bone sorcerer."

"To trapping the bone sorcerer," Ross agreed gravely, clinking her bottle against Vivian's and taking a long swig of beer.

Chapter 19

Opening a Gate was not as simple as Tess had thought it would be. It seemed like hours since the Queens had gathered around the silver bowl in the center of the pavilion and begun their incantation. She'd tried to take advantage of the time by conferencing quietly with the company who would be following her through the portal into the mortal world: Niall, his pale hair tied into a neat ponytail at the nape of his neck, wearing a breastplate emblazoned with the Seelie sigil; Ramel, who hadn't so much as smiled at Tess when he greeted her; the three Glasidhe, Forin, Farin and Haze; Calliea, with her golden whip coiled at her hip; and Molly, her cat-like eyes observing the proceedings attentively, her hands brushing the hilts of the slim twin daggers at her belt every so often. Jess observed the other fighters with his flinty eyes, and Kianryk stood uneasily at Tess's side.

They obediently arrayed themselves in a crescent around her, but Tess noticed that Niall stood as far away from Ramel as he could, and Calliea kept an eye on both of them. Just as Ramel hadn't smiled, Molly didn't say a word, but her pale face was alight with keen interest.

"We'll be wearing concealment runes," said Tess in a low voice, just loud enough to be heard over the incantation of the Queens. The voices of Vell, Titania and Mab twined together in a strange harmony, reminding Tess of snakes wrapping about each other with sinuous elegance. They were chanting, not quite singing, but the congruence of their voices sounded almost like a hymn. The air in the pavilion rippled with power, compressing and releasing in time with the rhythm of their chant.

Niall nodded and pulled up his sleeve, baring his forearm. "I've already inked mine, Lady Bearer, and I'd be happy to assist any others who require it."

"We have no need of concealment runes," said Forin calmly, speaking for the Glasidhe as a whole. "We have a long history of remaining unseen when we wish it."

Tess nodded. She wasn't about to start questioning the Glasidhe's judgment moments before diving through a portal into the mortal world. She turned her attention to Calliea, Jess, Ramel and Molly.

"I will draw mine now, with you, if you wish it, Lady Bearer," Calliea said. Tess nodded again, grateful for Calliea's subtle offer of assistance. She'd sketched the concealment rune dozens of times and thought she'd memorized it, but with the adrenaline churning in her stomach, it was a relief to rely on someone with steadier, more experienced hands than she.

"I would be grateful for your assistance, Seelie Vaelanseld," said Molly in a velvety smooth voice. Tess tried not to show her surprise, and she thought she saw a flicker of something like anger in Ramel's eyes before he recovered his stoic mask. He silently showed Tess the rune inked on his wrist.

Calliea produced a black grease-stick – or at least that was what Tess called them mentally. Her best guess at its formulation involved charcoal, perhaps some ink, and some sort of tallow. It was a special tool used to inscribe runes on skin, designed to be resistant to water, sweat and dirt. Tess wondered idly whether waterproof eyeliner would hold the rune-magic and almost laughed aloud as she held out her left arm to Calliea. She preferred not to ink the rune over her war markings. Molly slid over to Niall and offered him her milk-pale bare arm…and a small, coy smile. Tess blinked and caught herself before she looked at Ramel to gauge his reaction. If there was trouble in paradise, it would only be made that much worse if they all acknowledged it.

Calliea pressed the rounded point of the grease-stick to Tess's skin. The pressure as she skillfully sketched the rune wasn't painful, but it wasn't entirely pleasant, either. By the time Calliea finished, the black lines were rimmed with red. "Sensitive mortal skin," she murmured, mostly to herself. Tess had to smile a little at that. She looked at her forearm and traced the lines of the rune with her eyes: Calliea had drawn it with bold, thick strokes halfway between her wrist and elbow. The concealment rune was not circular, unlike most of the all-purpose runes that Tess had learned. She couldn't decide if it looked like a serpent, a bird or another creature. Perhaps it was part of its power that she couldn't pin down exactly what it looked like. It was clear enough while she was sketching it, but as soon as the design was complete it shimmied away from her, sliding into different forms beneath her gaze. *It means it's working*, she thought.

Calliea inked a second rune higher up on Tess's arm, above her elbow. "Closer to your heart and your head," the Valkyrie leader explained in a quiet voice. "This one is for clear sight. The concealment rune that the others are wearing won't try to twist your vision with this one counteracting it. And if we come upon anyone else wearing runes, you should be able to see true."

Tess cleared her throat. "Thanks."

"Of course." Calliea gave her a small, encouraging smile that lasted only an instant. She stepped back and turned to Jess, inking the concealment rune on the mortal fighter's arm before stowing her grease-stick in her belt pouch.

With the runes completed, the company gazed at Tess expectantly. She drew back her shoulders. "I'll be the first through the portal.

Niall, you'll be right after me, then Calliea, Jess and Molly, then Ramel to guard our flank. Haze, Forin and Farin, you may go through at any point after me."

Forin saluted her gravely.

"I'll be honest, I don't know what to expect in the mortal world," Tess continued in her quiet, intense voice. The air in the pavilion undulated faster as the Queens quickened the tempo of their chant. "But what I do know is that from this moment on, we are all responsible for each other. We will *all* watch each other's backs and defend against whatever evils the bone sorcerer has prepared to throw against us." She took a breath and forced herself not to look obviously at Niall and Ramel. "And after we defeat the bone sorcerer, I will bring the Lethe Stone back into this world as agreed." She thought she saw a flicker of something cross Niall's face at the mention of the Lethe Stone, but she wasn't sure. In any case, he bowed his head gracefully to her, Calliea nodded, and Ramel gave a curt gesture of understanding. Tess wondered whether Mab had placed some sort of spell on her onetime sword teacher.

But now was not the time to wonder about changing friendships and hurt feelings. Tess turned to the center of the pavilion. The three Queens stood about the silver bowl, their hands raised and palms pressed together, creating an unbroken ring. White smoke rose from the silver bowl, reaching out with sentient tendrils to touch each of the Queens, wreathing their shoulders with silvery ropes of mist. The pace of the Queens' chanting increased again, and an unnatural wind stirred the scarlet drapes at the boundary of the pavilion. Tess thought briefly of the vision of the woman in the scarlet gown, but then she refocused on the present. She'd have to wonder about her vision later.

The Knights standing behind each Queen braced themselves as the wind increased to a gale. The white smoke writhed untouched by the wind. Tess widened her stance and squared her shoulders as she strode toward the Queens. The wind reached a crescendo as the

Queens' voices rose to almost a shout, beautiful and commanding. The white smoke swirled up in two columns on either side of the silver bowl, and a thin spire reached from one column toward the other. The wind sloughed away the smoke to reveal two shining silver columns and a delicate arch uniting them into an unmistakable doorway. The wind slackened, the Queens brought their shouting chant down to a crooning hum, and then there was silence.

Tess gazed breathlessly at the Gate. It was beautiful and beckoning, but her skin prickled with goosebumps as she strode toward it. The air between the columns turned opaque, shadows moving through it every now and again. It reminded Tess of cloudy water and the sleek dark shapes of predators moving beneath the surface. She shivered and touched the hilt of the Sword for reassurance as she became aware of her company moving into alignment behind her as she'd directed. Kianryk padded to her side, his golden eyes fixed on the portal, the scarlet collar a striking contrast to his pale pelt.

Vell leaned over and swept up the silver bowl with two hands, her movements dance-like. Her voice, when she spoke, sounded like there was still a chorus echoing in the reaches of the pavilion. "Lady Bearer, step forward to be marked."

Tess obediently strode over to Vell, her heartbeat increasing steadily as the power of the Gate crackled through the air like lightning through storm clouds overhead. Vell dipped two fingers into the bowl and drew a line down Tess's forehead from her hairline to the bridge of her nose. Vell's fingers were cool, but the liquid felt warm and thick on Tess's skin. Vell marked each of the company, even the Glasidhe and Kianryk, and then placed the bowl back on the ground, dark liquid dripping from her fingers onto the silvery floor.

Another shadow rippled in the opaque pane between the silver columns of the Gate. Tess looked at Vell, who nodded slightly, golden eyes grave. Behind her, Liam gave Tess his own nod and a small smile. She smiled at him in return, then turned to the Gate, took a deep breath, and stepped over the threshold into the strange white mist.

The Gate felt nothing like the portal that had been opened between the Northern mountains and the Queen's camp on the Deadlands. That portal had offered some slow, elastic resistance, like swimming through thicker water. This Gate, though, grabbed Tess and violently threw her into a whirling, hot limbo, spinning and turning her until she stopped her futile attempts at controlling her motion. She grabbed the strap of the Sword at her chest, pressed her elbows into her sides and shut her eyes, every part of her body protesting at the impossibly fast and forceful turns, twists and somersaults as she hurtled through whatever ether filled the space between the worlds. The Queens' blood on her forehead burned her skin. She clutched the leather of the bandolier and tried to breathe in the hot maelstrom. Blinding light and black darkness whirled around her, piercing her eyelids with brutal power.

Just when Tess thought that she couldn't bear any more of the raging tempest, the sense of rushing speed slowed, and the invisible force stopped tossing her about like a hapless rag doll. Before she could open her eyes or take a breath of shuddering relief, gravity took over, and she felt the distinct sensation of being *dropped*. She instinctively protected her head with her forearms, and she landed hard on the ground as if thrown from the sky by a vindictive god. *Or a vindictive Queen*, she thought dizzily, the breath knocked out of her. She gripped the long grass in which she'd landed in both hands, dragging in a long, noisy lungful of hot and humid air. She heard rather than saw the rest of her company being dropped onto the ground. An unhappy yelp told her that Kianryk had made it through, and then indignant Glasidhe voices reached her ears. She rolled to her side and managed to get onto all fours, her head swimming.

A splash and a curse caught her attention. She opened her eyes, shut them unsteadily as the world spun around her, and promptly emptied her stomach into the long grass. As she spat bile disgustedly, trying to clear her mouth of the foul taste, she heard Calliea speaking to the voice that had cursed after the splash. Niall. She swallowed hard and tried opening her eyes again, rewarded this time by significant but manageable vertigo. The Sword's power stirred in her chest, but somehow that made her feel even more nauseous. She stumbled to her feet, took two wobbling steps and lowered to one knee, tears of frustration gathering at the corners of her eyes. If the rest of the company was this sick from going through the Gate, what use would they be against the bone sorcerer?

But when Tess managed to look up, she saw that the Sidhe members of the company seemed a bit shaken but functioning. Calliea supported a soaked Niall, who was grimacing and holding one arm protectively against his side. Molly was talking in a quiet, intense voice to Ramel. Out of all of them, Molly seemed the least affected by the travel through the Gate – perhaps because she was a child of both worlds, thought Tess. Jess, at least, looked a little sick, but he must have already taken care of his vomiting because he stood pale but solid next to Calliea and Niall. His sharp gray eyes traveled over the landscape with practiced speed. Gwyneth's pendant heated against her throat, and Tess hooked a finger through it. Its warmth traveled through her hand and up her arm, helping to banish a bit of the sick feeling spreading throughout her body.

The grass parted and her heart jumped before she realized it was Kianryk. The big wolf inserted himself beneath her free hand. Between the warmth of the pendant and the warmth of the wolf, Tess felt almost steady as she stood again.

That was pretty terrible, she remarked silently to the Sword, but it didn't reply. She swallowed down another wave of nausea.

"We shall scout," announced Farin, her bright voice giving no indication that she was suffering any ill effects from the journey through the portal.

Tess forced a smile. "I expect no less."

"Lady Bearer." The indefatigable Glasidhe saluted her jauntily and zoomed off to join her twin overhead.

Calliea didn't look up from examining Niall's arm, conferencing with him in a low voice. Molly and Ramel stood off to the side, Ramel watching Tess stiffly. Molly caught her eye and gave her a strange, brilliant smile, the stripe of blood down her forehead gleaming wetly. Another moment of vertigo overtook Tess, but not from the journey through the portal – she felt suddenly that she didn't know Molly or Ramel. They seemed like strangers, and now they were here in the mortal world with her. What kind of leader did it make her if she felt such odd detachment from two companions who had once been her friends?

"Well, Lady Bearer, what next?" Niall asked in his smooth, courteous voice, his pale gaze taking in their surroundings. They stood by the banks of a river, the air heavy with moisture and the scent of growth and decay. The sun shone brightly overhead, almost at its noon zenith, but heavy, dark clouds rolled with unnerving speed across the sky toward the sun, and the wind began to pick up as the bright sunlight faded. Tess looked down at Kianryk. She hoped the wolf would still be able to track Luca after the storm…but then again, perhaps he didn't need to track by scent. Already he kept gazing off to the west, whining low in his throat. Vell must have instructed him to stay with the company and lead them to Luca rather than take off on his own through an unknown world.

Thunder rumbled warningly in the distance. "We'll find some shelter from this storm," she said, hoping that Forin and Farin returned quickly. Surveying the horizon, she picked out the flat thread of a road no more than a mile distant. A large, gnarled oak rose in the field of long, swaying grass. They couldn't shelter under a tree during a thunderstorm, but Tess felt drawn to the tree for some reason she couldn't articulate. Calliea must have felt it too: the Valkyrie commander had already struck out toward the tree, her strides quick and sure, and one hand on her coiled whip. Tess followed at a manageable pace, stopping every few moments to take long breaths and push down the bile rising in her throat. No one commented on her strange behavior, but she didn't have the energy to feel grateful.

Jess matched her strides. "Looks like there might be something in the way of shelter up the road to the west," he said to Tess. She nodded, oddly out of breath and feeling like the long grass tried to tangle around her feet to trip her with every step. Calliea, though, had no problem traversing the grassy expanse to the gnarled tree. The Valkyrie commander disappeared from sight for a few long moments under the canopy of the tree's outstretched branches. Then she emerged from the shadowy thicket and bounded back to Tess, springing over the grass with light feet.

"They were here," Calliea said, eyes shining with a fierce hope. "They were here, and they were alive."

Tess used the opportunity to pause, taking long, deep breaths. "How do you know?"

"I spoke to the tree, though its nymph was very slow to awaken," Calliea replied.

"Probably because not many people talk to trees anymore in this world," Tess said.

"The nymph said they headed west," Calliea continued.

"Convenient," remarked Tess, glancing at Jess. "Let's find this shelter off to the west."

Jess gave a single curt nod. "Are we concerned about being seen, or will these magic tattoos take care of all that?"

Tess smiled a little but looked to the Seelie Vaelanseld. "Niall, what do you think?"

"The runes will disguise our true appearance and help discourage curiosity in any mortal," he said, "but they do not render us invisible."

"Pairs, then," said Jess, glancing at Tess for approval but confidence in his voice. "If we go by twos, it'll be easier to conceal ourselves if there's any trouble."

Tess nodded. "Good plan. Keep each other within sight but at a good distance." The group had already coalesced neatly into pairs: Jess at Tess's side, Calliea with Niall, and Molly with Ramel. Kianryk circled in the grass, nose scenting the wind. Thunder rolled through the approaching clouds. Without any further delay, Tess turned toward the road cutting through the grass. Jess stayed a few steps ahead of her, his flinty gaze constantly sweeping their surroundings. The grass swayed in the rising wind and the air smelled like rain.

Tess focused on putting one foot in front of the other. Dizziness still hovered like a cloud around her head, and every time the Sword stirred, a new wave of nausea rippled through her body. She kept their immediate goal in the front of her mind: find shelter from the storm. It shortened into a mantra recited silently in time with her steps. *Shelter from the storm.* Five steps. *Shelter from the storm.* Five more, following Jess, trusting him to find the path. She forced herself not to dwell on the disorienting sickness of passing through the Gate, or the fact that Calliea hadn't fully explained her conversation with the tree nymph. She could think about all that later, when they had found safe haven, both from the storm and the unknown creatures that could lurk in the hours of the night.

Just as they reached the road, Tess spotted the Glasidhe rocketing across the darkening sky. Her boots crunched on the gravel as they began walking along the shoulder of the country road. She stared down at the crumbling asphalt beneath her feet, stepping carefully over a broken beer bottle. The sharp edges of its amber glass glistened like daggers in the fading sunlight.

"Lady Bearer!" Haze bowed with a flourish at eye-level. She blinked as the brightness of his aura swirled into the surrounding air. "There is an abandoned dwelling along this road, a quarter hour as we fly." He flicked his wings. "Forin and Farin have entered it and found no threats, though they remained there to perform a more thorough inspection."

"And what were they gonna do if they found someone inside?" asked Jess.

"If it was a Dark creature, they would kill it," answered Haze seriously, keeping pace with them. "If it was a mortal, they would observe unseen and report their findings."

"You're capable fighters, but size *does* matter, especially in a strange world," Jess told the Glasidhe messenger.

"I shall take your advice into consideration," replied Haze with courtly grace, "as this is your world, and we are but scouts."

Jess glanced at Haze with consideration on his weathered face, but then shrugged slightly and took the Glasidhe's words at face value. He turned his attention back to Tess. "Think you can pick up the pace a little?" Thunder, close enough to shudder through the asphalt beneath their feet, underscored his question.

"I'm in no shape to run, but I can walk faster," said Tess, gritting her teeth and forcing her legs to cover more ground with each stride. Jess nodded and adjusted his own speed. Tess glanced over her shoulder and glimpsed Calliea and Niall walking unconcernedly along the road, heads turned to one another and each one occasionally making a hand gesture to accompany their conversation. She stumbled on a crack in the road as punishment for her distraction. Jess grabbed her arm with a bruising grip to keep her from falling. She winced and thanked him. Somehow she was grateful that he hadn't offered to carry her. Struggling through each step was preferable to underscoring her helplessness.

The first fat raindrops pattered onto the pavement as they drew closer to a shabby doublewide trailer. Tess wondered how Jess had known it existed. Had he spotted it somehow from back near the riverbed? The grass rippled as Kianryk passed them, slinking with predatory intent toward their destination. She tried to quicken her strides as the rain began in earnest, quickly becoming a torrential downpour. Water sluiced down the back of her neck and soaked into her braided hair. Haze landed on Jess's shoulder and the older man raised his cupped hand to shield the Glasidhe from the worst of the rain.

When they reached the trailer, Jess motioned for Tess to wait outside as he slid with practiced ease through the front door, a dagger held ready in his hand. After a moment during which Tess peered miserably into the gray, waterlogged landscape and jumped at a crack of thunder, Jess reappeared and motioned her inside. He offered her his hand when she slipped on the first step, and she took it wearily, sodden and tired. At least she had a dry set of clothes in her pack, she thought as she stood dripping in the dreary interior of the trailer.

"Definitely been empty for a bit, used by squatters here and there," said Jess, surveying the dim dwelling. "But safe enough, and dry."

Tess nodded. Now that her relief from being out of the storm had faded somewhat, she noticed the overwhelmingly musty odor in the trailer. Everything seemed damp from the humidity, water stains darkened patches of the faded floral wallpaper, and mold speckled the tarnished sink. A small table with one chair stood to the side of the kitchenette.

"Tess-mortal, you are soaked through!" said Farin, swooping down from the ceiling. Her bright aura caused a cockroach to scuttle for darker shadows. "You should change into dry clothes," the fierce little scout added solicitously. "I will make sure that none of the men see you."

Tess chuckled. "I'm sure you'll guard my virtue zealously, Farin."

"Only until we find Luca again," Farin replied with a wicked giggle. At that, Tess could only shake her head as she gingerly made her way into the bedroom of the trailer. Farin's aura provided the only light. Tess still felt so sick that the thought of something even as simple as a *taebramh* light, conjured without conscious command in Faeortalam, seemed impossible. Farin seemed to understand her predicament and focused more on providing Tess with ambient light than guarding the doorway.

Tess almost placed her pack on the lumpy bed, but then thought better of it. The floor seemed no better, but then she spotted a folding chair in the corner of the room. She set her pack on it and peeled off her wet clothes, hanging them over the back of the chair for lack of a better alternative. As she pulled on her dry shirt and trousers, she heard the door of the trailer open again. Calliea's voice traveled through the thin walls.

"This is the changing room, eh?" the soaked Valkyrie commander commented a moment later, her grin white in the shadows as she took in the shabby bedroom.

"Something like it," replied Tess with an attempt at a smile.

"It's enough to get us out of the storm," said Calliea. "I'd say I've slept in worse, but I haven't." She chuckled. "Although it's better than draping our cloaks over a tree branch and calling it a tent."

"True." Tess pulled her own cloak out of her pack and checked to ensure that her books were still dry in their oilskin wrapping. She glanced at the concealment rune on her arm; it had stood up to the rain admirably.

"Are you still feeling sick?" Calliea asked, voice muffled as she pulled her shirt over her head. Tess glimpsed the knotted scar on Calliea's side from a poisoned wound taken at Brightvale. She averted her eyes, despite the fact that Calliea was her friend and the *Vyldgard* did not offend easily.

"Yes," she answered honestly. "And it's not just from coming through the Gate. Every time the Sword stirs, I feel like I'm going to throw up."

Calliea made a face in the flickering light of Farin's aura. "That sounds entirely unpleasant. Perhaps it will fade."

"I certainly hope so," agreed Tess. She glanced again at the lumpy bed, the frame broken and the mattress uneven. It looked more appealing the longer she stayed on her feet. The door to the trailer banged on its hinges. Wind howled around the dilapidated structure and rain pelted the dirty windows so hard it sounded as though it was hailing, making Tess glad that Molly and Ramel had made it to shelter. Thunder rolled deafeningly around them.

"Certainly a storm," murmured Calliea. She dug in her pack for a moment and produced a little lantern, lighting it with an old-fashioned wooden match. After setting it on the dusty bedside table, she grinned at Tess. "Don't look so surprised. We prepared for a few different scenarios."

"So this is the girls' room," said Molly brightly from the doorway, her manic delight unhampered by her drenched clothes and soaked hair.

"Looks like it," replied Calliea coolly, surveying Molly.

Tess frowned as she watched Molly. Her last encounter with her old friend at the practice grounds on the journey through the Deadlands had been serious, even somber, where Molly had commented on feeling like a half-mortal castaway, her words accompanied by an enigmatic smile. But this new Molly with a feverish light in her eyes and a too bright grin on her face had eclipsed the Molly in Tess's memory.

The little lantern gave off a flickering golden light. Tess couldn't decide if the light made the room look better or worse. Her bones ached with a strange weariness – it was not the *absence* of the Sword's power, or the expenditure of it, as she'd felt after Brightvale and the Dark Keep. Somehow she felt simultaneously wrung out by the violent journey through the Gate and full from an uncomfortable feeling of expansion. Recognition clicked into place. That was it – *that* was why she felt sick. The Sword's power pressed into her stomach, venturing out past its usual bounds in her chest. She swallowed and wondered if it would go away.

The room stank suddenly of wet dog. Kianryk prowled along the shadowy walls. His blue eyes glowed pale in the lantern light. Tess watched the big wolf move, frowning. The scarlet collar that Vell had fastened around his great neck gleamed, making the dinginess of the room all the more apparent. After completing his inspection, Kianryk ghosted away.

"He looks better already." Calliea gave voice to Tess's thought.

Tess nodded. "I know I should feel relieved, but…" She trailed off and shrugged, wishing suddenly that Liam had accompanied her through the portal. They'd been able to spend more time together in the White City than they'd managed since before Liam completed training and Tess went off to college. Now she felt his absence more keenly than ever.

Farin dipped through the doorway for a moment and then returned, addressing the three women. "The men wish to know if you are all dressed."

Molly finished pulling on her shirt and tossed her wet hair over one shoulder. Calliea observed her with a neutral expression and then nodded to Farin. Jess, Niall and Ramel entered the room, Ramel staying conspicuously close to the door. He remained in his soaked clothing and dark breastplate, coppery hair plastered wetly to his head. Tess tried not to let her gaze linger on her onetime sword teacher – he had always been fastidious in his appearance, to the point of cheerful vanity. What was wrong with the two emissaries from the Unseelie Court? She resolved to ask Calliea her opinion if they found a moment alone.

The thunderstorm raged in spectacular fashion. The wind rocked the trailer slightly during particularly violent gusts, and Tess heard a few leaks dripping through the ceiling as the rain pounded down on the roof.

"Lady Bearer," said Niall, "it seems as though we will be here a few hours at least. If the storm lasts until sundown, I propose that we stay the night."

"Time is of the essence, is it not?" Molly asked in her bright, hard voice. "Why don't we travel at night?"

"Because we are in unfamiliar territory. It would give the bone sorcerer an advantage if we were to meet in terrain that he already knows," Niall replied smoothly.

Molly grinned. "The mighty Seelie Vaelanseld, afraid of the dark?"

Calliea rested her hand on her whip, though Niall merely smiled.

"We do not befriend the darkness, but we do not cower from it," he said. Tess couldn't piece together what he meant, exactly, but it was enough to make Molly's grin fade. Ramel remained strangely silent.

"I agree with the plan to stay here," Jess said. "It would do us all good to get some rest while we can, and I wouldn't travel in a storm like this unless I had to."

"We would not be able to scout in such conditions," Farin contributed.

"I don't like the idea of hunting this mage blind," said Calliea finally.

Tess nodded. "Then we'll wait out the storm here." She looked meaningfully at each member of her expedition. "I know we might not all agree with certain aspects of this journey, but let me make one thing clear: fighting with each other will only make this entire experience more difficult." The Caedbranr's power shifted and she had to pause, swallowing hard. "I'm not going to take the bone sorcerer lightly. Our first priority is to find our three fighters. They're easy targets and from what I've been told, he will most likely try to glean power from them."

"Opening the Gate might have attracted his attention," said Niall.

"It's a possibility," allowed Tess. "In that case, we'd be leading him to the other three, but I still think we'd all be stronger together."

"*We* are stronger together," said Molly. "The others will only weaken us, especially if they are wounded."

"Mind your tongue," said Calliea. "If you're suggesting that we leave our fellow warriors to their fate rather than rescue them, you'd better sleep with one eye open." Her voice trailed into a growl.

"Where is your sense of loyalty?" Niall said to both Ramel and Molly in a low voice.

"I have none," Molly replied, a fierce light in her eyes. "I am a child of two worlds and I belong to neither. No one has any loyalty to me, so why should I return the favor?" She smiled chillingly as she looked directly at Tess.

"We'll stay here for the duration of the storm and possibly the night, and we will scry for both our fighters and the bone sorcerer in the morning," Tess said firmly. She knew Niall had some skill at scrying – nearly all the older Sidhe had honed three or four useful skills in addition to the basics of warfare, and Tess came to understand that the Sidhe Queens did not choose their Three out of caprice or emotion. They all had very concrete talents that each Queen used to her advantage.

Niall nodded gracefully in acknowledgement. "I will take first watch."

"I'll take second," said Jess.

"Third," said Calliea. She looked at Molly and Ramel with hard eyes. "We'll let you know if we need you on the watch. You should probably sleep in another room."

Tess almost intervened, but her skin still crawled from Molly's hostile glare. She beckoned to the observing Glasidhe after the two Unseelie had silently left the room. They hovered about her like a trinity of miniature stars. "Keep a discreet eye on them, please," she said quietly. Farin bared her sharp little teeth, Forin saluted and Haze bowed. Niall left the room to begin his watch by the front door of the trailer, leaving Tess with Jess and Calliea. She sighed and rubbed a hand over her face. This was certainly not the start to this venture that she'd hoped for. Molly seemed determined to set the Unseelie against both the Seelie and *Vyldgard*. No, not merely set them against each other – put them at each other's throats. Why had Mab sent Molly to accompany Ramel in the first place? Merely to stir up trouble for the Bearer?

"Here." Calliea spread her cloak over the lumpy bed. "You should get some rest."

Tess eyed the decrepit, uneven bed suspiciously. "On the one hand, that journey through the Gate was rough. On the other hand, I really don't want to get lice or fleas."

Calliea chuckled. "There are runes for that."

"For warding them off or getting rid of them once I get them?" Tess raised an eyebrow.

"To make sure you don't get them in the first place. At least not while you're sleeping on *this* cloak."

"Aren't you tired?" Tess pulled the strap of the Sword over her head, leaning it against the chair. She thought better of it and laid the battered sheath on the bed.

"Going through the Gate affects us less when we're prepared," Calliea replied with a shrug.

Jess nudged the door of the bedroom shut. "I'm feeling pretty rough, too. Think I'll join you in that nap." He settled down with his back against the door, pulling his ubiquitous tan ball cap down over his face despite the fact that it was wet.

Calliea grinned. "See? You have permission. The tough old salt is taking a nap, too."

Tess shook her head with a smile at Calliea's slang. "You've been hanging around Liam and the others for too long." She slid onto the bed, keeping her boots on and daggers in place, careful to lie only on the portion of the bed covered by Calliea's cloak. She pulled her own cloak over herself as a blanket. Calliea settled cross-legged against the wall by the bed, producing her own small book from her pack. Tess slipped her hand into her belt pouch as she listened to the storm lashing the trailer mercilessly. The river stone imprisoning a piece of Malravenar's spirit felt cool to her touch, and beside it was the silken pouch with the components to Summon the Gate for their return to the Fae world. She tied the pouch shut again and closed her eyes, waiting to slide into sleep.

"Do you trust her?" Calliea's quiet question barely reached Tess's ears.

"I don't know," Tess replied in a voice barely louder than a whisper. She sighed. Between the storm, her sickness and the strange behavior of the Unseelie portion of her company, their expedition into the mortal world had certainly not begun on a promising note. But if she could travel across Faeortalam with a few *ulfdrengr*, an Unseelie Knight defying his Queen, and an inexperienced young navigator, she could find the bone sorcerer in the mortal world and destroy him. One hand reached out and rested on the hilt of the Sword. It warmed beneath her skin, a physical token of its alertness that she'd never felt in Faeortalam. It comforted her. As she slipped into a weary sleep, she finally relaxed enough to feel the tiny thrill of hope that had been hiding behind all her anxiety and adrenaline. Luca was alive, and she would find him. No matter who she had to strong-arm – or destroy – along the way.

Chapter 20

"There'll probably be a storm this afternoon," said Vivian as they trudged through the greenery behind the house. The air hung heavy and humid around them, the sun beating down mercilessly overhead. All of them, even Merrick, were already drenched in varying levels of sweat, though the *Vyldgard* navigator retained his pale complexion and didn't seem to be bothered much by the heat. Duke almost cheerfully resigned himself to sweating through his t-shirts. "Lets me know I'm really back in the South," he drawled with a smile. Ross couldn't help but smile at him as she pulled her ponytail out of the back of her ball cap.

They reached the shed at the edge of the property. Ross opened the door of the shed and began to hand out the heavy, old-fashioned gardening tools that had probably been in the shed for half a century or more. Despite their age, they were well maintained. Merrick took a step back and shook his head when Ross held out a shovel to him. She glanced down at the heavy head of the shovel and realized that it probably contained some amount of iron. Luca took it without a second glance.

"My granddad used to have a big vegetable garden back here," said Vivian as she accepted a trowel. "Even when he got older, he still grew Creole tomatoes. Have to grow them by the river for them to really be true Creole tomatoes." A fond smile appeared on her lips. "They even have a Creole tomato festival in the city."

"They have a festival for everything down here," said Ross with an answering smile.

"Any excuse for a party," agreed Vivian.

Ross disappeared again into the shed and emerged with an armful of tall cans with colorful lids. She adjusted her grip on the cans of spray paint and looked at Merrick. "Does it matter what color?"

Merrick shook his head. "No, not for the initial marking. I'll consecrate it later, after we're done crafting the trap."

"Okay." Ross looked at Vivian. "Are the extra stones from paving the front path in here?"

"No, I gave them to one of the neighbors down the road." Vivian shrugged. "Let's pull up some of the border stones from the garden. They can always be replaced."

"We'll get on that, if you two want to help Merrick with the initial drawing," said Duke, nodding at Luca. The *ulfdrengr* still looked terrible, but he at least stood steadily in the punishing midday heat. "How many you need?"

"Four," said Merrick. Then he quickly held up a hand, thinking. "Make it eight. Cardinal and ordinal points both."

"Points of the compass," said Vivian to Ross.

Ross looked at her friend in consideration. "You're picking all this up faster than I am."

"I read a lot," replied Vivian with a grin. "As opposed to lifting heavy weights and growling at everyone."

"I only growl at some people," Ross clarified, leaning on her shovel. "And they usually deserve it."

Vivian smiled. They watched as Luca and Duke decided which stones would be easiest to extract from the raised garden beds around the house, heading over toward their chosen quarry with shovels over their shoulders.

"Just a moment," Merrick said. "I'll need to decide on the best placement."

"No rush," Vivian said easily. She tossed her trowel next to the cans of spray paint and slid into the narrow shadow at the side of the shed, fanning herself. She wore a floppy-brimmed canvas hat to protect her pale skin in the vicious sun. "Lord, it's hotter than the hinges on the gates of hell today."

Ross laughed aloud. "I'll have to remember that one."

"Yeah, you could use it at the fire station! Speaking of the fire station, how'd the interview go?" Vivian raised her eyebrows.

"Considering the fact that I got a call from Noah five minutes before I walked into the chief's office…I think it went pretty well." Ross made a face. "I should probably give them a call today to let them know that my phone's broken."

"Use my phone and give them my number to call you," said Vivian immediately. "I wasn't supposed to be back for another two days, so they're not expecting me at the shop."

"You're in the running for best friend of the year award," replied Ross, only half-joking. "You came home to blood on the door and strange men in the house and handled it pretty well."

"Oh, *pretty well*? Not *amazingly* or *fantastically*?" Vivian grinned.

"I think the fact that Luca and Merrick are easy on the eyes helped their case," Ross pointed out with a practical air.

Vivian shrugged. "Didn't hurt. Plus, I always liked to think that some of the stories I've read could be true. You know, magic and other worlds and everything." Her voice trailed off dreamily. Then she glanced at Ross. "I'm more surprised that you seem to be accepting it pretty easily."

"Nothing easy about it." Ross shook her head, watching Merrick pace across the back yard, counting his long steps with concentration.

"At first, I just let them *think* I accepted it. It seemed easier at the time. Still does."

"What, you think they belong in the loony bin?" Vivian asked. They could still see Luca and Duke at the side of the house; apparently the easiest stones were located beneath Ross's bedroom window. Or maybe they wanted Merrick to use the stones that the bone sorcerer's lackey had stained with his blood.

"No. Maybe. I don't know." Ross sighed. "It's enough to handle Noah coming back, you know?"

"I'm surprised you can even function, honestly," remarked Vivian. She crouched and began arranging the spray paint cans in a row, sorting them by the order of the colors of the rainbow.

Ross started to reply with sarcasm but then reconsidered. "I am too." She shrugged. "I guess that's just how I am. Something needs to be done, there's a problem that needs to be solved, and that's on the front burner right now."

"As opposed to having a nervous breakdown because your fiancé is back from the dead. Sensible." Vivian nodded and stood up to survey her handiwork. "But really, how's it going to work? He can't hide out here at the house forever. Doesn't he have any family that would like to know he's alive?"

"An older brother and his mom," replied Ross. She'd been thinking about that too. How exactly was Duke supposed to live when he was supposed to be dead? "He hasn't talked to his dad in years, and apparently his home situation wasn't great. He didn't talk about it much."

Vivian hummed thoughtfully. "Well, it's a weird scenario for sure. But better than the alternative."

"The alternative?" Ross didn't follow.

"Him being dead," replied Vivian.

Ross didn't have an answer for that. She felt oddly numb. At random intervals when she glimpsed Noah, she kept remembering snippets of his memorial service: the polished coffin with the

American flag draped over it that really only held a few handfuls of ashes; the somber expressions of the other members of his unit; the murmured condolences whispering about her like moths in the darkness. On that day she'd been frozen in grief, thinking about the last time she'd seen him, the last hug he'd given her on the tarmac before joining the other men in the cargo plane, the last feel of his lips against hers. All of it gone.

She'd done her own research into fires – how hot they burned, how long it took bone to crumble to ash, how long a person could feel pain while they were trapped in a fire. Morbid, but somehow necessary. Somehow it made her feel connected to Noah, trying to understand his last moments. Trying to fathom how it happened, because nobody could explain *why* it happened. She'd been working as a paramedic at one of the firehouses on the outskirts of the city, and the firefighters had patiently answered her questions. Eventually, they'd suggested she become a firefighter, because she seemed so interested in the topic. The first time they'd said it, it had been almost a joke, but they'd gotten serious when they put her through some preliminary drills and understood that she could pull her own weight…literally and figuratively.

Ross watched Duke lever one of the large, flat paving stones up from the ground with his shovel. Did his survival invalidate the pain she'd felt over the past months? Shouldn't her joy over his appearance eclipse her anger? She couldn't make sense of what she was supposed to feel, so it was simpler to…not feel. Gather it all up and squeeze it into the black box in her chest. She had to hand it to her therapist. It was a handy trick once she'd mastered it, although the good doctor had admonished her that it was a tool to cope with things when they became overwhelming, not as a daily ritual.

Merrick strode back over to them. "The larger the rune, the more powerful it is, but I don't want to overextend myself, especially not for this trap. If it goes awry, I want to have some fight left."

"Makes sense." Vivian nodded gravely, as if she discussed the particulars of runetraps during daily business at the coffee shop. "You need a circle for the outer boundary, right?"

"Yes, like on the door," Merrick affirmed. His dark hair curled at his temples, damp with sweat. Vivian held up a hand and disappeared into the shed for a moment. She reemerged triumphantly with a roll of twine and a garden stake, a cobweb caught on one of her curls. Merrick stepped forward and delicately disentangled the dusty strands from her hair. Ross didn't miss Vivian's blush, and she made a mental note to ask Duke if Merrick was spoken for back in his own world.

"We'll drive the stake in the center of your circle," Vivian explained, sounding a little breathless, "and measure out the radius on a length of twine. Then we can tie one of the paint cans to it and – voila!" She grinned.

"It's an idea with merit," said Merrick, nodding slowly. Vivian happily followed him as he showed her where to place the stake. Ross picked up the mallet that they'd both neglected to take along to drive the stake into the ground, following a step behind them. She handed it to Vivian with a little smile when her friend realized the mistake and turned back toward the shed. Merrick and Vivian worked intently on marking the outer circle for the rune; Merrick paced out the length of twine while Vivian finished driving the stake into the ground, and Vivian demonstrated how to work the can of spray paint.

"It won't be a perfect circle," she amended, looking at their setup.

"Perfection doesn't exist. Flaws are always expected in the runes. They're built for it," explained Merrick.

Ross stood by the stake, feeling superfluous. Luca walked toward her with two stones stacked on his shoulder. She raised her eyebrows. For someone who couldn't stand up on his own the day before, the blond giant was still freakishly strong. She wondered about his capabilities when he was fully rested and healthy. Merrick handed over the marking of the outer circle to Vivian, who took over with enthusiasm. The dark-haired elfin man directed Luca to place the stones at the cardinal points of the compass, checking the sun overhead and a strange little device that he kept in a case on his belt.

"I have a compass in the house if you'd like to verify," Ross offered.

"This should be sufficient," said Merrick, carefully wrapping his device and sliding it back into its case. He flashed Ross a quick smile. "But thank you."

Ross nodded with an answering smile, studying Merrick while he directed the construction of the rune circle. He'd explained that just marking the runes, like he'd drawn with chalk on the doorway, was the most basic level of power, but actually constructing them lent another level of permanence and strength to runes, hence why they'd often be carved into a surface like wood, or engraved in metal. And since they lacked the tools to do either of those, he'd settled on carving the runetrap into the earth. That method would also let him expand the physical size of the rune, he added.

Now, in the middle of the project, Merrick looked livelier than Ross had yet seen him, but she watched him with a critical eye. His gray eyes shone with a feverish brightness, and there was a hesitation to some of his graceful movements, as though his joints pained him. Luca had said he was sick because of the cutoff between him and his wolf; was Merrick sick because he had no connection with the Fae world, or was it just a consequence of his being in the mortal world? Ross shook her head.

"Listen to you," she muttered to herself. "You don't even know whether you believe these guys and you're thinking about magical connections between men and wolves." She surveyed the circle that Vivian had triumphantly finished painting in the grass. "And you're building a runetrap in your back yard." She sighed and picked up one of the shovels.

They worked through the punishing heat as the sun rose higher in the sky, beating down on them mercilessly. Vivian disappeared into the house and reappeared with her tube of sunblock, explaining its purpose to Merrick and offering to apply it for him, a cheeky glint in her eye. He courteously declined and went back to supervising the construction of the runetrap. He tried to help dig – gallantly offering to give Vivian a break – but turned pale from just holding the shovel, and after a few feeble shovelfuls, Vivian wrested the shovel back from him. He disappeared behind the shed. Ross grabbed Vivian's arm when she went to follow him.

"Let him keep a little of his dignity," Ross advised her friend in a low voice. She shook her head at Vivian's half-formed protest. "He's not like one of your boys from the city. He doesn't want to be babied."

Vivian sniffed. "The boys from the city are boring compared to him."

Ross rolled her eyes as she dug her shovel into the ground again, maneuvering it around a tough clump of grass roots. "You've known him all of a day, V."

"I'm a very good judge of character," Vivian replied defensively. She swore effusively as she tried to pry up a tangle of weeds.

"Here." Luca walked over, sliding his axe from his belt. Vivian stepped back and watched with wide eyes as the *ulfdrengr* dealt the clump of vexing plants a few decisive blows, his muscles rippling beneath his tight, sweat-soaked t-shirt. He nodded in satisfaction to Vivian.

"Well, you certainly killed those weeds," she murmured, her eyes traveling over his undeniably attractive musculature.

Luca seemed not to hear, sliding his axe back into the loop on his belt after cleaning its edge of dirt. He returned to his sector of the circle, digging with placid determination.

Ross chuckled. "Weren't you *just* singing Merrick's praises?" she teased Vivian.

"There's nothing wrong with looking," Vivian replied. She waggled her eyebrows at Ross.

Ross smiled at her effervescent roommate and then almost unconsciously glanced at Duke. He'd taken off his shirt soon after they started digging, only grinning at Vivian when she offered him sunblock. Now Ross watched him and felt a prickling of desire: his deployment and adventures in another world had done her fiancé's physique good, whittling off the slight beer belly that he sometimes acquired during slack training periods. He wasn't as broad-shouldered as Luca or as slender as Merrick, but Ross liked his sinewy build. Most men towered over her, but he was just the right height, only about half a head taller than her; and just as she preferred his wiry body over more muscular men, he liked her compact, lean muscles, distinct from years of lifting heavy weights to build her strength and keep up with the men.

"Ross and No-ah, sitting in a tree, k-i-s-s-i-n-g," sang Vivian softly, grinning as she dumped another shovelful of dirt to the side of the circle.

Ross shook her head but smiled as she refocused on digging. Count on Vivian to dredge up some childhood rhymes to underline the humor in their situation. "Pretty sure *you* want to 'sit in a tree' with a certain elf," she said slyly in a low voice as they sliced their shovels into the dirt.

"I'm fairly certain he doesn't like being called an elf," replied Vivian with elegant disdain.

Ross shrugged. "I'm still waiting to find out that his ears are just really good prosthetics like they use in the movies."

"I could feel them to make sure they're real," Vivian suggested with a giggle.

Wiping the sweat from her face with one forearm, Ross rested her foot on her shovel and inspected her hands for blisters, not that it would deter her from finishing the task. "Let me know how that turns out for you."

"Is that a *dare?*" Vivian cocked her head to one side, grinning.

"Sometimes I think you're still thirteen," said Ross with a chuckle.

"I'll take that as a yes. Challenge accepted." Vivian went back to shoveling, glancing at Merrick every so often with a calculated look in her eye. He didn't seem to notice, completely absorbed in the construction of his runetrap. Since he couldn't dig with the shovels, he took a can of spray paint and attempted to sketch a rune on the first of the eight flat paving stones that Luca and Duke had pried up from the landscaping. A gust of wind interrupted his precise gestures, scattering the paint. He stopped, frowned and flipped the paving stone over onto its clean side, but then he looked at the can of spray paint with mistrust.

Ross leaned on her shovel, tucking a sweat-soaked tendril of hair behind her ear. "I have a paint brush and some regular paint, I think."

Merrick looked at her with relief. "Thank the gods. I was about to use my own blood."

She narrowed her eyes. "I hope you're joking."

"Not in the slightest," he replied calmly. He accepted the brush and a half-full little can of paint gratefully, waving Ross away when she apologized for not having any paint thinner or brush cleaning supplies.

They finished digging the circle as Merrick finished painting the last flat rock. Ross collected the shovels and Vivian disappeared inside the house. Mayhem bounded through the grass, greeting Ross before sniffing her way around the freshly dug circle. Duke pulled his shirt back on and convinced Luca to sit with him in the short shadow of the shed. Ross found one of Mayhem's rattier tennis balls in the long grass and idly threw it for the dog, tossing it almost across the large yard.

"You shouldn't let her overheat," said Vivian, walking back to them bearing a pitcher and large plastic cups.

"She'll be fine. She's been in Afghanistan and Iraq, with a lot more gear on than this."

"Yeah, well, so have you, but that doesn't mean you can't get heat stroke," Vivian replied, holding out a plastic cup to Ross. She poured ice water into it with the skill of a seasoned waitress. Ross had to admit that the sound of the ice cubes filling her cup was quite appealing.

"You are an angel sent from the good Lord above," said Duke as Vivian poured him water, his Southern twang coming through strongly as it often did when he was laying on the charm. "Second only to my lovely fiancé over there." He toasted Ross with his cup. She chuckled, drinking her water as Mayhem bounded after the airborne tennis ball.

Luca accepted his water with sincere thanks. He drank a few large swallows and poured a good portion of the rest over his head. Merrick mused aloud about runes to keep water frozen so that they could have ice-cold water with these strange cubes in his world as well. Ross finished her water and glanced up at the sky: the wind was picking up and the air felt heavy.

"What else do we need to dig, Merrick? And will this hold up in a downpour?" She thought of having to dig the whole runetrap over again. Her arms and back protested as she picked up a shovel again.

Merrick hastily finished his glass of water and swept up the spray paint that he'd abandoned for the runes on the stones. He drew a series of straight and curved lines in the circle. Ross tried to visualize the rune in her mind's-eye, but she couldn't seem to hold the image in her head. She shrugged slightly. It didn't matter if she knew what it looked like. All that mattered was that it worked – and even that she wasn't sold on. But it was better than sitting dejectedly in the house, waiting for another attack.

"Once I seal the lines, the soil will resist erosion," said Merrick as he stepped outside the circle. "Just these lines left to dig, and I'll seal it."

Luca, Duke, Vivian and Ross each took one of the lines inside the circle. The wind plucked at Ross's shirt and tossed Vivian's curls as they worked quickly, both of them glancing up at the sky every few minutes. Dark clouds gathered at the seam of the eastern horizon, still distant. Mayhem settled down in the long grass, watching them and panting.

They heard the rumble of thunder as the men finished their lines and went to help with the small remaining work. Ross almost snapped at Duke that she could finish it herself, but the approaching dark clouds made her swallow the words and her pride. Vivian and Luca finished her line, and Duke and Ross finished shortly afterward. Ross and Vivian each took two shovels and put them back in the shed, Mayhem trotting after them. Wind whipped around them as they locked the shed and turned back to the circle. Ross stopped and grabbed Vivian's arm. "I think we should stay back here," she said, watching Merrick drawing a dagger from its sheath at his waist.

"He's not going to hurt us," replied Vivian sensibly, pulling free of Ross's grasp. "Besides, you don't believe in the mumbo jumbo, right? I want to watch from a closer spot."

Merrick had already started murmuring an incantation. Vivian walked over to Luca and Duke.

"What's he doing now?" she asked Luca in a low voice.

Luca looked at the pale redheaded girl and smiled a little at her incessant curiosity. She was certainly a different creature than her reserved and practical roommate. "He is activating the rune and sealing it."

Merrick drew the dagger across his left palm in a sharp motion. Vivian winced. "With blood," she stated.

"Yes. If we were in our own world, there would be other ways, but blood is certain," replied Luca.

She narrowed her eyes. "His blood isn't red. It's…it looks *blue*."

"A difference in the Sidhe body. They are not made as mortals or Northmen," replied Luca. He looked like he was about to say more, but then stopped. Vivian glanced at him but remarkably didn't press him for more. Instead, she looked back to Merrick thoughtfully.

"Can it be anyone's blood?" she asked.

"Willingly given, yes," he said. He could see the calculation on her face. "It isn't much blood," he said, "and this is not the first time that Merrick has sealed his work in this way."

Vivian pressed her lips together and folded her arms over her chest but stayed put. The wind knocked her canvas hat askew. She muttered curses as she tried to pull it down on her head and eventually just tore it off, the wind playing gleefully with her mane of corkscrew curls.

"You remind me of a Sidhe warrior who became *Vyldgard*," Luca said. "Her name is Moira."

"Moira," repeated Vivian. "She's a good fighter?"

"One of the best," he replied, watching Merrick walk the perimeter of the runetrap, murmuring softly and scattering blood from his closed fist.

Vivian tried not to show that she was flattered, but she felt her face grow hot with a blush of pleasure. "Do you think…maybe you could teach me to fight like her?"

Luca chuckled. Her blush turned to one of mortification. She felt gangly and awkward. Of course this golden-haired Viking demigod wouldn't teach *her* to fight.

Luca realized that Vivian had taken his chuckle as ridicule. "Yes, you remind me of her. You're eager." He nodded, still smiling. "I will see what I can make of you, given the time that we have."

For once, Vivian was speechless. She swallowed down her excitement and turned her attention back to Merrick. He had moved on to the rune in the center of the circle, leaving himself an exit point in the perimeter. Strange silvery steam began to rise from the runetrap as he finished tracing the center design; when he stepped out of the circle and completed it with his blood, a silent explosion and burst of hot wind made them all stagger. Vivian blinked at the ringing in her ears. Then she felt the earth begin to shake beneath her feet. She looked with eyes round as saucers at Merrick.

"What did you do?" she shouted above the sudden wind and the roaring in her head. She couldn't hear his answer – he shook his head and his lips moved, but it was as if sound didn't exist anymore. In this white silence, Luca collapsed beside her. Duke awkwardly caught him as he fell, ended up going to a knee and then lowering the big man to the ground. Ross sprinted toward them from her vantage point by the shed, giving the steaming runetrap a large berth. She grabbed swaying Merrick and pulled him away from his creation. The silver steam turned black and the grass nearest the runetrap shriveled away, charred.

The ground shook for what seemed an eternity, but it couldn't have been – Vivian couldn't hear her own breathing, but she could feel her heartbeat thumping in her chest as she took Merrick from Ross. Everything seemed slow and ponderous. Each pause between her heartbeat felt like minutes. She didn't even feel any excitement at the touch of her bare skin on Merrick's as she grabbed him around the waist to keep him from falling. Her head ached – pressure built, and the ground shook, and then there was relief like slicing into a blister, strange and painful but undeniably better. Sound rushed back. Ross and Duke were yelling, trying to claw through the void of silence by brute force. They stared at each other and stopped, stunned at the sudden volume of their own voices. Vivian became very aware of Merrick's labored breathing, his arm over her shoulder, and her hand about his waist.

Ross made a strangled sound of disbelief and sat back on her hands. Vivian followed her gaze and couldn't hold back her own gasp: Luca was *glowing*. Not in the way that someone said a bride glowed on her wedding day or a new father glowed as he held his child for the first time. He was *physically emitting light*. Vivian swallowed hard and felt a crazy smile starting to overtake her face as she drank in the sight. If Merrick's runetrap hadn't convinced her, the vision of Luca shining like one of those illustrations of a saint rising heavenward cemented her willingness to believe in their fantastic story. She tore her eyes away and glanced at Ross, who stared transfixed with a mingled expression of shock and a strange relief.

The aura emanating from Luca quickly faded. Duke stood up, rubbed the back of his neck and watched the *ulfdrengr* warily. Luca opened his eyes and sat up. He no longer looked haggard and worn. The circles beneath his eyes had disappeared, and his icy blue eyes seemed more vibrant than just moments before. He flexed his hands, took a deep breath and stood, the simple movement conveying supple strength. Thunder rumbled overhead, closer now. He looked at each of them in turn: Ross and Duke, then Vivian, and lastly Merrick, still leaning on Vivian for support.

"A Gate was opened," Luca said. Merrick's breath hitched as a desperate hope surfaced in his eyes. "A Gate was opened," repeated Luca, rubbing his hands over one another as though to assure himself that his renewal was real. "And Kianryk is now in the mortal world."

The sky darkened and fat raindrops began to fall around them, breaking their collectively astounded trance. Ross appeared on Merrick's other side, and between them they managed to get him quickly across the yard to the house, reaching the door just after it began to pour in earnest. The dark-haired Sidhe collapsed onto the couch.

"Why are you better and he isn't?" demanded Vivian, looking at Luca desperately. While Luca looked sound and whole, Merrick's condition had worsened with the sealing of the runetrap. A gray pallor lurked beneath his pale skin, his lips tinged with blue.

"I don't have a wolf in the mortal world," replied Merrick with an attempt at a smile.

"You're still bleeding," said Vivian, touching the hand that Merrick still clenched in a fist. He didn't reply but laid his head back wearily as she spied the first aid kit in the corner of the living room and swooped down on it.

Ross checked the lock on the door and leveled a severe look at Mayhem when the dog shook the rain from her coat. The Malinois merely grinned innocently at her and loped over to Luca. "So what do we do now?" she asked the room at large.

"Every creature with any sense of our world within hundreds of leagues will have felt that Gate opening," said Merrick, obediently opening his clenched fist for Vivian. He winced as she dabbed at the cut gently with gauze, glancing surreptitiously at the dark blue blood.

"Yes." Luca nodded. He grinned and Ross realized how very wolf-like he looked with his teeth bare and gleaming. "Kianryk will not have crossed into this world alone. He is a wolf, after all." Luca's pale eyes flashed with humor.

"You think Tess is here with him?" asked Duke.

Luca laid one of his hands flat against his chest. "Yes. I feel it here."

"How convenient," remarked Ross dryly. She ignored the reproachful look from Duke. "Nobody has answered my question yet. What do we do now?"

"Now we wait," said Luca.

"Wait for what?" Vivian asked, looking up from fitting a clean square of gauze over Merrick's hand.

"We wait to see who reaches us first," said Luca. "The Bearer, or the bone sorcerer."

They all absorbed this announcement. Then Ross rubbed her face and sighed lightly. "I don't know about you, V, but I need another beer." She headed toward the fridge, thinking that perhaps a nice, cold beer would take her mind off being the bait in a trap for a psychotic wizard. It was already shaping up to be an interesting day, and she was fairly sure that they still had time for more craziness before it was over.

Chapter 21

"I need to speak to the Bearer." The voice was low, almost frantic. Tess didn't recognize the speaker immediately, the fog of sleep still shrouding most of her senses.

"She's sleeping." Calliea used her carefully neutral voice.

"I know," came the first voice again, this time tinged with something like desperation. "And I'm sorry to wake her, but I need to speak to her when *she* is asleep."

"First of all," Calliea replied, her voice closer to a growl now, "you're not making any sense. And second of all, it looks like sleep is the only thing that might help the Bearer…recalibrate. So we intend to let her have as much of it as she needs."

"You don't understand. *Please*. This isn't what you think. It's not what any of you think. I *need* to talk to her."

Tess stirred. If someone needed to see her that badly, she might as well oblige them – they'd awoken her already. She opened her eyes and blinked fuzzily: with the dissipating gossamer threads of sleep still entwining her mind, she *thought* she saw bits of *taebramh*, small and featherlike, drifting in an invisible wind that funneled the glowing silver specks down to her skin. And she thought she felt them, each one a tiny spark of warmth like the opposite of a snowflake hitting her skin. But then she blinked and her vision cleared. Rain still lashed the sides of the trailer and wind howled around the windows.

"Who is it, Calliea?" she asked in a rusty voice as she sat up. Her muscles ached as though she'd trained for hours with Luca, but it was a better kind of discomfort than the sickness she'd felt right after coming through the Gate. She brushed her fingers against the sheath of the Sword, still propped against the broken headboard. The Caedbranr warmed to her touch and *fawned* beneath her hand. She felt the liquid heat of the silky pelt it wore when it appeared as a primal wolf.

Calliea turned slightly from her post by the door. "It's Molly. She says she needs to speak with you."

"Yes, I heard that." Tess nodded as she took a deep breath. She didn't feel like vomiting every five seconds, so that was an improvement.

"But she is not making very much sense," Calliea said, tilting her head.

"If you let me in, I can explain," Molly said from the other side of the door.

Tess rubbed one hand over her face and glanced around the room. She wasn't *afraid* of Molly, but she still had the uneasy feeling that something wasn't right with her friend.

"Jess is on watch," Calliea said. "I'm staying."

"Sounds like a good plan. Let her in." Tess stood as Calliea opened the door slightly, forcing Molly to slide against the wall to enter the room. The Valkyrie commander took two steps back and settled one hand on her coiled whip, watching Molly dispassionately.

Molly shut the door with a soft click. She'd grown her hair long during her time in the Fae world, wearing it in a braid over her shoulder; Tess watched her friend for the manic grin or strange flash in her gaze, but Molly seemed…afraid. She moved with Sidhe grace but her cat-like eyes darted around the room, peering into the shadows, as though waiting for a trap to be sprung.

"Molly," Tess said, trying to make her voice calm and reassuring. "What's wrong?"

Thunder rumbled overhead and a particularly strong gust of wind shook the trailer. Molly jumped and glanced nervously at the window, licking her lips.

Tess frowned. "Molly?"

"What do you know that we do not?" Calliea asked in a low voice, stepping toward Molly again.

"I…give me a moment." Molly put up a hand as though to ward off a blow from Calliea. "Please. I need to explain to the Bearer…to…Tess." She turned and looked at Tess with wide eyes. After a moment of silence, she took a deep breath and said, "I remember. I have my memories back."

It took a moment for Tess to absorb the meaning of Molly's words. When they finally sank into her brain, she found herself grinning despite the strangeness of the situation. "Molly! That's amazing…isn't it?" Her smile faded as Molly shook her head, looking over her shoulder at the door again.

The dark haired, half-mortal girl took a few steps toward Tess. Calliea slid sideways, staying between Molly and Tess, her delicate face hard with purpose. Tess moved to wave Calliea away, but Molly began talking in a low voice, words tumbling out of her so fast that it took all of Tess's focus to understand them.

"Tess, she's punishing Ramel. He found a way to restore my memories, but he couldn't find a way to help the princess. Mab is slipping. She's resorting to…to methods that are cruel even for her." Molly took a breath and plunged on, her pale face earnest in the darkness. "She's paranoid. She began to think that I was a threat. I thought she was going to have me killed, Tess. This was my ticket out."

"So you've been acting crazy to seem like less of a threat to Mab?"

Tess asked slowly, the pieces of a strange puzzle finally beginning to take shape in her mind.

"Yes and no," Molly said quickly. "I don't know how much time I have, she only allows him to sleep when *she* sleeps, and if we are not asleep when that happens, then he doesn't get to sleep at all." A flash of anger crossed her face, erasing the fear for an instant. "It's monstrous, even for her."

"When you say 'she,'" said Calliea, "you mean Mab?"

"Yes." Molly nodded.

Tess felt her stomach drop, and this time the nausea wasn't from the Sword's expanding power. The image of Ramel in his light-swallowing dark armor and lifeless eyes flashed in her mind. "What has Mab done to Ramel?"

"I don't know exactly," Molly said, her words tumbling over one another, "but it has something to do with his armor, I think." She grimaced. "Whatever it is, she's spying on us. She's controlling him. He fought against her enough to warn me once. I don't think she realized that he'd been able to tell me anything, but it was enough that I understood him." She took a shuddering breath. "And...that's not all."

"Of course it isn't," muttered Tess. Aloud, she said, "What else is there?"

"As the price for my passage through the Gate, Mab gave me a mission." Molly grabbed her own elbows, hugging herself in an abrupt movement.

Calliea narrowed her eyes. "To retrieve the Lethe Stone for her?"

Molly shook her head. "No. But please...I never *meant* to do it. I only agreed to be free of her. I only said yes because it was the only way out."

Tess's stomach sank even further. "So what's this mission?" Her voice came out flat and cold.

Molly looked at her with a plea written across her pale face. "After you defeat the bone sorcerer and the Lethe Stone is in our possession, I'm supposed to kill you."

Tess didn't see Calliea move, but the Valkyrie commander suddenly gripped Molly by the throat, pinning her up against the wall with a dagger pressed to her ribs. Molly didn't move to defend herself, wheezing, "If you kill me, Ramel will do it."

"Then I'll kill him too," snarled Calliea, a savage light in her eyes.

"That's what she wants," choked Molly.

"Let her down," said Tess sharply. Calliea tensed and stared at Molly for another moment, but then released her grip and backed away. Molly dropped to her knees, coughing.

Tess took a step closer to Molly. "Why is that what Mab wants?"

Molly coughed and swallowed. She looked up at Tess, a few tendrils of dark hair escaping her braid and draping across her face. Her voice was a hoarse whisper. "Mab wants war."

"Why?" pressed Tess. "We just finished a war. The Unseelie Court lost as many as anyone. Why would Mab want another war?"

"She's afraid she's losing control," Molly whispered. Her eyes darted between Tess and Calliea. "She's afraid. She's afraid that with the *Vyldgard*, more of her people will realize that there are other ways to live. She's afraid that there will be another uprising."

A thrill coursed through Tess. "Another uprising like the one that ended with the Exiled being cast through the Gate."

Molly nodded. "And it might be true." She winced as she swallowed, standing unsteadily.

Tess took a deep breath. "So...you've been acting insane to try and throw Mab off your scent. You agreed to kill me as price for your passage to the mortal world." She shook her head. "And Ramel is somehow even more of a spy for Mab than one of her Three usually would be?"

"She's using him as her own eyes and ears," whispered Molly, casting another terrified glance at the closed bedroom door. "She's *controlling* him."

Calliea murmured an oath.

"How?" asked Tess brusquely.

Molly jumped at the sudden change in tone and wrung her hands together nervously. "I…I'm not entirely sure."

"Why should we believe you?" Calliea said in a low voice.

Molly straightened and her eyes flashed. "Why would I lie about something like this?"

Calliea shrugged one shoulder. "I don't know. But I don't know you and I don't trust you."

Molly turned back to Tess, her eyes glimmering too brightly in the shadows. "Please, Tess. Please believe me. I don't know how, but Mab is controlling Ramel and if she finds out that I've told you anything, she'll probably force him to kill me."

"And then kill me," Tess said grimly. The Sword's power circled in her chest. She rubbed at her breastbone with the heel of one hand. "I don't understand why Mab wants to start another war, but then again I've never fully understood Mab anyway."

"There's talk…within the Court, that she *is* going mad," Molly whispered.

"I wish I could send a message to Vell," Tess said, almost to herself. "But if I open the Gate without the Lethe Stone, Mab will just say that I've broken my word and use that as leverage to start a conflict too." She pressed her lips together and then took a deep breath.

"So what do we do?" Calliea asked Tess, her hand still resting lightly on her coiled whip.

"We continue with the mission. We don't let Ramel or Molly stand watch." Tess raised a hand at Molly's half formed protest. "If Mab is watching through Ramel…that means that I can't act as if I know anything is wrong. So keep on doing the crazy act and sowing discontent."

Calliea snorted softly. "That doesn't take much effort."

"And being courteous doesn't take much effort either," returned Molly with a rebellious flare.

"I don't make a habit of treating insane traitors with courtesy," said Calliea, smiling coldly.

"Enough," said Tess. She leveled a hard look at Calliea. "Even if you don't trust her, you know that she's in a difficult position. Try to be more understanding."

The Valkyrie commander had the grace to look slightly chastened. "Aye, Lady Bearer," she said with reluctant repentance.

"I need you to help me watch Ramel, in any case," continued Tess.

"Niall should know," said Calliea.

"As long as it's made clear that it is *not* an alliance against the Unseelie, or anything of that sort." Tess shook her head. "If Mab is controlling Ramel, physically controlling him, then I want to figure out how to break the spell."

Calliea opened her mouth, then thought better of whatever she was about to say and settled for a vaguely disapproving look.

"I didn't want to ask that of you," said Molly softly, "but...Tess, I'm in love with him. That's part of why I made the deal." She swallowed. "Mab was already going to send Ramel. This way, at least I'm here...at least I could tell you." Her eyes caught the dim light of the flickering lantern, wide and beseeching. "Please believe me, Tess. I'm not going to kill you." Molly's face settled into a determined expression. "Even if she kills me, I'm not going to kill you."

"I won't let her kill you, and I won't let her kill Ramel, either," Tess said. The Sword rumbled in her chest as the words left her lips.

Molly smiled sadly. "Thank you for saying it. I know that it's a long shot, but I can't leave him."

Tess smiled in reply. "I know a thing or two about being stubborn when it comes to the man you love."

After a short moment of silence, Molly said, "I should get back. If I'm not there when he wakes up, it might go badly for him."

Tess wanted to ask what exactly Molly meant by that. Would Ramel hurt her? Had Ramel already been hurting her? She felt sick at the thought of her cheerful friend being forced to lay hands on the woman he loved. But before she said anything, Molly darted away, sliding through the cracked door and moving quietly down the hallway of the trailer.

Calliea relaxed, her hand leaving her whip. Her heart-shaped face was grave as she looked at Tess. "It's not easy to accept, but you can't save everyone."

"What kind of person would I be if I didn't try?" Tess replied wearily, sitting on the bed again. "Molly used to be my best friend…if she has her memories back, she's the Molly that I knew before I became the Bearer. That should mean something."

"History doesn't always mean something, just as friendship doesn't always mean something," Calliea said.

"When did you become such a misanthrope?" Tess asked.

Calliea frowned slightly and then sighed. "Probably after seeing so many good warriors die in the battle for our freedom. Or what we thought was our freedom."

Tess thought for a moment, trying to ignore the prickling of the Sword's power in the spaces between her vertebrae. The expansion didn't make her feel sick anymore. The comment she'd overheard from Calliea made sudden sense. Her body was adjusting to this new world and new power as she slept. She brought her thoughts back to the conversation. "Have you heard of the Exiled, Calliea?"

Calliea looked at her for a long moment and then nodded. "Yes. I have heard the tales of the Exiled. And the rebellion."

"Do you think they were right to rebel?" Tess watched her friend carefully. The Sword went still, seeming to listen for the answer.

"In a sense, yes," said Calliea. "But I have what measure of freedom I wish within the *Vyldgard*. The *Vyldretning* will not abuse her power. I place my full faith and trust in her. And in you."

"Is joining the *Vyldgard* seen as an act of rebellion?"

"Not in the strictest sense," said Calliea slowly, "because it is the High Queen's Court. It is rooted in the First Queen's power that Vell is owed the choice of willing warriors from the two Courts. Perhaps in the future it will be different, if we can have children within the *Vyldgard*."

"But Mab resents her warriors choosing to go to the *Vyldgard.*"

"Mab has always been a jealous Queen."

"And Titania?" Tess asked. She thought of the battle at the Dark Keep, when the kind and loving exterior of Titania evaporated into a fierce, battle hardened fighter. Did the same jealousy simmer beneath the Seelie Queen's beautiful visage?

"Titania is as good to her subjects as she seems," said Calliea with a rueful smile. "I felt a bit guilty about leaving, to be honest."

"You felt called to be one of the *Vyldgard*," replied Tess. "It's only right that you follow that calling."

"True. But…what's that mortal expression…biting the hand that feeds you?" Calliea raised an eyebrow. "It felt a bit like that."

"Titania was the one who brought me to the Saemhradall," Tess said with a slight smile at the memory.

"I think it was a test," said Calliea. "She was surprised that you saved me. I think that truly made her believe that you were chosen to be the Bearer."

Tess frowned. "Titania *wanted* me to save you. Why else would she have brought me there?"

"Revenge is a powerful motivator, is it not?" Calliea asked calmly. "If you had watched the monsters slaughter me while you were helpless to stop it, you would have leveled the Dark Keep to compensate for your failure to save me. Which is what happened anyway." She smiled. "I'm grateful that you pulled your blade out of thin air and gave me a fighting chance. But I guess what I'm saying is that it would have served Titania's purpose whether I lived or died."

"That's…incredibly callous," Tess said, searching for words.

"It's brutal, but ruling the Courts has never been easy."

"Brutality seems to be a common theme between both our worlds." Tess rubbed one hand over her face.

Calliea sat down beside her on the bed. "I never thought I'd be a warrior," she said quietly, staring at the flickering lantern and the shadows dappling the water stained walls. "But sometimes the path is already laid before our feet, and we only need to take the first step. I'm glad that I could make a difference in the battle."

"Wouldn't it be different if Mab and Titania went to war against each other?" Tess asked. "Killing monsters is one thing. Killing Sidhe is another."

"Brother against brother," agreed Calliea grimly. "It has almost come to war before, but we've always managed to step back from the brink."

"Like when the rebels were exiled?"

"Like when the rebels were exiled." Calliea nodded. "There's always a price to pay."

"But what price is too high?" Tess murmured, almost to herself.

Calliea sighed. "I wish I knew, Tess." She stood and walked back over to the door, settling against the wall and extending one leg across the threshold so that any attempt to enter the room would also alert her. "I think the best thing now is to get more rest. I'll talk to Niall tomorrow."

"I'll talk to Jess," Tess said. "Just so that he's on the same page with everything. I don't think he much cares about Sidhe politics anymore." The emerald in the pommel of the Sword blinked at her as she rearranged the cloak on the bed. Though her mind whirled with questions about Molly and Ramel, she slid surprisingly quickly into sleep. As her eyes closed, she thought she saw small, glowing flakes of *taebramh* appearing in the air about her, swirling like snow, but then sleep claimed her and she drifted into a dreamless slumber, the rain and thunder her lullaby.

Tess woke again to a strange tingling in her right arm. She blinked the sleep from her eyes and rubbed at her skin – it felt like when the Sword had marked her with her war markings in the Royal Wood, its power biting into her skin like the sting of a tattoo gun. She noticed the silence as she sat up. The storm had passed, and the weak gray light of early dawn seeped through the less blemished portions of the dirty window. Then why were the shadows so sharp on the wall beside her, every detail of the broken headboard thrown into sharp relief? She realized belatedly that her war markings glowed hotly through her shirtsleeve, and the Caedbranr's emerald swirled with a fierce, bright light. As the sleep faded from her mind, her war markings faded into a less intense luminescence, pulsing slightly with her heartbeat.

"Oh, good. You're awake," said Calliea. "You're like a miniature sun when you sleep now. Or maybe a star would be a more apt comparison."

"What?" Tess asked. Why did everyone insist on bombarding her with riddles in the first five minutes of waking up?

"You have an aura!" pronounced Farin, leaping from the small nightstand into the air. "But only when you sleep."

Tess frowned slightly…and then she remembered the strange bits of glowing *taebramh* drifting around her as she let sleep swallow her. She experimentally reached for her *taebramh* and jumped off the bed in surprise as a roaring inferno greeted her. Sparks crackled from her war markings – real sparks – singeing their way through her sleeve. The Caedbranr's power swirled around her well of *taebramh* and helped compress it into a smaller whirlwind. "Thanks," Tess gasped.

"So I take that little display to mean that you're back at full power?" Calliea asked, looking at the little scorch marks on the floor where the sparks had showered down from Tess's arm.

"More than full power," Tess replied. "I think I've been…*absorbing taebramh* while I was asleep."

Calliea nodded. "Yes. It looked a bit like snow."

"Or tiny feathers," contributed Farin.

"How?" Tess shook her head. She reached out silently to the Sword. *This would be a great time to explain something to me for once.*

The Caedbranr's reply knocked the breath from her chest. Its voice was deeper, more resonant and layered. *You seem to imply that I have not been gracious in helping you.*

Tess sucked in a breath. *So we get supercharged and you get cheekier. Fantastic.*

You do not need me to explain something so simple, said the Sword, its power twining around her spine.

Tess blinked. She let her mind absorb the facts, mull them over, and then she smiled slowly. *Taebramh is the stuff that gives mortals dreams. I just came into the mortal world, with billions of mortals dreaming every night.* A little thrill of foreboding shivered through her as she thought of the sheer numbers of people in the world. *What happens if I can't hold all the taebramh? It won't just keep filling me until I…explode, will it?*

Don't be ridiculous, admonished the Sword in a somewhat bored voice. *You are merely the conduit. You will balance the flow between your world and Faeortalam.*

But there's not a Gate, she returned silently.

There is – in you. *You are the connection between the two worlds right now. The pressure might lessen if the Queens build another Great Gate, or something more permanent than their silly revolving door.*

"Great," muttered Tess. She took a deep breath and smiled at Calliea and Farin. "Apparently I'm the filter for all the *taebramh* flowing from the mortal world into the Fae world now."

Calliea grimaced. "That sounds uncomfortable."

Tess chuckled. "A little. But if it gives me the juice we need to blast this bone sorcerer, I'm alright with it."

"And you look quite beautiful when you are glowing and sleeping," added Farin seriously.

"That helps, too," Tess allowed with a smile. Somehow the revelations of the night didn't seem as dire with this molten stream of *taebramh* flowing through her. "All right, let's gather everyone for our morning meeting."

"Niall took another watch. It seemed like you needed a bit more sleep," said Calliea.

Tess smiled. "More time to soak up *taebramh*. But I think from here on out, I'll be fine with our usual traveling schedule." She stood and slipped the strap of the Sword over her head. "Time to go see where this bone sorcerer is lurking."

Chapter 22

The clash of metal on metal echoed throughout the practice yard. Finnead leapt away from a sweeping sword, bringing his own blade up to counter with a strong, fast stroke. His feet danced lightly over the packed dirt as he avoided another onslaught, his dark hair curling at his temples, damp with sweat. The air pressed in around him as his opponent launched a savage attack – three crisp strokes and Finnead stumbled, the Brighbranr wavering in his hand as he felt the cold sting of the tip of a blade digging into the soft base of his throat.

"Where is your head?" snapped Vell, her golden eyes flashing as she lowered her blade. She shook her head and pointed her sword at Finnead. "Stop thinking about her and *focus*."

Liam and Gray watched from just outside the circle, having just finished their own preliminary bout. Liam suspected that the remnant of Arcana had given him some skill with a blade, but he still wouldn't call himself evenly matched with Gray. She still had the edge on him when it came to experience and strategy, and her body slid with fluid, unconscious grace through the movements that Liam still found challenging. Usually, Finnead presented a challenge to

Vell in swordplay. Whereas the *ulfdrengr* were skilled at various forms of combat – from bow to axe to sword and any weapon in between – the Sidhe knight had been trained for centuries in the art of wielding a sword. So Vell usually matched herself against Finnead when she was fresh, then Gray and then Liam.

"The Queen is not happy this morning," Gray murmured to Liam. One of the Glasidhe spies had reported to Vell that he'd caught the barest hint of an assassination plot against the Bearer in the murmurings of the Unseelie Court. The High Queen had gone white with rage. She'd silently buckled her sword about her waist, grabbed the leather jerkin she wore for practice and stormed from the palace. Her Three followed, having quickly learned that the *Vyldretning* vented her fury through the physical strain of the practice ring. Target shooting with her bow sufficed when she was merely annoyed with the courtesies of Court life, but real anger required swordplay. The practice yards usually emptied at the first warning of the High Queen's fury. The *Vyldgard* weren't cowards, but they weren't fools, and no one was eager to place themselves in the *Vyldretning*'s path when she was angry. The violent clash of blade on blades usually mollified her. Liam watched her solidly muscled body and wondered if she would ask him to help her reach another kind of release later, when they were alone. His blood heated pleasurably at just the thought.

"You are *useless* with your head in the clouds," Vell growled at Finnead. She tilted her head, eyes narrowed. "Perhaps a sting to your pride will snap you out of it."

Gray had already stepped forward, thinking that Vell would dismiss Finnead as her sparring partner and call on the next of her Three. But Vell motioned sharply for Liam to enter the ring. Liam strode past Gray, who raised an eyebrow at him and grinned as she turned back to her spectator's position. He stood opposite Finnead and drew his sword, eyeing the Sidhe fighter.

Vell stalked out of the ring and sheathed her sword with a decisive snap. Beryk loped into sight, trotting around the wall of the practice field with a large white rabbit limp in his jaws. The sable wolf found a patch of shade and settled down with his kill, scarlet blood staining his mouth as he grinned toward the practice ring.

"First blood wins the match. Begin," commanded Vell.

Liam didn't allow her proclamation to startle him. Their practice sessions had never involved drawing blood, but he was conditioned to respond calmly to the unexpected. He lowered his body slightly into a predatory crouch, watching Finnead's chest for signs of his first movement. The Sidhe knight seemed weary. Usually he attacked with lightning speed, but Liam recognized the pattern of his opponent's strokes and blocked the attack easily. Something stirred strangely within him as he locked blades with Finnead. The scar on his side where the Crown Princess had slid a blade between his ribs vibrated like a plucked string, and his vision wavered. He recognized the misty overlay gathering at the corners of his eyes. It was the first sign of a vision, but before he could stop the match – he'd prefer not to be accidentally run through because he keeled over in the throes of his Sight – the mist flashed copper. He heard a voice whispering in his ear, and his sword arm responded instantly to the voice's commands, moving faster than he'd ever managed on his own.

Left. Right. Reverse crescent. Low block to the right. Counter. Now attack.

The whisper contained no inflection, no emotion. Liam felt as though he was not fully in control of his body, a sensation familiar to him from Seeing, but he'd never experienced this finely focused, nuanced form of his Sight. Again he felt that strange thrum in his side, the sensation rippling over his ribs. Everything seemed to slow. The coppery mist pulsed at the edges of his vision. He knocked aside a blow from Finnead as though it were no more than an annoyance. The Sidhe Knight countered his attack, but only barely. Liam advanced across the ring relentlessly. He saw a flash of surprise in Finnead's dark eyes and it spurred him to push harder, leaning into the feeling of the Sight wrapping around his limbs.

The sapphire in the pommel of the Brighbranr flared as though to ward off Liam's vicious assault. Liam felt his lips pull back from his teeth in a grin. Finnead tried to block the sweep of Liam's blade a breath too late. Liam felt his hand twist the blade, and the impact shuddered up his arm as the flat of his sword hit Finnead's cheek with resounding force. He heard Gray mutter an oath as Finnead fell to his knees, the Brighbranr skidding across the dirt.

The copper mist vanished. The force of the Sight twining around his body evaporated. The voice whispering directions in his mind quieted. Liam blinked and looked at the kneeling fighter in front of him. He swore under his breath, tossing his sword aside and moving to help Finnead. But the Sidhe knight shook his head slightly at Liam's offered hand. Finnead planted one foot and levered himself back to his feet, using his elbow against his knee. Ink-dark blood slid down his cheek, the cut splitting an already vivid weal. Vell watched silently as Finnead wiped at the blood with the heel of one palm and looked at the darkly glistening stain on his skin. He bowed with painful elegance to Liam.

"First blood and victory," he said, his expression inscrutable. He retrieved the Brighbranr from the dirt, sheathed his sword and turned to Vell. He bowed more deeply, a few drops of dark blood spattering the dirt. "My Queen."

Vell gave a single nod, her eyes hard. Finnead turned and walked away with stately poise. The High Queen looked at Gray. Without a word spoken, Gray followed him, her strides long and languorous.

"Well done," Vell said to Liam, her gaze hooded. "Though perhaps a bit more violent of a lesson than I had envisioned."

Liam held a hand flat and watched as his fingers trembled. "I didn't mean for it to go that far."

"You were the one holding the blade." Vell arched an eyebrow. Beryk looked up from the split carcass of the rabbit, licking his chops.

In reply, Liam lifted his shirt and stared down at his scar. It rippled with a slight copper incandescence. "I was holding the blade, but my Sight was calling the shots." He almost said *Arcana* was calling the shots, but something made him change the word.

Vell took a few steps toward him, brows drawn together as she examined his scar. "Interesting. Well, at least we know that Arcana didn't burn your Sight out of you."

"I've never had a vision like that before," Liam said, taking a deep breath. He was trained to expect the unexpected, but nothing had prepared him for the realm of the Fae.

"Perhaps it felt threatened," Vell said thoughtfully. "Your Sight, I mean. I think it's more of a separate entity than you realize."

"Or maybe it's part of the separate entity that pulled me back out of death," Liam said, pushing back his hair with one hand.

Vell looked at him sharply. "What makes you say that?"

"I heard it. Her. A voice." Liam shook his head and flexed his hands. "Telling me how to counter Finnead's next moves. It was like a narrated vision."

"That could come in handy," commented Vell. Then she sighed, her eyes traveling over the large, empty practice yard.

"I'll find Finnead later and make my apologies," said Liam. "Even a match to first blood didn't have to end that badly."

"If he had been focused on his blade rather than his lost love, he wouldn't have faltered in the first place," said Vell.

"Are you saying you expected him to beat me?" Liam asked with a hint of a grin. He wiped Finnead's blood from his blade and slid it into its sheath.

"Soundly," replied Vell without any hint of remorse. "But apparently you'll keep evolving new abilities if I place you under stress. So I'll keep going down that path." She raised her eyebrows suggestively. "Shall we head back to the palace?"

Liam considered. Vell still looked restless. To most observers she would seem calm and collected, but he noticed the tense cast of her shoulders and the quick flash of anger surfacing now and again in her gaze, despite her lighthearted words. "We could see if my archery has also improved," he suggested, motioning to the practice targets at the far end of the practice yard. A few pairs of Seelie fighters had quietly begun to warm up in the practice rings farthest from them. They would keep a respectful distance from the High Queen, affording her the courtesy they extended to their own Queen.

"I doubt it," said Vell dryly, arching an eyebrow as she strode toward the archery range. A few bows of different styles were always kept in readiness at the practice yards for communal use. Vell looked over the rack of weapons and selected two longbows, handing the shorter of the two to Liam.

"Well, I'm in no danger of feeling too prideful over that victory in the ring," he said a little ruefully as they inspected their bowstrings and chose a handful of practice arrows from the quiver at the side of the bow rack. After they had each shot five arrows at the target, they set their bows on the ground and walked to retrieve them. Vell's arrows clustered in a neat circle in the center of the target. Liam's arrows were erratic, but they had all hit within the third ring of the bull's-eye.

"You're getting more consistent," said Vell.

"That's the idea," Liam replied. He hadn't yet tired of watching Vell display her considerable skill with a bow. She looked like a statue of a warrior goddess in the still moment when she held the bow before her, arrow nocked and drawn back. He thrilled to her warrior talents, but he also cherished the moments when she let her guard down and allowed him to see her vulnerability.

"Glira said that Mab might be plotting an attempt on Tess's life," Vell said quietly after they had shot the second flight of arrows.

Liam nodded. He couldn't help the instinctual anger that raged through him at the thought of someone trying to hurt his baby sister. "There's nothing we can do about it right now. She's in the mortal world."

"She's in the mortal world and she's more than capable of defending herself against any that Mab might send against her," said Vell firmly. Liam wasn't sure if she was trying to reassure him, herself, or both of them. "And she has Calliea with her as well. The Laedrek certainly isn't the assassin."

"Jess would die before he'd hurt Tess," said Liam. "So I think it's safe to rule him out as well. Niall?"

"I don't think Titania would conspire with Mab to cause the Bearer harm," Vell said quietly, stabbing her arrows point-down into the earth.

"That leaves Ramel and Molly." Liam shook his head. "What a tangled web we weave."

Vell nocked an arrow, smoothly drew it back and raised her bow. Liam watched her as she sighted down the shaft of the arrow and exhaled. At the pause in the bottom of her exhale, she released the arrow. It cut through the air and sliced unerringly into the center of the target. She smiled slightly and then sobered. "No more tangled than Finnead and the Unseelie Princess."

"Why would Mab want to kill Tess? From what I was told, there was always some tension. But how would Mab benefit from the death of the Bearer?"

"I can't say that I know," Vell said quietly. "Perhaps she just wants chaos. Perhaps she thinks that if she kills Tess, she could influence the next Bearer more easily." She shook her head. "I don't know."

"I know that she won't succeed," Liam said steadfastly, "but...what would happen? If Mab...killed Tess." The words tasted like ash in his mouth.

Vell nocked another arrow to her bow, aiming with still, concentrated precision. The arrow sailed across the distance to the target and split her last arrow in two. The sundered halves of the ruined arrow shaft fell to the ground. She stared at the splintered arrow as she spoke. "If the Unseelie Queen were to kill the Bearer, then I have no doubt that there would be war."

A chill ran through Liam. A quick series of memories flashed through his mind's eye, seared there through his years fighting an amorphous war in a foreign land: a village built with mud bricks and thatch, dirty children watching with wide eyes as the convoy passed through, the eerie green glow of the world through night-vision goggles as his unit crept toward a targeted building, the stillness of the dark suddenly shredded by whistling bullets; his own hands, blood soaked through the protective gloves as he tried to staunch the wound in the chest of a little girl; the gray face of a friend, a classmate from his training days, eyes open and sightless under the glaring lights of the military medical facility, his uniform ripped first by the shrapnel of the explosion and then by his teammates trying to save his life.

Liam blinked. The memories surfaced unpredictably, but he'd learned to ride out the moment of recollection without giving too much away. He thought he smelled cordite and smoke and the sickly sweet smell of burning flesh, but he anchored himself to his surroundings and pushed away the sensation. His voice was steady when he spoke. "Do you think Tess would want war?"

Vell watched him closely with sharp golden eyes and shook her head. Beryk cracked one of the rabbit's leg bones between his teeth, licking at the bloody marrow. "I don't want war either. But killing the Bearer would be unforgiveable." She raised her chin. "It would prove that Mab isn't fit to lead her people."

"So who would lead the Unseelie Court?" Liam asked. "You can't remove a leader and leave a power vacuum. Even if that leader is a ruthless tyrant." His mouth thinned. "That's a lesson I don't need to learn firsthand again."

"War is a terrible thing," replied Vell, "but what would it say of us if we allowed her to keep her crown?"

Liam shook his head. He pulled one of his arrows from the earth, inspected the arrowhead and then nocked it to his bow. He focused on drawing the arrow back, feeling the steadiness of his stance and the strength in his arms as he aimed. The arrow struck only one ring outside the center of the target, but he felt no satisfaction. "All of this is still theoretical," he pointed out. "Unless we have actionable evidence that Mab plotted against Tess."

"She's smarter than that," said Vell. "I don't have anything concrete. But now we know to be on the lookout."

They shot the remainder of their arrows in thoughtful silence. After gathering the projectiles and returning their bows to the rack, they walked back to the palace. The streets of the White City still seemed empty, the statues still faceless and the wind moaning against the walls. But the filth of Malravenar's creatures had been stripped away, and Sidhe artisans had begun to craft golden masks to replace the statues' defaced visages. As they neared the palace, Liam looked up at two statues guarding the arched entrance of a smaller building, standing fiercely atop two pillars. The golden masks reminded him of the death masks of the ancient pharaohs, but he doubted any of the Fae would recognize the resemblance

The cathedral still contained the huge tent that housed the healers' ward and the living quarters for most of the *Vyldgard* and the healers. Most of the Seelie had withdrawn into their own camp in the east of the city, though Maeve and her healers still shared the task of caring for the many wounded. Titania had found a lofty structure, little more than a marble platform and pillars supporting a magnificent domed roof that had survived the occupation intact. She had established her own Court there; the Seelie were delighted with the airy, bright pavilion. Mab, on the other hand, had found what had once been an armory, built halfway into a hill on the western perimeter of the city. Liam hadn't seen it for himself, but he imagined that the dark, ancient passageways underground would suit the Unseelie Queen.

Vell strode through the massive doors of the palace, acknowledging the salute of the two *Vyldgard* warriors standing watch at the top of the great steps. Liam followed half a step behind Vell. For all that they were equals in private, he was still one of her Three and fulfilled his role impeccably in public, as they'd agreed was best.

The *Vyldretning* entered the healing ward, as she did every time she returned to the palace, whether she had been gone for half an hour or the entire day. The initial frenzied pace after the battle had finally slowed. By this time, most of the gravely wounded had either succumbed to their injuries or were on their way to recovery, however long a road that might be.

"My lady." Maeve greeted the High Queen with a deferential bow. The Seelie healer had looked experienced before the last battle. Now, after the loss of one daughter and an uncertain future for the other, she looked old, new lines framing her eyes and mouth.

"Healer Maeve." Vell returned the greeting. She swept her eyes over the antechamber of the healing ward, several long tables holding neat piles of supplies and records. "How is Niamh?"

A raw pain surfaced in Maeve's eyes. Any mention of Niamh no doubt brought to mind her dead twin. "She is slowly coming back to us." As the pain receded, a flicker of humor crossed Maeve's face. "Though I think it is a combination of her own stubbornness and the sheer will of that mortal boy."

Vell smiled slightly and glanced at Liam. "Quinn does have a certain amount of determination." She turned back to Maeve. "I'll walk the ward for a while, if it's all right with you."

"You are always welcome here, Majesty," said Maeve firmly, the stronger honorific underscoring the approval in her voice.

The healers on duty nodded respectfully to Vell, but they didn't pause in their tasks as she walked down the center aisle of the first ward. Liam knew her routine: – she'd silently observe the healers at work, offer a few well-placed words of praise and encouragement, and check on her *Vyldgard* wounded. Though the Wild Court had been by far the smallest force to enter the final battle, scores of wounded still owed their allegiance to the High Queen, and she made it clear that she hadn't forgotten them. A warm glow of pride suffused Liam as he watched her for a moment. He knew that it was still difficult for Vell to accept her position at times, but she was determined to be a good leader. She had been born *Herravaldyr*, raised with the expectation that she would follow in her mother's footsteps to become a *volta*; but after she had been chosen by Beryk – a *Herravaldyr* wolf, and a male at that – the path of her life had shifted. She expected to become the leader of a pack of *ulfdrengr* and the wolves bonded to them, warriors all. The harrowing of the North had changed her life yet again, but her heritage and the lessons of her youth still stood her in good stead as the High Queen.

Liam caught her eye and silently motioned to a bed farther down the ward. Vell nodded in understanding and he left her to continue her quiet conversation with a Seelie fighter who had lost a hand in the battle.

Quinn sat by Niamh's side, as he had for every day since they had returned from the Dark Keep. In the last few days, he'd adopted the habit of reading aloud to the Valkyrie warrior. He sat on a small stool, wearing his camouflage pants, which he'd washed thoroughly and meticulously patched after the battle, sewing with precise, neat stitches next to Niamh in those early hours when she hovered between life and death. Now he read in a quiet voice from a book with a blue leather cover, glancing at Niamh's pale face every now and again. He glanced at Liam as his teammate joined him, but he didn't stop reading until he came to the end of the chapter in the book. He marked his place before closing the little volume.

"What are you two reading today?" asked Liam.

"Memoirs of one of the Knights that travelled extensively in the mortal world," replied Quinn. He reached over and gently closed his hand around Niamh's motionless hand, holding the gesture for a long moment before he sat back and stood up. "Finished the volume of poetry this morning. I'll give them one thing, those suckers can really write some good love poetry."

Liam chuckled. "Listen to you, giddy and reading sonnets."

"Hey, brother, the ladies love the sonnets," replied Quinn with a grin. The two men looked down at Niamh. Her white-gold hair was neatly braided on one side of her head, and she was still undeniably beautiful, her golden coloring slowly returning after the pallor of near death.

"Anything new?" Liam asked. Niamh still hadn't regained consciousness, but her wounds were slowly healing. She hadn't been dosed with any of the sleep inducing, pain relieving elixir used by the Sidhe for fear that she wouldn't awaken from the effects of the medicine.

"I felt her squeeze my hand this morning. Or at least I thought I did," said Quinn. "But I don't want to get my hopes up too soon, you know?"

"Maybe you should switch back to the love poems," suggested Liam, only half in jest.

Quinn smiled. "Maybe I'll do just that." He rubbed one of his tattoos idly. "I just hope she's not in pain."

"She'll be able to tell you herself when she wakes up." Liam gripped Quinn's shoulder reassuringly. "Want me to take over for a bit so you can grab something to eat?"

"Nah, I made a supply run this morning. Thanks though." Quinn motioned to a satchel. Liam assumed it held the typical bread, meat and cheese that comprised Quinn's diet nowadays. "How'd the portal opening ceremony go? Or whatever it was called. Jess stopped by before he stepped off."

"It went well," said Liam. "Tess has her work cut out for her in our world, though. From what Vell told me, the bone sorcerer is no joke."

"All the nasties in this world seem to be super charged," commented Quinn.

"All the heroes are, too ,though, " Liam replied, looking down at Niamh and remembering the awe inspiring sight of the beautiful, fierce Valkyrie wreaking havoc from their winged steeds.

Quinn nodded. "Including Tess. She'll be fine, brother."

"So will Niamh." Liam knew this exchange was a carefully choreographed routine, but sometimes it helped even the most stoic of men to hear reassurance spoken aloud.

"She's a fighter." Quinn nodded and reached down to grip Niamh's hand again. Liam saw Niamh's fingers tighten around Quinn's hand. Quinn froze. Liam clapped him on the back.

"I don't think it's too soon to get your hopes up," he said as Niamh stirred slightly, her eyelids fluttering. An unabashed grin spread over Quinn's face as he knelt by Niamh's bedside, never letting go of her hand as he spoke to her in a quiet, encouraging voice. Liam felt an answering smile on his lips as he watched his friend's sudden joy. He took a few steps back and watched from a respectful distance as Niamh's eyes opened, glimmering in the light of the *taebramh* lantern. A crease appeared between her eyebrows and Liam saw the telltale strain of deep discomfort surfacing on her face as she swallowed thickly. But a weak smile appeared on Niamh's lips as she recognized Quinn. His tattooed friend spoke to her softly and then kissed her gently on the forehead. Liam caught the gleam of a tear tracing down his teammate's face as he turned to leave, giving them their privacy. He wondered if Quinn would tell Niamh about Maire's death, or if Niamh had seen it herself. Or perhaps Maeve had requested that she be the one to tell her daughter. In any case, he found Vell about halfway down the ward. She smiled at the news that Niamh had finally awakened and shared the good news with Maeve as soon as they came across the healer.

They visited with Robin and Sage for the better part of an hour. The Seelie healer was now well enough to sit up, though he still tired easily and wore a sling about his injured arm. Sage had freely admitted that he'd told the Bearer about the Exiled, even going so far as to suggest that Vell should make him part of the *Vyldgard* to spare him Titania's displeasure. And what had started out as a remark made in jest had turned into a serious consideration. Just as they counted on seeing Quinn by Niamh's side, so too had the healers learned to expect Robin sitting by Sage's bed. The red-haired *Vyldgard* fighter often brought work with him, daggers to sharpen, armor to clean and shine, a saddle to mend, any of the sundry tasks a warrior performed to keep his gear ready for battle. He also brought Sage books to read, though Sage refused to let him read them aloud as Quinn did for Niamh.

"So do you want to be Seelie or *Vyldgard* today, Sage?" asked Vell light-heartedly. She'd explained to Liam that much of her early interaction with Sage had been in the early days after Brightvale, when she still felt angry at everyone and everything around her that had somehow contributed to her crowning as High Queen. Sage had been one of the healers assigned to care for Tess, and Vell had admitted that he was a skilled and patient healer…if a bit easy to intimidate, she'd added.

"Don't patronize me, my lady," replied Sage with a half-smile. "I know I need to toughen up before you'd even consider baptizing me as *Vyldgard*."

Vell stepped forward and teasingly gripped Sage's uninjured arm, measuring his bicep with her hand. "Seems like you've got a good foundation."

"I'll second that," contributed Robin with an impish glint in his eyes.

Liam chuckled. He'd quickly learned that the Sidhe, especially the Seelie, were not as rigid and complicated as mortals in their view of love. Sidhe could marry, or they could be lovers, or they could be merely friends who decided to have a child together. The entire Court contributed to raising children, though there had been few Sidhe children in the last centuries. During the journey to the Dark Keep, he'd picked up on the fact that Robin was attracted to men, but none of the Sidhe had ever said anything that led him to believe it was considered anything other than perfectly natural and acceptable. He'd mentioned it to Vell recently after one of their particularly intense sessions of lovemaking, and she had laughed at him.

"Why would it be wrong?" she'd asked. "You and I, we fell in love with each other's souls." She'd trailed one hand down his bare, muscled chest, eliciting a shiver of pleasure from him. "It is no different with them. Love is love." She had effectively silenced any further questions by capturing his mouth with her own, her strong hands gripping his shoulders as she nipped at his lower lip and straddled him playfully.

Liam only half-listened to the conversation between Vell and the two men, instead letting his mind drift into daydreams as he watched Vell. He'd never before met a woman who so perfectly balanced strength and beauty. Sometimes he thought that Vell resented her beauty or tried to hide it. To her, it wasn't a tangible advantage like her physical strength. But he liked to think that with every kiss and every caress, he was convincing her that her beauty was as much a part of her as her toughness. They were equals in every way, and she even surpassed him in the skills of warfare required in Faeortalam. That in itself excited him beyond anything he'd felt with a woman in the mortal world.

After they left the healing ward, they returned to the High Queen's quarters. For the rest of the afternoon, Vell reviewed messages and received different members of her Court to discuss the progress of certain projects. Thea sought approval to build a bigger forge and take an apprentice, and Maeve had sent two of the younger healers into the grasslands springing up around the White City to report on the rejuvenation of the wild medicinal herbs. Liam spent much of that time contributing to the conversation when Vell asked it of him. In his free moments, he spoke with the leaders of his reconstruction teams and consulted different books on the history of the White City, gleaning details about building methods and materials, taking painstakingly meticulous notes.

After she had concluded her receiving hours for the afternoon, Vell sealed the entrance to her quarters with a quick flick of her wrist, the gesture ensuring that the tapestry would not admit any visitors without first seeking her approval. She stood and stretched languorously, linking her hands above her head. Then she removed her golden circlet, setting it on the table unceremoniously. Liam looked up as she unpinned her braid, glancing at him mischievously as she shook out her dark tresses. He carefully marked his place in his book and set it aside, watching as she stalked toward him with predatory intent. Her hands traced his broad shoulders and slid under his shirt; he obligingly raised his arms and she divested him of the garment. He stiffened slightly when her fingers found the scar on his side, playing lightly over the sensitive area.

"Visiting the healing wards reminds me of how lucky I am," she said softly. Without her crown, with her hair curling gently around her face, she did not wear the mantle of the High Queen in this moment. She was a young woman speaking to the man she loved. Liam caught her hand and tenderly kissed her knuckles. She shivered. He pressed her palm to his chest over his heart.

"I would die all over again for you," he said earnestly, his green eyes serious.

Vell smiled, a puckish edge to her voice as she said, "You say the sweetest things, my love." She leaned close and kissed him deeply, her hands traveling down the hard planes of his chest and abdomen, dipping lower, teasing until he growled and stood, sweeping her off her feet and grinning at her girlish squeal of surprise as he carried her over to her sleeping furs.

Chapter 23

Ross wrapped her hands around her steaming mug of tea and gazed out at the stormswept landscape beyond the living room window. She couldn't make out more than silhouettes in the inky blackness. At first she'd thought that the storm would just be a typical summer cloudburst, intense and then quickly swept away by the winds from over the lake. But the storm rumbled and shuddered over them all evening and into the night.

"Can't sleep?"

Ross turned at Vivian's voice. Her roommate had changed into her pajamas, long gym shorts and a soft, loose t-shirt emblazoned with a phrase from Tolkien: *Not all who wander are lost.*

With a crooked smile, Ross replied, "Was that a rhetorical question?"

Vivian shrugged. "Mostly. Since I can see that you're staring out the window in the middle of the night – or I guess it's really early in the morning, isn't it – and therefore can judge for myself that for whatever reason, you're not sleeping." She nodded to the ceramic teapot sitting on the stove. "Still warm?"

"Should be warm enough."

"Excellent." Vivian busied herself with selecting a mug and rifling through their stash of tea. "You know," she said as she poured steaming water into her mug, "I'm surprised that Noah trusts the runes enough to sleep."

"I was surprised too." Ross sipped her tea and added thoughtfully, "He trusts Merrick and Luca."

Merrick and Luca slept in the study again, while Duke slept in Ross's bed. She'd tried to sleep, and normally the solid warmth of him at her back lulled her into slumber. But her thoughts kept racing around the events of the day. She managed to catch a few hours of restless sleep, but then she'd slipped out of bed in the early hours of the morning. Duke hadn't even stirred.

"You think this plan is going to work?" Vivian asked, dipping a finger into her mug to test the temperature.

"The men seem to think it will." Ross shrugged. "I don't really care about this wizard or whatever he is. I just want us all to be safe."

"I think that eliminating one might help with the other," Vivian commented.

After they'd finished the runetrap and the skies had opened up, they'd sat sodden in the living room for a few moments. Then Merrick had asked Ross if she had any glass bowls. She willingly if suspiciously produced a set of four small glass bowls.

"No more blood," Vivian had said to Merrick firmly, her concern written across her expressive face as she finished bandaging his cut hand.

Merrick's chuckle had turned into a cough and then a wheeze. Ross glanced at Duke; the dark-haired Sidhe sounded like a pneumonia patient.

"I couldn't do any more work with blood even if I wanted to," Merrick had finally gasped with a game smile. "Just the chalk." He held out his hand. Luca picked up the chalk that Merrick had used to mark the doorway and handed it to him.

"Do you have to do anything else? You don't seem strong enough," Vivian said. "And if you need blood…take mine."

"V," said Ross sharply. As much as she didn't want Merrick to overextend himself, she certainly didn't want her roommate throwing herself into the dubious exercise of this magic that involved blood.

Vivian smiled at Ross. "You don't even believe in magic, right? So what's the harm?" She turned back to Merrick. "I'm guessing these are going to be something like alarms, aren't they? Placed by the road and then back by the river."

"Are you sure you aren't a sorceress?" Merrick asked guilelessly, his luminous gray eyes considering Vivian. "I'd heard that there weren't many left, and none so young as you."

Vivian blushed fiercely. "No. At least, I don't think so. I mean, there's family stories and whatnot. But I'm not part of a coven or anything. My gran would have had a cow if she'd found out I dabbled in any of that. She went to Mass every Wednesday and twice on Sunday."

"Devotion and dedication come in many forms," Merrick replied vaguely. He looked down at the chalk and then at Vivian. "You offer willingly?"

"Yes," she replied.

"Perhaps my blood would be more appealing to Gryttrond," suggested Luca.

"Don't steal my moment," Vivian snapped at him.

The *ulfdrengr* raised his hands as if to ward her off. "If the *raedhaerdyr* wants to prick her finger, far be it from me to stop her."

Vivian narrowed her eyes. "What does that mean? *Raedhaerdyr*?" She pronounced the word seamlessly.

Luca chuckled. "You are a silver-tongue, I think. It means…" He searched for the right words. "She of the red hair."

She tossed the hair in question over her shoulder. "Well, at least you're accurate."

Merrick lined up the bowls, dome up, on the living room carpet.

"Don't worry, Ross, we won't get blood on the rug," said Vivian with a grin.

"That's the least of my worries," Ross muttered. She watched skeptically as Merrick traced symbols on the bottoms of the glass bowls. He paused after the last one, closing his eyes briefly as though resting. Then he produced a little silver dagger. Vivian held out her hand unflinchingly. Merrick flicked the dagger expertly and a fat drop of blood welled from Vivian's middle finger.

"Just one drop on each bowl is enough," said Merrick. "But give me a moment."

Vivian balanced the drop of blood on her finger with concentration until Merrick took a breath and nodded to her. He murmured under his breath as she carefully dropped the blood onto the first bowl. The air in the room tightened, and Vivian shivered, but her eyes lit up. She squeezed another drop of blood from her finger with single-minded intent, repeating the procedure with the remaining glass bowls. A shudder ran visibly through her body as Merrick said a word in a commanding voice and the symbols on the bowls flashed scarlet. Little wisps of white smoke curled from the bowls. The runes now looked as though they'd been engraved and painted red.

Merrick sat back, his face gray. "Two by the road, and two by the river." He nodded at Vivian. "You'll be able to feel it, too, when the line is crossed." Sweat pearled his forehead. "For everyone else there will be a red flare."

"I'll place them," said Luca.

"I'll go too," said Vivian, raptly tracing the rune on the nearest bowl. Luca hadn't protested, and they'd both gathered their bowls, returning from their mission soaked but satisfied.

"What did it feel like, when Merrick did that thing with the bowls?" Ross asked now as they watched the storm together in the early hours of the morning, swirling the tea in her mug.

"You could let him use your blood in his next spell and you'd find out," Vivian said teasingly. Then she sobered. "It felt like little bits of me expanded and…I don't know. It's hard to describe. Like sparks in my veins but a cool rush through my chest when he finished the spell. It actually felt really…good."

Ross groaned. "Please don't become addicted to magic or whatever it is that makes up his hocus pocus."

Vivian laughed and then quickly lowered her voice as she remembered that the others were still sleeping. "I won't lie, I want to learn how to do it myself."

"*Can* you do it yourself?" Ross asked skeptically. "I mean, I know that there are Wiccans and such. Ouija boards and voodoo and all that. But this…*if* it's real," she pronounced deliberately, "this is on a whole new level."

"Pretty cool, isn't it?" Vivian grinned. She took a deep breath and sighed happily. "I mean, seriously Ross. Didn't you ever read Tolkien or Anne McCaffrey or any of the other great fantasy books when you were a kid? Didn't you ever investigate the back of your closet for a door into Narnia?"

"No, but I'm betting *you* did," Ross replied, smiling as her friend grinned brilliantly.

"Well, yeah, of course I did. I always wanted it to be real, you know? And now…now I can be a *part* of one of those stories." Her eyes shone with the same light that had appeared when Merrick sealed the spell on their warning-bowls.

"I thought you were going to write about it," said Ross.

"I mean, *afterwards*, yeah. But I'm along for the ride now." Vivian tilted her head, joining Ross by the window. "The rain is slowing down."

As the rain slowed, the predawn twilight washed the storm soaked land in weak gray light. From the living room window, she could see most of the side of the property, from the tangle of brush and trees by the river up to the gravel drive that snaked through their yard from the main road. Ross noticed that the wind had torn down a few small branches from the trees by the river. She frowned. "V, can you still feel those little warning runes you put your blood on?"

"Yeah, why?"

"Has anyone tripped the alarm?" Ross asked. She felt her heart speed up.

"Nope," said Vivian confidently. "No alarm bells jangling in the noggin. Or maybe in my chest. I don't know where exactly to pinpoint it, but…"

"Go get Luca and Merrick," Ross said in a low, tense voice.

"Why? They need their sleep, or at least Merrick certainly does…" Vivian trailed off as she saw Ross's knuckles whiten on her mug and followed the direction of Ross's focused gaze. "Oh." She swallowed. "You're two for two with seeing the creepy things first, Ross." And with that, she quickly set her mug on the counter and disappeared down the hallway. Ross stared out the window for another moment, and then she followed, wrenching open the door to her bedroom. Not that it locked anymore anyway, since Duke had kicked it in the night before.

"Noah," she said without preamble, "we've got company."

He muttered a curse and threw back the blankets. "No flare?"

"No flare." She shook her head as she picked up her Glock from the dresser, checking the magazine perfunctorily. Two extra magazines weighted down the left pocket of her mesh gym shorts. She clipped her folding knife to the waistband as extra insurance.

Duke grunted, already checking the Beretta. "Then what is it, if it didn't set off the alarm?"

"I don't know," replied Ross grimly, "but it didn't look human."

When they emerged into the living room, Luca was hefting an axe in both hands, and Merrick held a naked blade in his hand. Vivian had convinced one of them to give her a long dagger. Luca spoke to her in a low voice. "Keep your weight balanced between both feet and don't stop moving. Go for the elbow or shoulder. If they can't hold a blade, they can't attack you. But stay behind us."

"You want all of us to go out there? Are you sure that's the smartest plan?" Ross said.

"Smartest, perhaps not. But these runes won't hold forever, and they may not hold at all against whatever is out there. It didn't set off the warning-runes," said Merrick.

Mayhem circled the room restlessly, her ears pricked. She stopped by Ross, staring at the door as if waiting for them to move out. "Vivian, you should stay in the house with Mayhem," Ross said. She felt like events were spiraling out of control First Vivian offered her blood for those stupid bowls, and now she thought she could go out and fight whatever creature was out there in the darkness.

"Like hell I will," Vivian said firmly, all trace of joking gone from her normally jovial voice.

"If anything's going to happen, it's going to happen out there," said Duke to Ross with a half-grin. She wasn't sure if he was trying to reassure her with one of the phrases they had uttered often on their deployments, or if he was trying to lighten the mood. Either way, it didn't work.

"Why don't we just take my truck? Get out of here and lose them on the road," she continued doggedly.

"Because they will not stop hunting us," replied Luca. His icy blue eyes caught Ross's gaze. "You are no coward. You wish to protect your friend, and that is honorable. But everyone here is a part of this fight now."

"I didn't ask to be, and neither did Vivian," she said in a low voice that was close to a growl, but she adjusted her grip on the Glock.

"I know," said Duke. "I know you didn't, and I'll make sure you both get through okay. I promise."

Ross looked at Duke for a long moment. She couldn't decide if she felt like crying or screaming, but regardless, she shoved her whirlwind of emotions deep into her chest and slammed the lid on the black box. Her voice came out gravelly. "The last time you told me that, you disappeared and I thought you were dead."

"I'm here now, ain't I?" Duke drawled. "I think that means I kept that promise. Just like I'm gonna keep this one."

Ross took a deep breath and nodded. "Okay." If she didn't believe in sorcery and another world and magic, why was her heart hammering so hard in her chest that she felt its pulse in every fiber of her body?

"Stay within sight of one another when we go out," said Luca. "Ross, what exactly did you see?"

"There was something moving near the road. It looked like a person, at least from the silhouette, I mean. But it moved wrong. Too graceful, too...predatory."

"If Tess and Kianryk had arrived here, they wouldn't be slinking around in the shadows," Duke said. He looked at Merrick. "Are there any more of your people in our world?"

"There used to be." Merrick looked uncertain. "But they were supposed to be dead long ago."

"Well," said Duke, "looks like they ain't so dead after all." He grinned humorlessly. "Kinda like me. Seems to be a pattern around here."

"So what do we do?" Vivian asked. "If they're like you, Merrick, will they pose a threat? Wouldn't they be, I don't know, happy to see you?"

Merrick shook his head. "Precisely the opposite. They will most likely want revenge of the most gruesome sort."

Vivian looked at the front door with slightly wider eyes. "Right then. So...what do we do?"

"Don't let them take revenge," replied Luca firmly. He looked at each of them in turn. "Ready?"

"As I'll ever be," replied Ross. She saw the dagger shaking in Vivian's hand, and she grabbed her friend's shoulder with her left hand. "Hey," she said in a quiet voice as Luca reached for the doorknob. "Stick with me, okay?"

Vivian swallowed and nodded. "I feel like I want to throw up," she whispered with a sheepish smile.

"If you do, get it over with and move on," Ross said. Vivian blinked and then nodded again. Luca opened the door, and they filed out into the weak light of dawn.

Mayhem stuck close to Ross as they crossed the porch. She motioned to Duke that she'd take their six – the rearguard of their group. He nodded and took a position to the left and slightly behind Luca. Merrick fanned out to the right, creating a rough diamond shape. Ross grabbed Vivian's shoulder again as she stumbled on the porch steps.

"Sorry," Vivian whispered, her eyes wide as saucers in the half-light.

"Just focus on one step at a time. Thinking too much will make you feel more overwhelmed," Ross advised quietly. "Stay to my left, right behind me. You can put your hand on my shoulder if you want. If I tell you to get down, get down and stay down."

Vivian nodded jerkily, her dagger gleaming in her hand.

A slight breeze brought the scent of the river with it. The air was uncharacteristically cool thanks to the storm. Ross felt her skin prickle into goose bumps. After weeks of scalding heat and heavy humidity, the light chill in the air felt unnatural. She clamped down firmly on her imagination as her thoughts tried to run wild at every rustle of grass. But it wasn't her imagination when the sounds of insects and birds slowly died into silence as they made their way across the front of the property toward the road. Every few steps, she turned to her right and scanned behind them, her gun pointed at the ground. Vivian jumped when a motorcycle rider sped down the main road, flashing by with a roar of his engine. But to her credit, she didn't make a sound and recovered quickly. The light brightened with every passing moment, but even the light of the sun didn't make Ross feel any better.

They had covered about half the distance to the main road, walking slowly and purposefully in the strange silence, when the explosion erupted behind them. Ross shoved Vivian down as she whirled and took a knee, weapon automatically coming up to aim at the source of the explosion. A wave of heat washed over them and their ears rang as the roar of the detonation filled the air.

"Son of a *bitch*!" Ross yelled as her truck crashed back down onto the driveway, fountains of flame pluming from its broken windows, oily black smoke roiling into the sky. But she didn't have time to contemplate the demise of her beloved truck. Mayhem spun and snarled. Ross followed the dog's gaze and saw that the three men were locked in struggle with two dark clad figures. Duke had already been knocked to the ground, though he was quickly regaining his feet. She scanned their surroundings and when she didn't see any other immediate threats, she released Mayhem with a quick hand signal. "Go!"

The dog shot through the grass, low to the ground and gaining speed as she selected the nearer figure attacking Merrick as her target. Ross blinked the spots from her vision and tried to clear the ringing in her ears with a shake of her head. Vivian still crouched next to her, but she sprang up when she saw the attackers. Ross grabbed her as she leapt forward, keeping her beside her with a firm grip.

"We have to help them!" Vivian protested, raising her dagger.

"If we rush in, we could distract them and someone could get hurt," said Ross, but she felt a warm flash of pride in her friend's bravery. They approached the brawl with measured strides. Vivian gave a little cry as she spied Merrick lying unmoving; Mayhem stood over him, teeth bared ferociously. That left Duke and Luca to grapple with their assailants. The one fighting Luca slid about like a specter, moving so quickly that the *ulfdrengr* couldn't land anything more than a glancing blow. Duke's attacker knocked him to the ground again with a long staff.

"Oh, hell no," growled Ross, sprinting forward. Vivian rushed to Merrick. Mayhem seemed to acknowledge that she had been relieved of her guard duty and rocketed forward to join Ross. Duke rolled away from the first blow of the staff but caught the second blow on his shoulder. Ross brought up the Glock, aimed at the attacker and pulled the trigger. The dark-clad figure jerked as Ross's shot hit home, the dark hood obscuring its head falling away. Mayhem's snarl rumbled through the shadows as the dog crouched by Ross's side, coiled and ready to attack the stranger but awaiting Ross's signal.

Duke struggled to his feet as Ross stopped beside him, her gun still trained on the figure. The weak light revealed an otherworldly face dominated by striking azure eyes and silver hair.

"Stay where you are or you'll get another bullet," Ross said commandingly. "And this time I won't miss."

A wet patch stained the shoulder of the strange woman. She grinned. Her teeth were filed to points. The woman raised her staff again and Ross tensed, pressing the slack out of the trigger; but then the woman hissed.

"Lay down your weapon, or he dies," said Luca, holding the second attacker by the throat. The *ulfdrengr* didn't strain at all as he lifted the struggling man bodily until the man's feet kicked futilely in midair. He seemed more boy than man, from the look of his face.

The silver-haired woman hissed again but lowered her staff. Her eyes blazing with hatred, she set her weapon on the ground and raised her empty hands.

"Look at their faces," whispered Vivian, kneeling beside Merrick. The skin of both the man and the woman bore layer upon layer of scars. Ross would have said that they looked like burn scars, but the skin wasn't rippled and contorted. Different shades of white, gray and pink mottled their faces. She saw that the woman wore black gloves along with a strange mix of modern and old-fashioned clothes – a long-sleeved emerald tunic that billowed a bit, held in at the waist by a leather belt adorned with a rhinestone pattern, the long black cloak that had concealed her face with its hood, leggings similar to any in Ross or Vivian's closet, and dark leather boots. A mix of stud and hoop earrings bristled from both the woman's ears. Ross couldn't see in the shadows if the woman's ears were pointed.

"Let him go," said the woman to Luca.

The *ulfdrengr* let the man's feet touch the ground and loosened his grip slightly on his throat, enough that the man gasped and stopped fighting so desperately. Luca held up one of his axes in front of the man's face warningly, and his captive's struggles subsided.

"You blew up my truck," Ross said to the woman accusingly, gun still steadily aimed at her chest.

The woman grinned. "Yes. It was rather spectacular, wasn't it?" She spoke with a slight accent that Ross couldn't place.

Luca regained the woman's attention by making the man choke as he tightened his hold again. "Why did you attack us?"

"Because we are hungry," said the woman simply. A chill crawled down Ross's back as she combined that statement with the woman's pointed teeth. "And we have not come across such a weak Unseelie knight in such a long time." Her voice dropped almost to a purr as she glanced over at Merrick, who Vivian was helping to sit up. Vivian glared at her and raised her dagger.

"I am not Unseelie," said Merrick in a deceptively strong voice.

The woman stared at him. "Aye, and I'm the Queen of England." She burst into maniacal laughter, seemingly forgetting about the peril of her companion at Luca's hands.

Ross raised her eyebrows and looked at Duke. He rubbed his shoulder and shook his head slightly. He didn't have any more of an idea about these strangers than she did. Merrick struggled to his feet, accepting Vivian's offered hand. His eyes never left the silver-haired woman. "I am not Unseelie," he repeated. "I am one of the *Vyldgard*." He paused. "And you are two of the Exiled."

Chapter 24

After sending Farin to wake Forin and Haze, Tess stood in the kitchenette of the abandoned trailer. The storm had finally abated, rain tapping only fitfully on the roof. Weak gray light filtered through the dirty glass of the window. Little curtains that had once been white but were now yellow with age and cigarette smoke hung limply on either side. A small animal had chewed a hole in the baseboard beneath the sink. Tess wondered idly if she'd been sharing her room with a nest of raccoons or possums for the night.

Niall sat in an old wooden chair that faced the door of the trailer, his sword leaned within easy reach against the leg of the table. The Seelie knight stood respectfully when he saw Tess. "Did you sleep well, Tess? You look much improved from yesterday."

"Well, we all looked like drowned rats yesterday," said Tess, "but thanks, and yes, I slept well." She contemplated telling Niall about the *taebramh*, but decided against it. "I know I can always count on you for honesty, even if it's unflattering."

Niall smiled slightly. Tess hadn't yet gotten used to the unsettling paleness of his eyes washed of color when he gave part of his lifeforce along with Titania's other Knights to keep their Queen alive.

Jess appeared, resettling his ball cap onto his head and rubbing the five o'clock shadow on his jaw. "Morning," he said to Tess, nodding to Niall.

Tess's stomach growled and she rummaged in her pack, producing some *kajuk* and bread. The dried meat, produced using traditional *ulfdrengr* methods, always made her think of Vell...and Luca. She chewed thoughtfully as Jess pushed aside the ratty curtains of the window over the kitchen sink, peering outside. Calliea pounded on the closed door at the end of the narrow hallway – Tess assumed that was where Molly and Ramel had ended up sleeping. She raised an eyebrow at the unceremonious summons. Calliea raised her chin slightly as she joined them by the little kitchen table, as if waiting for Tess to comment. Tess shook her head and finished her breakfast.

"Good weather today," commented Jess, letting the dingy curtain fall back into place as he leaned against the counter and crossed his arms over his chest.

"Then we'd better find out which way to travel," said Tess, brushing crumbs from the front of her shirt.

Niall silently laid his scrying tools on the chipped tabletop: a protective cylindrical case about as long as Tess's forearm, a circular case that reminded her of Merrick's scrying compass, and a stick of the charcoal that looked similar to what Calliea had used to draw the runes on their arms. Tess surreptitiously pulled up the edge of her left sleeve; the rune had remarkably survived the journey through the portal and the torrential downpour, as well as her time asleep.

Ramel and Molly joined them as Niall spread a map on the table. Jess held down one corner and he used the case to anchor the other side. Tess glanced at the map of Faeortalam – it was a detailed view of the Deadlands and the Dark Keep. She resisted the urge to ask exactly how a map of Faeortalam would be useful in the mortal world. If there was one thing she'd learned, it was that her questions were often answered even if she didn't ask them aloud.

While Niall prepared his other materials, sharpening the charcoal stick and unclasping the circular case, Tess looked at Ramel. He showed little interest in the proceedings, staring into the distance with blankness in his eyes that sent a chill through her. He still wore the dark breastplate, and his clothes seemed to be the same from the day before. Molly stood slightly behind him, glancing at the profile of his face every few moments with something like nervousness or perhaps even fear in her eyes. She seemed more subdued this morning but offered Calliea a manic grin when she caught the Valkyrie commander's eye. Calliea pressed her lips together and looked away, a trace of disdain on her face.

Niall drew a rune on each corner of the map and then made a complex gesture in the air over the table. Tess leaned forward slightly, watching in fascination as the detailed map disappeared, the parchment drinking up the ink. Niall laid a few blades of rain wet grass and sprinkled damp earth on the center of the map. Tess felt the air in the room tighten as Niall's spell gathered force. She blinked. The grass and earth had certainly been *real* just a moment before – she'd seen them in Niall's hand. But in an instant they had sunk into the blank parchment, becoming an incredibly realistic *drawing*. Then the map swallowed the inked blades of grass and scattered sprinkle of earth. Niall pricked his finger, pressed a bloody print into the center of the parchment, and from the center of his fingerprint a thin black line threaded out onto the blank expanse. It split into three, four, five and then ten little lines, drawing a detailed depiction of their trailer, and the trees dotting the landscape.

"My blood allows it to center on our location," said Niall, mostly for Tess's benefit, she surmised, since she'd drawn in her breath in admiration at the rapidly growing map. Perhaps she'd study scrying when she returned to Faeortalam, she thought as she watched the image bloom across the blank parchment.

"Handy," commented Jess.

Niall smiled. "Exceedingly."

"Parlor tricks are all well and good," said Molly brightly, "but I haven't seen anything that a child couldn't produce with a few prompts."

"You're welcome to try, my lady," said Niall with cool courtesy. Tess glanced at Calliea – had she been able to talk to Niall about the situation with Molly and Ramel? Calliea nodded slightly.

Molly, though, seemed not to hear Niall's reply, her eyes darting to Ramel's face. Tess glanced at her sword-teacher and caught his slight grimace. His eyes weren't far away anymore and sweat curled the hair at his temples. She shifted her gaze and noticed that he gripped the hilt of the Brighbranr with white knuckles.

"We don't really need to be here for this, do we?" said Molly, her voice petulant now.

"Keep scrying," murmured Tess to Niall, turning toward Ramel and Molly. As much as she wanted to watch the captivating progress of the self-drawing map, a prickle of unease warned her that her instincts about the Unseelie emissaries took precedence. Out of the corner of her eye, she saw Calliea quickly hand something to Niall – a locket of some sort? – before sliding around the edge of the table to stand by Tess.

"If this doesn't interest you, I'm sure you can find something to amuse yourself," Tess said to Molly, putting a light layer of annoyance into her voice.

Molly looked at Ramel again and Tess recognized the determined set of her jaw. Ramel stared down at the map. He took a step forward, closing the distance between him and the table. A faint scent of hot metal reached Tess, turning her stomach. Something twisted and surfaced in Ramel's eyes, an alien consciousness not his own. *Mab*. Tess felt her heart drop. She pushed away the memory of the ghosts in Emery's gaze after she'd brought him back from death. Ramel wouldn't end up like Emery. She wouldn't let that happen.

"What do you say? Shall we go *amuse* ourselves while the children play with their magic tricks?" Molly said to Ramel, sliding in front of him and running a hand through his hair. Despite the lascivious suggestion in her voice, Tess didn't miss Molly's tense shoulders or her slight hesitation before she touched Ramel.

Ramel didn't reply. The hand gripping the hilt of his sword shook with the intensity of his grasp. Calliea began to say something, stepping forward, but Ramel exploded, grabbing Molly by the shoulders and throwing her bodily down the narrow hallway. She crashed into the wall and fell. Ramel turned back to the map without a second glance, saying in a flat voice, "Interfering little wench."

Calliea crouched to leap at Ramel, but Tess shook her head sharply. She couldn't afford for Calliea to be injured or worse in a fight with Ramel. Clearly he wasn't in control, and she didn't want to contemplate what his considerable strength could do with Mab at the reins. Jess pushed past Ramel, clearly not caring that he could incite violence by such a slight, walked down the hallway and helped Molly up, talking to her in a low voice. She seemed shaken but unharmed thanks to her Sidhe blood. Tess felt a wave of relief, then she refocused on Ramel. He had changed his stance so that he could see over her shoulder to the map. Tess moved to block his view. Calliea quickly understood her intent and shifted as well. They heard Niall murmuring behind them, his words accompanied by the soft clicks of adjusted gears and wheels on his scrying compass.

Molly returned to the tense gathering, brushing dust from the side of her body that had careened against the wall. "Well, you could have just told me that you weren't interested," she said to Ramel with a too bright grin.

Ramel ignored her and stepped toward the table. Calliea uncoiled her whip and Tess reached over her shoulder, gripping the hilt of the Caedbranr. She unsheathed just a sliver of the Sword, but that was enough to send a wave of power rolling through the room, making everyone except Jess stagger.

Ramel looked at Molly. His movements reminded Tess of Arcana, like a puppet with a particularly skilled master, an imitation of living movement. "Telling them will not save you. Or him." A smirk twisted Ramel's mouth.

"Then it might save *them*," flared Molly hotly. "And you won't get away with this."

A chill slipped down Tess's spine as she recognized Mab using Ramel's voice.

"You thought you were so smart, little mutt," said Mab to Molly. "And it was a very good try, but you forget that I have centuries more experience in playing this game than you." Shadows flickered across Ramel's face, creating a sketch of Mab's features.

"And what game is that?" demanded Molly. "Screwing over your loyal subjects?"

"Loyal," sneered Mab. "That is not exactly a word that I would use for either of you."

"Oh, that's right…why would I owe any loyalty to the person who wiped my memory when she unbound my Fae half?" Molly's cat-like eyes glowed with rage.

"So self-centered," murmured Mab with a deadly smile. "And yet I have control of your…*lover*." She said the last word disdainfully.

"This isn't going to end well," said Calliea under her breath.

"He's your eyes and ears," spat Molly. "You're not going to give that up."

"No…but I am quite skilled in inflicting pain." The shadow reflection of Mab's face faded, and for a quick moment it was Ramel, the *real* Ramel, looking at Molly.

"I won't stop fighting," he said in a strained voice.

"Neither will I," she replied, flying into his arms and kissing him fiercely.

Calliea winced at the display of affection but then leapt forward and pulled Molly away as Ramel went rigid.

What can I do? Tess asked the Caedbranr desperately as tremors began to travel through Ramel's body.

"No," Molly moaned in protest as a choked sound of pain escaped him. Calliea held her back with a none too gentle grip on her arm.

You could kill him, replied the Sword with a practical air.

That isn't an option, snapped Tess angrily. She watched helplessly as blood trickled down Ramel's chin. Wisps of dark smoke curled from the black breastplate.

Quick as a striking snake, Jess landed a perfect right hook to Ramel's jaw. The Unseelie knight's eyes rolled back and his body went limp. Jess grunted as he caught him, sliding him down to sit against the wall.

Or you could do that, commented the Sword with something like amusement in its voice.

If you're not going to be helpful, you can just be quiet, Tess replied, reaching her limit of patience with the sentient weapon. *He taught me to hold a sword before I was anything but a mortal girl dragged into Queen Mab's Court as repayment of an honor debt. He was my first introduction to the Fae world when I was just a child.*

"Well, this is all a bit dramatic for my taste," commented Calliea as Molly knelt by Ramel's side, smoothing his hair back from his forehead.

Tess sighed. "Any more dramatic than leading an expedition into the mortal world to rescue *our* lovers?"

"Technically we're here to kill the bone sorcerer," Calliea pointed out as she recoiled her whip and clipped it back to her belt. "So now the question on everyone's minds...what do we do with him?" She motioned to the unconscious Ramel.

"The bond between Mab and Finnead was broken when Finnead drowned," Tess said. "She had to let him go before she was dragged down with him."

"That was probably a one in a million kind of chance," said Jess. "She might have gotten smarter since then."

"How? Place some sort of invincibility spell on her Three? We already know that isn't the case, or else you wouldn't have been able to lay him out like that."

Jess rubbed his chin thoughtfully, looking at the matte black armor encasing Ramel's chest. "He hasn't taken off that armor since we've come through the portal."

Calliea frowned. "It's barely been a full day."

"But soaked through in a rainstorm and sleeping in it?" Jess shrugged. "It's a little weird, is all I'm saying."

"He's been wearing the armor since right after he helped me regain my memories," said Molly slowly. "I knew it had something to do with her control over him, but I could never figure out how. Mab got…angry…after Ramel helped me. He tried to help her sister, and when it didn't work…" She swallowed. "I only saw him a few times between then and now. He had the armor on every time."

"It's a possibility," allowed Tess. Could she cut away the enchanted armor just as she'd cut away the cursed dagger that had controlled Luca? She filed the thought for later contemplation. "I don't want him to know our plans," she said finally. "Mab knows that we know, so the element of surprise is gone. But we can't afford to leave someone here to guard him, and honestly, I don't know what he's capable of now that Mab is in control." Even as she pronounced her words calmly, more questions surged through her mind. Would Mab retaliate against anyone in the Fae world if they foiled her plans in the mortal world? What was more important to her, the Lethe Stone or killing the Bearer, if what Molly said was true?

"We can blindfold him," suggested Calliea.

"That might work as a temporary solution when we make camp, but I want him in the fight against the bone sorcerer," Tess replied.

"It's not guaranteed that he'll fight on our side," said Calliea.

"Mab usually loosens her hold when he's fighting, I think," said Molly. "She doesn't know as much about it as he does. She doesn't want to lose him as her eyes and ears, like you said. And she wants the Lethe Stone."

Tess closed her eyes for a moment and rubbed her forehead. A bone sorcerer, the Exiled, the Unseelie Queen possessing Ramel…it seemed there was no end to the complications.

"Tess, you'll want to see this," said Niall.

"We're watching him," said Jess, widening his stance as he stood over Ramel. Calliea nodded.

When Tess turned to the map on the table, she found the three Glasidhe studying it intently, their auras dimmed as they stepped carefully around Niall's scrying glass.

"We thought it best not to interfere," said Haze, looking up at Tess.

"That was a most impressive explosion," said Farin approvingly as she peered down into the scrying glass.

"Explosion?" Tess repeated in alarm.

"Yes," said Niall. "A…truck." He remembered the word after a quick moment of thought.

Tess leaned over the table next to Niall. His scrying compass looked like it was crafted from carved white bone. She looked down through the lens and the blurred figures resolved, the picture widening in her mind's eye until she could see far more than just the initial field of view offered by the scrying glass. Admiration for Niall's skill surfaced in the back of her mind.

Sparring figures dominated the foreground of the chaotic scene, the backdrop a crackling fire spilling black smoke into the sky. Tess quickly picked out Duke and Merrick, her heart leaping into her throat as she scanned the rest of the scene. She froze as she saw Luca. The joy that surged through her at the sight of the *ulfdrengr* was so intense that it was painful. She couldn't breathe as she watched him try to capture a quicksilver figure blurring around him with the speed of its movements. Something would have to be moving supernaturally fast to make Luca look so slow, she thought, turning her attention back to Merrick and Duke. A lanky red-haired girl crouched over Merrick's prone figure, her face pale as she clutched a dagger in one hand. An exotically beautiful woman stood beside

Duke as he regained his feet, pointing a pistol at their opponent. Her lips moved but Tess couldn't hear her – no sound accompanied the scrying glass's picture.

Niall turned one of the small knobs on the side of the scrying glass, and Tess experienced a moment of vertigo as she rose above the scene. The Seelie Vaelanseld moved the picture at a slow enough speed that she didn't feel sick, but nonetheless the scrying glass swooped over the trees, following a small river until it settled on a little glade a moment later. Despite the early morning light illuminating the trees, the glade remained cloaked in darkness. Strange shadows writhed like mist over the ground. At the edge of the glade, a girl was tied to one of the trees. She couldn't have been more than fifteen, and she looked as though she had been terrified for so long that she was exhausted. Anger roiled in Tess's chest. Something moved through the glade. The scrying glass kept sliding away from it, and Tess couldn't see the figure properly. She only got a sense of a predatory darkness. The girl's eyes widened and she whimpered against the gag in her mouth, twisting against the ropes binding her to the tree.

Niall's fingers found the knobs at the side of the scrying glass again, and Tess stumbled back from the table. She blinked and shook her arm, settling the blaze of her war markings into a manageable glow. "We need to go. Now."

"It's too late for the girl," said Niall, almost gently.

"It's not too late until she's dead," retorted Tess.

"That glade is about fifteen miles away as the crow flies," said Niall. "Even if we found a ride, we would be too late."

Tess swore softly. Haze tilted his head and turned to Forin and Farin, conferencing with them in a low voice.

"Killing the bone sorcerer will ensure that it doesn't happen to anyone else," said Calliea.

"That doesn't help *her*, though," said Tess.

"Sometimes you can't save everyone," said Jess softly.

"What good is this power if I can't use it?" she replied in frustration. First Ramel possessed by Mab, now this girl about to be gutted by the bone sorcerer mere miles away.

"Lady Bearer," piped Haze, sweeping his trademark bow. "With your permission, we will mount a rescue mission."

Tess blinked and stared at the diminutive Fae. "The three of you want to rescue that girl?"

"We can fly very fast," said Haze seriously.

"We can distract him," said Farin, baring her pointed little teeth.

"Free the girl from her bonds and guide her through the forest," finished Forin.

"It would be easier if the bone sorcerer were distracted already. If he left her there while he pursued someone else." Tess thought quickly.

"You'd best act fast," said Niall, watching again through the scrying glass.

"What would appeal to him more than that girl?" Tess paced a few steps in the cramped trailer.

"He draws power from his victims. So…a more powerful victim," said Calliea. She looked at Tess's glowing war markings meaningfully.

"Well, I'm being a little slow today," muttered Tess. She motioned to the Glasidhe. "Start heading toward the glade." Farin let out a shrill war cry and even Haze grinned fiercely. Tess rolled up her sleeves as she opened the door of the trailer and stepped out into the cool morning air. Kianryk stood and stretched from his makeshift den just beneath the trailer. The trio of Glasidhe rocketed past her. "Keep watching the bone sorcerer," she called to Niall over her shoulder. She held up her sword arm and examined her war markings. "Let's see if I can send up a flare that he won't be able to resist."

Chapter 25

"So what now?" Ross kept her gun pointed at the sharp-toothed Fae woman. Her mind had suddenly stopped struggling to accept the reality of this other world. This magic, this existence that ran parallel to her own, had remained safely out of her sight…until now. Ross stared at the Exiled woman and knew that if the fight had gone the other way, she and her companion would probably be drinking Merrick's blood right now.

"You are lovely," said the woman appraisingly, tilting her head. "Like a South Sea dancing girl."

"Shut up," growled Ross. Mayhem echoed her growl.

"And with such a well-trained little wolf. But you are not *ulfdrengr*," the woman continued. She clasped her gloved hands together thoughtfully, her long sleeves falling down over her wrists.

"Hands up!" commanded Ross, finger tightening on the trigger. As her voice rang out, the woman tossed something into the grass and a blinding flash of light seared white across Ross's sight. She stumbled and went down to one knee, cursing. A strange mist lingered in the wake of the flare, and as Ross blinked the spots from her eyes she heard Vivian cry out. She turned toward the sound and only her quick reflexes allowed her to brace herself as Vivian crashed into her.

"Stupid girl," said the Exiled woman derisively, pulling Vivian's dagger from her leg. Merrick lay before her, gasping, a dark chain laid across his throat. The woman tilted her head, looking at her own blood on the dagger. "Brave girl," she amended, as though arguing with herself. She shook her head and growled. "Focus."

Merrick writhed on the ground, seemingly held immobile by the chain on his throat. Ross scrambled to her feet; she glanced at Vivian, who blinked at her dazedly, blood running down her face from a cut on her forehead.

"What are you waiting for?" Vivian said hoarsely, motioning to Merrick. "He needs help more than I do!"

Ross turned back to Merrick and the woman, cursing from between gritted teeth when she saw that the woman straddled him now, stroking his throat with one gloved hand. The woman was too close to Merrick for her to take a shot. Ross exchanged a quick glance with Duke and he nodded. She looked down at Mayhem, the dog met her eyes, and she released the Malinois with a firm word and gesture toward the woman.

Mayhem sprang forward, covering the distance to the woman in two long bounds. The woman hissed and threw herself flat onto Merrick; Mayhem's jaws caught only the fabric of the woman's cloak, but the dog held fast as she twisted. It was enough to jerk the woman off of Merrick, enough for Ross to leap over Merrick and tackle the woman. It felt like she had tried to tackle a statue of solid marble. She jammed her forearm into the woman's throat, and it seemed to stun her slightly, but then they rolled and Ross found herself fighting from her back, the woman's gloved hands closing about her throat. She delivered a blow to the woman's temple with the butt of her gun that would have knocked out a full grown man, but the woman grinned manically and licked her pointed teeth. Choking as her air supply was cut off, Ross freed her legs and delivered a vicious two-footed kick to the woman's midriff. It would have been enough force to do internal damage to a human, but it only succeeded in making the woman release her hold on Ross's throat momentarily.

Mayhem's jaws closed on the woman's arm. Ross's kick hadn't injured her, but even the strange Fae wasn't immune to the crushing power of the black dog's grip. She screeched and tried to fling Mayhem away, lifting the dog bodily, but the working dog snarled through her jaws and kept her grip on the woman. Ross lunged forward and tackled the woman's legs. She fell heavily and Ross saw her gloved hand moving toward her wrist again, the same gesture that had preceded the flash of light that had started this whole mess. Mayhem jerked the woman's arm, keeping her other wrist out of reach, and Ross seized the woman's free hand, pinning the arm under her knee before the Fae could break her hold with her unnatural strength. The woman howled, a sound so keening and loud that it hurt Ross's ears, but she snugged the Glock under the woman's chin and said firmly, "Stop fighting."

The woman went limp, laying panting under Ross, her azure eyes blazing and her teeth bared. Growls still spilled from Mayhem's closed jaws. Ross gave a low command, and the dog released her hold. "Don't get any ideas," Ross said to the woman, pressing the gun harder into the underside of her chin. "I'm pretty sure that no matter what kind of magic you have, you won't survive a point blank shot to the skull."

An incongruously high-pitched giggle escaped the woman. "Nearly four centuries I've survived this blasted world, and I'm executed by a little mortal whelp." She licked her teeth and grinned. "At least you're pretty."

"Stop talking," Ross said. She glimpsed movement out of her peripheral vision but didn't let it distract her from the woman lying beneath her.

"Bet you've been itching to fight like that for a while," Duke said with a grin from beside her. He pointed his Beretta at the woman's head. "I got security. See what she's got up her sleeves."

Ross kept her Glock under the woman's chin but used her free hand to pull up one of the woman's long green sleeves. Several dull metal chains looped about her wrist, mixed with a few silver bracelets and a dirty length of twine that had several small glass orbs tied to it. Different colors swirled within the orbs like smoke.

"Don't touch it," rasped Merrick. Vivian held the chain that had been across his throat between two fingers, as though she'd caught a snake. "They're spells."

"More than you could probably manage at this point, my boy," said the woman, eyeing Merrick hungrily as he lurched over to them, kneeling in the grass by the woman's arm.

Luca calmly deposited the second Exiled onto the grass, and Ross glanced between the *ulfdrengr* and the unconscious Exiled questioningly. Luca shrugged. "He wouldn't stop struggling. So he got the flat of my axe."

"Effective," allowed Ross.

Merrick carefully cut the twine holding the spell orbs around the Exiled woman's wrist. Ross and Duke still held both their weapons on her and Mayhem settled watchfully onto her belly in the grass, panting in satisfaction. Dark blood gleamed wetly against the dog's muzzle.

Merrick cut another bracelet of spell orbs from the woman's other wrist, carefully avoiding the chains of dull metal. He took two daggers from her boots, and then he paused, glancing at the woman's torso.

"Oh, such a proper gentleman," purred the woman, squirming suggestively beneath Ross and grinning. "Doesn't want to search the enemy below the neckline, eh?" She giggled again.

Ross sighed. "The pointy toothed bitch does have a point." The woman made an affronted sound. "Can't be squeamish when it comes to searches. Got her?"

"Got her," affirmed Duke, his weapon still pointed surely at her head.

"Aren't you going to even ask a girl's name when you've got your hand down her shirt?" asked the woman. Ross just rolled her eyes as she searched the woman's torso for any more chains or spell orbs; she found a short dagger in a rib sheath and a strange little leather pouch, but no more spells.

"What's your name?" asked Merrick, staring down at the white-haired Sidhe.

"So polite. Too bad you'd make a nice meal." The woman tilted her head. "Corsica. That's Tyr." She motioned with her chin toward the limp man.

"All right, I think that's all her weapons," said Ross. Luca retrieved Corsica's cloak and carefully moved all the chains and spell-orbs onto it. Vivian contributed the chain that had been laid on Merrick's neck. After relieving Tyr of his various blades and another spell orb tied with a thin strip of black leather, Luca wrapped it all into a neat bundle.

"Now that you've defanged me, *must* you point that at me still?" asked Corsica, looking up at Duke and his gun.

"We still gotta figure some things out, sweetheart," Duke replied. "So do yourself a favor and stay put."

Ross carefully stood and backed away. Her body ached. She pushed the discomfort aside and adjusted her grip on the Glock, looking at Luca. "What's next?"

Luca looked at Merrick. "She is one of your people."

Merrick swayed. Vivian inserted herself under his shoulder. "I didn't think the stories were true," he said.

"Oh, we're bedtime stories now, eh?" said Corsica. She sighed. "I suppose there are worse things."

"Worse things like being vampires?" Vivian asked sharply.

Corsica laughed delightedly. "Oh, my dear girl, *you* are sharp." Her nostrils flared as she sniffed the air. "I thought the South Sea girl was the one that smelled of the Old World, but it's you."

"I have no idea what you're talking about," said Vivian. The dawn light blooming through the trees made the blood on the side of her face luridly dark. She made no move to wipe it away, and it trickled in a thin line over her cheekbone.

"Bedtime stories in both worlds, how about that, hmmm, Tyr?" said Corsica, though Tyr hadn't stirred. Ross wondered just how hard Luca had hit him with the flat of his axe. The burgeoning light caught the silver rings bristling from Corsica's ears and transformed her silver hair into a glowing nimbus spread behind her head. Even with the scars dappling her face, Corsica was still ethereal.

"We should move them," said Luca, scanning their surroundings.

"He'll be here soon, I think." Corsica grinned.

"The bone sorcerer?" Vivian asked.

"Yes," the Exiled replied. Her eyes went half-lidded. "We were the first to arrive, you know. I think others will have felt it. First him coming through, and then you, and then *her*."

"Her?" repeated Luca.

"Don't be coy," said Corsica. She licked her lips. "I can hear your heart thumping faster at the mention of her."

"What's with the blood thing? Are they really vampires? We need to get moving with this plan, whatever it is," said Duke. "I don't like sitting out here in front of the house."

"You and me both," Ross muttered.

"Perhaps I was not thinking ahead enough," said Corsica softly, tilting her head to the side. "So long since we had a good meal, perhaps hunger was making me hasty..."

"This is making my head hurt," said Ross. "Merrick, please explain it to us."

"From what I think I understand," said Merrick slowly, "they somehow survive by taking blood. By *drinking* blood." A faint trace of disgust colored his voice.

"Corruption is the price of survival," said Corsica. "We had to...improvise."

"So you *are* vampires," Vivian mused.

"Those silly fanged creatures that can't stand the light of day?"

Corsica snorted. "Hardly." She shifted her shoulders and crossed her legs as if she were lounging in bed rather than lying in the grass with a gun pointed at her head. "It's gotten harder throughout the centuries. The dreamers taste the best."

"*Taebramh*," Merrick said. "You've been…taking the *taebramh* of mortals through their blood."

"Clever boy." Corsica grinned.

"All right, this is all very informative, but we need to make a decision," Ross said. "What are we doing with these two?"

"I think they'll jump us the first chance they get," said Duke.

"What about the 'gruesome revenge?'" asked Vivian, craning her neck to look at Merrick.

"Revenge is a lofty goal, but I'd settle for a good meal," said Corsica. "Tyr, too, though he won't tell you that himself." Her vivid eyes traced the patterns of the clouds in the sky, backlit now by the sunrise. She stared up into the sky for a moment and then shifted her gaze to Merrick. "What are you going to do with the dark mage, hm? He's going to use you as bait, you know. For *her*."

Merrick stared down at Corsica, his haggard face unreadable. "Let's bring them inside."

Something flickered in Corsica's eyes. Ross frowned. After centuries of fighting to survive in the mortal world as outcasts, could the Exiled be made allies by a slight gesture of mercy? Were their souls so starved that empathy would restore them, or were they so far gone that they would still plot the death of Merrick and, perhaps, all of them?

Luca sank to his haunches near Corsica, one hand still gripping his axe. Her eyes traveled over his muscled body appraisingly, but his face was grim, his blue eyes icy. "If either of you lift a hand against any of my companions, I will kill you."

Corsica watched him intently for a long moment, a cunning intelligence surfacing in her calculating gaze. "I believe you," she murmured. "*Ulfdrengr*," she added, a crooked smile pulling up one side of her mouth. In that instant, she looked almost human, the memory of some long past experience softening the taut planes of her body.

Luca nodded gravely. "Yes. So you know that my word is my bond."

Corsica didn't reply. Luca stood and took a step back, gesturing for her to stand as well. Duke still kept a watchful eye on her, but he lowered his Beretta to an alert position rather than directly pointing it at Corsica. The Exiled woman slid to her knees and then silently offered her wrists, bowing her head. The motion looked natural, and she held carefully still, waiting.

"We will not bind you," said Luca gruffly.

Corsica raised her head warily, her eyes darting between Luca, Merrick and Ross as though she expected someone to counter Luca's statement. After a moment she lowered her hands and stood, still looking between all of them guardedly.

"Take security," Duke said to Ross. "I'll get the other one."

Ross nodded, widening her stance slightly and focusing her attention on Corsica. Mayhem's ears swiveled forward and the dog stood at Ross' side. Duke pulled the unconscious Tyr onto his shoulders, hefting him once to settle the weight properly. Corsica watched but said nothing.

"Come on," Duke said, trudging past them. "Let's go inside before we get any more nasty surprises." He looped his left arm around Tyr's leg and grasped the unconscious man's arm, freeing his right hand to wield the Beretta without any interference. Vivian and Merrick followed him.

"You next," said Ross to Corsica, expecting some slightly unhinged grin or comment in reply, but Corsica mutely followed them toward the porch of the house. Ross trailed a step behind her. Mayhem circled back and trotted alongside Luca. Ross glanced over at the smoking wreck of her truck. The flames from the explosion seemed to have some sort of time expiration, thankfully. "I still don't understand why you blew up my truck," she muttered.

"To distract you so we could attack," replied Corsica bluntly. Then she grinned a little. "And I've never blown up a truck before. I thought it would be fun."

"Yeah, well, you're not the one who has to figure out how to explain it to the insurance company," Ross retorted as they reached the porch steps. How in the world was she supposed to fill out that insurance claim? Did magical spells count as an 'act of God?' She'd always thought that little clause was archaic and ridiculous but now she wasn't so sure.

Vivian held the screen door open for Merrick and then it banged shut behind her. Corsica reached unconcernedly for the wrought-iron handle, opening the door without so much as a flinch. Ross followed her quickly, feeling the frown crease her forehead. She wasn't an expert on the effect of iron on Fae, but she thought that even with gloves, Merrick would have avoided gripping the iron handle. Luca shut the door behind them. The sound of the deadbolt clicking home wasn't much of a comfort.

Vivian had already rolled the living room rug into a corner and spread a blanket on the wood floor. Ross smiled a little. Trust Vivian to adapt quickly to the appearance of the Exiled while still managing to keep their little house free of bloodstains on the carpets. Duke squatted and carefully slid Tyr from his shoulders. Without prompting, Corsica sat cross-legged by Tyr. His hair was as silver as hers, cut in a sort of shaggy, puckish way.

Merrick settled onto the couch. Vivian stood in the corner of the room, crossing her arms over her chest. Luca slid his axe back into its loop on his belt.

"I can take a look at your shoulder and arm," said Duke to Corsica. "I'm a medic. A…healer."

"I know what a medic is," she replied without taking her eyes from Tyr. "The bullet passed straight through the muscle. And our flesh is resilient. The dog's bite didn't do much damage."

"I could at least clean them," said Duke.

Corsica looked at him sharply, narrowing her eyes. "What do you care? I'm no friend of yours."

Duke shrugged. "Fine. Have it your way."

"You said the bone sorcerer was on his way here," prompted Merrick.

"You said you'd give us a good meal," countered Corsica, licking her lips. She kept glancing at the windows and the door, as if checking to make sure that the exits to the room still existed.

Merrick looked at Corsica for a long moment. "You don't use blood magic? Giving you my blood won't give you a hold over me?"

"You can't be serious," said Vivian. "You're not strong enough to give her any of your blood."

"I'll determine what I'm strong enough to do," Merrick replied, a bit sharply. Vivian looked away and Merrick sighed wearily, shifting his focus back to Corsica.

"No," Corsica said, staring hungrily at Merrick. "No, we just use the blood to survive. Not for sorcery. Not for a while, at least. We've barely been scraping by, these past years. We didn't have the runes and we were bound and banished."

Luca touched his axe. "Give your word that you won't use our blood against us."

Corsica laughed. "What good is my word, Northman? I am one of the forsaken. Our bond has been broken all these centuries. We were bound by iron and banished." Anger blazed up in her eyes again, extinguished just as quickly by a lost expression. "Bound and banished to wander in the darkness."

"I am not Sidhe," said Luca almost gently. "I am *ulfdrengr* and I am *Vyldgard*, as he is. And I will take you at your word."

"Such grand gestures," said Corsica with a hint of a sneer in her voice. She looked away and spoke to herself again. "Only time will tell if they are friends. Only time will tell."

"Give us your word," Luca repeated.

"You have it," Corsica replied. "For what it's worth," she added to herself.

Ross shook her head. "I don't like this."

"Smart girl," said Corsica with a grin. "Calculating and cold, yes, you're a smart one too. Why give something for nothing when that's not the way of the world? Mercy met with betrayal, that's the usual script, isn't it?" She tilted her head. "You're trying to catch him, aren't you? With that little runetrap in the back of the house."

Merrick leaned forward. "Yes." He rolled up one of his sleeves.

Corsica stared at his pale forearm, her eyes tracing the blue veins beneath his skin. Ross's skin crawled at the hunger written across her face. "It won't hold him. He'll just laugh," Corisca said without taking her eyes off of Merrick's pale arm.

"And how exactly do you know that? It's not as though there've been bone sorcerers running amuck in the mortal world before," Ross said acidly.

"Skeptical, skeptical," said Corsica in a chiding voice. "Not a bone sorcerer, no, but we have hunted other things. Other beings. Some from this world, some from the next, some from none at all." One of her black-gloved hands sketched an arc through the air. "Traps require certain things. You have the right idea, yes, a good foundation, but not enough." She shook her head.

"I give you my blood, you tell us how to fix the trap for the bone sorcerer so that it will hold him," said Merrick firmly.

Vivian pressed her lips together unhappily but said nothing.

"What will you do with him when he is caught in your little web?" asked Corsica, cocking her head to the side.

"Kill him," replied Luca simply.

"Perhaps…perhaps you would allow me to talk to him first," said the Sidhe woman with a strange note of pleading in her voice.

"Why?" asked Ross suspiciously.

"It is maybe a chance for us to come closer to what we once were," said Corsica. She glanced at Merrick's arm again and licked her lips. "It is not easy."

Ross raised her eyebrows. "Sounds like you made the choice to become what you are."

"Would you choose to live or die?" replied Corsica with a mad glint in her eyes. She looked Ross up and down. Ross shifted uncomfortably; she felt like Corsica was peering past her skin, into her soul. "You chose to live. You chose to kill. Are you a monster, same as me?"

"Maybe," Ross replied calmly. "But I fight against it every day. I try to *help* people now."

"Recompense for your deeds?" suggested Corsica, arching a pale eyebrow.

Ross clenched her jaw and tried not to let the words bother her, but they stung…because they were true. She looked away.

"Perhaps now we will…help…too," said Corsica. She looked down at Tyr and then nodded. "Yes. We will help."

Merrick drew one of his small daggers from its sheath.

Vivian paled. "I can't watch this," she said to Ross. "Make sure she doesn't kill him."

As Vivian strode from the room, Corsica called after her, "I like the quote on your shirt! Tolkien is one of my favorites." She grinned her sharp-toothed grin as Vivian told her, in some choice words, what she could do with her opinion.

"Improvements to the runetrap, and no sorcery with my blood," said Merrick, holding the blade over his skin.

Corsica nodded. "Yes, yes, I'll be good." She slunk toward Merrick on her hands and knees, clambering over Tyr's prone form, her eyes fixed on the throb of Merrick's pulse in his wrist.

"Are you all right with this?" Duke asked Luca.

"It's not my choice to make," the *ulfdrengr* said in a low voice. He moved forward and stood within easy reach of Corsica and Merrick.

"If he goes unconscious, you stop," Duke said firmly to Corsica. "If you don't stop, I'm gonna pry you off. And if I can't pry you off, I'll shoot you."

Corsica nodded, kneeling in front of Merrick like a supplicant. Merrick took a deep breath and sliced through his skin with the dagger. His blood welled up dark as ink, and Corsica seized his arm, her tongue darting out between her pointed teeth to catch the first drops before they fell. She lapped like a cat at first, and then pressed her mouth to the wound. Merrick sucked in his breath.

Ross felt sick but she swallowed hard and stood her ground. At least Vivian hadn't offered her blood this time. Merrick leaned back, sweat standing out on his forehead. Duke stepped closer, putting a hand on Merrick's shoulder and talking to him in a low voice. Merrick nodded. Corsica pressed her body against Merrick's legs, leaning over his lap as she drank his blood.

Duke stepped over Tyr and quickly retrieved a packet of gauze from the first aid kit. Merrick closed his eyes, his skin pale as bone. Corsica hummed in pleasure, her throat working as she swallowed.

"All right, that's enough," Duke said as Merrick began to slide sideways. He steadied the *Vyldgard* Sidhe and expertly gripped Merrick's arm just above the elbow, putting pressure on the veins and arteries supplying Corsica with blood. "Enough," he repeated tersely. To Ross's surprise, Corsica drew back, panting and licking the blood from her lips. Duke quickly bandaged the cut on Merrick's forearm. The navigator's eyes fluttered open again.

"That was…unpleasant," he said hoarsely.

Corsica rolled onto her back, part of her body draped over Tyr. She closed her eyes, chest heaving, a dreamy smile on her face. Ross looked at Merrick and then down at Corsica, still licking her bloodstained mouth, and she wondered what kind of deal they had just struck with these Exiles from the Fae world.

Chapter 26

"Tess, wait!" Calliea leapt out of the trailer, the door banging shut behind her. "Niall says that he thinks Luca and Merrick have already laid a trap for the bone sorcerer. From what he can see, anyway." She glanced at Tess's rolled sleeves and the bright burn of her war markings. "What's your plan?"

"Light myself up and make me the target instead of the girl," said Tess. It sounded too simple. She took a deep breath and thought quickly.

"But if you send up a flare here, what good is that going to do? We're just going to confront the bone sorcerer here?" Calliea eyed the trailer and the surrounding grassy land skeptically.

"We came here to kill the bone sorcerer and retrieve the Lethe Stone," Tess replied. "That's about as basic a plan as I can come up with." Her war markings pulsed a little brighter, looking like rivulets of emerald fire sliding over her skin. "Do you have a better idea?"

"Use the runetrap that Merrick and Luca have built," said Calliea. "It'll give us some time to think, if we have the bone sorcerer trapped."

"I'd be leading him straight to them," said Tess impatiently. "I don't like that."

"They're already expecting him. They may not know that we're here," pointed out Calliea.

"But how would I cover the distance..." Tess stopped as the Caedbranr plucked a memory from the back of her head and displayed it for her in her mind's eye – a dark forest flashing by, her body pressed against the muscled body of a black wolf, Beryk's musky scent filling her nose as he raced toward the battle in the clearing at the Royal Wood, her first battle as the Bearer of the Iron Sword. Tess almost laughed. Kianryk's ears swiveled as he met her gaze with intelligent blue eyes. The scarlet collar flashed against his golden pelt as he moved. Tess wondered suddenly if the collar would prevent him from doing whatever it was that the Northern wolves did. Beryk had seemed as large as a small horse when she'd ridden him through the forest.

"We'll come as fast as we can," said Calliea. "Hopefully Jess can keep up."

"He'll keep up," Tess said confidently. Her *taebramh* surged in her chest, stretching the bonds that she unconsciously placed on her power, but she didn't feel nauseous. She felt stronger than she'd felt since she was first bound to the Sword. "As soon as I know that the bone sorcerer is locked onto me as a target, you can start for the house. If we do it right, we'll arrive at about the same time."

"There's a lot of moving parts to this, and it might not work out exactly as we plan," cautioned Calliea, her hand resting on her golden whip. "But it's a better plan than simply trying to draw him here."

Tess nodded. "I'll burn the flare for a bit here and try to buy you some time. Then I'll haul ass toward the trap."

"What if he catches you before you get there?" Calliea asked.

"Then I'll kill him," Tess replied. The Caedbranr rattled in its sheath. She turned to Kianryk. "What do you say, think you could stand being the Bearer's noble steed for a few hours?"

Kianryk shook himself thoroughly and grinned. Tess blinked and suddenly he was larger than usual. It wasn't quite as shocking of a change, since the golden wolf was bigger than Beryk normally, but she smiled and said, "I'll take that for a yes." She turned back to Calliea. "Go let the others know the plan. I'll need Niall to confirm that the bone sorcerer locks onto my *taebramh*, so you can start toward the house with the others."

Calliea nodded briskly and disappeared inside the trailer. Tess shouldered her traveling pack, adjusting it to rest alongside the Sword's sheath. "You know where Luca is, right?" she asked Kianryk. He straightened and bounded off confidently through the grass, straight as an arrow, pausing and looking back at Tess. "All right," she said, striding over to him. "Just wanted to make sure. We're not heading that way right away, but after we make sure he's got our scent, we'll swing in that direction." She didn't know how much Kianryk really understood, but she let herself feel optimistic as she watched his nearly human eyes. She stood and breathed in the cool early morning air, watching dawn lighten the clouds to the east. After a few moments, Calliea, Molly, Ramel and Jess filed out of the trailer. Jess propped open the door with an old chunk of cement so that Tess could see Niall at the table. Ramel looked dazed, an impressive bruise blooming across his jaw from Jess's punch.

"You've got the coordinates to the house?" Tess asked, feeling strangely nervous. Her palms tingled as she wiped them on the front of her breeches.

"Yep," replied Jess.

Calliea nodded. "Both of us looked at the map and traced out the route."

"Good." They all stood and looked at each other for a long moment. Jess still had a firm grip on Ramel's arm, whether to keep him upright or keep control or both, Tess wasn't certain. "Well," Tess said awkwardly, "see you on the other side."

Calliea smiled slightly. "I'll tell Luca you're on the way."

That brought out an answering smile from Tess. "Thanks."

Calliea strode away in the direction that Kianryk had pointed out just moments before. The tawny wolf watched the Valkyrie commander go, but stood still in the long grass. Jess gripped Tess's shoulder with his free hand, his gray eyes grave. "Do what you have to do to make sure you're the one left standing."

She nodded. "I always do."

Ramel didn't meet her eyes. Jess prodded him forward, following Calliea's path. Tess wished briefly that they'd had the time to figure out the solution to Mab's takeover of Ramel, but she pushed away the regret. If they didn't act now, an innocent girl would die at the hands of the bone sorcerer. There would be time enough to sort out that mess afterward. And perhaps it would placate Mab to see them procure the Lethe Stone.

Molly and Tess were left alone in front of the trailer. Tess suddenly felt an echo of that same joy that had surfaced within her when she'd learned that Molly had regained her memories. She felt like she should say something momentous and serious, but instead she said, "I like your hair longer. It looks good."

Molly smiled. "Thanks."

"Why didn't you come find me when your memories were restored?" she asked, wincing internally. Great, sound accusatory to her best friend who just recently regained the memory of them ever being friends at all.

"Mab was watching me," said Molly, the smile fading from her face. "I didn't want to put anyone else in danger."

"I'm sorry." Tess waved a hand. "That was dumb. I shouldn't have asked that."

"It's fine. Really." Molly smiled. Her gaze wandered to Ramel. "There'll be plenty of time to talk after we figure out this mess."

"Good point." Tess nodded. "We should…celebrate."

"Fine by me," Molly said. She suddenly lunged forward and hugged Tess hard. Tess froze and then returned the hug a bit stiffly. "Kick ass!" Molly said into her ear. She released Tess and slid away.

"Oh, and you know what's the best part?" she called over her shoulder as she began walking after Ramel and Jess.

"What?" Tess said, smiling despite herself.

"Our celebration can include ice cream and beer!" Molly flashed a thumb's up, and loped away after the group.

Tess grinned and then sighed. Time to get a move on with this plan. "Still got him, Niall?" she said loudly. "I'm about to spin up this flare."

"I'll let you know when his attention is diverted," said Niall.

"You might want to look away," said Tess to Kianryk. She didn't wait to see if the wolf complied. There wasn't any more time to lose. She closed her eyes and slowly released the bonds of her power. She felt the Sword surge eagerly, and then the world went white.

The strength of the raging inferno that roared from her war markings nearly knocked her from her feet. A column of striated white-and-emerald fire shot up into the sky, brighter than any beacon she could have imagined, and she stood at its base, watching the world through a wavering curtain of flame. The *taebramh* didn't burn the grass or throw off heat like any normal fire, and to Tess's surprise she felt a slight tug but nothing like the depletion she'd anticipated. She grinned a little. The power felt *good* as it swirled through her bones and danced along her skin.

She barely heard Niall's shout through the swirling tendrils of fire. Finally, his distorted voice reached her. She gritted her teeth. Now for the more difficult part. Releasing her power was rarely the problem. With great effort, she began to pull the column of fire back into herself. It felt as physically taxing as hauling a heavy rope. Sweat slid down her back as she glanced up and saw that the beacon was about half its original height. She bore down and compressed the rest of her *taebramh*. For its part, the Sword helped. Finally, with a burst of wind, the last of the fire disappeared and the white fire faded from the edges of her vision. She rested her hands on her knees for just a moment, breathing hard.

Niall emerged from the trailer, clipping the case of his scrying glass back to his belt. He nodded to Tess, his pale eyes grave yet lit with a strange excitement. "He is coming."

"Good." Tess straightened and rearranged the Sword's strap over her chest so that she didn't have the time to find out if her hands were shaking.

"I will stay with you, if you wish it," said Niall. A faint smile touched his mouth. "I may not be able to keep up with a Northern wolf, but it would be a close race."

"Thanks, but I'd like you to stay with Calliea and Jess. If Mab takes control of Ramel again, I want to know you're there with them." Tess was touched by the offer, and for just a moment she let herself consider taking it, but she reminded herself that the bone sorcerer was her responsibility. She'd been the one to bargain with Mab to open the Gate.

Niall nodded. "He left the girl in the clearing. He was moving at a good pace."

Tess swallowed. "What does that mean, a good pace?"

"About as fast as a Northman can run. Fifteen miles…that would probably take him perhaps an hour and a half," replied Niall. He bowed to her slightly. "With your leave, Tess."

She nodded. "Thanks, Niall. Keep them safe, if you can."

Niall nodded and then turned, breaking into a measured, graceful run. The others were already out of sight. She took a deep breath and looked at Kianryk. "Well, now we wait."

Kianryk huffed in agreement. Tess brushed her knuckles against the red collar, and the sorcery ingrained in its leather fizzed up onto her skin. It wasn't an unpleasant feeling, but there were strong wards on the collar, which weren't unexpected, given its origins. Tess tugged her sleeve up and checked her concealment rune again. Then she paced as she waited, walking a line parallel to the trailer. Kianryk watched her for a few minutes and then gazed off in the direction that the others had taken. Tess wondered if the Glasidhe had freed the girl yet. She sent up another smaller beacon and ate a few more pieces of *kajuk* despite her roiling stomach.

"I'm assuming you approve of this plan, since you didn't object," she said out loud to the Sword.

I have no objections, as long as you do not get yourself killed, it replied.

"Thanks for the overwhelming vote of confidence," she said.

Why do you think I am not confident in you? You are the Bearer.

"I know, I know." Tess kicked at a rock. "Sorry. I just don't like waiting. It's too much time to think."

Apparently, replied the Sword drily.

When she had kicked at all the rocks within a ten pace radius of the trailer, Tess got out her little reference book and read the section on the Lethe Stone again, studying the diagram. It looked a bit like an egg, smooth and dark blue like the waters of the mythical River Lethe, or at least that's what the description said. She replaced the book in her pack, squinted up at the sun and took a deep breath. The bone sorcerer would be close enough now, and she had given the others over an hour's head start. She loosened the bonds on her *taebramh* enough to send sparks flickering from her war markings. Kianryk raised his head and sniffed the wind that lifted the hair from Tess's neck. A low growl rumbled from his throat.

"I'm guessing that's my cue," Tess said, although she wasn't sure why she was even talking out loud. She looked at Kianryk. "Ready?"

During her time in Faeortalam, Tess had become a very proficient rider. She wouldn't go so far as to call herself skilled, but she'd ridden Nehalim charging into battle up the side of a mountain. Yet she was still reminded of how different a wolf was from a *faehal* as she clambered onto Kianryk's muscled back. "I hope Luca will eventually forgive me," she muttered, lying low with her belly against Kianryk's back as she'd done when riding Beryk.

When she felt fairly confident in her stance, she said, "All right, let's..."

Her last word was lost in a squeak as the tawny wolf leapt forward, not needing to be told twice to close the distance between him and Luca.

The sparks from Tess's war markings flared and snapped in the wind, streaming back like fireworks behind them, but she didn't have time to contemplate the effectiveness of her trail for the bone sorcerer. She clutched at Kianryk's ruff with white-knuckled hands, her knees tight around his sides. She grabbed the scarlet collar when he sprang over a stream with a gravity defying leap, and nearly slid off his side. The sorcery in the collar prickled on the skin of her hands, but she kept her grip anyway, reasoning that a bit of discomfort from the runes on the collar was better than falling. Her heart hammered against her rib cage, but she also thrilled at the rare feeling of accompanying something so swift and wild. She felt Kianryk's muscles flexing beneath her, rippling as he stretched his great body to mind numbing speeds. She wondered, in the small part of her mind that wasn't preoccupied with *not falling*, whether the others had reached Luca and Merrick yet. She wondered if they should be leading the bone sorcerer on a more circuitous route.

Kianryk slowed slightly as though sensing Tess's hesitation. She still didn't dare look behind them. Would the bone sorcerer appear as a cloaked figure, like the sorcerer at the bridge? Or would he be a shadow sliding across the ground, speeding to its destination and then taking corporeal form? What if the runetrap didn't hold, and she wasn't strong enough to protect all the others from the dark power of the bone sorcerer?

If you give voice to your doubts, you give them strength, cautioned the Sword. *Think of the task ahead, not of all the ways it could go wrong.*

You make it sound so simple, replied Tess, but she swallowed hard and cleared her mind. The Sword was right. She couldn't charge into the fight worrying about everyone else. It was just like before the battle at the Dark Keep. She had to focus on the task at hand, not on all the ways it could go wrong.

Kianryk slowed enough that Tess caught glimpses of the scenery around them, oaks draped with Spanish moss and the wild lush greenery of the land near a river. The scent of growth and decay hung heavy in the air. The sun burned brightly on its way to its noon zenith. Perhaps it was a good sign, Tess thought, that they would be battling the dark mage in broad daylight. They emerged from a copse of trees and Kianryk was suddenly trotting unconcernedly along a paved road. Tess glanced around in alarm. She didn't see any cars. It looked like a quiet country road, but that didn't loosen the knot of sudden panic in her chest. Kianryk either didn't understand or didn't want to listen when she attempted to guide him back toward the trees with her knees like she would have guided Nehalim or any other *faehal*. He loped by the edge of the road where the ground was flat and the grass sparse.

Tess noticed that an eerie silence had fallen around them. She twisted and looked over her shoulder, trying to keep her body low on Kianryk's back. The sound of a car engine grated against her ears, sounding new and unfamiliar. But it wasn't the car in the distance that turned her stomach. Only a stone's throw behind them a faceless figure swept along the road…about as fast as a Northman could run.

"We better not be far away, because we've got company" she said to Kianryk. The wolf lurched forward and she nearly fell again. Only her desperate grip on the scarlet collar saved her. Kianryk picked up speed, bounding across the dirt and then turning sharply onto a smaller street. Tess's heart caught in her throat as she leaned hard to the opposite side of the turn. Kianryk hurtled along the lane. A mailbox suddenly loomed before them and he dodged, but his feint failed to take into account the extra space required for Tess. The post hit her right knee as they hurtled by it. She held on grimly through the starburst of pain, gritting her teeth. Kianryk seemed to belatedly realize his miscalculation, giving the other mailboxes a wide berth as he flashed past small houses set at country lane intervals. He surged up a winding driveway, gravel flying beneath his paws. Tess's thoughts had disintegrated into a single repeating stream: *Don't fall off.* She couldn't breathe and her knee pulsed with Kianryk's every stride and she could *feel* the bone sorcerer behind them, a black shadow that greedily sucked in the trailing sparks from her war markings.

Smoke tinged the air as they rounded a bend in the long driveway. Tess glanced up and saw through her streaming eyes the burned remnants of the truck that had exploded in the scene Niall had shown through the scrying glass. Relief washed through her chest. They were here. They'd found the house and they'd found Merrick and Luca and Duke, and the runetrap would be behind the house.

But her relief vanished as the ground rolled beneath Kianryk's paws. The wolf stumbled, regained his footing, but another wave caught him unawares from the side and he fell. The gravel rushed up to meet Tess, a bone jarring impact rattled her teeth, and her vision went black.

Chapter 27

Ross crossed her arms over her chest and nudged Corsica with her foot. "Hey. Merrick held up his end of the bargain, now it's your turn. We don't know how much time we have."

Corsica grinned drunkenly up at Ross. "Such impatience. Let me bask a moment." She stretched like a cat against Tyr. The man stirred for the first time since Luca had knocked him unconscious. Corsica turned and whispered in Tyr's ear. Ross's skin prickled and she took a step back.

Tyr opened his eyes, which were a clear, dark gray that was nearly black, a startling contrast to Corsica's blue gaze. His hair, though, was just as silver as that of his companion, and his skin bore the same mottled layers of white, pink and reddish scars. He looked sharply up at Merrick and Duke, and then his gaze settled accusingly on Luca. He didn't wear gloves, and Ross saw that his hand was scarred more heavily than his face as he touched his throat delicately with two fingers, exploring the mottled bruises left by Luca's grip. Ropes of scar tissue circled his wrists. Ross wondered whether the bracelets of scars were from manacles.

"If you hadn't fought, I wouldn't have had to do that," Luca said unapologetically. He held one of his axes almost casually.

Tyr said nothing, his eyes lingering on Merrick's bandaged arm. Corsica giggled and fell onto her back, flinging her arms wide, eyes closed again. Tyr pushed himself up onto his forearms, still silently staring.

"Sorry, bud, not enough for two right now," Duke said firmly, stepping in front of Merrick.

For a moment, the silver-haired man leaned toward them anyway, a primal hunger written across his face. Ross sidestepped to get a better angle on him, her finger slowly sliding toward the trigger of the Glock. Then Tyr grunted and grimaced, shuddering as he closed his eyes. He turned and touched Corsica's shoulder, making an inquiring sound.

"They have a runetrap in the yard for the bone sorcerer," Corsica said languorously. "But it's not quite right."

Tyr sighed audibly and stood. He gestured between Corsica and Merrick, a question written on his face. Everyone stared at him. Tyr mimed cutting his arm, and held the arm toward Corsica.

"Yeah, she drank his blood," said Duke.

Tyr raised his eyebrows.

"She said she would fix the runetrap in exchange for the blood. Or...I'm guessing that *you* could fix the trap," Ross said.

The slender Exile rubbed both his hands over his face but said nothing.

"He doesn't talk," murmured Corsica. "I talk for both of us."

Tyr sighed again and raked one hand through his shaggy silver hair. He pointed toward the door and swept his hand around toward the back of the house.

"It would be really helpful if you'd actually tell us what he's trying to say, then," said Ross in irritation.

"Stop being so dramatic," replied Corsica. "He's the one who will fix the runes. He wants to go see them. And if you have supplies, he would like those too."

Ross heard Vivian rummaging in the kitchen. Her stomach growled incongruously, reminding her that she hadn't had a chance to eat breakfast before all hell had broken loose that morning.

"How do we know that you won't sabotage the runetrap?" Ross asked, forcing her mind away from the thought of food.

Corsica blinked at her with wide eyes, and then she grinned. Merrick's blood darkened a few of her sharp teeth. "I gave my word, didn't I?" She rolled to her belly and then to her hands and knees, sinuously stretching. "Wouldn't want the Northman to put that axe in my pretty chest. No, no, that's not what I would want at all."

Tyr offered Corsica his hand with a glint of impatience in his slate eyes. She sat back on her haunches and linked her arms overhead, taking her time before she delicately placed her gloved hand in his and stood. Luca watched impassively. Duke still gripped Merrick's shoulder, the dark-haired Sidhe's color more gray than white now.

"Merrick can't supervise the rune corrections," said Duke. "We'd have to carry him out there."

"I'm not so far gone as all that," protested Merrick weakly.

"I will supervise," said Luca. "I know enough of runes to see any malicious intent." He hefted his axe as he looked at Corsica. "And I know enough of trickery to see that as well."

"I gave you my word," said Corsica, "and my word is good for both of us."

Tyr nodded. He winced and touched the back of his head. His fingers came away stained lightly with blood, but he darted to the side when Duke stepped closer to look at his wound.

"He doesn't like strangers," Corsica said. "Neither of us does." She wrinkled her nose. "And you smell strange. Not like the Old World. Like…like fire and gunpowder and iron."

"'Long as he doesn't fall over before he fixes our trap," drawled Duke with a shrug. He glanced at Ross. "You stayin' in here?"

"If that's what's needed," she replied, though she didn't want to leave Duke alone with Corsica for some reason. Maybe it was the hungry way the Exiled woman kept glancing at Merrick. "I'll keep an eye on Merrick."

"I don't need a wet nurse," grumbled the navigator.

"That argument would be more effective if you could stand on your own," Ross retorted. She nodded to Duke and Luca. "Give a yell if anything goes wrong." Catching Corsica's eye, she held up the Glock. "This might not look as intimidating as an axe, but I guarantee you I'll put you down if you hurt them."

"Threats, threats," said Corsica. "Axes and guns, knives and spells." She clicked her tongue. "No trust, but that's to be expected." Tugging at her gloves, she motioned to Tyr. "Come, come, time to go look at the runes. Time to catch a bone sorcerer." She giggled brightly and murmured something else to herself in a low voice.

"The paint and brushes are in the shed," said Ross, watching as Luca opened the door and motioned to Corsica and Tyr. "And take my set of keys for the door. I'm going to lock it behind you."

Duke nodded and stashed the Beretta in his waistband. Ross winced at the makeshift holster, but didn't comment as she handed him her set of house keys. Their hands touched briefly, and he gave her his signature cocky smile. She locked the door behind him.

"Are the creepy ones gone?" asked Vivian, emerging from the kitchen with half a peanut butter sandwich in one hand.

"For now. And only Corsica is *really* creepy. Tyr didn't talk at all." Ross eyed the half-eaten sandwich.

"Glad I didn't watch." Vivian shook her head. "I wouldn't have been able to eat anything afterward, and you know how I am when I get hungry. Looks like it didn't spoil your appetite, though. Come on, I made extra."

Ross unloaded the Glock, locking the slide back and checking the chamber before she placed the gun on the kitchen counter. She fairly inhaled two peanut butter sandwiches, pausing only when her first bite of the second sandwich yielded a strange crunch. "V...what's in this?" she asked slowly.

"Bacon," replied Vivian brightly. "There was some left over from yesterday morning's breakfast. It's a good combo. Salty and sweet, you know?"

Ross started chewing again, squinting slightly as she evaluated the taste. Either Vivian was right and it actually tasted good, or she was just too hungry to care.

"Well, we have to make a grocery run. That's all the bread we've got in the house," said Vivian as she finished arranging another dozen sandwiches on a plate. A smaller plate sat to its side, already bearing its own two sandwiches.

"Jeez, V, think you made enough?"

"Have you *seen* Luca eat?" retorted Vivian. "He's like Thor's younger brother or something. And besides, Duke eats a lot too. You know that." She covered the platter of food with plastic wrap and pushed it back slightly on the counter. "That should be good for now. I don't know what we're going to do for lunch, though."

"I haven't thought that far ahead," admitted Ross as she filled a glass with water to wash down her last bites.

"Well, someone has to," said Vivian with an air of practicality. She took the smaller plate and walked into the living room. Merrick opened his eyes and looked warily at the sandwiches. "I know you might not be hungry," said Vivian, "but I think you need to eat, especially since you just gave Corsica some of your blood."

Merrick took one half of a sandwich and peered at it curiously.

"Peanut butter and bacon," said Vivian. "Pretty good, if I do say so myself."

Though he ate slowly, Merrick eventually finished both of the sandwiches. Vivian looked satisfied as she brought the empty plate back into the kitchen. Ross changed into different shorts and a t-shirt, prodding at the bruises she'd received in the fight with Corsica. None of them were any worse than what she'd experienced in her other sparring matches. She rubbed the scar on her arm unconsciously as she contemplated their next moves. How was Duke going to live when he was supposed to be dead? He couldn't just hide out here at the house forever...though *theoretically* she supposed he could. Suddenly she straightened. Was he going to tell his teammates' families that they were all alive? She couldn't decide if it would be crueler to let them continue to believe that the men were dead, or tell them that they were alive, but just in another world of magic and Fae. It would probably hurt more than it helped, unless the men came back themselves. She sighed and rubbed her forehead, walking back into the main room.

"Is there anything we can do to help you?" Vivian was asking Merrick as Ross rejoined them. "I mean, I know you said that Luca is better because his wolf is in this world now, but isn't there *anything* that can, I don't know, make you any better?"

"Keep feeding me peanut butter and bacon sandwiches," Merrick said lightly, but his haggard face belied his attempt at humor.

Vivian crossed her arms. "Seriously, Merrick. There must be *something*." She pressed her lips together. "Could you...I mean, Corsica and Tyr, with the blood..." She rubbed her own arm, trailing off.

"No," said Merrick vehemently. Vivian jumped guiltily at the sudden strength of his voice. Merrick shook his head and looked very tired. "Sometimes a choice between life and death turns into a choice between surviving as a monster, or dying as yourself."

"You're...dying?" Vivian whispered.

Merrick nodded. "I have a few days, a few weeks maybe. But I don't have the protections afforded to the travelers sanctioned by the Queens." He took a breath and paused. Even talking seemed to tire him. "Without the traditional runes, this world...it strips away at us. It's like..." He grimaced as he tried to find the words. "It's like a dust storm, wearing away at my skin."

Vivian shivered. "So that's why Corsica and Tyr drink blood?"

"They might have known the runes," admitted Merrick. "In the days before the Great Gate was sealed, many more Sidhe knew the runes to protect themselves in the mortal world."

"Then how did they become what they did?"

"I don't know." Merrick shook his head. "They've survived for centuries. Far longer than any Sidhe who has made the mortal world their home…at least as far as I know. And I am not a Scholar."

"Could I…do you think I could come with you, when you return to the Fae world?" Vivian asked hesitantly. She couldn't hide the spark of hope that shone in her eyes.

Merrick frowned. "Why…why would you want to come to my world?"

"Because it would be an adventure." Vivian grinned and then saw Ross's disapproving expression. "Not *forever*, I don't think. I'd probably come back."

"It was law until not so long ago that no mortals could travel into our world," said Merrick slowly. "But then there was the Bearer, and her brother and his teammates. So I don't rightly know. Perhaps."

Vivian's face flushed and her eyes shone with excitement. "That's all I wanted to hear."

Ross sighed. "V, if you go into the Fae world, who will take care of the shop?"

Merrick looked questioningly at Vivian, who fidgeted with the empty plate on her lap.

"There's a coffee shop in New Orleans," she explained. "My great-grandparents started it, and my grandparents ran it, and now it's mine." She shrugged and said defiantly, "I could just say that I'm traveling. Going away for a while. Backpacking across Europe or something. Mike and Evie are good managers, they take care of mostly everything anyway."

"And what happens when they can't get ahold of you at all – you know that there are very few places where you can't answer email nowadays," Ross pointed out.

"Don't crush my dreams!" protested Vivian.

Ross shrugged and shook her head, smiling even as she gave up the argument. "I'm going to go check on everything out back, if you two are okay in here."

Merrick nodded wearily and leaned his head back, closing his eyes. Vivian watched him worriedly for a moment and then shook herself slightly, grabbing the empty plate and walking into the kitchen.

"I'll take that as a yes," said Ross as she followed Vivian, retrieving the Glock from the counter, replacing the magazine and chambering a round.

"Yeah," said Vivian distractedly, deep in thought.

"It's never good when I can see the hamsters running at full speed," said Ross, nudging Vivian with her shoulder as she passed by her on the way out of the kitchen. She paused. "Hey."

Vivian looked up at her. A corkscrew curl escaped her braid and she tucked it behind her ear.

"We'll figure something out," said Ross in a low voice, with more confidence than she felt. She just didn't like seeing the worry written across her friend's face.

"You're just trying to make me feel better." Vivian smiled slightly. "I know you think I need protection, Ross...and you're right, I haven't done what you have. I haven't ever shot a gun, much less shot *at* anything." She shrugged. "But this...this feels like what I've been waiting for. It just feels like everything is falling into place." She sighed. "But I hope you're right. I hope we figure something out with Merrick. It makes me feel so...helpless."

Ross nodded. "And that sucks. But trust me. We'll find something. Does Luca seem like the type of guy who'd leave his buddy hanging out to dry?"

Vivian shook her head. "No. You're right." She grabbed a glass and filled it with water. "We're good. Go check on the progress of the crazies at making our trap sorcerer proof."

"I wouldn't call them 'crazies' to their faces," cautioned Ross with a smile as she left the kitchen. "I'm taking the spare key with me."

After pulling her black Converse shoes onto her feet, she grabbed the key from the dish on the table by the door and ventured out into the humid midmorning air. Now that she wasn't hungry, she enjoyed the feeling of stretching her legs as she walked with long strides around the side of the house. She ignored the urge to check her bedroom window for scratch marks left from the crazed gas station cashier. As the back yard came into view, she glimpsed Corsica turning a few graceful cartwheels in a circle around Tyr, who crouched at the perimeter of the runetrap. Luca stood near Tyr, and Duke was watching Corsica with an expression somewhere between bemused and irritated.

"How's it going?" Ross called, the long blades of grass tickling her ankles as she walked toward them.

"Well, I don't really know," confessed Duke, "since he doesn't talk and she's just been doing acrobatics like a rejected Olympic gymnast ever since we got out here."

Ross raised an eyebrow as Corsica switched to back walkovers, leaning back in a graceful arc until her gloved hands touched the ground, then neatly flipping her legs overhead and landing upright. "She's certainly…flexible." As Corsica passed them, still following her circular path, Ross heard the Exiled woman humming a strangely unsettling tune. She frowned. Maybe Vivian's description wasn't so off the mark after all.

"I believe he is about halfway done with his improvements," said Luca without looking away from Tyr's work. "He is using a few archaic runes that I have never seen, but all are for our purpose."

Ross wasn't entirely sure, but she thought she saw Tyr roll his eyes at Corsica as she passed him. What was the bond that had brought the two of them together? She tried to pick out any similarity between them, and decided they weren't siblings. Had they been lovers, or were they still? She mulled over the possibility as she watched Tyr painting on the flat rock with sure, quick strokes. He'd fashioned his own brush using a stick and a few black, glossy feathers. For a reason she couldn't name, the sight of the strange little brush sent prickles down Ross's spine.

Luca suddenly straightened, looking sharply at the house. Ross instinctively followed his gaze and her pulse quickened as she saw the five figures making their way toward them. But she glanced at Luca and Duke and realized they were both grinning in recognition.

"Well, knock me flat with a feather," said Duke. "Looks like the rescue expedition finally found us."

"Rescue expedition?" repeated Ross as the other group closed the distance between them. A tall, fair woman led them, her hair a gold so light that it was almost white, her heart-shaped face beautiful but fierce. She rested her hand on a golden whip coiled at her hip. Behind her, a pale man wearing black armor walked between a dark-haired woman and a man almost the match of Liam in stature. The man wore his long pale hair tied back in a neat ponytail, the woman kept glancing at the man in the dark armor, who walked mechanically, his face expressionless. At the rear of the group, a tall man with a scar across one side of his face raked his fingers through his sweat-soaked hair, trying to unobtrusively catch his breath.

Corsica paused in her acrobatics, crouching in the long grass on the far side of the runetrap, watching the newcomers cagily through the curtain of her silver hair. Tyr continued working without sparing them so much as a glance. He seemed almost happy as he dipped the black feather brush in more paint.

The fair woman raised a hand in greeting to Luca, but she increased her pace and Ross saw her smile fade as her eyes travelled between Luca and Duke, glossing over her and the two Exiled. She was clearly looking for someone else, and a trace of worry crossed her face.

"Calliea," said Luca warmly as she approached. Ross eyed the strange woman and thought that she'd want to be on her side in a fight.

Calliea didn't return Luca's greeting this time, uneasiness plain in her voice. "We saw the fight earlier – please don't tell me that

Merrick…that he…" She stopped and swallowed, as though the words choked her.

"Merrick is inside," Duke replied quickly. "He's…well, he's not fine, but he's alive."

"Thank the White Wolf," breathed Calliea, closing her eyes briefly. Then she gathered herself and looked back at Luca. "Tess will be here soon with Kianryk. She's going to lead the bone sorcerer here. Niall saw the runetrap when he was scrying this morning." She glanced at the sun making its way overhead. "Maybe half an hour, maybe a bit more time. We were in the abandoned trailer by the river."

"You walked here from there?" said Ross in surprise. "That has to be at least ten miles."

"We ran most of the way," replied Calliea. Then she seemed to look at Ross more closely.

"Calliea, this is Ross," Duke offered. "Ross, Calliea. We fought together in the Fae world."

Calliea merely nodded at the introduction and turned back to Luca. "Where is Merrick?"

"Inside," Ross said. "I can take you to him."

"Are those lost runes you're working with?" asked the dark-haired woman, tilting her head as she watched Tyr work.

"He doesn't talk," said Duke.

The dark-haired woman nodded as though that was a perfectly logical answer, and then turned to Ross. Her eyes were cat-like, dappled green and brown and gold. "I'm Molly. That's Niall and Jess." She gestured to the pale-haired man and then the one with the scar across his face, who had stepped forward to meet Duke's brotherly hug. "And this is Ramel." She looked at the man in the dark armor. "Or Mab, maybe I should say," she muttered.

"Nice to meet you," said Ross automatically, feeling as though she'd just jumped into the deep end of a strange and shifting ocean. She recognized Jess, thinking that maybe she'd met him before at one of the homecoming events or team barbeques. Somehow she knew he was human, even if she couldn't quite place his face.

"Mab?" Luca repeated, frowning.

Molly sighed. "She's not taunting us right now, but she basically has control over Ramel." She rubbed at a chain of bruises around her arm that Ross recognized as the imprint of a hard grip.

"You said you could take me to Merrick?" Calliea said to Ross, impatience plain on her face.

"Follow me." Ross led the strange woman around the side of the house again, Molly's explanation to Luca fading behind them. Jess and Duke were talking in low, rapid voices. "Are you Sidhe too?"

Calliea glanced at her in surprise. "Yes. I am *Vyldgard*, just as Merrick is."

"Well, I'm glad you arrived when you did. Hopefully you can help him," she said, too focused on fishing the house key out of her pocket to see Calliea's look of concern. "Don't touch the handle, it's iron," she cautioned as she propped the screen door open with her foot, unlocking the deadbolt. "V, Merrick! We've got visitors!" she called into the living room. When she stepped into the house, she stopped short. If her suspicion was correct, Calliea was *not* going to be happy.

Vivian looked up from where she straddled Merrick on the floor. At first glance, it looked like an interrupted tryst. But then Ross saw the panic in Vivian's eyes. Calliea slid past her and she let the door close.

"He had...some kind of seizure or something," Vivian said quickly, her face pale. "I don't know if he's breathing, I don't know if...I was trying to check..."

"Move," said Calliea brusquely. Vivian scrambled to the side. Calliea knelt by Merrick's prone form and promptly ripped the front of his shirt open, brushing the cloth aside to bare his chest. Vivian hugged herself as she watched Calliea produce what looked like a slender stick of charcoal from a pouch on her belt. She began drawing complex runes on Merrick's skin. To Ross's practiced eye, Merrick's chest looked ominously still.

"Fetch Niall," Calliea said to Ross. When Ross didn't move, she paused and looked up at her. "Please. I may need his help."

Ross nodded and Calliea bent back over Merrick. When she finished the first rune, Merrick gasped in a breath and Vivian made a sound of relief.

"V, they're friends," said Ross reassuringly as she turned back to the door. She ran around the side of the house. Corsica was nowhere to be seen, and Ross knew she should have felt alarmed but she said without preamble, "Niall, Calliea says she needs you in the house. For Merrick."

"I will watch Ramel," said Luca with a nod, and Niall ran back toward the front of the house.

"Don't touch the handle of the screen door!" Ross called after him. She shook her head. "Maybe I should stop thinking that the day can't get any crazier, because then it does."

"The bone sorcerer will probably be here soon," replied Luca in agreement.

Ross sighed. "Well, is that runetrap going to hold him?"

Tyr held up a hand and pinched his thumb and forefinger together, indicating that he needed a small amount of time to finish.

"Corsica went down to the river. She said something about gathering mud." Duke shook his head. "No idea what she meant, but Tyr is still working so I'd say it's a safe bet she'll be back."

Tyr nodded silently. Molly peered over his shoulder. Contrary to Corsica's earlier assertion that he didn't like strangers, he seemed fine with Molly's proximity. Then he paused in painting and glanced hungrily at Molly's pale wrist.

"Molly, step away from him," Ross said, not entirely sure why she cared so much about someone she'd met mere minutes ago. Molly slid back without a question, and Luca pulled her behind him. Tyr watched her for another moment, his nostrils flaring; then he grimaced and turned back to his runes.

"What's his flavor of weird?" Molly asked Ross quietly as she walked over to stand beside her.

"He drinks blood. They prefer Fae blood over regular old human, apparently," replied Ross. Then she frowned. Molly had sounded entirely too much like Vivian with that question. The wording didn't match the slightly formal speech patterns of the Sidhe. But the Exiled had already shown that they were more attracted to Fae blood. "Are you...Fae or human?" Ross asked, feeling somehow rude but voicing the question nevertheless.

"Half and half," replied Molly matter-of-factly. She grinned at Ross's nonplussed look. "It's a long story, but I'll tell you afterward if you want." She turned back to watching Tyr from this safe distance. "Tess and I are going to celebrate with beer and ice cream. You're welcome to join."

"Sounds like a good celebration," Ross said, beginning to genuinely like the other woman. "What's the occasion?"

"Stomping the bone sorcerer, of course," Molly replied. She glanced over her shoulder at Ramel.

Ross followed her gaze. "Is there something wrong with him?"

"Yes," Molly said bluntly. "Queen Mab is using him like a puppet."

"Queen Mab...like...Shakespeare Queen Mab?" Ross felt again like she was swimming in a vast, dark sea.

"Like ruthless Queen of the Unseelie Court Queen Mab," affirmed Molly.

"Well...okay," Ross managed.

"They didn't tell you?" Molly motioned to Duke and Luca.

"They did...I just..." Ross shrugged.

"You didn't really believe them. That's reasonable." Molly nodded, then she smiled puckishly and lowered her voice. "My guidance counselor thought I was crazy in the seventh grade because I told her about the Small Folk."

"The Small Folk?" Ross repeated weakly.

"The Glasidhe. They're about as tall as your hand, very beautiful, like all the Sidhe. They're very good scouts and fierce warriors."

"Right." Ross blinked. "Of course."

Molly smiled again. "It's a lot to take in, but just go with it. Don't think too much about it, especially in the next day or two. You'll only make your head hurt."

"Okay." Ross couldn't think of anything else to say. They stood in silence watching Tyr, Molly looking at the motionless Ramel every now and again. Then Tyr stood and surveyed his work. He nodded and snapped his black feather brush in two, tossing the halves into the grass.

"Guess that means he's done," commented Molly. She glanced at Ramel and pressed her mouth into a thin line. "And I guess that means I should try to get him inside."

"Is he like a zombie or something?" Ross tried to understand what Molly meant by *puppet*.

"No, he's just a little slow to move sometimes. I think it's because he's fighting Mab every step of the way now." Molly sighed slightly, rubbing at the bruises on her arm.

"Sounds kinda like a zombie to me," said Ross under her breath. Louder, she said, "The front door should be unlocked. Niall and Calliea are inside with Merrick." She felt slightly proud that she remembered all their names.

Molly nodded and spoke in a low voice to Ramel, who turned woodenly and began walking toward the front of the house with her.

"Has Corsica reappeared?" Ross said.

"No." Duke shook his head.

"Should we go looking for her?" she asked reluctantly. She didn't relish the prospect of searching for the unhinged Exile through the swampy brush of the riverbank, but she also didn't like the idea of Corsica lurking around the house unchecked.

"You know the land," Luca said to Ross. "I do not think her intention was escape, but do you think she could have gotten very far if it was?"

At Luca's words, Tyr shook his head emphatically. Ross wasn't sure which part of the question he was answering.

"The river isn't very deep, at least not right now. After it rains sometimes it will get pretty high but it's not much more than a creek at this point in the summer." She considered. "I don't know. It just depends."

Luca looked at Tyr thoughtfully, but then his face suddenly lit with strange anticipation. "They're coming," he said, looking back at the house.

"The bone sorcerer?" asked Duke quickly.

"Yes. And Tess," Luca said.

"Since when do you have a spidey sense like that?" Ross asked.

Luca grinned. "I can feel Kianryk. He is bringing Tess, and Gryttrond is chasing them. They are going to spring the trap on him."

"Fantastic," muttered Ross. "What's the plan?" She thought quickly. Calliea and Niall were in the house. She assumed they were players in the fight against the bone sorcerer. Merrick and Vivian she counted out, along with Corsica and Tyr just on the grounds of trustworthiness and sanity. She wasn't sure if Jess was going to fight the bone sorcerer, but she wished they had time to set him up in the house with a weapon to protect Vivian.

Luca looked at Duke and then to her. "Take Tyr to the shed by the river and stay there until the fight is over. Corsica will probably go to where he is."

"What?" Ross felt slightly affronted, though she recognized the logic.

"You are mortal and this is a dangerous fight," said Luca. "Let us handle this threat from our own world."

"What about Vivian?" she asked. "I can't just leave her."

"We'll make sure she is protected. She'll stay in the house along with Merrick," said Luca, speaking more quickly now. He nodded to Jess. "And Jess, to watch them." Duke's teammate nodded wordlessly.

She looked at Duke. "Noah, what do you think?"

"I think we'd better let him call the shots on this one," Duke replied slowly and seriously. "We don't have the firepower they do. I've seen the damage they can cause."

"Well, yeah, I've seen that too. They blew up my truck," Ross reminded him peevishly. She sighed. "All right. Guard duty it is. Come on."

Tyr began walking toward the river without question. Duke fell into step beside her.

"He's much less difficult than his partner," Ross commented as Tyr picked his way through the brush, his silver hair catching the sunlight that struggled through the boughs of the trees overhead.

"I'm guessing he's actually the brains of the operation," Duke agreed drily. "It's the quiet ones you really need to watch."

Ross snorted and stepped over a fallen branch as the shed came into view among the tangle of greenery. Then the earth suddenly shifted beneath their feet with a faint rumble. Ross froze and held her free hand in front of her as though preparing to be knocked off balance. She glanced at Duke with wide eyes, and they hurried into the green undergrowth. Tyr stood against the small building, his gray eyes worried and perhaps a bit frightened as he gazed back toward the house. Duke took up a position along the side of the shed, holding security on the river side. Ross faced the house, her eyes scanning the yard. They stood for what could have been minutes but felt like hours, the humid air pressing heavily around them. An explosion erupted in front of the house, and a moment later a scream pierced the heavy, humid air. Tyr crouched down by the shed and covered his ears with his hands.

"Well," said Duke, glancing back at the house. "Sounds like the big showdown just started."

Chapter 28

Tess clawed her way back to consciousness. The whirling power of the Caedbranr reached into the blackness and looped about her, pulling her back to her body like a rescue line. She felt rough rock beneath her cheek. Her right knee throbbed, and the entire left side of her body prickled with strange numb spots that she knew would flare into pain when the shock of her fall faded.

The bone sorcerer. Luca. Kianryk. The house by the river. Trees flashing by as they ran. The girl tied to the tree.

Her fractured memory rushed back, the fragments quickly reassembling into a recognizable mosaic. She struggled to her hands and knees; vaguely she noticed that her shirt and breeches on her left side were shredded, her skin studded in places with small rocks from the gravel. Traces of blood trickled from her wounds, mixing muddily with the dirt staining her body. She dragged in a breath and heard Kianryk snarling with staggering ferocity.

The bone sorcerer. The runetrap.

The pain clouded her mind and her vision wavered. With a wordless growl, she released the bonds of her *taebramh*, letting her power expand, filling her limbs with cool white fire that soothed the sharp, immediate pain. Time enough for pain when the bone sorcerer was trapped. She staggered to her feet, unsteady despite the roar of her *taebramh*. The power of the Caedbranr swelled in her chest, curling into the space where her caged *taebramh* had burned. She turned and faced the bone sorcerer.

The faceless black figure reached up and pulled at the hood of its dark cloak. Tess panted and licked the blood from her lips as the hood fell away, revealing the sorcerer's face. She took a step back, stunned.

The bone sorcerer looked like a Northman.

About as fast as a Northman can run.

Had Niall known that the bone sorcerer was a Northman? The thought flitted through her mind. She couldn't have put words to exactly how she knew, but she could see it in the high planes of his cheekbones and the line of his jaw. He was short and slender for a Northman, but there was still unmistakable strength in his shoulders and legs. But unlike any Northerner Tess had ever seen, the bone sorcerer bore a pattern of blood-red runes on every visible inch of skin: his face, his neck, his hands where they emerged from his sleeves. A black mark like a thumbprint of ash stood out on his forehead. His eyes were still blue, though. A blue almost like the blue of Luca's eyes, save for the chilling deadness in them.

The bone sorcerer took no notice of the bristling, snarling wolf standing between him and Tess. He folded his hands and said, "Quite the chase you led me on. But I would expect no less from a Bearer of the Iron Sword." He stepped toward her. Kianryk tensed to leap and the bone sorcerer knocked him aside with the flick of a hand. Tess swallowed hard against the bile rising in her throat. She reached for the hilt of the Sword.

"Ah, no, I think not." The bone sorcerer said a word that sounded *wrong* to Tess. Its syllables flew sharp as daggers into her arm, arresting its movement. Tess felt her war markings flare as her *taebramh* thrashed against the bruising grip of the dark mage's spell.

She tested her legs. If she couldn't draw the Sword, she could at least draw him closer to the runetrap. She gritted her teeth at the burst of pain from her knee, but her legs worked. She stumbled backwards, clumsy but moving.

The bone sorcerer matched her pace unconcernedly. "Now, what is the Bearer doing in the mortal world? Hopefully you are not here on my account." He smiled. Blood stained his teeth.

Keep him talking, keep him moving. "Malravenar is defeated. We're hunting down all of his minions."

"Minions." The bone sorcerer smiled again. "You know, most mortals are dull creatures. Hardly worth the blood I can drain from them. But you…you are interesting, Tess O'Connor."

Tess fought the urge to ask him how he knew her name, focusing instead on lengthening her strides. Her right foot caught on something, wrenching her knee, and she stumbled but managed not to fall.

"Tess!"

She heard her name again, this time in a voice that made her heart leap despite the pain, despite the bone sorcerer advancing on her, despite the spell immobilizing her sword-arm overhead. But she kept her gaze focused on the bone sorcerer, even though every instinct told her to turn her head, to resolve that movement in her peripheral vision into Luca. There were more footsteps, a door opening, sounds that swirled around her.

The bone sorcerer stopped, his cold eyes traveling along a line behind Tess. She knew without looking that the rest of the warriors who had traveled through the Gate with her stood behind her, ranged across the green expanse of the yard.

"So this is the *we* you speak of," he said to Tess, smiling slightly. "A veritable feast. I shall enjoy it. And I will start with you, *ulfdrengr*." He turned his gaze to Luca.

Tess felt her *taebramh* explode in protest, a snarl spilling past her clenched teeth. As the bone sorcerer said another sharp word, she broke through his spell on her arm, lurching forward with the force of her movement as she drew the Sword. It blazed bright as a star, but the bone sorcerer sucked in its light, becoming again that faceless black figure.

"Foolish girl," he said, his voice rippling on waves of searing heat. Tess slashed with the Sword, cutting through a piece of the shadow; a solid cold force smashed into her and knocked her to the ground again, igniting the pain of her wounds. She blinked stars from her vision and the bone sorcerer suddenly stood not a stone's throw away from her, watching her with his cold eyes as he advanced. Holding the Sword before her like a shield, she scrambled backward, scrabbling at the ground with her good leg and her elbow. The grass slid coolly beneath her skin. Then there were hands under her arms lifting her. The dark mage came inexorably closer.

Many things happened at once – Luca heaved Tess bodily into his arms, careful to keep the Sword pointed toward the bone sorcerer as he started to run; Ramel appeared from behind the hulk of the burnt truck, sprinting with grim intent toward the bone sorcerer; and a small glass orb sailed overhead, flashing in the light as it tumbled through the air. Ramel tackled the bone sorcerer at the same instant that the glass orb shattered on the ground at his feet, erupting in a violent explosion.

Luca threw Tess to the ground and shielded her with his body. The Caedbranr skidded through the dirt, torn from her grasp. She heard Molly scream. It sounded the same as when Molly had screamed during the *garrelnost*'s attack in the Hill Country of Texas. That seemed like years ago, and she shook off the memory, focusing on the task at hand. She pushed herself to her hands and knees as Luca rolled to the side.

"Kianryk," she coughed. "And Ramel."

"Kianryk is fine," said Luca tersely. For a split second, his blue eyes softened as he pushed Tess's hair from her face. "Gods, I'm so glad to see you again."

She coughed again and grinned. Her voice came out as a croak. "Same." Then she sobered quickly, stumbling to her feet and grabbing the Sword. She turned and saw Ramel lying against the frame of the truck, his black armor horribly mangled. Molly was already beside him, pressing her hands to his blackened face. A red-haired girl stood by the steps of the front porch, her eyes round as saucers and her right hand still frozen in the final gesture of her throw. She held a glimmering string of glass orbs in her other hand. A witch? Tess thought. She was too tired to feel surprise or alarm at that prospect.

"Go," said Luca. "*Go!*"

"What about you?" she protested.

"It's you he wants now," Luca said.

The bone sorcerer slowly rose from the ground. The explosion had blackened parts of his face, but it looked like smudged ash and nothing more. He pointed at the stunned red-haired girl and barked a word. The girl crashed into one of the pillars of the porch and tumbled to the ground.

When the bone sorcerer's eyes fixed again on Tess, she turned and ran. Her gait was limping, but her *taebramh* swept her along and the Sword pulled with unyielding insistence at her hand. She felt him following her, and she rounded the side of the house into the back yard. The point of the Sword swung like the needle of a compass toward the runetrap. She pushed aside all the doubts suddenly clotting her mind. What if the bone sorcerer sensed the trap? What if he caught her before she reached it? She grimly focused on stretching her legs into longer strides, ignoring the drumbeat of pain in her knee and the sharp tug of the stones embedded in her skin.

"You cannot run fast enough to escape me." The bone sorcerer's voice vibrated through her head. Tess gritted her teeth and spied a flat stone inscribed with runes. Her breath caught. And then he seized her shoulder, wrenching her to face him. He smelled of blood and salt and the sickly sweet odor of decay. She swung at him with the Sword, but he caught her wrist in an iron grip, the Sword blazing between them. His nails bit like talons into her skin.

"Foolish girl," he whispered again.

She threw herself away from him, his fingers tearing into her shoulder as he grabbed at her; the shoulder of her sword arm screamed in pain as she hit the ground and he kept his bruising hold on her wrist. She rolled to one side, kicking at him with both feet. He grunted in surprise when her boots crashed into his legs. She wasn't sure if it caused him any pain, but it was enough to make him release his grip on her. He lunged for her again, she brought up the blazing Caedbranr, and a golden whip snaked around his chest. Tess kicked him again for good measure as Calliea gave a mighty haul on her whip, her entire body arching with the force of her pull. The bone sorcerer wavered, balanced at the edge of the runetrap for an instant, and then fell.

The flat stones flared with blue light, which arced up and connected each stone to its opposite point on the compass. Wind rippled through the grass and Tess's ears popped as the runetrap blazed. The bone sorcerer scrambled to his feet, suddenly seeming much less threatening. His lips moved, but Tess didn't hear his voice. She smiled wearily as she levered herself to her feet. The mage gestured, but his spell merely created a slight ripple in the invisible dome connecting the blue light arches. He screamed, the cords in his throat standing out as he raged uselessly, and silently, from her viewpoint. Tess indulged herself and gave him a very choice mortal gesture with one of her fingers. Even if he couldn't see her, it felt satisfying.

"Well, that was interesting," said Calliea as she coiled her whip, examining the end for damage and apparently finding none.

"Thanks for the backup," Tess replied, her voice hoarse.

"That's what friends are for, isn't it?" Calliea clipped her coiled whip to her belt and surveyed the bone sorcerer, folding her arms over her chest. "You look like you were dragged for miles behind a galloping *faehal*," she continued as she looked Tess up and down. "Come on, we should get you inside."

"What about Ramel? And the red-haired girl?" Tess protested.

"Molly and Jess are working on Ramel. The red-haired girl, brave little idiot, got away with a broken arm as the worst of it," Calliea replied. "And Merrick is quite fine too, now that we have the runes on him."

"What did you say about the red-haired girl?" said a dark haired woman holding a pistol as she emerged from the trees behind the runetrap. Tess knew she recognized the woman peripherally, but her pain fogged mind refused to supply her name.

"Vivian used one of Corsica's spells," Calliea explained.

The glass orb, Tess thought dully. She suddenly recognized its similarity to the glass orbs that she carried in her belt pouch, and she wondered with detached curiosity if they had survived the fight intact. She hoped they had, because otherwise their ticket back to Faeortalam was null and void.

"She did *what*?" the woman said sharply. Then she looked at Tess and did a double take. "Tess! You look terrible. You should probably sit down."

Tess could only manage a crooked smile as she gathered her strength to sheath the Sword. After the Caedbranr slid home into its scabbard, she did sit heavily on the ground, wincing and keeping her injured knee mostly straight.

"Mud from the river," said a silver-haired woman, stepping into the noon light along with another silver-haired man slightly behind her. "Mud from the river to soothe fire and flesh. Flesh and fire."

Duke appeared last, holding a gun as well. He gave a low whistle as he took in the sight of the activated runetrap. "Like catching a cockroach under a glass bowl, eh?"

"That's one way to put it," agreed Tess in a scratchy voice.

"I have to go," the dark haired woman said to Duke. "Apparently Vivian used a spell and got herself hurt. Glad you made it through, Tess." She nodded as she strode purposefully past.

"Good to see you too," Tess managed. She grimaced and then remembered. Ross. That was the dark-haired woman's name. She was Duke's fiancé. The pieces fell into place – Ross must have been the tether that drew Duke to this place when he fell through the Gate, and the others had been pulled along in his wake.

The silver-haired woman held a dripping bundle in her wet, gloved hands, trailing river water as she crossed the yard. She paused to grin with pointed teeth at the bone sorcerer in the runetrap. The silver haired man stopped and surveyed the domed prison, the blue columns of light faded somewhat from their original brilliance but still shining with a steady, somehow solid power. Every so often a ripple of color emerged from a rune on one of the stones, curling lazily over the dome. The mage had stopped screaming and instead threw himself against each bar of light successively. The silver-haired man watched and smiled as the runetrap rebuffed each attempt without even so much as a flicker.

The strange woman walked purposefully past Calliea, who regarded her with a sort of suspicious fascination. As she neared, Tess saw the layers of scars on her face. One of her ears was exposed, and after the bristle of studs and rings, it came to a delicate point. They were Sidhe, the silver-haired man and woman, but unlike any Sidhe that Tess had ever seen. Her tired mind supplied the answer: The Exiled.

"Can you walk?" Calliea asked, watching the Exiled make their way around the side of the house.

"I can, but I don't want to," said Tess truthfully.

"Then I'll carry you," Luca said. Kianryk walked by his side, limping slightly but otherwise seeming none the worse for his encounter with the bone sorcerer.

This time, Tess let his voice unlock all her relief and joy. Tears gathered in her eyes as he knelt beside her, and she pressed her hands to his shoulders. She stared at him for a long moment, her mouth quivering. "I *missed* you," she said in a shaking voice.

"You came for me," he said, his beautiful eyes staring into hers. His huge hands cupped her face with infinite tenderness, and she leaned into his touch.

"How could I not?" she whispered with a shaky smile. "I love you."

He gathered her carefully against his chest. She didn't protest. The pain of her wounds as her body shifted was a small price to pay for feeling his solid warmth again.

"I love you, too, Tess," he said softly, smiling as he pressed a gentle kiss to her lips. She shivered and smiled contentedly. He lifted her with little effort and strode smoothly toward the house. She laid the uninjured side of her face against his chest and listened to his heartbeat, feeling complete for the first time since the battle at the Dark Keep.

Chapter 29

Liam finally found Finnead in a remote room of the palace, a room that the Seelie Scholars had been using as a library. A few stacks of books rose from the floor around the single table where Finnead bent over a large, old tome. He didn't look up as Liam approached – they were both bound to Vell, and most of the time they could sense each other's presence. A bloodstained square of cloth draped over one corner of the table, as though Finnead had used it to blot at the cut on his face and then tossed it aside.

"Time for a break from the research," said Liam, setting a satchel on the table. As he opened it, a savory scent drifted into the air. "Thea made her meat pies today. They're pretty fantastic." Finnead said nothing and didn't even look up. Liam continued speaking unconcernedly. "You wouldn't think that a smith would be so good at cooking, but I guess there's a kind of symmetry there. Fire and metal, fire and food."

Finnead turned the page of the ancient book, the volume so large that it covered half the table. He handled the yellowed, brittle page carefully. Liam watched him, noticed that the cut on his cheekbone still glared red and raw, no stitches or poultice from the healers or of his own making. Liam sighed inwardly. Of course Finnead was going to make this as difficult as possible. Sometimes he wondered how his sister had thought she was in love with the dark haired Sidhe – he always seemed to be in one sour mood or another these days. He felt a flash of guilt at the uncharitable thought.

"Look, brother, I know times are tough, but you still have to take care of yourself. You're one of the High Queen's Three, and we can't have you looking like you were on the losing end of a bar fight and then just kept drinking afterward," Liam said, deciding to use the tough love approach that worked well on his stubborn teammates…most of the time.

Finnead looked up from the book, his face devoid of emotion. "First of all," he said smoothly, "you are not my brother. Second of all, I do not need you to remind me of my duty to the High Queen. I have been serving the rulers of this realm for far longer than you have been alive." Finnead's eyes flickered. Liam couldn't discern the emotion…disgust? Disdain? In the mortal world, he had grown proficient at interpreting facial expressions and emotions, adjusting his own voice and dialogue to match. It still irked him sometimes that he couldn't always read the Fae.

"Fair point," he allowed, unwilling to let Finnead lapse into his moody silence again. He decided to take a more hardnosed approach, see if that produced any results. "But now we're at the same level, aren't we? Both bound to the *Vyldretning*."

Finnead merely raised an eyebrow and then looked down at the old book, preparing to ignore Liam again.

All right, well, time to swallow his pride, Liam thought. "It got out of hand this morning in the practice ring. I'm sorry for that."

Finnead looked up again. "It was my own fault," he said, no rancor in his voice. Then something shifted in his expression. "And Vell is right. I am…distracted."

"It's understandable," said Liam.

"But that doesn't make it acceptable," Finnead said, shaking his head. He finally seemed to be emerging from his icy fugue, thawing a bit into the man that Liam remembered from their ride across the Deadlands to the Dark Keep.

Two chairs had been pushed to the side of the table and Liam went to retrieve them. "Come on. Sit down and eat with me. Let's talk – see if there's anything I can do."

Finnead looked at the chairs for a long moment, then sighed and walked around the table. They both sat down and began to eat, the silence companionable now rather than cold.

"Thea does cook exceedingly well," admitted Finnead as he finished his second meat pie. The smith had formed light, flaky bread into an echo of a piecrust, filling the palm-sized creations with a delicious mixture of meat, roasted vegetables and cheese. Liam couldn't name some of the unfamiliar flavors, most likely because those particular ingredients didn't exist in the mortal world, but it was delicious nonetheless. He brushed the crumbs from his fingers and reached inside his satchel again, producing a little jar of salve.

"For your cut," he said, pushing it across the table toward Finnead. "I'd offer to stitch it up for you, but I'm afraid my stitches would leave a worse scar than if you just let it be."

"I'll find one of the healers," said Finnead. He paused for a moment. "Thank you."

"No problem," replied Liam. "It's part of it, you know? We've got to look out for each other. The world is tough enough without making more problems for ourselves."

Finnead looked at Liam with contemplation in his ocean-colored eyes. "I thought you would hate me for breaking your sister's heart."

Liam smiled a little. "Tess is tough. A lot tougher than either of us have given her credit for at times, I think." He shrugged. "I'll admit I wasn't a fan at first. But I got thrown into the situation well after it had already started to go south." He rested his elbows on his knees, contemplating how far he should take the conversation.

"Affairs of the heart have never been my strong suit," said Finnead with an air of confession. "I never meant to hurt Tess."

"Well, what's done is done. Poking at it now doesn't change anything," said Liam firmly. "She's fine, Finnead. Tess, I mean." He hoped that she'd found Luca after stepping through that shimmering portal into the mortal world.

Finnead seemed to sense his thoughts. "Yes, she will be fine. She loves Luca, and he loves her." He nodded. "It is a good match."

Liam wasn't quite sure how to reply to that, so he didn't. Instead, he tried to guide the conversation a bit more. "The Unseelie princess," he ventured quietly. "You're trying to find something in these books to help her?"

Finnead nodded. "Yes. I do not think that the Lethe Stone is the solution."

"What else are you thinking?" Liam glanced at the open book. He didn't recognize the language and assumed it was written in an older version of the Sidhe tongue.

"There might be a way to restore her memories through the use of others' memories of her," Finnead said slowly.

Liam took a moment to work through that statement in his head. "Without using the Lethe Stone?"

"I don't know. The Lethe Stones have been outlawed for so long…the Queens themselves might be the only ones who remember how to use them." Finnead ran a hand through his raven's wing hair.

"Mab isn't going to use the Lethe Stone," Liam said quietly. They both knew of Vell's plan to use the Lethe Stone in Mab's stead, to prevent such a potential weapon from falling into the possession of the Unseelie Queen. They didn't speak of it out loud very often, because it felt like admitting that Vell didn't trust Mab. Which was the truth. None of them did, not even Finnead, who had been one of her Three.

"I know," agreed Finnead. "And I think that is for the best. But I also think that she could use it as another excuse to harbor ill will against the *Vyldgard*."

"Titania is already unhappy with the deal," Liam said, shaking his head. "We can't afford to alienate the Seelie any further." He thought for a moment. "Have you spoken to Vell about what you've found?"

"A bit, yes, but I'm not entirely sure that it will work," he replied.

"I hope it does," Liam said honestly.

Finnead smiled humorlessly. "If it does work…if it succeeds, taking others' memories to build hers…then I probably won't remember her enough to rejoice in her restoration."

Liam frowned. "Wait, it's not just…you'd be *giving up* your memories of her permanently? As in, they'd be erased?"

Finnead nodded. "A small price to pay." He looked at Liam. "Wouldn't you do the same for the woman you love?"

"Yes," said Liam without hesitation. He took a deep breath. "It just seems particularly cruel."

"Crueler than thinking she was dead for centuries, when she was really held captive by Malravenar?" Finnead shook his head. "I think not."

"Will you still love her, after your memories are taken?" Liam asked. "I mean, couldn't some memories be taken from others, leaving you *something*?"

"From what I have read, this technique works best when the memories are all from the same person. There are only a few accounts of its use, mostly because of its implicit price – its…*cruelty*, as you termed it." Finnead glanced back at the ancient tome. "The memories must be from someone who loved the person who is to be restored. A father, brother, sister or lover."

"And you were lovers," said Liam, almost to himself.

Finnead nodded, his gaze faraway. "Yes. Our love was chaste at first, like most young love…and Andraste feared her sister's displeasure. She wanted to please the Queen in all things."

"I don't know what young love looks like in your world, but in my world it's hardly chaste most of the time," said Liam with a chuckle. Then he considered. "That's the first time I've heard her name. Andraste. It's a beautiful name."

"It is the name of an ancient moon goddess," said Finnead. He smiled a bit wryly. "Appropriate, I suppose, for a princess of the Court of Night and Winter."

"Tell me about her," Liam said softly. "All everyone ever talks about is how she's broken. How she did terrible things because of Malravenar's hold over her. Tell me about her when you fell in love with her."

Finnead searched Liam's face for a long moment, as if trying to divine his intentions. Finally, he nodded and settled back in his chair, taking a deep breath. "It was almost three centuries ago, I think, that I met Andraste. She was little more than a girl, just barely a hundred years old. She was already beautiful, as you'd expect from the younger sister of Mab. Mab herself was a gay and bright young Queen. She went Maying with Titania every year, and they exchanged gifts on the Winter and Summer Solstices."

"That certainly sounds like a different world," said Liam.

Finnead nodded. "It was. I was a young squire then, working toward becoming a full Knight. It was my heart's desire...until I met Andraste." A slight smile appeared on his lips. "One day I was at the practice yards and there was a commotion. The princess had grown tired of her tutors, carefully selected by her sister the Queen to ensure the young princess grew into an educated young woman. Andraste had asked Mab to allow her a swordmaster, and the Queen indulged her. But the old Knight sent to teach Andraste would not spar with her for fear of the Queen's displeasure if the Princess were injured, and he taught Andraste some pretty flourishes with a blade but no real swordsmanship. So, she braided her hair and pinned it up under a cap, put on her plainest shirt and breeches and stole away to the practice yards." His smile widened. "She was a very pretty boy, to be honest, pretty enough that some were suspicious. But she lowered her voice with a simple rune and cast a bit of a glamour over the rest of her, so that she was not immediately recognizable. And then she proceeded to insult everyone within earshot until one of the young pages lost his temper and challenged her to a sparring match."

Liam chuckled. "It sounds a bit like what Tess would do." A slightly pained expression crossed Finnead's face, and Liam resolved not to mention his sister again. He pressed his lips together. "I'm sorry, I won't interrupt again. Please go on."

Finnead nodded. "Well, the pretty flourishes that Andraste had learned from the old Knight didn't stand up very well to even a page, and he promptly knocked her into the dirt. They were using quarterstaffs, as pages aren't allowed to use practice blades. But she sprang up again and demanded a rematch. He knocked her down again, and then a third time, but she lasted longer with each bout. And she had pluck, so he finally took a few minutes to show her some of the mistakes that she was making. And then Mab's Vaelanseld swept into the practice yard on a thundercloud, looking for her on Mab's orders. Thankfully, the Vaelanseld didn't see that page knock Andraste down, or else he probably would have been executed right then and there."

Liam thought that the Vaelanseld could have probably inferred that the young princess had been knocked down from the dirt on her breeches, but he kept his word and didn't interrupt.

"The Vaelanseld couldn't very well lay hands on Andraste, and she knew it, but I remember her staring defiantly at him all the same when he roared that if she were a squire and not a princess, he'd have whipped her for her deceit. She replied in a very prim voice that if she were a squire and not a princess, no one at all would care that she was in the practice yards." Finnead chuckled softly. "She had such fire in her eyes. I think a few of the pages fell in love with her right then." He paused, lost in his recollections. "It was almost half a year before she slipped away to the practice yards again, but the second time we recognized her and spirited her away to a far corner. One of the pages kept watch for the Vaelanseld." He chuckled again. "When he came looking for her, the pretty slim squire was nowhere to be found. Oh, he was furious, but he couldn't very well bring us *all* up on charges of treason with no evidence."

Liam tilted his head to the side. "I know I said I wouldn't interrupt," he said with a grin, "but I do have a question. Couldn't Mab have just listened in on your thoughts? From what I've heard, that's the baseline for the Sidhe Queens."

Finnead shook his head. "It was a different time then, you must understand. The rebellion shook both Courts to the core. To prove our loyalty, we had to take the blood oath to Mab and accept our baptism from the fountain by the Dark Tree."

"So she was Queen, but not all-powerful," said Liam.

"Powerful, but not so suspicious," said Finnead. "In those days, Queen Mab trusted her subjects. Loved us, even." His voice lowered regretfully. He stared at his hands for a moment before continuing. "So Andraste learned how to fight with a sword. A few of the older squires became Knights, and they instructed their own pages and squires about the mysterious squire that appeared every so often in the practice yards. None of us exposed her secret." He sighed. "I was the best with a bow out of the older squires. Andraste asked me to teach her archery."

"She became very good at it," Liam murmured.

"Yes," said Finnead heavily. "Neither of us could have known at the time how her talent would be twisted. She was a natural. Her practice with the sword had made her strong, and she devoted herself to archery wholeheartedly."

"Still keeping it a secret from Queen Mab?"

"At first. But archery is a more ladylike pursuit than swordsmanship, and archery practice didn't require her to scuffle with the page boys in the dirt." Finnead shook his head. "Andraste loved Mab, but she began to chafe under her sister's watchful eye. As the princess neared her age of majority, the subject of a suitable marriage began to be a topic of conversation."

"I thought the Sidhe were not so strict about the idea of marriage," said Liam, thinking of his conversations with Vell.

"Andraste was not any girl," said Finnead. "Mab could not have children. So it would be the princess's son or daughter who would inherit the throne, centuries hence."

"Mab and Titania aren't immortal?" Liam asked skeptically.

"Immortal in a sense, yes. But, as with the First Queen, they might well tire of their throne and this world someday. So Mab thought it prudent to create a line of succession. Andraste was furious at the thought. She loved reading mortal mythology – ironic, I know, as we are a part of the lore in your world," he admitted with a smile. "She was particularly fond of the Greeks and Romans. She thought to be like Artemis or perhaps one of the Amazons." Finnead paused. "I had loved her for a long time already. Maybe even since that first day in the practice yards. I didn't dare hope that she felt the same, especially since she so often railed against the idea of marriage and children when she stole away to meet me in the Royal Wood. We met to practice archery," Finnead clarified with a raised eyebrow.

"Of course," said Liam, chuckling.

"Though she wanted to secure her line, Mab could afford to wait. Andraste had not yet even reached her age of majority. She hoped that perhaps her sister would choose a suitable lover of her own accord."

"Which she did," guessed Liam.

Finnead nodded. "Yes. It was the natural progression, I suppose. We had been friends for years, and I became a Knight just as she reached her age of majority. Her love spurred me to work hard to rise in Mab's favor, to be considered worthy of her sister's hand." He fell silent, staring down at his hands. Liam waited for him to continue, but he remained lost in his own thoughts. Perhaps that was the point at which the story became painful. Liam knew from Vell and Tess that Finnead had been escorting the princess with her ladies when they had been attacked and taken prisoner. Beyond that, the story contained nothing but regret and sorrow.

"Do you still love her?" Liam asked quietly. He knew the answer, but he wanted Finnead to say it out loud to banish the dark thoughts visible behind his eyes.

"Yes. I have always loved her," said Finnead. He drew in a long breath. "Sometimes, though…it is more difficult now than when I thought her dead."

"Now you have to think about all the terrible things she endured," said Liam. Others shied away from the subject. The least he could do was offer Finnead a listening ear.

"Yes. All the terrible things she endured because I told Mab that she was dead." A heavy note of bitterness and self-loathing leavened Finnead's voice.

"You know that's not entirely true," Liam said firmly. "Look, you can wallow in self-pity if you want. But you can't change the past." He nodded to the book on the table. "All you can do is try to change the future." He stared at the book for a long moment, considering. "Maybe this is a crazy idea. But…if you're going to give up your memories of Andraste so that Vell can put her back together with the Lethe Stone…what if you told me those memories before they're erased?" He looked at Finnead steadily.

Finnead frowned. "What would that accomplish?"

"Maybe," said Liam slowly, "I could tell you those memories again, once she's herself. I can be your failsafe. Your backup. And since we're both bound to Vell, you can sense when I'm lying. You'd be able to tell that I was telling the truth."

"Being told my memories will not restore them," said Finnead, his brow furrowed slightly.

"No, but maybe…maybe I could help bring the two of you together again," said Liam. The gravity of his proposal settled heavily onto his shoulders.

"Why are you making this offer? You owe me nothing," said Finnead. "And I haven't been particularly pleasant, these past weeks since the battle."

"You're one of Vell's Three. Your happiness – or unhappiness – affects us all, in a way," said Liam truthfully. He shifted in his chair. "And why do I need to have an ulterior motive? Maybe I just want the story to have a happy ending."

Finnead smiled briefly. "You have the same soft spot for romance as your sister."

Liam laughed. "Well, that's the first time I've been told that. I'll take it as a compliment."

"You should. The Bearer's heart of gold is already a bit legendary." Finnead grinned. "And…I accept your offer. I will tell you my memories of Andraste, but they are only for your ears," he cautioned. "It will be difficult to bring all of those memories into the light."

"Better you tell them to me before you lose them," pointed out Liam.

Finnead nodded. "You're right." He looked up at the ceiling, considering where to start, when Liam straightened, feeling the sudden tug on the invisible string that stretched from his chest back to Vell. Finnead looked at him sharply as he felt it too. Their Queen was calling them.

"She's usually not this insistent," Liam commented as he stood and slung the strap of the satchel over his shoulder again.

"Something must be happening," Finnead replied ominously as the summons sharpened painfully.

"Something big," agreed Liam as they stretched their legs into long strides, leaving the ancient book behind them on the table. Vell's beckoning call increased yet again, spurring them into a run. They reached her chambers just as sweat began to slide down Liam's back from the headlong sprint. Gray was already in the Queen's chambers, fully armored and tightening the straps on Vell's breastplate. When she finished, Vell turned to them and swept a hand to their armor, laid out neatly on the table. Beryk paced restlessly about the perimeter of the chamber, backlit briefly by the embers of the fire.

"Get ready," the High Queen said, her golden eyes grim. "Mab has asked for a Council. Something significant has happened in the mortal world, and we might be on the brink of war."

Chapter 30

Ross hadn't felt this exhausted since her last double shift on the ambulance in the city. She thought disjointedly that she needed to call the firehouse and leave Vivian's phone number for her contact information since her phone was still fried from its close encounter with Luca. The lights in the house had gone out after the fireworks display put on by Tess and the bone sorcerer. She'd reset the breakers in the fuse box on the side of the house after making sure that Vivian was taken care of – the red-head had been carried inside very gently by Niall, and the pale-haired Sidhe had set her broken arm quickly and easily while she was unconscious. Ross had shuddered at the terrifying strength in his quick movement. Someone that strong could as easily snap a neck as set a bone back into place, but she thanked him quietly as she splinted Vivian's arm. A full-body check didn't reveal any other obvious injuries. Every instinct told her to take Vivian to the hospital, but her friend surfaced into consciousness for long enough to tell her fuzzily but firmly that she did *not* want to go to the hospital. Vivian had a phobia of hospitals, and doctors in general and, luckily for her, Ross was fairly confident that she and Duke could handle this injury with their own skills.

She'd found Merrick bare-chested in the study, runes covering his torso and his arms. He looked better than she had ever seen him, closer to his true self, she guessed, his gray eyes luminous and alert. He'd promptly slipped outside to help with whatever he could. Mayhem had been shut inside the house for the duration of the battle and consequently had left scratch marks in the paint of the door from her attempt to dig her way through to her mistress. When Luca reappeared with the big tawny dog by his side, introduced fondly as Kianryk, Ross had blinked as her eyes tried to tell her that it wasn't a dog, it was a *wolf*, a huge golden wolf. But then her double vision had settled and a peculiar buzz whispered over her skin. She suspected it had something to do with Kianryk's red collar, which Luca regarded with equal parts resignation and loathing. Strangely, Mayhem had bellied up to the big tawny dog, head low in supplication. She'd licked Kianryk's chin, causing Luca to chuckle. Ross had raised her eyebrows but shrugged. Far be it from her to understand the inner workings of her faithful canine.

Luca carried a grimacing Tess into the house. She had some impressive road rash from her fall on the driveway. The gravel had gouged furrows into her left arm, hip and thigh, with a few stones stuck in her skin for good measure. Kianryk followed them into the house and lay by Tess's feet as she sat on the couch. Her right knee was swollen and bruised, from a mailbox post, Tess explained a bit sheepishly. Duke pulled the first aid kit over and sterilized a pair of large tweezers in anticipation of digging the gravel from Tess's wounds. She frowned but stoically extended her arm.

Ross looked at Duke. He nodded to indicate that he had the situation under control. She checked on Vivian again, and then ventured out into the yard. A smoking crater marked the impact of Corsica's spell-orb. And about twenty years away from that sat her poor, burned out truck, now the center of industrious activity. The dark-haired one with the black armor – Ramel, she remembered – lay flat on his back, pale as death, his head lolling to the side as Molly and

Jess worked to remove his mangled breastplate. Jess pressed two fingers to Ramel's jaw every few minutes. Ross felt relieved that Ramel was alive, though she couldn't have said why she felt relieved that a total stranger was alive. Her shoes crunched through the flash fried grass.

"What happened?" she asked, though she had an idea just from the damaged breastplate and the blackened shreds of Ramel's shirt.

"He was tackling the bad guy and got caught in the blast," said Jess tersely. He made a sound of triumph as he succeeded in cutting through the last strap on the breastplate, made hard to access by the twisted metal. Ross took a deep breath and tried not to breathe through her nose. The scent of burned flesh always stirred up memories that she'd rather remained buried.

"Can I do anything to help?" she asked.

"See if Niall can come out," said Molly in a voice thick with repressed emotion. "I think we'll need him when this comes off."

"Already here," Niall said, striding across the yard.

Corsica appeared around the side of the house, still bearing her sodden cloak in her arms. The silver-haired woman paused to watch a bird flit from one tree to another, her face filled with childlike wonder. Tyr passed her and tugged her onward.

Ramel jerked when Jess and Niall carefully pulled the breastplate from his chest. Molly hissed through her teeth as she saw Ramel's skin, swearing effusively in a language foreign to Ross's ears. The breastplate had protected his chest from the fire of the blast, but beneath the bruises already blossoming on his ribs, Ross saw a raw red wound over his heart. She traced the shape with her eyes. It was a rune, but unlike any of the ones that she'd seen Merrick or even Tyr draw. It was sinuous and serpentine, and it sent a shudder down Ross's spine without her quite knowing why. She just felt the *wrongness* of it. Then she glanced at the breastplate, resting on the grass where Jess had tossed it in disgust. The underside of the breastplate, the part that fit snugly against Ramel's chest, bore the same rune as the wound on Ramel's chest, except that on the underside of the breastplate the rune was crafted from a length of thin, gleaming metal. The breastplate had punched the rune into Ramel's chest, and no doubt he was reminded of it every time he moved.

"What monster would do something like that?" she said, mostly to herself.

"Queen Mab," replied Molly in a hard voice. Then she bent over Ramel and talked to him in a quiet, quick voice, brushing back his ash-laden hair.

"Mud from the river to soothe fire and flesh," said Corsica, approaching and holding her cloak out before her like an offering.

"That's ridiculous," said Ross before she could help herself, but it seemed like Corsica didn't hear her.

"Not if they've bespelled it," said Niall. He stood and carefully peeled back a corner of the cloak, dipping his fingers into what Ross assumed was swamp mud. Instead, his fingers came away coated in a white substance flecked with shimmering silver. Tyr motioned urgently from the cloak to Ramel. Jess looked skeptically at Niall.

"They are from a different time," the Seelie Vaelanseld said. "Not many in our world have the knowledge to make this anymore."

"If you say it's good, I trust you," Jess said with a nod. He caught Ross's wide eyes and gave her a quick grin. "Would you believe me if I said this wasn't the weirdest thing I've seen lately?"

"Strangely, yes," murmured Ross. She watched for another moment as Niall and Jess began applying the white mud to Ramel's chest. Molly stiffened and pressed her hand to Ramel's cheek when the prone man gasped, but he settled after a moment, and they encased his entire torso in the stuff. Tyr nodded in satisfaction. Corsica set her stained and muddy cloak down within reach of the men and wandered toward the trees at the side of the house where she'd been watching the bird.

Ross walked back into the house, feeling strangely numb. On the couch, Tess waved off Duke, who was trying to remove a particularly stubborn bit of gravel from her arm.

"Just give me a minute," Tess said firmly, taking a shaky breath and looking anywhere but the shredded skin of her arm.

"We could wait a few hours," said Luca. "A few little stones won't do you any great harm." He turned his pale eyes to Duke when the medic began to protest. Duke raised his hands in defeat and dug out some gauze from their rapidly dwindling first aid kit. Ross felt oddly grateful that she'd spent the time to stock it so extensively. Vivian had called her a worrywart.

Tess nudged aside the bag of frozen peas that covered her knee. She grimaced at the sight of the livid bruise and pushed it back into place as Duke bandaged her arm. They didn't have any gauze pads left that were big enough to cover the abrasion on her side and thigh – Duke muttered something about making a supply run as he was forced to settle for cleaning the tattered skin as best he could.

Satisfied that everyone else had a medic or healer of some sort to tend them, Ross sat on the edge of Vivian's bed and watched her friend, checking her vitals every few minutes. She left the bedroom twice, once to pilfer one of the slightly stale peanut butter and bacon sandwiches, and the other to check on the progress of the others. The study had been turned into an observation room for Ramel. Ross couldn't bring herself to feel irritated that the strange silver speckled mud now adorned a good portion of the futon mattress. Her adrenaline began to wear off and she snuck in a nap sitting beside Vivian's bed. Every time her mind tried to make sense of all the events of the past days, she firmly turned to a concrete task, checking the splint on Vivian's arm for the tenth time, or rearranging the blankets about her friend. As the afternoon sun slanted golden through the bedroom window, Vivian's eyelids fluttered. She squinted, wrinkled her nose and muttered, "Ow."

"About time you woke up," said Ross.

Vivian stuck out her tongue at Ross and moved to push herself into a sitting position before realizing her arm was splinted. She growled every curse she could think of and even let out a whimper to top off the stream of invectives.

"You probably need some painkillers," said Ross, reaching for the bottle on the bedside table.

"That is the understatement of the year. No, the century," said Vivian hotly, groaning as she arranged her arm across her stomach and gingerly pushed herself up against the headboard with her good arm.

"You're lucky you only have a broken arm," said Ross severely. "And it wasn't a tibia fracture, it's just your radius, so that's a good thing."

"Speak English," Vivian told her. Then she squinted. "Oh. My forearm versus my bicep." She grinned. "See, high school anatomy and physiology coming back."

"I'm so proud," said Ross. "Here, take these with some water."

Vivian swallowed the pills and drank half the cup of water that Ross handed her. She grimaced. "Those tasted like shit."

"Well, you'll be floating on cloud nine in a few minutes, so I think it's a tradeoff worth making."

"Did you just give me illegal drugs?" Vivian narrowed her eyes in comical suspicion.

"First of all, no, and second of all, you should have asked that before you took them."

Vivian nodded. "Good point." She winced. "Ow. My head hurts too."

"Yeah, well, apparently you got slammed against the porch pillar by the bone sorcerer," said Ross.

"Did we get him?" Vivian straightened. "Did the trap work? Is anyone else hurt?"

Ross suppressed a smile. "Yes, the trap worked. Tess got scraped up, but it's not too serious. Ramel got caught in the blast from that spell you threw, though."

Vivian paled. "I thought maybe I was remembering wrong. He's not…I didn't *kill* him, did I?" She swallowed hard.

"He's still hanging in there," Ross replied quietly. "But he's not out of the woods yet. Corsica made this weird white mud and that seems to be helping."

"I want to talk to them more," said Vivian. "Corsica and Tyr." She smiled dreamily and then blinked at Ross. "Tess. She was the one with the sword made of fire, wasn't she?"

Ross had no idea what Vivian was talking about, but she remembered the well-worn scabbard on Tess's back. "Yeah. She was the one with the sword."

Vivian nodded woozily. She wriggled down until she was lying on her back again. "It was pretty awesome." Her eyes, glossy now with the painkillers, slid half-shut. "Very progressive, you know, seeing the girls…kicking ass…" Her eyes closed. Ross stood. Vivian stirred at the movement of the bed. "Calliea…has a whip…d'ja know that?" she slurred.

"That *is* kick ass," agreed Ross softly. Her answer seemed to satisfy Vivian, who sighed and turned her head to the side, settling into sleep, her arm held carefully across her stomach.

The door to Vivian's bedroom opened slightly. Duke slid into the room and smiled at Ross. He looked about as weary as she felt. "Hey. We made some dinner, if you want some." He nodded to Vivian. "Looks like she'll be fine, right?"

"Yeah, just the arm and some bruises. Maybe a slight concussion," allowed Ross in a quiet voice. Though her first instinct was to keep her station by Vivian's bedside, she knew that she needed a break. Her body ached as she stood. "Who do you mean when you say 'we made dinner?' Because the way I remember it, your culinary specialty is Ramen noodles."

He caught her around the hips as she passed through the doorway. She reached back and made sure the door didn't slam before giving in to her grin.

"Well, when I say 'we,' I really meant that Jess cooked. I just found the pots and pans for him," he said, resting his chin on her shoulder. "You smell good," he murmured into the soft curve of her neck.

His breath sent shivers through her body. She chuckled and

leaned back into his embrace. "I smell like sweat and ashes and God knows what else."

Duke growled playfully. "Sounds pretty perfect to me."

"You always did get rowdy when I smelled like the shooting range," she murmured, sliding around in his embrace until she was facing him.

"I'll take the smell of cordite over a lacy thong any day," he grinned. Then he tilted his head in consideration. "Although cordite *and* lingerie, that's like a one-two punch..."

"Shut up," she chuckled, leaning close to kiss him. For a moment, her exhaustion fell away as the world narrowed to just them, just his lips on hers and the familiar feel of the rough stubble on his jaw, a delicious contrast to the softness of his lips.

Jess cleared his throat at the end of the hallway. Though Ross jumped slightly and went to pull away, Duke gently but insistently continued their kiss. She could feel the blood rushing to her cheeks – for all her boldness, she wasn't an exhibitionist – but all the same, she smiled slightly against Duke's lips. No doubt it was just his way of annoying his older teammate while making up for lost time.

"If you want any dinner, you better come get it before Luca comes back for seconds. And Merrick, for that matter," Jess said dourly.

Ross chuckled as Duke drew back dramatically.

"You tell Luca that I'll hogtie his ass if he eats everything," Duke said with severity. He winked at Ross and kept hold of her hand as they walked down the hallway. "Seriously, I was a hog tyin' champ in high school, lasso and everythin'."

Jess merely returned to the kitchen, but Ross saw him trying to hide his smile.

Dinner turned out to be a more than passable gumbo, with rice on the side. Jess had even managed to whip up a batch of cornbread.

"I didn't even know we had all these ingredients," Ross said, her eyebrows lifting in surprise.

"You didn't," Jess said. "I took the liberty of making a supply run."

He handed Ross a bowl. She served herself a generous portion of rice, ladled gumbo over the top, and selected a square of cornbread from the corner of the pan.

"Well, I would have been *more* impressed if you'd made all these ingredients appear magically," said Ross as she settled at the table with her food. "But color me impressed all the same." She spooned up some rice and gumbo, nodding in approval as she tasted it. "Guessing you used V's car for the groceries?"

"Yours is kinda toast," said Duke. He shook his head. "Cryin' shame."

Ross sighed. "I still don't know how I'm going to list that on the insurance claim."

"Act of magical arson by crazed Fae rebel?" suggested Duke. His grin only grew wider when Ross punched him lightly in the arm.

"Yeah, that'll really go over well," she grumbled. "Let's not talk about it anymore. This food is too good to spoil with worrying." She glanced into the living room and glimpsed Luca ensconced on the couch, spooning rice and gumbo from what Ross was pretty sure was supposed to be used as a mixing bowl. Tess dozed on the other side of the couch. For a moment, Ross thought she saw something like glimmering snowflakes swirling around Tess, but then she blinked and the strange sight faded. "Where's everyone else?"

"Molly is in the study with Ramel. I believe Merrick is sleeping there as well," said Jess, stirring the gumbo in its huge pot and replacing the lid. "Calliea and Niall are keeping watch on the asshole in the glowing dome. The other two, I don't know."

"By 'keeping watch,' do you mean plotting how to crush him like a bug?" asked Duke through a mouthful of cornbread. "Because that's what I wanna do."

Jess opened the refrigerator and selected a beer. He sat down at the table with them as he took a contemplative sip. "I don't know if it's that simple." He rubbed his chin, which was covered in the beginnings of an impressive beard.

"It seems like nothing is simple anymore," agreed Ross. She scraped the last of her rice and gumbo from the bowl. "Except good cooking. This is really good, Jess. Are you sure you didn't grow up here?"

"Hunger is the best seasoning," said Jess with a chuckle. "And my grandma was from down here. Over near Shreveport, I think. It's her recipe."

"Well, it's fantastic," Ross said firmly, heading back into the kitchen for another helping. As she walked back to the table, she saw the glowing snowflakes – or feathers, maybe they were feathers – drifting lazily around Tess *again*. And this time they didn't disappear when she blinked. She placed her bowl carefully on the table, shut her eyes for a moment and then looked again.

"You're seein' it too?" Duke asked quietly. "Good. I was beginning to think I'd done damage to these pretty baby blues."

"Your eyes aren't blue," replied Ross automatically. She squinted. "What *is* that?"

"Well, based on our experience, it's some kinda magicky thing," he replied with a wave of his hand.

"A...*magicky* thing," she repeated skeptically. "That's really what you're calling it?"

"I'm sure it's not the technical term, but..." Duke shrugged and grinned.

"It's called *taebramh*," said Luca as he surveyed the pan of cornbread. He opted for more rice and gumbo instead.

"What's *taebramh*?" asked Ross.

"What you would call magic, I think," replied Luca. Duke raised a hand at the validation of his description. Ross rolled her eyes at him. Luca held up his bowl in Jess's direction. "This stew is very good. Very different than anything I have tasted before. It is like delicious fire."

"Delicious fire," repeated Ross with an uncharacteristic giggle. Duke grinned.

"It's got a true Southern kick to it, for sure," agreed Jess gravely.

Luca stood for a moment in the kitchen, looking over at Tess where she lay dozing on the couch. Ross could see his devotion written plainly across his face – it made her like the big Northman that much more. As she finished her second helping, Ross went to the refrigerator and raised her eyebrows as she opened the door. "Jeez, do you expect an army or something?" she commented, poking at the overflowing shelves.

"Have you seen how much Luca eats?" Duke deadpanned. The *ulfdrengr* chuckled.

Ross grabbed a soda, though she didn't usually indulge in the sugar laden drink. Her body still hurt from the post-adrenaline crash, and a bit of sugar would help to take the edge off. Luca looked at the can suspiciously as she popped the tab and the drink fizzed a little.

"V is gonna have a lot of fun introducing you guys to all this mortal stuff," Ross said with a smile.

"Who says *I* can't introduce everyone to mortal stuff?" Tess asked good naturedly, smoothing down her sleep-ruffled hair as she padded into the kitchen. She yawned and then frowned, testing her weight on her right leg. Luca watched her silently as she prodded her knee, gingerly at first and then more forcefully. "What in the..." she muttered, pulling up the side of her shirt. Shiny red scars dappled her ribs.

"Your side looked like ground beef a few hours ago," said Duke, raising his eyebrows.

Tess tugged at the gauze on her left arm, unwinding it to reveal the tender pink of just-healed flesh. She stared at it for a moment and then walked back over to the couch, swiping her hand over the cushions and coming up with a few pieces of bloodstained gravel.

"Well, that's...neat," said Duke anticlimactically.

"I guess absorbing all this *taebramh* in the mortal world has its benefits," murmured Tess, looking at Luca with raised eyebrows.

"I cannot say that I object to anything that makes you a more formidable warrior," he said with a glint in his blue eyes.

"Yeah, well, that means I kinda have to get sliced and diced before this takes effect. But…I'll take it." She shrugged. "Weird that I'm stronger in the mortal world than in Faeortalam, huh?"

"Not necessarily," Luca said.

"Don't tell me it's because I'm mortal, because you and I both know that's not quite true anymore," she said. They both grinned like it was an old joke between them. Then Tess grimaced, patting her stomach. "I hope there's food left, because apparently healing myself like a glowing mutant requires some refueling."

Before she finished her sentence, Luca had refilled his giant bowl and held it out to her expectantly, spoon and all. She smiled at him, kissed him on the lips and took the food. She slid into the last chair at the table, testing the temperature of the gumbo with an experimental bite and then beginning to wolf it down with impressive speed.

"So," she said between bites. "Any ideas on how to get that psychopath in the glowing cage to give us the Lethe Stone?"

Chapter 31

After every battle, food tasted better. It was a rule that Tess had learned during her time in Faeortalam. But even without the post-fight euphoria, she was pretty sure that Jess's gumbo was blue ribbon at the county fair special, and she told him as much between bites. When she wasn't complimenting the cook, she spent the time between mouthfuls explaining the Lethe Stone and the Council of Queens to Duke and Luca. Duke seemed abivalent about the Lethe Stone, and Luca merely absorbed the information in a stoic and thoughtful manner. Neither of them had offered any questions, so she moved on to musing aloud about the bone sorcerer. "I mean, we have him hemmed up, so that's a point in our favor. But I'm not sure how to make him give up the Lethe Stone."

"Tell him we'll kill him if he doesn't," rumbled Luca.

Tess hummed thoughtfully. "That's an option," she admitted, "and that was the original plan."

"You should probably talk to Merrick," Duke said. "Tyr – he's the silent one, not the weird one – helped him with the runetrap. And Corsica said something about the bone sorcerer being able to help them."

"Help them how?" Tess asked sharply. "The bone sorcerer is a monster. He had a teenaged girl tied to a tree and he was about to cut her heart out." She scooped another spoonful of gumbo and rice into her mouth. "Speaking of…where are the Glasidhe? I'd have thought they'd returned by now."

"They are out with Niall and Calliea," replied Luca. "They said they didn't want to intrude during the busy hours after the battle."

"That was probably Haze," said Tess with a fond smile. "They didn't bring the girl here, did they?"

"No." Luca shook his head. "Haze reported that they led her to the road and watched over her until a passersby stopped to help her."

Tess interrupted with a frown. "They shouldn't have just left her with anyone passing by. How would they know that he wasn't a creep too?"

"If you would let me finish," continued Luca. Tess smiled a little sheepishly and gestured with her spoon for him to continue. "Haze reported that they followed the car into a small town, staying out of sight. The girl went to a place that looked very official, and had men with uniforms and shining gold stars pinned to their chests. Haze's words, not mine," said Luca with a hint of doubt, as though he couldn't envision what Haze described.

"A police station," said Ross. "They followed her to a police station. They did well."

Tess nodded. "We can cross reference with any news reports of a missing teenaged girl, make sure she got home all right."

"Well, you're a regular Sherlock," said Jess with a trace of a wry smile. "I can do some searches, let you know what I find."

"Thanks." She sighed and sat back in her chair, leaving her spoon in her empty bowl. "All right. Seriously, I have to figure out how to get the Lethe Stone from this bonehead."

"Bonehead…bone sorcerer. I see what you did there," Duke said with an approving grin.

"It was unintentional, so that's even better," said Tess. She stood and collected her bowl. "Time to go talk to Merrick. Thanks for the food."

Luca followed her as she walked across the living room. She turned and smiled up at him. "Am I going to have an oversized shadow for a few days?"

He grinned and stole another kiss. "Yes. I may never let you out of my sight again."

She chuckled, marveling at the warmth that his simple statement kindled in her chest. They both moved toward each other at the same time, and she slid into his arms with a sigh of contentment, resting her cheek against his muscled chest. "I think I can live with that," she murmured.

"You have returned Kianryk to me twice now," he said, his voice a low rumble.

"And you've carried me away from battles twice now," she replied, tilting her head up to smile at him. "I think we can call it even."

He lowered his lips to hers. "Perhaps we shouldn't keep score."

"Mmm. Keeping score could be perilous," she agreed mischievously. She tightened her arms around him, relishing the feel of his broad back under her palms and the flat plane of his stomach pressed against her. Then she drew away with a sigh. "Duty calls."

"If you kept your arms around me for much longer, you wouldn't resist my charm," he agreed. "And then we would get nothing done, duty be damned." He kissed her forehead and smoothed her hair back with one large hand. "I should go see that Kianryk isn't teaching Mayhem too many bad habits."

Tess chuckled as she watched Luca go and then opened the door to the study as quietly as she could. Her smile faded as she saw Ramel, his chest covered in strange white mud. His skin, where it was not the angry red of minor burns, was gray. Molly dozed beside him, sitting on the floor by the futon with her head pillowed on her arms by his side. Merrick slept under a blanket on the air mattress that took up the rest of the floor space. He, at least, seemed to be improving. Luca had told her about the difficulties that they'd had once the portal had dropped them on the banks of the river. Tess swallowed past the lump in her throat. She looked at her own newly healed scars and wondered if she could heal Ramel with her new abilities in the mortal world.

It does not exactly work like that, the Sword murmured in her mind. *You are the vessel.*

Anger flared in Tess at the Caedbranr's words. *Oh, my life is worth more than his because I'm the Bearer?*

That is not what I said, the Caedbranr replied almost gently. *It is merely that your abilities in the mortal world correspond to your duties as the Bearer.*

Will you ever stop speaking in riddles? Tess demanded. The Sword fell silent and didn't answer her. She sighed and stepped further into the room. Molly stirred and looked up, her feline eyes alert the instant she opened them. For a moment Tess and Molly stared at each other. Ramel's harsh breathing filled the silence.

"I didn't mean to wake you," Tess said softly.

Molly nodded and chewed on her lower lip as she checked on Ramel.

"How is he?" Tess asked. The words felt inadequate, but she searched for something larger to say and her mind remained blank.

"Not dead," replied Molly curtly. Then she heard the aggression in her own voice and sighed. "Sorry. It's been…a long day."

"A long couple of days," agreed Tess. "And then whatever you were dealing with in the Unseelie Court."

Molly nodded. "It's strange. I should feel relieved. I'm here, I escaped Mab." She shook her head. "But now I don't know what to do."

"Not kill me, I hope," Tess replied dryly, arching an eyebrow. She winced internally, wondering if it was inappropriate for even that small joke with Ramel lying unconscious. But she'd learned that sometimes humor was needed in the most incongruous of circumstances. To her relief, Molly's lips twitched with a small smile.

"I mean, that *was* number one on my to-do list," Molly said, crossing the small space between them. "But, you know…I figure that Mab can suck it." She shrugged and her smile threatened to blossom into a grin.

Tess chuckled quietly. "I wish I could see you tell her that to her face."

Molly rolled her eyes. "And get frozen into a human Popsicle? No thanks."

"Half-human Popsicle," Tess corrected her with a smile. She wondered, not for the first time, if Mab really punished unruly subjects by encasing them in columns of ice. It wouldn't surprise her.

Molly took a deep breath. "I know that I should probably be mad at…what's her name, the redhead. The one who threw the spell."

"Vivian," offered Tess.

Molly nodded. "I feel like I should be mad at her, but that explosion busted the spell that Mab had put on him." She grimaced. "There were some pretty nasty runes on the surface of it, from what Niall could tell. Runes to burn anyone's fingers if they tried to remove the breastplate, runes to blind anyone who tried to draw a counter-spell." She shook her head. "And then on the inside of the breastplate…did you see it, Tess?"

Tess shook her head.

"The master rune was on the inside of the breastplate. She made it so that it cut into his skin, Tess, so that it was like there were knives constantly marking the rune into his chest." Anger flashed in Molly's eyes. "How could she do that to one of her own Three?"

"The explosion damaged the rune enough to free him?" Tess asked carefully. She shivered. While they were all prepared for gruesome tasks, she doubted any of them would have been able to knowingly detonate that explosion next to Ramel, even if they'd suspected it would free him from Mab's curse.

"As far as we can tell. The armor was the key to it, and we destroyed what was left of it." Molly nodded firmly. They stood in silence for a moment.

"So..." Tess began slowly. "You have your memories back?"

Molly kept her eyes on Ramel. "Yes. There are still a few patches that are fuzzy, but I have enough to remember who I am. Who I was."

"Who you *are*," Tess corrected her softly.

"I'm definitely not the girl that got knocked off the *garrelnost* anymore," Molly said in a voice so soft that it was almost a whisper.

"Well, I'm not the girl that stabbed the *garrelnost* in the eye with the horseshoe anymore, either," replied Tess. She smiled a little at the memory. She'd seen enough terrible things and fought enough battles that the thought of the *garrelnost* and its stinking mottled fur didn't turn her stomach anymore. She wasn't sure if that was a good thing.

"Remember retrieving that horseshoe from the little stone cave?" Molly asked, a nostalgic smile now on her lips as well.

"The one you and Austin thought was an outlaw's camp," said Tess with an answering smile. She remembered climbing up the stone wall, the dust gritty under her palms, as they retrieved the iron objects that they thought would protect them against the perils of the Fae world.

"Yeah." Molly said fondly, though her eyes were sad. "That's part of what I have to figure out, I guess. If I want to stay here in the mortal world. And if I do, what do I say to Austin? Or do I just leave him alone?" She turned her head to look at Tess. "If I go back, I think Mab will kill me."

"For not killing me?" Tess tried to change gears to match Molly's thought process.

"Partially, I think." Molly sighed. "It's complicated."

Tess watched her friend's face, beautiful and smooth like the Sidhe at times and then shifting into the expressions of human emotion. "If you stay here, won't you have trouble like Merrick did?"

"I'm a half-blood," replied Molly with a crooked smile. "The runes that are used for travel will be just fine for me. I might even get them as tattoos so that I don't have to worry about rubbing them off."

"Tattoos? Scandalous," said Tess, widening her eyes in mock dismay.

"You're one to talk!" said Molly with a chuckle, tugging at Tess's sleeve to reveal the complex emerald swirls of her war markings.

"Fair point," conceded Tess. She crossed her arms thoughtfully. "Ramel is still bound to Mab, right?"

Molly nodded. "As far as we know. He didn't…it wasn't like with Finnead. She had to release the spell on him, but he's still bound to her as one of her Three."

Tess kneaded at her forehead with a knuckle. "Life would be much easier if my friends weren't all so powerful and important."

"Again…you're one to talk," said Molly dryly.

"I know. I'm just trying to think. If you stay here in the mortal world, will Mab hold him accountable for that? Will she punish him for not ensuring that you killed me?" Tess shook her head.

"I wouldn't put it past her," said Molly grimly.

"He's not strong enough to travel through the portal now," said Tess, "and he probably won't be well enough for at least another few…weeks?" She shrugged and pressed her lips together. "I think that I'll need to return with the Lethe Stone before that. I'll tell her that he wasn't strong enough to go through the portal, and I wanted to fulfill my end of the bargain."

"She could still kill him," whispered Molly. She swallowed hard. "I'm still frightened of what she might do to him, Tess. Even here in another world."

"I know." Tess looked over at her friend. She couldn't quite believe that it was really *Molly*, that she was talking to her best friend again as though they hadn't both traveled into another world and been separated for months, first by the loss of Molly's memory and then by Tess's binding to the Sword. It felt like they'd traveled across the world, but they'd ended up back at their own familiar doorstep. After a moment, Tess let the feelings of familiarity and fondness wash over her. "But what I also know," she said slowly, "is that we'll figure it out together."

"You're a true friend," said Molly, her voice clotted with emotion.

"More like a sister," corrected Tess.

"More like a sister," agreed Molly, smiling through her unshed tears. "I know we've never really been big on hugs and you were wounded in the battle…"

"Super awesome healing powers unlocked," said Tess with a flourish, pushing up her left sleeve to show Molly the fresh scars. Then she smiled. "Get over here. Everyone needs a hug once in a while."

As she hugged her best friend for the first time in a long time, Tess thought that Luca wasn't the only person she loved who had been returned to her on this journey into the mortal world. Then the seriousness of the moment was broken when Merrick stirred and sat up, his dark hair sticking up wildly in all directions. He blinked at them as they stepped back from their hug. Tess raised her eyebrows bemusedly – the *Vyldgard* navigator, a very capable warrior, looked remarkably like a particularly handsome college student awakening after a night of revelry…if college students had delicately pointed ears and flawless alabaster skin.

"What is that amazing smell?" he asked with a yawn.

"Gumbo," replied Tess. "Apparently Jess has some impressive culinary skills." She looked at Molly. "If you'd like, I can sit with Ramel while you eat."

Molly shook her head without any hesitation. She began to say something but then pressed her lips together.

"I'll grab you a bowl," offered Tess.

"I can take care of that," Merrick said as he stretched. "I should make myself useful."

Tess smiled. "It's good to see you, Merrick."

He bowed slightly to her. "And you, Lady Bearer."

She scowled at him in mock reproach as they headed toward the kitchen. "If you call me Lady Bearer, I'll be forced to call you the Arrisyn."

He grinned. "I have no issue with the name given to me by the *Vyldretning*."

"The Arrisyn and the Laedrek, together again," said Tess teasingly. To her delight, Merrick blushed, two faint spots of color appearing high on his cheekbones. He was saved from having to reply by the lively shouts of greeting from the kitchen table. Duke sat with his arm around Ross, Luca had been enticed to try a beer, and Niall had come in from his watch over the bone sorcerer. Haze sat on the table with his own miniature portion of gumbo. Ross kept glancing at Haze as if to reassure herself that there was really a small, fierce Fae eating gumbo out of a thimble-sized bowl with fastidious manners.

"You're lookin' fit as a fiddle now," said Duke approvingly, toasting Merrick with a can of beer.

"Yes, well, now I'm covered with the proper runes," replied Merrick, lifting the edge of his shirt to show Duke the pattern of runes that Calliea and Niall had inked on his skin. He smiled a little abashedly. "They're simple, but you have to know the correct pattern. Runes to fortify against the strangeness of this world and protect us from the forces that would strip us of our power."

"They should have continued to teach those protection runes to young ones, even if the Gate was closed," Niall said. "But that wasn't for me to decide."

"I am eminently grateful that you knew them," said Merrick. His gray eyes darkened as he ladled his bowl of gumbo from the steaming pot on the stove. "It was a close call."

"Too close," agreed Niall. The Seelie Vaelanseld also had a beer on the table in front of him, though he'd opted for a bottle rather than a can. Tess leaned against the wall and smiled a little as she watched the interactions between the Sidhe warriors who had come through the portal with her and the fighters who had been here...not to mention Ross. Other than her surreptitious glances at Haze, Ross seemed to accept the Sidhe with less incredulity than Tess would have expected from a practical, no-nonsense woman like her. It probably helped that Duke and Jess had verified the outlandish story. In any case, everyone seated around the table acted as though they'd known each other for years rather than hours. Deadly peril had a way of bringing people together, she thought wryly.

Luca gave up his seat to Merrick, waving aside the other man's protests. "It is time for me to go look at this corrupted Northman," he said as he finished his beer.

Tess made a face at him as they walked side-by-side toward the front door, leaving the hum of easy conversation behind them. "You know, if you're going to make a habit of drinking beer, you should at least drink *good* beer."

Luca chuckled. "I'll let you be my teacher in that, if you wish."

"Well, I wouldn't say I'm an *expert*, but I'm sure we can figure it out between us," Tess replied. The sun balanced on the top of the gnarled oak trees as they walked past the blackened crater and burned-out skeleton of Ross's truck. "We're going to have to do something about all this," she muttered. "It looks like a war zone out here, and it would be best if we can keep a low profile." She glanced down the country road in consideration. "Though it looks like we're not too close to anyone, so that's good."

As they passed the side of the house, Luca told her briefly about Gryttrond's possession of the gas store clerk and his attempt to claw through Ross's bedroom window with his bare hands. Tess shivered a little at the description. She could imagine the blood-curdling terror at encountering such a strange creature in the night all too easily. In turn, she told him about the girl tied to the tree that Niall had seen while scrying that morning. Luca squeezed her shoulder as the bone sorcerer's glowing cage came into view. They paused.

"I am proud," he said seriously, looking down at Tess. Kianryk appeared out of the brush at the edge of the yard, Mayhem trailing happily behind him.

"Proud of what?" she asked, warmth rippling through her at the undeniable love in his eyes.

"Proud of you," he said with a smile. "You saved that girl in the forest at your own peril without a second thought."

"Well, *I* didn't save her. Haze, Forin and Farin did that, technically. I was just the diversion to bait him into chasing me here," she replied with a smile, though her face heated at his earnest compliment. "And…I mean, we were going to track down the bone sorcerer anyway, so it was really just speeding up the timeline." She realized as she spoke that she was downplaying his compliment, but rather than exhort her to recognize her accomplishments, Luca just smiled. He just let her be, let her think out loud, talk without any fear of judgment. She sighed. "I missed you," she said quietly.

"And I missed you as well," he said. His hand lingered on her shoulder and his thumb traced the curve of her neck. As if it were the most natural thing in the world, his hand slipped softly up her neck to the side of her face, his calloused palm gently cupping her cheek. She closed her eyes for just a few breaths, feeling the roughness of his hand against her face, wondering at the comfort that blossomed at such a simple touch. Then she turned her face, kissed his palm and smiled at him.

"Time to go figure out what to do with this bone sorcerer," she said. Luca nodded, and the Sword hummed in its sheath on her back.

Gryttrond paced his cage angrily, throwing a curse at the glowing bars every few minutes with a flash of rusty red sparks. The invisible dome that comprised his cage between the shining arches absorbed his power with little more than a ripple. Calliea sat in the grass a few paces away, cleaning her daggers, and glancing at the mage with a mixed expression of disgust and amusement when he threw his spells fruitlessly at the cage. The two Exiled – Corsica and Tyr, Tess remembered – also observed the bone sorcerer. Corsica crouched on her haunches on the side of the cage closest to the river, watching the bone sorcerer much as a cat watches a caged bird. Her brilliant azure eyes tracked his movements, and she cocked her head to the side with a smile at his spells. Tyr walked the perimeter of the cage, glancing down at the runes on the stones and nodding to himself.

"They've been doing that for hours," said Calliea, standing to greet Tess. She narrowed her eyes. "You look remarkably spry after your spill on the rocks and whatever else you managed to do to yourself during the fight."

"You mean what the bone sorcerer did to me during the fight," Tess corrected. Calliea arched an eyebrow. "Seriously, I didn't just *fall* off Kianryk! I'm clumsy, but I'm not *that* clumsy...at least, most of the time. He made the *earth* move."

"Ah, that was the shudder we felt in the house." Calliea nodded.

"And I guess being the Bearer in the mortal world means super healing powers." For what felt like the hundredth time that day, Tess pulled up her left sleeve and showed Calliea the shiny new scars on her skin.

"Convenient," she remarked. "At least I won't have to be your nursemaid."

Tess shook her head. "And here you let me believe that you did that out of the goodness of your heart."

"The goodness of my heart and a direct order from the *Vyldretning*," Calliea said with a smirk.

With an answering smile, Tess fell silent, staring at the trapped mage. She remembered his coppery hot metal smell and the brutal strength in his hands. The Caedbranr's power stirred restlessly in her chest.

"He can't see us," Calliea said. "Or at least that's what she says." She gestured with her dagger to Corsica.

Kianryk bounded over to Luca, the *ulfdrengr* bracing himself as the big wolf leapt on him. Calliea watched them wrestle with dry amusement. Mayhem joyfully leapt into the scuffle. Tess smiled and then walked closer to the bone sorcerer's cage. She wondered how long he would rage impotently against the impermeable dome.

Tyr noticed her approach and he paused in checking one of the rune-stones, his eyes traveling over her with interest. When she turned slightly to better view the bone sorcerer, he saw the beaten scabbard of the Sword on her back. He looked sharply at Corsica, who glanced up at him and stood with lazy grace. As Corsica skirted the edge of the runetrap, Tyr turned back to Tess and bowed elegantly.

"I…thank you," Tess said, unsure. She hadn't known what to expect from the Exiled, but it certainly hadn't been such a respectful greeting. Tyr straightened. A small smile curved his beautiful mouth, and his gray eyes glimmered with something akin to reverence. Tess had no doubt that Tyr recognized the Sword.

"I speak for both of us," said Corsica silkily. She gave a deep curtsy, her gloved hands delicately holding the edges of her long tunic in place of skirts.

"Why?" The question escaped Tess before she could stop herself.

Corsica straightened and looked at Tyr, who motioned to Tess with an impatient gesture. He was giving Corsica permission to answer, Tess realized.

"We do not speak of it often," Corsica said. "It was many centuries ago and it was what gained us our binding and banishment." She plucked at her mud-stained black gloves uneasily. "Betrayal and binding and banishment. Burning and bloody and bereaved."

Tess waited for Corsica to stop talking to herself. She wondered if the Exiled were indeed insane as Sage had warned. They didn't seem to want revenge, as he'd suggested, but the part about the long years in the mortal world driving them mad, Tess could believe.

"Burning and bloody," Corsica said, her blue eyes staring. She rubbed at her wrists. Tyr touched her shoulder and she shuddered, shaking herself free of whatever memory had dragged her back into its clutches. She raised her gaze to Tess again. "Before," she said. "Before the banishment, Tyr spoke for us."

"Tyr spoke for the rebels?" Tess asked, trying to follow.

Corsica hissed and displayed her pointed teeth. "Rebels! Queens who burn and bind and banish write the legends to please themselves. Freedom fighters. Not fighters until they forced us." She shook her head and her face became strangely open as she continued. Tess easily read the yearning and sadness in her eyes. "Tyr was the best of us. The best of all of us who only wanted to be free." Tyr stared at the nearest rune stone silently. Anger chased away the sadness in Corsica's expression. "And the cold Queen, she took his words, his beautiful words and his lark's song voice." She showed her pointed teeth again.

"You're saying that Queen Mab…took Tyr's voice," Tess said slowly.

Corsica had retreated back into her own head. "Betrayal and binding and banishment," she repeated, the words closer to a growl now. "Burning and bloody and bereaved." She gripped her own wrists, her fingers circling her wrists like manacles.

"I'm sorry that happened to you," Tess said quietly. Tyr looked up and nodded solemnly. She didn't think Corsica heard her at all. With a deep breath, she looked back at the bone sorcerer. "Thank you for helping to trap him. I was told that you improved the runes and made sure that the trap would be strong enough."

Tyr nodded again. Corsica suddenly stopped muttering and dropped to her haunches, assuming her watchful position again, her eyes tracking the mage hungrily. Tess decided to speak to Tyr directly.

"I need to find a way to retrieve an object that Gryttrond has on his person," she said. Naming the bone sorcerer made her feel as though she pulled aside part of the veil of mystery shrouding him. And the Glasidhe had taught her long ago that names held power—including fear. She would name the bone sorcerer without a tremble in her voice.

Tyr raised his eyebrows and tilted his head questioningly to the side. For a moment, Tess hesitated. Was it the right choice to trust the Exiled? But really, what other choice did she have? Tyr had helped build the runetrap, so she assumed he would have to help with any modifications. She didn't relish the thought of releasing the bone sorcerer from the cage to search for the Lethe Stone, and she hoped it wouldn't come to that.

"It's called a Lethe Stone," she said. She thought she saw a flicker of recognition in Tyr's eyes, but she wasn't sure, so she dug in her belt pouch and produced the palm-sized little book that contained the description of the Lethe Stone. She flipped easily to the correct page, her fingers finding it of their own accord. She'd read the description and looked at the illustration dozens of times in the past days.

Holding the book out to Tyr, she watched as his dark eyes traveled across the pages. He reached out with one scar-mottled hand, looking at her inquiringly. She nodded and he took the book carefully into his hands. After reading the pages again a few more times, he nodded.

"You'll help?" asked Tess, but Tyr was already moving. She watched as he retrieved a rune-stick from the grass near one of the flat stones. Her skin prickled as he began to write runes directly on the illustration of the Lethe Stone, and she was too busy trying to decide if she'd made a mistake in trusting Tyr to protest at the defacement of the little tome. Corsica paid no attention to Tyr, licking her sharp teeth as she stared at the bone sorcerer. Tess reached back and gripped the hilt of the Sword, its power vibrating reassuringly through her palm. Tyr wrote furiously for a moment more, then nodded. He stood up straight and then threw the little book into the nearest beam of blue light.

Tess jumped at the crack of thunder that split the air. The whole dome shuddered and the earth beneath their feet vibrated. A high-pitched whine emanating from the dome made her teeth hurt. She slid the Sword a few inches from its sheath, preparing to draw it if the runetrap failed. Swirls of light flickered faster and faster across the surface of the dome, like slick oil spreading over the surface of water. The vibration of the ground increased as the whine became almost a shriek, loud enough that Tess had to resist the urge to clap her hands over her ears. She gritted her teeth and watched as the dome flared brighter and brighter until it looked as though the sun had been lassoed and embedded into the earth.

Another crack of thunder sounded and Tess saw a miniature comet streak out from the dome. She drew the Sword, its power expanding in her chest and racing down her war markings as she prepared to defend against one of the bone sorcerer's spells, but Tyr reached up and plucked the little comet from the air as it arced toward her. As soon as he touched it, the shrieking ceased and the dome slowly faded back to its previous appearance. Everything looked as it had in the moment that Tyr had thrown the little book into the blue arc of fire…except the trapped mage lay motionless in the center of the cage.

"Did you…is he dead?" Tess asked breathlessly. She wasn't sure if she felt triumphant or disappointed that she hadn't been the one to finish Gryttrond.

Tyr shook his head unconcernedly. Tess looked harder and after a moment picked out the rise and fall of the bone sorcerer's chest. She sighed. When she turned back to Tyr, the white-haired Fae knelt before her. He held his cupped hands up to her like an offering. Nestled in his palms, glistening as if freshly pulled from the river, was the Lethe Stone.

Chapter 32

Liam strode one pace behind Vell on her right side. Finnead walked at her left side, with Gray as the rearguard. They wore their armor and didn't speak as they walked. The Three could feel the tension of the High Queen through their bond. Liam drew a sense of familiarity and security from the weight of the armor on his torso. It reminded him of the weight of his body armor, the panels of Kevlar that would in theory protect him from enemy bullets or shards of metal from an IED blast. He'd worn his vest like a second skin, the fabric soaked with his sweat and the dirt of a land thousands of miles away from his home. In a few places, the fabric had born a rusty stain. It was nearly impossible to truly remove blood, and they didn't try very hard anyway. Gear that was too shiny and new with no marks of use was one of the telltale signs that you were the new guy, fresh out of training and eager as a kid on his first day of school.

Since the day that his Sight had taken over in the practice ring, Liam had actually forged a strange sort of friendship with Finnead. After that first long session of laying the groundwork of Andraste's story, Liam and Finnead met nearly every day so that Finnead could continue to give his memories to Liam. The hardest part had been convincing the dark haired Sidhe Knight that he wasn't going to anger Liam by recounting his relationship with the Unseelie princess. Finnead's guilt over how his relationship with Tess had ended had put a halt to the memory sessions for a few days. It had perhaps been a bit heavy-handed, but Liam had resorted to reminding Finnead that Tess loved Luca, she had struck a deal with Mab in order to open the portal to the mortal world and find him, after all. Liam had heard enough ribald stories from fellow warriors that he didn't flinch away from the story or become embarrassed when it came to the physical aspect of the tale. He merely pointed out to Finnead that whatever details he left out, he ran the risk of losing forever. Finnead, however, countered that it would hardly be proper for him to discuss such intimate knowledge of the princess with another man. They finally struck a compromise when Liam suggested that Finnead write it all down and leave the book in his safekeeping.

So Finnead told Liam the broad sketches of his courtship of the princess, and her progress as a truly gifted archer. He had spent some of his time writing down other memories in a small journal bound with red leather. Liam had told Vell of their project when she asked. She'd merely shrugged and said grimly that Finnead's memories were the least of her problems. The tension between the Courts was growing. Titania had sent a messenger to Vell with a letter written in the Seelie Queen's own beautiful flowing script. She again reiterated her disapproval of the bargain struck by the Bearer and the High Queen with Mab.

"I have to tell her," Vell had said, with a dour look at the letter on the table. "Much as I don't want things to ignite between Mab and Titania, I'm not going to put the *Vyldgard* in the middle."

"The *Vyldgard* isn't in the middle," Liam had reminded her, folding one of the large architectural sketches into a neat square packet. "You're the High Queen."

"Yes, but that doesn't mean I get to smack Titania and Mab on the snouts like unruly pups," Vell had replied with a bit of a growl in her voice. She sighed. "Even if I'd like to sometimes," she added to herself.

The Glasidhe messenger had accepted Vell's reply with a bow, zooming off to find Queen Titania to deliver the missive. Now, Liam knew that Vell suspected that perhaps a spy for Mab had betrayed her plan to use the Lethe Stone herself. What would happen if Mab challenged Vell…and would Titania support the High Queen, or watch from the sidelines?

As they walked and Liam mulled over the possibilities, he suddenly felt his muscles tighten and his stomach flip, his warning signs that a vision was about to assault his senses. Since his Sight had returned, he'd had fewer visions but they were all the more intense for their scarcity. He reached out for the wall as the white fire swirled over his sight and he lost perception of his body.

All of the visions had multiple threads, multiple futures stemming from every possible decision. Lately, they had been a bit more focused. Liam thought that it was probably a side effect of his healing at Arcana's hands. When he had these new and more intense visions, he felt the sliver of the Morrigan awaken in the back of his skull. The remnant of the deity slid like a snake through his head and down his spine, a physical sensation that heightened the nausea brought on by his Sight. Perhaps it was the Morrigan directing his Sight now, focusing his ability with her power. Liam felt Finnead and Gray supporting him on either side. Vell slid her strong, calloused hand beneath his chin. He waited for the vision to coalesce in the blank brightness.

"What do you See?" Vell's voice reached him as a soft echo.

He took a breath and focused. After another moment of vertigo, his Sight presented him with a kaleidoscope of images. First he saw Mab, her eyes alight with a cold fury, holding a blade above the head of a kneeling Knight with copper hair. Liam jerked as Mab brought down the sword with savage force. He couldn't look away or close his eyes as he saw the Unseelie Queen execute Ramel. And then the scene shifted to a dark haired girl that he vaguely recognized. He realized after a moment that he was looking at Tess's best friend Molly…but the woman Molly, not the girl he had known. She knelt in the long grass beside a river, tears streaming down her face, rage and searing sorrow in her eyes.

Liam connected the two images: in one future, Mab would execute Ramel, and she would make an implacable enemy of Molly. His brow furrowed. What did Mab care if a half-mortal girl hated her? The image shifted again to a man with blood-red runes inscribed on his skin and a black mark on his forehead. The man spoke to a silver-haired woman who watched him with rapt azure eyes, and then Molly strode up to the three of them, determination written across her face. His Sight blurred again, like a reflection disturbed by a ripple, and showed him a final image of chaos and carnage. In a great hall carved of dark stone, the bodies of slain Seelie and Unseelie fighters lay side by side…but this was not the Dark Keep. It was the future, and it was Darkhill, the center of Mab's kingdom. Molly strode toward Mab's throne, red runes now written on her pale skin, a hard light in her eyes.

His Sight rushed away, leaving as abruptly as it came and rendering him breathless with nausea. He blinked and regained his feet, nodding to Finnead and Gray in thanks for their support. Their faces were pale and drawn, too – though they recovered more quickly than he, they felt a bit of the sickness brought on by the Sight through their bond. Vell's hand was still under his chin.

"What did you See?" she asked urgently, her golden eyes intent on his face.

He drew in a shuddering breath. "I Saw Mab execute her Vaelanbrigh, Ramel." His hoarse voice gained strength as he continued, and he didn't miss the flicker of shock that appeared for an instant in Finnead's eyes. "And Molly, the half-mortal girl who came through with Tess. She'll seek revenge. I Saw her speak to a man with red runes on his face, and a silver haired woman." He frowned, trying to remember any other details about the wild-looking woman, but she seemed to be the least important. "And then…the last thing I Saw was Darkhill. Mab's throne room, littered with bodies. Molly advancing on Mab…except this time she also had red runes on her face."

"The bone sorcerer," murmured Finnead.

"Why should we care if Mab makes an enemy that spells her own doom?" Gray asked in her bright voice, eyes flashing. "Mab has not been a friend to the *Vyldgard* of late."

"And do all Mab's subjects deserve to be consigned to the same fate?" asked Finnead. "As much as we may dislike Mab, not all of her subjects are as cold or hard-hearted."

"Bold statement, from one who used to serve her," said Gray.

"Enough," said Vell calmly. "Finnead is right. No matter the sins of their Queen, the Unseelie do not deserve to be drawn into another war needlessly."

"There were Seelie corpses in the throne room too," said Liam in a low voice.

"The silver-haired woman," said Vell, almost to herself. "One of the Exiled. Perhaps she will lead them in a war of revenge against both Courts."

"This is only one future," Liam said heavily. "It seems to stem from the Vaelanbrigh's execution." He took another deep breath as the last of the sick feeling drained from his stomach and the shard of the Morrigan settled into stillness in the back of his skull. "It looks like that's the proverbial straw that breaks the camel's back. I didn't see all the details, and I don't know what else happens. But it was a dark vision."

"Ramel is well-liked," said Finnead thoughtfully. "Perhaps his death would incite a rebellion."

"What does it mean for the *Vyldgard*?" Gray pressed. "That should be our focus."

"For too many years, we have all been focused on the well-being of our own people, isolated in our own parts of the world," Vell said after a moment. "I watched my own people annihilated by evil because the Sidhe Queens did not act. They thought that an evil that threatened the North was an evil to be fought by the North. And when the North fell, they drew back into their strongholds and thought that the evil would not come for them as well."

"All it takes for evil to succeed is for good men to stand by and do nothing," said Liam.

"We have fought for our world once," said Vell, looking at each of her Three in turn. "But there will always be another battle."

"So what will we do?" asked Gray in a more subdued voice. "We could capture the girl Molly."

Liam shook his head, wincing slightly at the headache building behind his eyes. "Someone else will lead the rebellion, I think. And we can't start imprisoning people for the things I See." He met Vell's eyes. "I don't want my Sight to be used as a tool for preemptive punishment."

"Preemptive punishment," repeated Vell with a little smile. "So educated, my Seer." She thought for a long moment. "For now, we will go to the council. We will listen more than we speak, and we will see what path Mab chooses. Ramel and Molly are still in the mortal world, and I would like to understand where Mab's order to assassinate the Bearer fits into this plot."

"That in itself makes me want to leave Mab to the wolves," said Gray in a low voice.

Liam chuckled. "I didn't know you were so fond of my sister."

"Well, it's more my opinion of Mab as a cold-hearted bitch that influences my viewpoint," replied Gray with a brilliant, predatory smile.

Finnead glanced at the golden-haired woman with ill-concealed irritation. "Must you be so rude? Even if you do not like her, she is still a Queen."

"You two bicker like brother and sister," Vell commented mildly. She shifted her attention to Liam. "Steady enough to walk?"

Liam nodded. "Yes."

"Good," Vell replied as she turned and strode down the passageway. "For all her faults, Mab is punctual, and it wouldn't do to be late to the council."

Chapter 33

Ross wasn't entirely sure *why* everyone felt the need to run outside at the two strident peals of thunder. If something supernatural was wreaking havoc in the back yard, why did everyone want to rush headlong into it? Niall and Merrick shot up from the table quicker than thought and disappeared through the front door. It was akin to soldiers or policemen running toward the sound of gunfire, she decided. Jess calmly turned the stove down to a simmer before following them, and Duke emerged from the bedroom with the Beretta and Glock.

"Wanna check on V before we go?" he asked her.

"Of course." Ross was already halfway down the hallway to Vivian's room. Though the two cracks of thunder had shaken the house, Vivian still slept peacefully, her red curls splayed haphazardly across the pillow. Ross glanced around the room and found nothing out of place. She shut the door quietly behind her and accepted the Glock from Duke.

"Maybe I should start wearing my holster again," she said, only half joking.

"Wouldn't be a bad idea," said Duke. They passed the door to the study and he nodded to Molly, who sat cross-legged by Ramel's side. Molly seemed to be the only one uninterested in investigating the unnatural thunder. Ross wondered if Merrick's runes on the front door were still enforcing his wards around the house. Either way, she thought that spending time in the Fae world probably meant that Molly could defend herself quite well on her own.

The late afternoon sky arched cerulean over their heads, a few woolly clouds breaking the blue expanse. The thunder had definitely been unnatural, thought Ross, adjusting her grip on the Glock as they rounded the side of the house. But what came into sight wasn't a scene of devastation or chaos – instead, it looked more like…celebration. Niall, Merrick, Calliea and Luca all gathered around Tess, who held a smooth blue stone in her cupped palms. She spoke animatedly to the Sidhe, her eyes bright with excitement. Jess stood a small distance away, surveying the glowing dome with his arms crossed over his chest. Corsica turned cartwheels around the bone sorcerer's cage, and Tyr knelt by one of the rune stones, staring at the still figure in the runetrap.

Ross looked at Duke. "Did they kill the bad guy? Is that what that was?"

He shook his head slowly. "No. He's still alive. Something else…I think it's that stone that Tess is holdin'. It's probably somethin' magic."

Ross snorted. "What do you mean, *magic*?"

Duke chuckled. "Don't tell me you're still holdin' out that this is all a fever dream or a hallucination or somethin'."

"Well, no," admitted Ross as they walked across the yard toward the knot of otherworldly travelers. "But that doesn't mean that I'm going to think that every little rock is *magic*."

He shrugged. "I'm just tellin' ya what I think. I mean, they had flying horses. *Valkyrie*, Ross. What's a measly magic stone compared to that?"

She smiled at his grin and shook her head. "Please don't tell Vivian about the flying horses. She already wants to go to their world, and that would seal the deal."

"Good luck tryin' to cure her of that bug," Duke said under his breath. He clapped Jess on the shoulder as they passed. "Hey, brother. Trying to decide if you're gonna get some red face tattoos like the fugly guy in there? I think you'd wear 'em better."

Jess chuckled dryly, the scar on his cheek creasing as he smiled. "And give up any chance of gainful employment after they retire my ass?"

"Hey, as far as they think, we're dead," pointed out Duke with entirely too much cheer. "And tattoos seem to be way more acceptable in Faeortalam, right?"

Ross left the two men to talk. She walked toward Tess, the long grass tickling her ankles. She really needed to mow the lawn, she thought distractedly as she approached. The others had arranged themselves in a loose half-circle about Tess, and they were listening to her intently.

"We could leave…well, now," she said as Ross approached. "I told Mab that I'd bring her the Lethe Stone in exchange for opening the portal."

"We also said that we would destroy the bone sorcerer," said Niall. "But that is not yet done."

"That's a good point," allowed Tess, "but he *is* trapped. Contained." She glanced over her shoulder at the dome.

"I know that you aren't constrained by the bargain I struck before you arrived," said Merrick, his luminous gray eyes serious. "But I would like to keep my word. Tyr assisted in the capture of the bone sorcerer in exchange for…well, really *Corsica* was the one who made the deal. She drank my blood and wanted to talk to him. She said that he could perhaps help them to undo some of the damage that's been caused by their time in this world."

Tess looked over at Tyr. "He helped me retrieve the Lethe Stone just now. Without any promises." She pressed her lips together. "I don't think they're evil."

Luca crossed his arms over his massive chest. "I do not think they are evil either, but I do not think they can be completely trusted."

Ross listened to the conversation silently. She didn't have anything to contribute, after all…although she supposed she was allowed to have an opinion on keeping an otherworldly villain caged in a glowing dome in her back yard. Then she realized she *did* have something else to bring up. "Corsica blew up my truck," she pointed out. "I agree on the not to be trusted part."

Tess ran a finger lightly over the smooth surface of the Lethe Stone. "Something just tells me that I should return sooner rather than later to Faeortalam."

"You have the makings of three Gates, do you not?" said Niall slowly.

Ross didn't quite understand what he meant, but she continued to listen.

"Yes," said Tess slowly. A small crease appeared between her brows. "Those will work in Faeortalam too?"

Niall smiled slightly. "I believe so."

Tess grinned. "That's brilliant, Niall! I hadn't even thought of that." She looked at each of the members of her little circle. "One portal to take us back to Faeortalam. It doesn't have to be everyone. Ramel isn't strong enough yet anyway. So I go back with whomever wants to join me, to give Mab the Lethe Stone." She nodded to herself as she continued. "And then I can explain about the Exiled and the bone sorcerer."

"You will tell the Queens that you bargained with the Exiled?" Niall asked with a hint of gentle skepticism. "I do not think either of them would take it well."

Tess held Niall's gaze searchingly. "Won't you tell Titania?"

He shrugged. "Not if she does not ask. I cannot deny my Queen the truth, but I will not volunteer it. She charged me to help you fulfill your task in the mortal world, and I have done that to the best of my ability. And as far as I am concerned, my fealty to you extends still, since our tasks are not yet complete."

Tess nodded and paused, thinking over her next words. She used the time to wrap the Lethe Stone in a square of white fabric and slip it into her belt pouch. Ross suspected that Tess had realized the prudence of keeping some parts of her plans to herself now. Finally Tess said, "All right. I've made a decision. I'm going to return to Faeortalam tonight."

"I am coming with you," Luca said.

Tess nodded as though she'd expected it, but Ross thought she saw a bit of relief in her eyes. Tess then turned to Merrick and Calliea, addressing them both at once. "What are your thoughts?"

Merrick and Calliea looked at each other, and then Calliea said with a little smile, "This world is fascinating, but I think we will return to the *Vyldgard*. We'll bring Vell some ideas on establishing a base in this world," Calliea said. Ross got the sneaking feeling that Vivian's house was currently the prime candidate for this base in the mortal world.

Tess nodded in approval.

"I'm staying," said Jess. He and Duke had drifted over, caught by the gravity of the serious discussion. "I have to figure some things out."

Ross stiffened in surprise and then relaxed as she realized it was Duke who had slipped an arm about her waist. She rolled her eyes at him as he squeezed her hip.

"I think it goes without sayin' that I'll be holdin' down the fort here," Duke said.

Something loosened within Ross at his words, a knot of anxiety that she hadn't recognized. She hadn't known until then that she feared he would want to return to this fantastic world of magic. She leaned into him slightly.

"You didn't think I was gonna leave again, did you?" he murmured just loud enough for her to hear.

"I hoped not," she said softly.

He pressed a kiss to her temple. "I'll always come back to you."

Ross smiled a little. "Or I'll just come with you."

"That's my girl," he chuckled. "But I think V would be pissed at you if you were the first one to score a ticket into the world of magic and mayhem."

Mayhem bounded over to them, pressing happily against Ross's legs, hearing her name even though Duke had spoken in a quiet voice. Ross scratched the Malinois behind her ears and turned her attention back to the conversation.

"I will oversee the guard on the bone sorcerer and the healing of the Unseelie Vaelanbrigh," said Niall with a graceful bow. "If the Bearer so wishes."

"That works out quite well, actually. So it will be Calliea, Merrick, Luca, Kianryk and I traveling back into Faeortalam," Tess said.

"Looks like it," Duke replied.

Tess looked at Ross. "Are you and Vivian all right with this? Us using your house as a sort of base, I mean."

"Does it matter if we're not?" Ross softened her words slightly with a smile.

"Of course it does," Tess replied with a frown. "You've already done so much for us. I wouldn't consider intruding on your hospitality any further if you objected."

"If Vivian spent time in the Fae world, would she come back talking all formal like you do?" Ross returned, trying to backtrack, but Tess merely waited for her response. She smiled slightly. "Well, it's technically Vivian's house, so you'll need to ask her the next time she wakes up. But I'm pretty sure she's been having the time of her life the last couple of days."

"I'll take that as a yes for now," Tess replied. She nodded and one hand brushed her belt pouch. "I have to set up the Summoning...preferably not too close to this cage." She tapped her lips with one finger. "Niall, if you'd discuss this with me?"

The circle dispersed into smaller groups as Tess walked away with Niall, already deep in discussion about the proper placement of the elements to Summon the portal to the Fae world. Kianryk appeared out of a shadow and leapt onto Mayhem, who gleefully wrestled the huge wolf. Luca said something to the wolf in a Nordic sounding language. Kianryk paused, grinning at the *ulfdrengr* and enduring Mayhem's attempts to flip him onto his back. Then he sprang away and led Mayhem in dizzying circles around the yard. Ross snorted when the two rebellious canines almost collided with the cartwheeling Corsica.

"I wonder if she's ever going to get dizzy," Ross muttered, watching the silver haired woman spin in circles around the glowing dome.

"Probably not. I mean, she's like a mutant elf, right? So..." Duke shrugged and grinned when she smacked his arm lightly. "What? You were totally thinking it."

"Yeah, well, that doesn't mean that you should say it out loud," said Ross with a laugh.

Duke squinted and tilted his head. "Don't tell me my girl grew a set of manners while I was away." He held up his hand, miming drinking from a teacup with his pinky out. "Are we gonna start using salad forks and shit?"

"Only when we're dining with mutant elves," she deadpanned.

"I think Corsica would rather stab someone with a salad fork than eat from it," replied Duke, raising an eyebrow. The Exile had stopped cartwheeling and had reassumed her cat watching the canary posture. "Are we sure they just wanna *talk* to the bone sorcerer? Because from here it looks like she wants to eat him."

Calliea glanced at Duke, a glimmer of amusement in her eyes. "And why would that be such a tragedy?"

Merrick smiled. The two of them looked entirely capable of fighting an entire battalion on their own, Ross thought. There was something in their relaxed yet watchful posture that reminded her of predators. Panthers and wolves, teeth and claws flashing in the night. After a moment, Merrick and Calliea walked away, both still looking to Ross's eyes like carnivores prowling through their habitat.

"Remind me never to get on their bad sides," murmured Ross.

"Honey, I learned that on day one," replied Duke.

"May I interrupt briefly?" Niall asked courteously, his almost-colorless gaze shifting from Duke to Ross, who gestured for him to continue. He offered her a little velvet pouch. "I hope this will cover your…truck." He said the word hesitantly but smiled when Duke gave him a thumb's up. Ross took the pouch, loosening its strings and frowning slightly as Niall glided away.

"What in the…" she breathed as a handful of coins slid into her palm. Some were gold and some silver, but they felt *heavy.* "I…what…these look *antique!*"

"From the way I heard it, last time that Niall was in the mortal world was maybe Elizabethan times," Duke replied.

"I guess we'll have to find an antiques dealer," Ross replied, stunned.

"For some of 'em," agreed Duke, pushing them about in her palm with his finger. "But look, some of 'em look to be just gold coins. No inscription or anything, just…gold."

"Just…gold," repeated Ross weakly.

"But hey, you must have some of my life insurance money left," Duke said with a grin.

"Don't even joke about that," admonished Ross, dropping the coins back into the purse. She weighed the purse surreptitiously in her hand. It felt like she'd only held maybe half of the coins in her palm. "Wait until V sees these."

Duke chuckled, following her back toward the front door. "Not like V needs the money."

"Well, you're just on a roll right now," Ross said, arching an eyebrow.

"It was your truck that got blown up," he replied sensibly, just as they were passing the charred wreck.

Ross sighed. "Can't argue with you there." She unloaded the Glock and left it on the kitchen counter, slipping the magazine into her pocket as she padded down the hallway to Vivian's room. After a light knock, she pushed the door open. Vivian sat in bed with a book on her lap, chewing absently on a strand of her hair. A sling held her left arm. She looked up only when Ross cleared her throat.

"Hey, V. How are you feeling?" Ross made sure there was still water in the pitcher on the nightstand.

Vivian blew the strand of hair away from her face. "Well, other than the fact that I didn't realize I was rereading *The Hobbit* for the millionth time because I was so high on those painkillers you brought me..." She giggled. "Other than that, fantabulous."

"Fantabulous, huh?" Ross raised her eyebrows. "You sure that's not the pain meds still talking?"

Vivian giggled again and then sighed. "I have no idea. Probably."

Ross chuckled. "All right. Well...I do have a serious question for you."

Vivian gasped and looked at Ross with wide eyes. Ross paused expectantly and Vivian lunged out of bed, throwing her arms around her roommate.

"Of *course* I'll be your maid of honor!" she howled gleefully. "It's about *time* you two tied the knot, all googly-eyed and cute..."

"I...well, we were already engaged," Ross protested, carefully disentangling herself from Vivian's embrace.

"I *knoooow* that," said Vivian. "But, you know, you *need* an awesome maid of honor. I mean, all the *planning!*" She grinned happily.

"Okay," Ross said soothingly. She glanced at Vivian's pupils and found her suspicion correct – her roommate was still high as a kite. "Apparently you're pretty sensitive to the stuff I gave you, so just try to relax, okay?"

"What do you *think* I'm doing?" said Vivian dramatically, motioning to the book on her lap. She sighed and then looked searchingly at Ross. "Did you say you had a question for me?"

"Yes," said Ross, trying not to smile. "Is it alright if we have a few guests for a while?"

"You mean the Sidhe? You'd better mean them," Vivian said severely.

"Yes. A few are going back to the Fae world, but others are going to stay here. Ramel is too injured to travel, so he and Molly will be here, along with Niall. And then Jess will stay with us for a while too, I think."

"What about Haze and the twins?" Vivian raised her eyebrows.

"I...actually, I don't know," Ross replied honestly. "But would it be all right if any of them end up staying?"

"Of course. I like them. They're little and fierce." Vivian nodded. Then she wrinkled her nose. "What about Corsica and Tyr? They kinda creep me out. Well, Corsica does anyway. But Tyr not so much. He's just really quiet."

"They're going to stay here, but probably not in the house." Ross debated whether she should tell Vivian about the bone sorcerer in his domed cage and decided against it. There would be plenty of time once the medication had worn off. "I'll tell them you're on board with it. Are you hungry or anything?"

"I had some of my emergency stash of chocolate," replied Vivian, turning back to her book. Ross glanced at the nightstand and spied the candy wrappers behind the water. She swept them into her hand.

"How about I bring you some actual food?"

"I can walk," said Vivian in an affronted voice. "My *arm* is broken, not my legs."

"Well, come on then." Ross stood close to Vivian as the redhead maneuvered out of the bed, tossing her book back onto the rumpled covers. Aside from a bit of wobbliness at first, Vivian was actually pretty steady on her feet. She surveyed her clothes with a frown.

"You put me in bed in my jeans?" she demanded indignantly.

Ross chuckled. "There was a lot going on. And I thought you wouldn't mind."

"I *do* mind," Vivian replied. She tossed her wild mane of curls. "Although now it saves me from having to get dressed."

"See? Convenient," remarked Ross.

With Vivian presiding over a table laden with several different food choices ranging from Jess's gumbo to a fresh peanut butter sandwich, Ross leaned against the kitchen counter and glanced out the kitchen window. The deep golden light of late afternoon was fading into twilight. It was strange to think of everything that had changed that day. Everything that had changed in the past week, she amended silently.

Two glows zipped through the living room and hovered over the kitchen table. Vivian swallowed her mouthful of gumbo and grinned with unrestrained delight.

"May we join you, my lady?" asked Forin politely.

"Of course," Vivian said. "Would you like anything?" She gestured to the bounty that Ross had laid out.

"Thank you for your kind offer, but we ate earlier," replied Farin as he and his sister alighted on the table.

"We saw you throw the spell at the sorcerer," said Farin with a fierce smile. "You were most brave!"

"Brave or stupid," Ross said to herself, but she smiled and left Vivian with her Glasidhe audience, who listened raptly as Vivian began recounting her (somewhat foolhardy) decision to use one of Corsica's spells. Ross nearly ran into Niall in the living room as she walked out of the kitchen.

"I apologize," said Niall with his typical gallantry. "I did not mean to frighten you."

"You didn't frighten me," demurred Ross, though her heart beat rapidly in her chest. She didn't like it when people suddenly appeared around corners. "Thank you, by the way, for the coins."

"It is only proper to pay for the damage that was caused," said Niall. He smiled slightly. "We haven't completely forgotten our courtesy." He glanced over her shoulder. Ross could still hear Vivian, and she suspected that Niall could glimpse the redhead through the kitchen.

"She's a little loopy on some painkillers right now," cautioned Ross. "Medication," she clarified when Niall frowned in confusion at her words.

"Ah." Niall smiled again. "Then I should go introduce myself properly. Ramel needs my supervision the most, but I would like to make sure her arm heals well."

It seemed that Niall didn't expect a reply, because he slid past her without waiting for one. Ross watched him for a moment. He selected a seat further down the table rather than one right beside Vivian, listening attentively as Vivian finished her story for the Glasidhe. Farin leapt up and greeted Niall affectionately.

"Look at us, a happy little family," commented Duke as he passed her on the way to the kitchen. He opened the refrigerator and grabbed a beer. "Want one?" He already had the second bottle in his hand before she nodded.

Ross accepted her beer and watched Vivian happily conversing with a patient Niall and the two Glasidhe. "One happy, weird little family," she agreed, taking a sip of her beer and letting herself lean against Duke again. He kissed her temple and she smiled. For all the weird happenings during the course of the day, she was all right with it. They had all survived, and she got to drink a beer with her favorite person in the world, watching her roommate have the time of her life with three Fae at the kitchen table.

Chapter 34

"I wish there were a way to send messages between the worlds," Tess said.

"I know, and you've already said that a dozen times," Molly replied. They sat on the floor of the study, each with a pint of ice cream and a beer. Tess was eager to return to Faeortalam with the Lethe Stone, but she also wanted to savor a small sliver of time with her best friend. Jess had somehow overheard their conversation – or Molly had told him – and he'd picked up a variety of ice creams along with the impressive inventory of beer that now resided in the refrigerator.

Tess sighed. "I just…I want to know you're okay."

Molly gave her a crooked smile as she licked her spoon. "I think I've done all right so far on my own."

"Don't remind me," said Tess.

"No, you're not going to start that guilt trip again," ordered Molly, pointing at Tess with her spoon. "You're the Bearer. You did what you had to do. If you'd talked yourself out of escaping Darkhill to go find the patrol in the forest, then I probably wouldn't be sitting here with you." She scooped a glob of cookie dough out of her ice cream. "I mean, none of us would be here. The Fae, I mean."

"You probably would've figured it out," said Tess with a shrug. To her surprise, the Caedbranr remained silent; apparently it wasn't interested in their conversation.

"Nope, not even a little bit." Molly shook her head and took a swig of her beer. "Just face it, Tess. You're a hero. You saved an entire *world*."

"With help," Tess pointed out.

Molly grinned at her discomfort. "Jeez, you're still not used to it, are you?"

"No." Tess shook her head and dug into her ice cream. "I don't know if I'll ever be." The Sword, laid on the floor nearby, eyed her lazily with its flashing emerald. Her traveling pack rested by the battered sheath, packed and ready for the journey back to Faeortalam.

"Eventually," Molly said with a confident nod. She glanced at Ramel every few minutes. The Unseelie Knight *looked* a bit better, but concern still etched lines into Molly's forehead.

"You're in good hands with Niall," said Tess.

"I know, I'm not questioning that," Molly said. She sighed. "I'm glad to be back but I also don't like not knowing what the future holds for us. After all, he's still one of Mab's Three. It's not like he can just quit."

"Just focus on getting him better," said Tess in encouragement. "And we'll figure out the next steps when I come back."

Molly nodded. "You know, Ross and Vivian are pretty cool. A little crazy, maybe, on Vivian's part…but they seem like good people."

"They are, as far as I know." Tess smiled. "When Vivian finds out that you're half-Fae she's probably going to ask you a million questions."

Molly gestured grandly. "Ask away. I've got all the time in the world, after all." She scraped the last of the ice cream from the bottom of her carton. "I win again!"

"Like I've always said, it's not a race," said Tess, repeating her timeworn argument. "You should *savor* your ice cream."

"Why?" demanded Molly.

"So you don't get a brain freeze?" suggested Tess with a chuckle.

"I think one of my Fae abilities is to eat ice cream as quickly as I want without getting a brain freeze," replied Molly. "No, seriously, think about it! Did you ever hear me complain about a brain freeze? Nope. Even that one time I drank a whole Cherry Coke Slushy without stopping because it was free slushy day and I wanted a top-off before we left."

Tess grinned at the memory. "You're right, I should have *totally* suspected that you were half-Fae when you didn't get a brain freeze."

Molly laughed. Ramel stirred at the sound of her mirth and she instantly set down her beer, sliding over to his bed. Tess finished the last of her ice cream and discreetly gathered Molly's carton and beer bottle. Ramel didn't open his eyes, but Molly murmured to him until he settled again.

"Take care of him," Tess said quietly. "And don't forget to take care of yourself, too."

Molly smiled. "I think that's a bit of the pot calling the kettle black, huh?" But she stood and hugged Tess. "Travel safe. Don't let Mab turn you into a mortal Popsicle."

"A not quite mortal Popsicle," said Tess with an answering smile.

Molly chuckled and then became serious. "We'll be waiting for you."

Tess nodded. "Beer and ice cream to celebrate my return," she said.

"That's a promise." Molly nodded.

Tess swallowed against the knot in her throat and slid the strap of the Sword over her shoulder. She wouldn't say goodbye because goodbyes meant leaving. She didn't want to leave Molly and Ramel. She was tired of goodbyes. Picking up her pack, she slid one strap onto her shoulder.

She moved into the kitchen and threw the ice cream cartons into the trashcan, rinsed the bottles and set them on the counter to be recycled. Such ordinary actions, just like the morning before the great battle at the Dark Keep. That was life, she supposed, ordinary actions bookending moments of chaos.

Vivian and Niall still sat at the kitchen table with Forin and Farin. This time, Niall was telling the story. He paused as Tess approached.

"Thank you," she said to Vivian. "Thank you for taking in Luca and Merrick, and helping us."

"Well, the taking in part was mostly Ross," Vivian replied with a smile. She looked a little tired now that the medication was beginning to lose its effect. "But you're welcome." She pressed her lips together as if debating on speaking her next words. Tess raised her eyebrows expectantly. "I was just…wondering. Merrick said that maybe…maybe I could travel into the Fae world. Someday." Though she tried to say it nonchalantly, Tess saw the hope flaring in her eyes.

"After your arm is healed," Tess said slowly, "I'll consider it." She smiled. "I have a feeling that a lot of things are going to change soon."

Vivian grinned and then remembered that she was trying to act casual about her inquiry. She swallowed and said in a measured voice, "Thanks. Good luck with traveling."

Niall stood and to Tess's surprise he clasped her hand. "Be strong," he told Tess, his fingers cool around hers. She nodded, though she had little idea of what he meant, and he took his seat again.

"Tess-mortal!" trilled Farin. "I shall stay, I think, to guard the dark mage!" She brandished a small blade.

"Very well. I am sure Niall will be grateful for your help," Tess said. Niall nodded gravely in agreement. "Haze?"

"I shall return with you," Wisp's cousin said. "I think I have now met more mortals than my esteemed kin."

Tess chuckled. "I would believe it."

Haze leapt from the table and followed her as she walked to the door. "Lady Vivian is very keen on traveling to our world," the Glasidhe said as they crossed the front porch. The shadows pooled around the house as the sun sank red behind the trees. Tess glanced up at the sun and thought it strange that she had only been in the mortal world for two days, and yet it felt like it had been weeks. To her surprise, she found that she missed Faeortalam. The air tasted different and the light of the sun struck her face just so in the Fae world. It *felt* strange to her now in the mortal world, like she was slightly off balance. Maybe it was simply the fact that she was absorbing much more *taebramh.* She wondered if the feeling would subside the longer she stayed in the world of her birth, or whether Faeortalam would always call to her now.

Luca sat on a stump near the tree line, sharpening one of his axes and glancing up every so often at Gryttrond in his glowing cage. Kianryk lounged in the reddening light of the sun, his eyes half-closed. Corsica crouched on the opposite side of the runetrap, still as a statue save for when she licked her lips, staring at the bone sorcerer like he was her next meal. Tyr still walked in his circuit around the glowing dome, pausing at each rune-stone.

Tess walked through the long grass toward Luca, savoring the sight of him. She quietly delighted in the way that the setting sun burnished his golden hair and outlined the broad strength of his shoulders. Being near him again settled her in a way that was difficult for her to describe even in her own thoughts, but she did know that the raw sorrow that had settled to an aching sense of loss since the battle had subsided. Luca's presence spread balm over the wounds that her *taebramh* was not able to heal. He sharpened his axe with skillful strokes and then tested the blade, pressing the side of it with one finger and then carefully shaving a small portion of the white-gold hair on his forearms, nodding as the blade apparently met his standards. After he slid the axe back in its loop on his belt, he caught sight of Tess. His pale blue eyes leapt with joy and he didn't try to suppress the grin that spread over his face. She felt an answering grin on her own lips – they had been apart for the better part of an hour, and he reacted as though he hadn't seen her in days.

Luca didn't leap up to meet her, but let her approach through the long grass, following her movements with his eyes. His gaze lingered appreciatively on the contours of her body, and though she wore a simple outfit of a white shirt and green breeches, the look on Luca's face made Tess feel as though she were wearing a ball gown spun of silk and diamonds. Even in her simple attire, his eyes made it plain that he found her beautiful. They had trained and traveled and slept together under the stars; they had ridden muddy and bloodied across the Deadlands and into the Dark Keep; they had hunted a dragon and escaped sirens and survived the greatest battle the Fae world had ever seen. And Tess somehow knew that through it all, Luca had seen her as *beautiful.* He had always emphasized her strength and her tenacity, but she understood now that he had been encouraging her in the way she needed most. They would never stop facing challenges, but Malravenar was broken and bound into the river stones, and Gryttrond was trapped in his glowing cage. She could let herself recognize her own beauty without the misplaced fear that it would make her weak or distract her from her duty as the Bearer.

Luca finally stood when she came within arm's length. She tilted her face up to him in invitation, and he obligingly kissed her. Tess closed her eyes and lost herself in the delicious sensation of his lips upon hers, his kiss gentle at first, kindling a warm glow within her. One of his strong, calloused hands found her waist and firmly drew her closer. She felt her knees go weak as a torrent of desire roared through her at the feel of his muscled body against hers. He held her with gentle strength and deepened the kiss, sliding her lips apart with his tongue. She pressed into him, sliding her hands under his arms and up his back. A very feminine satisfaction rose up within her as she caught his lower lip between her teeth, eliciting a low growl of passion from him.

Tess vaguely heard a trilling laugh from Corsica and a whistle of approval. She struggled out of the haze of desire and they both drew back, smiling. Luca brushed a thumb over her tingling lips, his eyes very blue as he said, "Tonight, we will sleep under the stars of Faeortalam again and we will delight in each other."

A pleasurable shiver ran through Tess at his words. She smiled crookedly and arched an eyebrow. "Is that a promise?" she asked huskily. He kissed her swiftly in reply and she drew back, laughing. They stood together and surveyed the bone sorcerer.

"Is it a mistake to leave him alive?" Tess asked softly. The Sword hummed in its sheath on her back.

"We will not leave Gryttrond alive for long," said Luca in a low voice. One of his hands stroked the handle of his axe. "He has many crimes for which he must answer."

Tess nodded. "I know. But I mean…do you think it's a mistake for us to travel back to Faeortalam with him still alive?"

Luca took a deep, measured breath. "All my instincts tell me to kill the kinslayer now." He bared his teeth. "But I would not force Merrick to break his word to the Exiled."

"Maybe we should wait until the Exiled have found out what they need to know and then kill him before we return," said Tess. She still shrank from the thought of executing Gryttrond. Thrusting her sword through Malravenar had been almost too easy, when it came down to it. Would sliding her blade into this dark mage offer her some twisted pleasure?

"You don't want to execute him," said Luca quietly, his voice free of judgment.

She swallowed. "No. I'm afraid that I'll…that it'll be too easy. That I'll enjoy killing someone in cold blood."

"Mab has executed those she deemed traitors," said Luca, following her train of thought.

"I don't want to be like her." Tess's voice shook slightly.

Luca laid his hands on her shoulders and turned her to face him.

"*Anganhjarta,* you will never be like her."

She let the assurance in his words wash over her. "What does that mean?" she murmured. "*Angan...*"

"*Anganhjarta,*" Luca repeated with a small smile. She tested her pronunciation of the word again and he nodded, brushing a strand of hair from her face. "It means...joy of my heart."

Tess blinked. Would this man ever stop surprising her with the depths of his tenderness and the wholeness of his love for her? She swallowed again, this time against a sudden tightness in her throat. Words didn't seem sufficient to express the emotions whirling in her chest, so she hugged him and repeated the word again into his chest. He kissed the top of her head and smoothed her hair. Then she drew back again and considered Tyr and Corsica.

"Are *you* all right with leaving the bone sorcerer alive and coming with me? Niall will be here to guard him, and Forin and Farin. But..." Tess sighed. It seemed like she had no clear good choice, although at first she hadn't minded the thought of leaving Gryttrond trapped within the cage built by Tyr and Merrick's runes. Now she began to second guess her decision as the time drew nearer for her to Summon the Gate. "I trust Niall," she said, "and I have no doubt as to his strength. He's Titania's Vaelanseld, after all."

"But it is Corsica and Tyr, and most of all Gryttrond, that you do not trust," Luca supplied.

"Exactly. More Corsica than Tyr," Tess muttered. The silver-haired woman's head turned sharply in her direction. The Exiled unfolded herself from her watchful posture and slunk toward them. "I think she heard me," Tess said, torn between embarrassment and defiance. She was the Bearer, but she still didn't want to be rude.

Perhaps it is not rude if it is true, the Caedbranr whispered insidiously in the back of her mind. She ignored it. Tyr joined Corsica, tilting his head at her in question, but her azure eyes flashed and he shrugged as he fell into step beside her.

"You do not trust me, daughter of Gwyneth?" Corsica demanded.

Tess drew back her shoulders. No use in denying the truth. "No. I haven't known you long enough to trust you, and I have heard...interesting things...from my companions back in Faeortalam."

"All suppositions and sordid half-truths," said Corsica. "The victors write history, do they not?"

"The victors or the survivors," said Luca, nodding once. "Sometimes they are one and the same, and sometimes they are not."

"Sometimes they are *not*," said Corsica. Her eyes blazed as she turned back to Tess. "The word of a wanderer is worthless. Yet we have not betrayed you. We have not slit the sorcerer's throat and supped on his blood."

"Is that what you plan to do?" A small, rebellious thought inserted itself into Tess's mind: perhaps letting the Exiled kill Gryttrond would not be such a bad thing. It would leave her hands clean.

"It is what I *want* to do," said Corsica. Tyr touched her arm lightly. "But what we will do is speak to him."

"Speak to him about reversing the effects of your exile," Tess clarified.

Tyr nodded gravely. Corsica didn't say anything, her eyes still burning like two blue flames. Gwyneth's pendant heated at Tess's throat. She tried not to let her surprise show on her face. The pendant didn't speak to her often anymore, and she felt like she didn't speak its language as fluently. Was it expressing approval or doubt? Was it trying to warn her or urge her to trust the Exiled? She wished that Gwyneth had imbued the pendant with the ability to speak...but then again, that wasn't always helpful with the Sword.

"After you speak to him," said Tess slowly, "you will return him to the runetrap until I return."

Tyr nodded again, his face serious. His dark gray eyes looked black in the deepening dusk. Corsica stared off into the trees until he touched her arm again; then she looked at Tess and grudgingly gave a little jerk of her head.

"You will swear on the Iron Sword," Tess continued. She carefully gathered the Caedbranr's power into herself as she reached behind her head for its hilt. With its fire compressed into a brightly burning star just behind her heart, she drew the Sword. The blade shone with its own soft light in the shadows as she held it flat over her hands. Tyr let out a sigh of wonder but Corsica stared at the Sword with an almost petulant cast to her mouth. Tess felt the many voices of the Bearers before her well up through her throat, and her *taebramh* raced down her war markings, shining brightly through her shirtsleeve. "Swear on the Sword that you will guard the bone sorcerer known as Gryttrond until my return."

A tendril of the Sword's power reached out in a tongue of white fire that split into two streams of brightness. Tyr held both his scarred hands toward the Sword, as if warming himself by its light. He nodded deeply, mouthing the words: *I so swear.* The fire licked his forehead and he shuddered.

Corsica drew her shoulders forward and hugged herself, shrinking back as the tendril of fire advanced on her. She shook her head and muttered to herself, the words too low for Tess to hear; but then Corsica suddenly threw her shoulders back and gritted her teeth. She looked at the Sword and said, "I so swear." The Sword's power brushed her skin for longer than it had with Tyr, and she winced as though its touch caused pain.

The fire funneled back into the Sword, then through its hilt and back through the circuitous path of Tess's war markings. She let out a breath as the remnants of the Bearers before her receded into quiescence, settling into the depths of her unconscious mind like a smooth stone dropping through the blue waters of a lake. The Sword settled back into its scabbard with a satisfied snap. Corsica shook herself as though trying to rid herself of a biting fly, while Tyr gazed dreamily at the hilt of the Sword, visible over Tess's shoulder.

"Now they have been bound by giving their word to the Sword," said Luca. He glanced over to Gryttrond. Tess hazily wondered at the thoughts lurking behind his now-somber eyes. Was he thinking of the family he had lost to the harrowing of the North? Was he thinking of all the innocents that Gryttrond had killed? She blinked and focused on the Exiled.

"Thank you for giving me your word," she said, though she wasn't sure it was customary to *thank* anyone for doing such a thing. The strange feeling in her gut that tugged her toward Faeortalam intensified and she pressed her lips together, looking at Tyr. "Take the knowledge you need from him, and no more."

The Exiled who reminded her faintly of Chael bowed elegantly in answer, his scarred yet beautiful face solemn. She nodded. She wasn't sure if there was anything more that she could do to allay her uneasiness at leaving Gryttrond alive while she delivered the Lethe Stone.

Tyr took her nod as a dismissal. He tugged at Corsica's sleeve as he turned back toward the runetrap. She followed him, but her eyes were hooded and she glanced sourly at Tess and Luca before resuming her watchful position.

"I should feel reassured that they swore on the Sword, shouldn't I?" Tess said quietly, almost to herself.

Luca shrugged slightly. "You can do no more."

Tess bit her lip in thought. "There *is* one thing more I could do. I could kill the bone sorcerer before I return to Faeortalam." She sighed and shook her head. "But that would deny Tyr and Corsica the chance to regain a bit of what they've lost." She pressed her lips together. "When I was told about the Exiles, they were painted as traitors who would be bloodthirsty for revenge. The traitor part…that's not for me to decide. But we wouldn't have been able to trap Gryttrond in the first place without them, and aside from the initial meeting, they haven't tried to exact their vengeance on anyone here." She looked up at Luca, who stared over at the bone sorcerer.

"It is not always black and white," Luca said quietly. "You could have killed me when I had the dagger bound to my hand, but you chose a different path."

Tess nodded. Though it was a timeworn argument by this point, it still rang true. Luca had been sent by Malravenar to kill her, controlled by a dagger imbued with a malevolent spirit. Their fight against Malravenar himself had been clear-cut – the ancient deity's desire to annihilate the Sidhe and wrest control of the Fae world and the mortal world was easy to oppose. After having faced Malravenar, Tess couldn't bring herself to consider Corsica and Tyr evil. They had spent centuries in the mortal world, accepting a slow corruption and painful existence over a quick death. She shivered. If anything, perhaps they deserved her empathy.

Finally, she sighed and met Luca's eyes. "I just want to be sure that I'm not making the wrong choice."

He smiled slightly. "You cannot See the future like your brother, but you are the Bearer and you have been trained well." One of his eyebrows arched slightly. "And I would tell you if you were being a complete…what is the mortal word…moron." His smile widened into a smug grin as she smacked his arm.

"You and your picking up mortal slang. Did Vivian teach you that one?" Tess shook her head, but a smile played on her lips.

"You'll have to get used to it, if we're to establish a base here in the mortal world," Luca said, following her as she walked toward the side of the house. She'd decided to open the Gate at the farthest point in the back yard from the trapped bone-sorcerer. Kianryk raised his great head, watched for a moment and then stood, yawning and stretching before loping after them. The shadows painted his tawny gold pelt a shade of darker gold.

"Let's focus on one thing at a time, shall we?" replied Tess. "I'd like to untangle this whole mess with Mab as best I can before we think about building a training base or something here."

"Many things happen at the same time," countered Luca. "We know that Gryttrond escaped into this world when Malravenar fell. We don't know if there are others. And there are creatures that were trapped in this world when the Gate was closed."

"That's a can of worms that I'm not willing to open right now," Tess said firmly.

"Worms have nothing to do with it," said Luca sensibly.

Tess chuckled. "Would you mind fetching the others who are coming with us while I set up?"

Luca nodded and walked toward the house, Kianryk at his heels.

Tess refocused her attention on the Summoning, opening her belt pouch and carefully withdrawing the little silken bag containing the spheres created by the Queens. The Lethe Stone nestled beside them, wrapped in its square of white, and beside that the river stone containing the shard of Malravenar's spirit rested. Perhaps it was appropriate that the instrument of his defeated henchman was stored next to a fragment of his spirit, Tess thought. She tugged the strings of the pouch loose and rolled the small marble-sized objects into her palm, selected one each from Mab, Titania and Vell – sparkling night sky, white rose suspended in brilliant noon-sky blue, and tiny tree surrounded by the white swirl of snow, all perfect and beautiful to the last intricate detail, sealed with a drop of the Queen's blood. With her three orbs in one hand, she carefully slid the remaining six orbs back into the pouch. Just as the last rolled over her palm, Corsica's voice purred into her ear: "Such beautiful things the bountiful ones have bestowed upon you."

Tess jumped at the sudden closeness of the Exiled woman and dropped the last remaining orb. Her heart flew into her throat as she dropped to her knees, scanning the long grass until she saw the flash of stars in the midnight sky against the dirt. Corsica bumped into her as the Exiled dropped to her knees as well, gloved hand effortlessly scooping up the orb. Tess stood jerkily, staring at the silver-haired Sidhe. She let her *taebramh* expand in her chest, ready to force the Exiled to return the orb that was their return ticket after the next visit to the mortal world. She didn't think that Mab would create any more orbs for a Summoned Gate.

To Tess's surprise, Corsica gracefully dropped to her knees again, offering the orb on her upraised hands. Her silver hair fell like a curtain about her face.

"I apologize, Lady Bearer," came Corsica's voice, sounding strangely subdued.

Tess reached out and took the orb between thumb and forefinger, sliding it back into the pouch. "No harm done," she said. Corsica stood and sank into her elegant curtsy. "I…there's no need for that, Corsica," Tess said, now feeling slightly ashamed that she'd thought she needed to unleash her *taebramh* on the Exiled to make her return the orb. The Sword's power stirred uneasily in her chest, and the strange tug toward Faeortalam intensified again.

"We look forward to your return, Lady Bearer," said Corsica. "We will remain loyal to you, no matter our scars or our reputation. Bound and banished, burned and bloodied. We are…grateful," she said, the word almost strangled. "Grateful to you, for allowing us a chance to become some of what we once were. Before."

Tess looked at Corsica's gloved hands, held in fists by her sides. She held up her empty left hand, the rippling scars left by the Crown of Bones clearly visible even in the fading light. "I have scars as well. I don't judge others for theirs."

Something flashed in Corsica's eyes before she lowered them and bowed her head, then she slid away, murmuring to herself. Tess watched her go and then blinked, shifting the strap of the Sword across her chest. The three orbs felt unnaturally heavy in her hand.

"We are all here," said Luca, approaching with Calliea and Merrick. Jess, Niall, Vivian, Ross, and Duke trailed behind them. Tess found that she was relieved that Molly hadn't left Ramel to come out and watch the Summoning.

"And all ready to return to Faeortalam," said Merrick, his gray eyes alight with anticipation. Haze rode on Calliea's shoulder, his small hand touching her ear every so often for balance as Wisp had once done with Tess. Forin and Farin hovered high over the group, watching from the air.

Tess nodded, the words of the Summoning rising in her mind. "All right then, let's go home."

Chapter 35

Ross watched as Tess performed the complex ritual that would open a portal between the worlds. A Gate, Vivian had told her excitedly. She hadn't been enthusiastic about her friend venturing outside so soon after her injury, but Vivian had stubbornly insisted, and Niall had reassured Ross that he'd stay close by the redhead. Ross still had her doubts about the whole business, but the events of the past days had all but forced her to grudgingly accept the fact that there were supernatural powers in the world about which she knew nothing…and that Tess, the little sister of Duke's teammate, carried one of those supernatural powers in the sword on her back.

Niall, while he kept his word to Ross about staying close to Vivian, positioned himself so that he was angled to intercept the Exiled should they attempt to throw themselves through the Gate. While Niall had said that travel through the portal typically required a mark from the creator of the Gate – a passport, Ross had thought with a bit of amusement – he was still wary of the ancient knowledge that the Exiled possessed. Tyr and Corsica, for their part, showed little interest in the Summoning. Tyr still performed his endless circuit around the cage, and Corsica crouched in her customary spot. She stared down at one of her hands, a look of childlike wonder on her face. Probably a bauble she'd found in the overgrown brush by the river, thought Ross. Bottles of colored glass and other oddments occasionally emerged from the tangle of greenery, borne downriver by the muddy water and deposited into the brambles.

The air tightened as Tess murmured an incantation. Ross worked her jaw to relieve the building pressure in her ears. Duke slipped his hand into the pocket of her shorts and she smiled. She wasn't much for public displays of affection like holding hands, so this was their compromise. For a tough as nails, sarcastic and at times cynical operator, Duke surprisingly enjoyed physical expressions of their relationship.

Vivian leaned forward, watching raptly as Tess raised a little glass orb in one hand, her chant almost a song. She threw the orb onto the ground and smoke that looked like a dark, star spangled night swirled up out of the shards. An unnatural wind raced toward Tess, plucking at their clothes as it rushed past, throwing Vivian's curls into a waving mass of fiery red that seemed to take on a life of its own about her head.

Tess smashed a second orb, and the mist roiling up from this one blazed bright as a summertime noon, twining with the dark smoke in two twisting columns. Goosebumps prickled Ross's skin as she recognized the outline of a door…or not a door, she thought. A Gate to another world. Luca, Merrick and Calliea stood behind Tess. Ross couldn't see their faces but she could read their eagerness in the set of their shoulders. Tess threw the third orb onto the ground and a gust of icy wind blasted back from the Gate. The columns solidified as if frozen by the white mist from the third orb, and a shivering pane of frost hung suspended between them.

"Come forward to be marked," Tess said, drawing a dagger from her belt. She pricked her finger and pressed her blood to the foreheads of the four traveling with her. Then she turned back to the

Gate, drew back her shoulders and slid her bloodied fingertip across the pane of frost. A silent explosion rocked the ground for an instant, and the pane rippled. Colors swirled behind a veil of mist. Ross strained her eyes and thought she made out the vague impression of a sort of pavilion. The veil kept shifting, whirling with a kaleidoscope of shadows and colors. She glanced at Niall, and he wasn't watching Tess. His eyes were trained on Tyr, who gazed at the Gate with naked longing on his scarred face. Corsica watched from her crouch, her gloved hands held against her chest as though she pressed something precious to her heart.

Tess turned back to the small group gathered behind her. Without a word, Calliea and Merrick walked forward. Merrick smiled and bowed slightly to Calliea, gesturing for her to go before him. She rolled her eyes at him but, with Haze on her shoulder, she gracefully slid into the mist of the Gate. Merrick followed as soon as she disappeared from sight. Luca said a Northern word, and Kianryk grinned his wolf grin. Tess looked relieved as Luca vanished through the Gate, the tawny wolf leaping after him. She turned to look at those remaining behind. Ross saw with a start that Tess's green eyes had been overtaken by white fire.

"Thank you," said the Bearer, her voice layered with hundreds of other voices. She nodded to them, her blazing eyes seeming to look at all of them at once. "Until we meet again."

"Until we meet again!" returned Niall and the two Glasidhe. Duke let out an exuberant yell and even Jess added his own holler. Tess smiled slightly, turned, and stepped through the Gate. The veil flashed silver as it swallowed her, and the columns silently and suddenly dissipated into curls of white, blue and gray smoke. The air smelled faintly like snow and roses.

"That's it?" Ross said, unable to keep the suspicion from her voice.

"It did seem a bit…anticlimactic," agreed Vivian.

"That is the way of it sometimes," Farin piped in her bright voice, swooping down to hover between the two women. She spun and addressed Niall. "Vaelanseld, I shall take the first watch on the bone sorcerer!"

Niall nodded. "As you wish, Farin. Forin, will you take second? I will take the dawn watch."

Corsica cocked her head as she slid toward them. "Watches to watch *him,* or to watch *us*?" She flicked her silver hair over one shoulder, combing through it with her grimy gloved fingers.

"Both," replied Niall unshakably. Ross didn't miss the considering glance that Vivian leveled at the Seelie man. She smiled to herself; perhaps Merrick had just been a target of opportunity for Vivian's affection, something beautiful and unique and, she had to admit, very courteous. Niall fit that mold as well, and it seemed he would be staying with them for a while.

"Seems like V might be settin' her sights on someone else," Duke said out of the side of his mouth to her as they headed back toward the house.

"As long as he doesn't make Vivian cry, I have no objections," replied Ross.

Duke chuckled. "Should I warn him?"

"Oh, he'll figure it out for himself if he hurts her," said Ross, raising her eyebrows.

"No doubt he will," muttered Duke with a smile. They reached the front door. Ross glanced behind them. Niall and Vivian followed at a small distance, Vivian asking Niall a question with an animated gesture and flash of her eyes. Ross watched them for a moment, noting the respectful posture of Niall as he listened to Vivian with his hands clasped behind his back. Perhaps it would be more than a passing fancy. Either way, it would be interesting.

Duke held the screen door open for her and followed her inside. She surveyed the chalk runes on the door as she kicked off her Chucks; smudges marred a few lines, but overall Merrick's handiwork had survived intact. She moved into the kitchen, staring at the disarray for a moment before she began placing bottles in the recycling bin and dirty dishes in the sink.

"Feels a bit like the letdown after a big party, huh?" Duke said as he walked into the kitchen with a stack of gumbo bowls from the table. Vivian and Niall came through the front door, and paused in their conversation to reopen the door for Mayhem.

"May," scolded Vivian as the dog tracked mud into the living room. Ross watched as her roommate tried to corral the dog with her good arm. Vivian looked at Niall for help. "Want to learn how to give a dog a bath?"

Niall chuckled, his pale eyes alight. "It would be my pleasure to help you corral this unruly canine."

Ross smiled as she turned on the faucet and the water drowned out the sound of their conversation. Duke placed the bowls on the kitchen counter.

"You know," Ross said as she squeezed dish soap into the sink, "I think it's just…a pause. A pause in the party."

Duke laughed. "Darlin', let's face it, we could use a pause."

Vivian slid into the kitchen with her phone held aloft like a trophy. "Ross! It's the firehouse!"

Ross winced at Vivian's exuberant shout as she dried her hands, eyeing the phone.

"Don't worry, I have them on mute," Vivian reassured her. "I called them this morning, at least I *think* it was this morning, to let them know that this was a good contact number for you."

Ross took a deep breath as she took the phone. "Thanks, V."

"Anytime!" Vivian smiled and then her eyes widened as she heard what sounded like Sidhe curses coming from the guest bathroom, where Niall was presumably attempting to convince Mayhem to get into the bathtub. She ducked her head to hide her grin as she exited the kitchen. "Never fear, help is on the way!" she called.

Ross sighed and looked down at the phone.

"Well, you gonna answer it?" Duke lifted an eyebrow. "Or you gonna make 'em wait forever?"

"Do I even want the job, with everything that's happened?" Ross said. "I mean…the gold that Niall gave me, that could last us for at least a couple of years."

"I think you need this job to stay sane," Duke replied seriously. "I know you and I love you, Ross, but you get kinda crazy when you don't get to kick down doors and save people."

Ross nodded and swallowed. "You're right. Besides, I don't even know if I got the job." She steeled herself and pressed the "Unmute" button, holding the phone up to her ear. "Hello?"

Duke watched her face as she listened.

"I'm fine, thanks," she said into the phone. "And I apologize for the switch in numbers, my old phone broke and, well, you know how that goes." Ross bit her lip as she listened. "Yes, ma'am. Yes." She blinked and a slow smile spread over her face, eclipsing the worried look. "Yes, ma'am, please tell the chief that I'd be happy to start Monday. Yes, ma'am, you have a good evening too." She hung up the phone, stared at it for a second and then looked at Duke. "I got the job." Her smile widened to a grin. "*I got the job!*"

"Knew you would," said Duke, grabbing her and spinning her around.

"You didn't even know I was applying for this job," said Ross teasingly, too happy to feel irritated at anyone or anything. Finally, she'd be able to pay some of her debt. She'd be able to save people, show up on their worst day and make sure they lived to see the next.

"Doesn't change how happy I am for you," said Duke. He set her down and kissed her soundly, leaving her giddy.

"Congratulations!" yelled Vivian from the bathroom. There was a splash and she squealed.

"Mayhem, behave!" ordered Ross, but she couldn't manage a stern voice. She felt…happy. Duke was alive. They'd survived the strange and terrifying events of the past days. And she had gotten the job.

She moved through the rest of the evening in a blissful daze, washing the dishes almost cheerfully and checking in on Ramel and Molly. Ramel's color continued to improve but he hadn't shown any signs of awakening. Molly, too, looked better, a little less haggard now that it seemed Ramel would survive. Mayhem emerged from the bathroom damp but clean, and Ross glimpsed Niall and Vivian sopping up puddles from the drenched tile floor, conspiratorial grins on their faces. She found that she even looked forward to Tess's return, and the mage in his runetrap didn't bother her as much as it had even hours before.

She changed into her t-shirt and shorts for bed after checking the lock on the front door. Duke slipped into the bathroom as she brushed her teeth, resting his chin on her shoulder as she leaned back against him. He wore only the thin shorts that he and most of his teammates inexplicably favored for running, but Ross appreciated the lack of clothing, running her eyes over his reflection as she rinsed her mouth and deposited her toothbrush into its holder. She leaned back against him again and their eyes met in the mirror.

"I think," Duke said in his slow drawl, his words laden with heat, "we need to properly celebrate this new job of yours."

She slid to face him. "And I think," she replied in a low voice, matching his tone, "that I need to properly welcome you home."

Duke grinned devilishly, a thousand promises in his desire-darkened eyes as he slid his wonderfully calloused hands beneath the hem of her shirt.

They fell asleep pleasurably exhausted, twined together on Ross's bed. She grinned to herself in the darkness, relishing the satisfaction that permeated every part of her body. She drifted into sleep with her back pressed against Duke's chest, his warmth solid and reassuring.

They jerked awake when a shrill scream pierced the stillness, both of them scrambling out of bed and grabbing for their weapons.

"God," groaned Ross in a scratchy voice, "what is it this time?"

A full moon bathed the back yard in silvery light. Ross shook the last of the sleep from her head as she followed Duke, feeling as though she were a swimmer trying to surface through water thick as gelatin. Her body ached in protest at the rude disruption of her rest. She almost ran into Duke as he suddenly stopped.

"What is it?" she said, scanning the back yard. Nothing seemed out of place...until she remembered that there was supposed to be a glowing dome near the tree line. "Oh God," she whispered. "He escaped."

The shrill scream came again, the sound slicing through the air. Ross scanned the ground. She saw a glow in the grass – the Glasidhe. Without stopping to think, she ran forward, stumbling as her foot caught an unseen rock. Duke silently grabbed her elbow and she regained her feet.

Farin keened again as Ross dropped to her knees in the grass. The fierce Glasidhe wailed as though her heart was breaking...and it was, Ross realized. Farin knelt over the crumpled body of her twin, her aura flaring as she gathered Forin's still form into her arms.

"Ross, what's going on?" Vivian called, a flashlight beam bobbing in front of her as she picked her way cautiously across the yard.

Niall knelt a few feet away from Forin and Farin, a softly glowing blade in his hand. He bent over another still form. Ross caught the glint of moonlight on silver hair. She stood and looked closer. It was Tyr, lying still with blood running down the side of his face.

"Oh, no," Vivian said behind her, reaching the Glasidhe. "Farin, is he...?"

Farin's wordless screams answered Vivian's question. Ross felt heaviness settle into her chest as she glanced down at the still, dark form of the lifeless Glasidhe. Duke strode past her and stopped by Niall.

"Is he dead, too?" he asked tersely.

Niall shook his head. "No." He stood and looked from the blackened rune-stones to Tyr, then to the grieving Glasidhe. His voice carried a deadly chill when he spoke. "Corsica betrayed us."

Ross took a deep breath. The Bearer had left them, returning to the Fae world. Corsica was gone, betraying her oath to the Bearer, and the bone sorcerer had been released again on the mortal world. She squared her shoulders and raised her chin, the Glock feeling comfortingly solid in her hand as she met Niall's pale eyes. The echo of Farin's keen laced her words.

"All right. The bone sorcerer is gone, and Corsica with him. The Bearer isn't here, so it's up to us. There's no way I'm letting that asshole wreck our world." Determination lit Ross's eyes. "So. What do we do now?"

OTHER NOVELS BY JOCELYN A. FOX,
AVAILABLE ON KINDLE AND IN PAPERBACK:

The Iron Sword
The Crown of Bones
The Dark Throne

The first three novels are also collected in a special edition, available on Kindle:
The Fae War Chronicles Omnibus Edition

Acknowledgements

As always, I must thank the team that polishes my book and prepares it for its final showing: Peter at Bespoke Book Covers for his amazing cover designs; Maureen Cutajar at Go Published Formatting Services for her impeccable formatting over several editions and platforms; Ilana Harkavy and her team at Nailed It! Media for her helping hand with social media management; and Joelle Reeder at Moxie Design Studios for the gorgeous, shiny new website that has helped the launch of this book.

To Ronn Dula and Erin Platt: once again, my unending gratitude goes to my editing team for their dedication and determination in finding every errant semi-colon and spelling error in my manuscript. Any error that remains at this point is my own. I cannot thank you enough for your eye for detail and your thoughtful recommendations on every twist and turn of this novel.

Finally, once again and always: thank you to all of my readers. I hope you'll continue to traipse gleefully through this fantastic world with me, marveling at these characters and enjoying the community that we've created. It is my fondest wish that we continue to grow into a group of readers who are willing to discuss the very human issues presented through the lens of fantasy, and by doing so make a difference in the world.

Jocelyn A. Fox, October 2016

About the Author

Jocelyn A. Fox is the bestselling author of the epic fantasy novels *The Iron Sword*, *The Crown of Bones*, and *The Dark Throne*, the first three books in *The Fae War Chronicles*. *The Lethe Stone* is her fourth novel. She is in the military by day and an author by night; she likes dogs more than she likes most people, drinks too much coffee for her own good and is constantly looking for her next adventure in real life or in a good book.

She is constantly awed and humbled by the courage, tenacity and sacrifice of the men and women with whom she has the privilege of serving. Their fighting spirit and sense of fellowship inspire her every day, and her military experiences provide her with ample material to ground her fantasy world in the reality of the modern warrior.

You can find her at *www.jocelynafox.com*, or on the following platforms:

Facebook: *www.facebook.com/author.jocelyn.a.fox*
Twitter: *www.twitter.com/jafox2010*
Instagram: *@jocelynafox*
Amazon Page: *www.amazon.com/Jocelyn-A.-Fox/e/B0051DX7G0*

Made in the USA
Lexington, KY
14 December 2016